T0277964

WE SHALL BE MONSTERS

ALSO BY TARA SIM

SCAVENGE THE STARS

Scavenge the Stars

Ravage the Dark

TIMEKEEPER

Timekeeper

Chainbreaker

Firestarter

THE DARK GODS

The City of Dusk

The Midnight Kingdom

WE SHALL BE MONSTERS

TARA SIM

Nancy Paulsen Books

Nancy Paulsen Books
An imprint of Penguin Random House LLC, New York

First published in the United States of America by Nancy Paulsen Books,
an imprint of Penguin Random House LLC, 2024

Visit us online at PenguinRandomHouse.com.

Library of Congress Cataloging-in-Publication Data
Names: Sim, Tara, author.
Title: We shall be monsters / Tara Sim.
Description: New York: Nancy Paulsen Books, 2024.
Summary: "Drawing from Indian mythology, a teen girl desperate to bring her sister back from the dead is forced to first resurrect the kingdom's fallen prince, but accidentally awakens the wrong boy"—Provided by publisher.
Identifiers: LCCN 2023056485 (print) | LCCN 2023056486 (ebook)
ISBN 9780593407424 (hardcover) | ISBN 9780593407431 (ebook)
Subjects: CYAC: Sisters—Fiction. | Monsters—Fiction. | Fantasy.
LCGFT: Fantasy fiction. | Novels. | Classification: LCC PZ7.1.S547 We 2024 (print)
LCC PZ7.1.S547 (ebook) | DDC [Fic]—dc23
LC record available at https://lccn.loc.gov/2023056485
LC ebook record available at https://lccn.loc.gov/2023056486

Printed in the United States of America
ISBN 9780593407424
1st Printing
LSCH

Edited by Caitlin Tutterow
Design by Nicole Rheingans
Text set in Dante MT Pro

For my mother, who crossed an ocean.
And for my father, who always knew.

It is true, we shall be monsters, cut off from all the world; but on that account we shall be more attached to one another.

—Mary Wollstonecraft Shelley,
Frankenstein

Chapter One

THE WORST DAY of Kajal's life was the day she broke out of her own coffin.

It wasn't even a nice coffin. It was one made to burn, to reduce unclean flesh to ash, to allow the soul to return to nature and be reborn. Traditions such as this reigned strong in Dharati, especially in the town of Siphar, isolated as it was against the crags of the eastern mountains.

Though tradition did not specify what to do when a girl's fist broke through rotting wood, terrifying the humble crowd assembled to witness the burning.

Kajal shoved the coffin lid off and sat up with a gasp. Everything in her vision slanted and slid. Blinking rapidly, she could do little more than stare at the second coffin beside her, then at the people who gazed back at her in horror.

"Get away," she rasped.

Half of them didn't need telling twice, outright running to the squat, pale buildings sitting under a dusk-flushed sky. The coffins had been placed far enough from the town that the smell of charring flesh wouldn't carry.

The man who held the flaming branch meant to light the pyre stood with rigid limbs and a slack mouth.

"W-Witch," he breathed. "Dakini."

Kajal ignored him and forced herself to move, teeth gritted as she gracelessly climbed over the side of the broken coffin and dropped onto the kindling. Her arms and legs were shaking and weak with disuse; how long had she been lying in there? Dust and dirt billowed around her, and she thought she saw a shape within it—a moth or a butterfly. Mindlessly, she reached out, but it dissipated between her fingers.

"How?" the man with the torch demanded. His voice was thick with the local country dialect Kajal had grown used to during the months she'd stayed here. "The medicine woman said you were dead!"

"The medicine woman was wrong," Kajal croaked. Her long black hair hung limp and unwashed on either side of her face. Someone had dressed her scrawny body in a plain white kameez, another detail dictated by tradition. White was pure. White was the color of renewal, rebirth.

"You . . ." The man pointed the branch at her, the fire reflected in his wary eyes. "We found you both outside the cave-in, surrounded by . . . by malevolent offerings. You were behind it, weren't you?"

Her head was spinning, but she recalled a cave. A plan.

It should have worked. She had been *so sure*. But all she remembered now was a flash of unbearable light, a cacophonous breaking of stone.

Screams.

"They're *dead*," the man growled, his wariness turning to fury. "Six of our miners are dead because of you, and we can't get to their bodies." He pointed at the second coffin. "Not even she was spared from whatever wicked spells you cast. You killed her."

The words slid off her like raindrops. She was sanded down, edgeless, without corners or niches to catch them.

She crawled over branches and roughly hewn firewood toward the second coffin, gathering stains on her white dress and splinters in her skin. Her chest constricted so painfully she could hardly breathe.

It wasn't true. It couldn't be true.

She waited for a fist like hers to break through the wood, but all was still and silent. Kajal's throat tightened as she pushed at the flimsy coffin lid.

"Don't," the man cautioned.

The lid fell to the ground. The girl within was swathed in the same white cotton as Kajal, but on her, it looked intentional, like she had chosen it from her clothes trunk that morning. Her glossy black hair had somehow maintained a hint of a curl at the ends. Her face was lovely even in death, lips pale against her brown skin.

Kajal's breaths were coming in short bursts, her lungs on fire, her stomach writhing. She fumbled at the girl's cold neck.

"See?" The man's country dialect drawled around a sneer. "Now move aside. We can't burn the miners 'cause of you, but at least we can burn her before rakshasas are drawn to the smell. There's already an aga ghora prowling the outskirts of town."

An eerie cry in the distance backed up his claim, followed by the shouts of what had to be hunters wielding crossbows with iron bolts.

Kajal barely had a thought to spare for them. The girl's name was a bright, burning spot in her mind, lodged in her throat, waiting to be cried out—but she couldn't, she couldn't, if she said her name it would make it true, and it couldn't possibly be true that she was . . .

Dead.

Kajal was alive, and she was dead.

It was an accident.

I'm sorry.

How am I alive and you aren't?

Wake up!

She slapped the girl's cheek. The remaining townspeople murmured at her disrespect, but when she bared her teeth they shrank back, unwilling to fight a feral, possibly undead creature.

Kajal shook the girl's shoulder until her head lolled. "Please. Please, you can't. La—"

The first sob caught her off guard. She slumped against the coffin as the cry tore through her like removing an arrowhead from her body, all agony and bloody mess.

"No," she moaned when the man with the torch approached her again.

"She needs to burn," he said. "Stay there, for all I care. You can burn with her and spare us the rope for a hanging."

For a moment, Kajal was resigned to let them have their way. She would sit here and let the flames consume her too. Have them finish what she had started.

Someone gasped, and another screamed. A high-pitched call shivered through her, breaking the fragile mountain air.

The horse appeared with little warning, leaving a trail of scorched hoof-prints in its wake. It stood with head bent and forelegs spread, snorting fire while smoke purled from its open mouth. The body was barely distinct under the roiling flame, its eyes unseeing orbs of brilliant light.

"The aga ghora broke through!" came a cry as the remaining townsfolk fled, followed by a warning to prepare weapons and water buckets.

Kajal moved without thinking. She scrambled to kneel before the coffin, arms spread. If the rakshasa wanted to eat the dead, it would have to eat Kajal first.

But it stood unmoving, unblinking. As if waiting for her to take charge.

A dark laugh rumbled in her throat.

They wanted fire.

She staggered to her feet, hauling the dead girl up by her armpits. The weight was more than she had anticipated, and nearly made Kajal topple to the ground. But she only had a few minutes before the townspeople would return with their crossbows to drive the demon away.

"If you're not going to eat us, then make yourself useful," Kajal snapped.

The flames engulfing the aga ghora ebbed. It fell to its knees, and Kajal hesitated despite the urgency coursing through her. But the rakshasa made no move to attack, so she pushed the girl's body across its bare back and scrambled up behind, the stained kameez shifting around her hips. The horse's flesh was hot, almost unbearably so, and threatened to burn the insides of her thighs.

Kajal fisted a hand in the demon's mane.

"Run," she commanded.

The body refused to grow colder with the horse's heat, but it did begin to stiffen. Kept in this state, it would continue to decay until flesh sloughed from bones and organs were reduced to fetid liquids.

But Kajal knew how to prevent it.

Several miles from the town of Siphar, Kajal pulled the girl's body off the rakshasa. The horse's flames sprouted and danced again, flickering against those uncanny white eyes.

Horse and girl stared at each other for an uncomfortable moment. Kajal wondered if it expected some sort of debt now, or if it was only drawn to her because she was seemingly a dead thing resurrected.

If she had even died, that is. If she had implausibly returned through a veil of darkness and unbeing, she had no idea how—or why the girl beside her hadn't returned too.

"Thank you," she said at last.

The rakshasa let out another cry and galloped across the plain, its embers singeing the ground.

She was at the edge of the mountains that bordered eastern Dharati, near a thick forest of looming evergreens. Beyond was swampland and a field tangled with scrub. Ghost lights bobbed between the weeds, pinpricks of pulsing blue.

Kajal slowly lifted the girl's kameez to reveal what it had hidden: a large wound slanted across the girl's abdomen, sewn shut to preserve her dignity. She winced and tugged the dress back down before dragging the body toward the base of a tree, far enough out to hopefully not run into roots.

Then she began to dig.

She had no tools other than her own two hands. Her kameez was a ruin and clung to her with sweat, and she had to pause every so often to vomit thin bile that made tears spring to her eyes. The moon had fully risen by the time she'd dug deep enough, her arms sore and wrecked, her insides scraped raw.

Kajal turned to the body. It looked so serene, so at peace, even while sprawled in the middle of nowhere with no heartbeat and no future.

For now, at least.

She pulled the girl into the grave. The arrangement was awkward, and Kajal had to readjust the arms and legs until they fit. When she lifted the girl's wrist, she stared at the snug copper ring on her pinkie finger, the skin around it tinged green. She debated whether to take it. In the end, she decided to leave it be.

Kajal flexed her sore hands; it was hard to imagine the dirt under her nails was the same soil blessed long ago by the nature spirits of the yakshas. Soil that would protect a body from devourment and preserve it from decay.

Of the flesh, that is. A human soul, if trapped within its vessel and denied release through the gift of fire, would warp into a bhuta—a wraithlike ghost. A specter that, once strong enough, could claim lives of its own.

This was why it was steadfast tradition in Dharati to feed their dead to flames.

Kajal sat straddling the body a moment longer, her breaths evening out. She had to make this right. She had to undo this before the spirit began to corrode.

More tears blurred her vision. Staring at the girl, Kajal finally forced herself to speak her name.

"Lasya," she whispered.

As she'd feared, saying it out loud made it worse. Something real she could not take back. Something she had to accept, with her whole miserable heart.

Her chest faltered under a sob as she leaned down and pressed their foreheads together, one cool and one burning.

"I promise this isn't the end. I'll bring you back, Lasya. I swear it."

The corners of her sister's pale lips were curved slightly upward, as if even in death she knew better than to trust Kajal's promises.

Chapter Two

Five months later

THE SOUND OF a snapping twig forced her head up.

Kajal was elbow-deep in the dirt, a position she now lamented as she thought of what all could be stalking the countryside at night. Rakshasas and wild animals—and, worse, other people—had proven troublesome in recent months.

Especially as more and more of the Usurper King's soldiers prowled the roadways.

She strained to hear anything in the darkness. Breathing, rustling, the slide of fur or skin over branches. But there was only the faint breeze through the leaves, her own racing pulse. And a strange odor, like murky, stagnant water.

Keep going, she urged herself.

Kajal flexed her sore fingers and grabbed the end of the burlap sack she'd unearthed. Clouds rolled across the sky, casting shadows over the town and the woodland on its outskirts. Perfect conditions in which to dig up the body.

But she'd forgotten how *heavy* it was. When it was halfway exhumed, she sat on her heels to catch her breath and sigh over the state of her hands. She had a tool this time—a small, rusty shovel she'd stolen from one of the local farms—but that hadn't prevented dirt from digging into every crevice and crease of her brown skin.

She was readying herself for another heave when voices brought her up short, followed by the crunch of boots on detritus.

Who'd be senseless enough to go strolling through the woods at night? she thought. Barring herself, of course.

Kajal searched the trees until she spotted a couple of figures moving amongst the scraggly trunks. A shaft of moonlight broke through the weak edge of a cloud and shone upon the hilts of their swords.

Biting back a curse, Kajal ducked lower. None of the villagers owned swords; these were either strangers passing through or, if she was exceptionally unlucky, soldiers.

She debated slipping away. Her right foot shifted, ready to creep off into the night, a habit she was on her way to perfecting.

Keep going.

Kajal took a fortifying breath. She wasn't going to abandon her experiment so easily, not when she'd gone through so much trouble for it.

Not when she had so little time to complete it.

The figures stopped and leaned against the trees. The smell of tobacco and betel nut reached her nose before one of them lit a match and ignited a clay chillum.

"How long do we need to stay here?" A man, his voice a weary tenor.

"As long as it takes," said his companion, her tone cheerier. "What, you're not liking our tour of the countryside? Take a moment to enjoy the scenery once in a while."

The man inhaled from his chillum and exhaled a smoky sigh. "I'll enjoy being done with our search."

"The good news is I think we're close."

"How do you know?"

"I have a feeling."

"Wonderful," the man muttered. "Because your *feelings* have been so reliable in the past."

The woman scoffed. "We get chased by a chimera *one* time . . ."

Kajal peered through the foliage to get a better look. Their clothing wasn't the light kurtas and trousers common in western Dharati or the blue-and-marigold uniforms of the Usurper's highest-ranking soldiers, but rather the thicker salwar kameezes of the northeast, plain and loose for riding. They both carried curved talwars on their backs over long-sleeved, skirted cloaks, still dusty from the road.

Whatever they were searching for, they had certainly traveled a long way to find it. But Kajal couldn't think of anything important enough in this tiny rural northwestern town that would attract people like them.

It was why she'd chosen Kinara in the first place: Far less chance of strangers passing through. Less chance of being interrupted—or discovered.

The travelers kept smoking and mumbling about inane things like the weather, how uncomfortable their beds were, the bug bites they had collected on their journey. Kajal curled her fingers into the burlap sack and glared in their direction.

Hurry up and leave already if you hate this place so much, she thought. *I have work to do.*

The breeze came back to tickle her cheek, bringing with it that scent of murky, stagnant water.

"What is that?"

She lifted her head to discover another shadow-draped figure standing between the trees.

Kajal's instinct was to call it a rakshasa—a demon—but that wasn't quite right. The creature was both too ordinary and too outlandish for such a word.

It was a buck, tall and strong and pelted in tawny fur. But the antlers growing from its skull were cracked and rust red, its eyes dark and weeping black liquid. That same viscous substance dripped from its lolling mouth. It staggered forward as a guttural keen left its throat, like the scraping of metal.

The travelers immediately reached for their weapons. Kajal reached for the shovel, little to no good it would do her.

"What is it?" the woman demanded. "Demon?"

"No, I think . . . I think it's blighted."

The woman swore, and Kajal tried not to echo her. She had never seen the blight infect animals before.

Life and death were always in flux, kept in careful balance so that one could not overpower the other. The blight—a worsening sickness that spread in unpredictable waves of black rotted fields, now seemingly jumping into any weak living thing that made room for it—was the cost of imbalance. One that spelled the gradual yet undeniable tilt toward catastrophe.

Kajal did not have time for catastrophe. Her sister's corpse was waiting for her in the east. If the blight reached Lasya's body first, like it had this poor creature . . .

Her throat tightened the way her hand did around the shovel's handle. *Stop it,* she told herself, cutting her thoughts off at the root before they could spiral. Fear would only delay her further. *What-ifs won't solve anything.*

The travelers flanked the diseased buck. Its mouth yawned wider, revealing teeth sharpened to fangs. With a quick turn, it made to sink those fangs into one of the traveler's throats, but the other came in and pushed his sword between its ribs. The creature gave another of those strange dissonant cries before folding toward the earth.

Even in death, its eyes were open. They were the absolute black of the night sky beyond its stars; it felt like tipping into a hole you'd never crawl out of. The dirt soaked with its blood formed dark tendrils, like veins sprouting from a sick heart. Kajal worried about them infecting her half-buried experiment.

The man cleaned his sword on his sleeve and sheathed it, giving the creature a disgusted yet pitying look. "Let's burn it before it spreads."

Kajal frowned and watched one of them gather dry brush and twigs while the other dug a shallow firebreak and coughed over the smell of the buck. Mere travelers wouldn't carry swords like theirs or remain so calm when facing something as abnormal as a blighted animal.

Unless they weren't mere travelers, but demon hunters.

They'd mentioned they were searching for something. Maybe they were searching for some*one*.

Kajal shivered while they lit the kindling before they turned to leave, the man complaining he'd have to burn his shirt. A thin ribbon of smoke curled like a beckoning finger from the first licks of fire, inviting Kajal to remember Siphar, the bob of a lit torch, the smile frozen on her sister's face.

Keep going. Her teeth chattered. *Keep going*.

She turned back to the burlap sack. She needed to be far away from this place before the flames rose higher.

With only weak starlight to see by, she dragged the sack through town. The mustard fields to the south swayed in the wind, waiting for the laborers to come at dawn and resume their harvesting. The town of Kinara was mostly self-sustaining, with enough livestock and hunters for meat and milk and furs, but the people here still needed something to bring to the city's markets to trade for metal and cloth.

Kajal had been traveling on her own long enough to know that a girl who did little else than pace her rented room at the boardinghouse, collect unusual supplies, and mutter to herself invited unwanted suspicion. So to appear less reclusive—and since she needed some way to pay the wrinkled potato of a woman who ran said boardinghouse—she had taken to those fields on a near-daily basis for the last several weeks.

As much as she hated standing under the wickedly bright sun for hours while picking greens, it was far from the worst job she'd had. She worked with her head down and her mouth shut, and it was enough to make the townspeople excuse her otherwise worrying behavior.

But if they saw her dragging a corpse through town, especially one that had been lying so close to the site of a blight attack, the illusion would be shattered without hope of repair.

Please don't be blighted, she begged. *This will have been a massive waste of time if you are.*

Kajal eased the front door to the boardinghouse open. The proprietor, who insisted everyone call her Gurveer Bibi, had a room right by the entrance. The woman snored like a fiend while Kajal dragged the body across the threshold as quietly as she could, wincing when it snagged on the jamb.

The boardinghouse was always drafty, and when the rains came, the building tended to absorb all the wet, making the ceiling drip for days afterward. That was likely why every single piece of wood decided to creak under Kajal's feet when she lifted the sack into her arms and staggered into the stair railing, earning herself a bruise on her hip. Holding back a grumble, she made her slow ascent.

Gurveer Bibi had a tendency of staring at those who displeased her with milky, captious eyes. The old woman especially liked to watch Kajal, waiting for the exact moment to chew her out over some trivial thing. Kajal could practically feel that gaze on her as she navigated the curling stairs, like Gurveer Bibi had enchanted the walls to keep track of her every movement.

By the time she tottered into her room and set down the bag, she was red-faced and trying to stifle her gasps.

The hardest part hadn't even begun.

She turned to her sparsely furnished lodging, containing only a low rope bed and a trunk to store her belongings. A small window peered out at the fields, half obstructed by the next roof over. A slab of pale limestone lay on the floor.

She'd learned the hard way that limestone was the best conduit for this type of work. An incident with common shale and a chicken had led to Kajal frantically cleaning up blood and feathers while Gurveer Bibi shouted at her through the door about the noise.

Kajal rolled the bag toward the slab (stolen from the nearest quarry), which she'd already soaked in water and salt (the latter nabbed from Gurveer Bibi's kitchen). She had used vinegar before (also taken from the kitchen—so, sure, maybe the woman did have a reason to keep an eye on her), but that had resulted in yet another tragic chicken accident. She kept telling herself it was all part of the scientific process, but each failure cost her days, if not weeks. If this new method didn't succeed . . .

Slow and steady, Lasya would have told her. Already, her voice was starting to fade from Kajal's memory, which sent a spike of panic through her stomach. *You're always rushing into things. Breathe and try again.*

Kajal inhaled deeply. Two bodies in this room, and only one heartbeat.

But not for long.

She opened the burlap bag, spilling dirt and fur. Ignoring her already aching limbs, she dragged the dog's filthy corpse onto the stone.

"Of course the first dead thing I saw had to be massive," she muttered. "You probably weigh more than I do." It was easily over a hundred pounds of muscle and long black and brown fur, its paws nearly the size of her head.

But there was no rot. As soon as she'd spotted the mongrel lying near Kinara's cremation grounds, she had buried it, buying time in which to gather the necessary components. Which meant now that it was out in the open, she raced against the ticking clock of decomposition.

She pried the dog's mouth open and pushed a zinc pellet past its large yellowed teeth. It hadn't been easy to obtain even a pebble of the mineral; she'd had to make a long trip to the nearest city on foot, limping on blistered soles to a market where she had traded stolen goods from Kinara. Then she'd crushed it into powder using a pestle, which had rubbed her palms raw.

All this effort for a dog. Kajal put a hand on its flank, its fur bristling between her fingers. *You'd better be worth it.*

Kajal's tongue felt swollen with anxiety as she reached for the jar of salt and sprinkled it liberally over the dog's body. She parted the dog's fur to rub chopped goldenrod and adder's-tongue against its pale skin, the herbs having been boiled in oil and suet (the used oil bartered from the dhaba down the street, the suet stolen from their kitchens when they were busy getting her the oil), then used a spoon to dribble more of the mixture into its mouth.

Pressure was already emanating from the limestone and seeping through the hunk of dead flesh like the charged air before a storm. Her skin prickled in response, the warning before a lightning strike.

Slow and steady.

Kajal massaged her hand over the dog's cold throat and chest. Her fingers tingled with the current. She followed the body's pathways, pressing against the focal points of its chakras, until she rested one hand over the dog's chest and pressed her other thumb to the center of its brow.

Reach its heart, she thought desperately. She visualized grasping the energy flowing between her and the dog, thick and smelling vaguely metallic, like blood. *Please. You must.*

One pulse, and then another. She gasped at the lick of pain that went up her arm from the contact. The only thing preventing her from recoiling was the thought of Lasya opening her eyes, of her looking up at Kajal and smiling.

Come on!

With the next lashing pulse, the limestone cracked nearly in two. The sound took her back to Siphar, to the gaping mouth of a mine entrance, to the echoing break of stone, bone, heart.

Six of our miners are dead because of you.

You killed her.

Kajal pushed down a cry as the dog spasmed again. Its paws twitched. Its fur stood on end.

And then it opened one amber eye.

Kajal scrambled away from the slab. The dog lumbered to its feet, salt flying as it shook its shaggy head. It began to growl.

"No, it's all right!" She reached under the patterned rope of her charpoy. "I don't mean you harm. See?"

She unsteadily held out a strip of dried lamb. The dog stopped rubbing at its face to inspect the offering.

"That's it," Kajal breathed when the dog cautiously padded over, head lowered. It didn't *seem* blighted. "Are you hungry, after being in the ground so long?"

Preserved as it had been, its organs should be functioning. But the dog sniffed at the lamb, took it gently in its mouth, then spat it out.

"Oh," she said. "All right. We can work on that."

The grin that stretched across Kajal's face was so wide and unfamiliar it made her cheeks hurt. She watched the dog nose around her room, sometimes growling, sometimes turning its head to make sure she hadn't moved. Her chest welled with the same warmth that stung her eyes.

"You're alive," she whispered to the shadows. "I brought you back."

I can fix this, Lasya. Just wait a little longer.

I won't let you down again.

Chapter Three

THE WORLD CHANGES when you have nothing left. The first impulse is despair: to lash out, fight, gnash your teeth in denial. But after a while it becomes a calm surrender, a realization that nothing can be as it once was, so what is the point in fighting? Kajal had been left in an empty house that had once been filled with comfort, and she had chosen to lie on the cold floor with the windows boarded up, entombed within her loss.

Then had come a fresh wave of determination, a door swinging open. She *could* fight. She *could* reclaim what had once been hers. Lasya was gone, but not forever.

And now Kajal was one step closer to getting her back.

The dog was restless the entire night, and neither of them slept. Kajal sat in the middle of the rope bed with her battered and stained notebook, taking notes with the nub of a charcoal pencil.

"Sure you don't want to eat?" she asked again. Without Lasya around, Kajal was out of practice when it came to conversation—not that she'd ever been proficient at it in the first place—but she found it oddly nice to speak to the dog, perhaps because it couldn't talk back.

The dog gave her a flat look in response.

"Fine, more for me."

She chewed on the dried lamb, making exaggerated noises of satisfaction and waving it around in a show of enticement, but the dog pointedly ignored her. She rolled her eyes and made a note of his lack of appetite.

In the first town she'd visited after the Siphar accident, she had worked a short stint as a butcher's assistant, plucking chickens and hanging up the bodies of other animals to drain them of blood. Whenever the butcher wasn't looking, she'd poked and prodded at the animals' insides, committing the layout of their organs to memory. Eventually, she'd saved up enough coin to purchase a pencil, as well as paper and thread to bind up a notebook, one of the few possessions she hadn't stolen.

Most of the pages were already filled with sketches and measurements and theories among the occasional doodle (her favorite being Raja Hiss, a mustachioed snake wearing a turban). Her handwriting was cramped and barely legible, but she had been lucky to learn her letters at all. Living as they had, she and Lasya hadn't received a traditional education. Instead, Kajal had hidden in classrooms, listened in on tutoring sessions for the brats she minded, and stolen books from libraries and homes.

If they weren't swarming with soldiers, she would have traveled to the cities of Malhir and Suraj to make use of their grand public libraries. At the libraries she *had* been able to access these last few months, she'd read essays published by the Meghani family, celebrated demon hunters who'd even traveled to the Harama Plain and lived to tell the tale. Although Kajal disapproved of the profession—there was simply no reason to hunt rakshasas that weren't actively trying to kill you—she'd found plenty of useful information.

Namely, what would happen if she didn't succeed. Six months after death, an unburned body would form a bhuta that would first target those it had known in life, then—once glutted with power from those kills—whatever unfortunate soul crossed its path.

Already, five months had passed since she had buried Lasya, and one of those months she'd wasted wallowing. Her window of opportunity was closing, but with this latest triumph, she was more confident than ever she could achieve what all the books in the libraries she'd combed through deemed impossible.

The dog settled on the floor and stared at her. She stared back, blinking slowly, but the dog only stared harder. Was he trying to tell her something? Was he hungry after all, and simply didn't like her offering? It would be just her luck to have resurrected a picky dog.

"You better not have expensive tastes. I can't afford to feed you prime cuts."

The dog's sides heaved with a sigh. His eyes were an oddly glowing amber, and the morning sunlight didn't lessen the effect. She couldn't help but think of the aga ghora with its uncanny white eyes.

Kajal had a shift scheduled in the fields that day. Unwilling as she was to go, she needed the money to travel to Lasya's body and gather the supplies for her revival.

"Don't even think about it," she said when the dog trailed after her. "You stay here." If the travelers-maybe-demon-hunters were staying at the boardinghouse, she didn't want to give them any reason to notice her if they crossed paths.

But the dog was large and stubborn, shoving her into the door as he stalked past. Kajal gave an incredulous huff and hurried down the stairs after him.

Gurveer Bibi was smacking her sunken lips over a bowl of rice at the communal table when she saw the dog and Kajal. Her eyes widened, and her frayed chunni slipped down to her shoulders, revealing a shock of gray hair.

"What's that disgusting creature doing here?" she demanded.

Kajal reached for an excuse and landed short. "It followed me home?"

"Take it out at once!" Gurveer Bibi rapped her spoon on the table, her iron bangle making an echo beside it. "Crawling with fleas like its master, no doubt."

"Fleas can't live in human hair."

"Don't you talk back to me! The mutt's an omen of misfortune. If I see it in here again, I'm kicking it *and* you out."

Kajal bit the inside of her cheek. She could hardly argue with the woman; she owned the damn place. But Kajal couldn't stop the wick of indignity from being lit, already charred from so many other exchanges like this.

"Be grateful I haven't done it already. I know you're up to no good." Gurveer Bibi's face twisted into a sneer. "Did I ever tell you what the Vadhia did to our fortune teller?"

She had, many times. Just a few months before Kajal arrived, the star reader of Kinara had accurately predicted the death of her cousin, an otherwise healthy man who'd ignored her warnings. When he'd died in a hunting accident, her own family had encouraged the soldiers passing through at the time to drag the star reader from her home and blind her. She'd then been exiled, forced to wander sightless through the countryside. It was the same propaganda Kajal had seen popping up everywhere lately; any connection to the preternatural, to death, would land you a final—and more often than not, fatal—meeting with the Vadhia.

"I'm sure the next Vadhia patrol would be interested in searching that room of yours," Gurveer Bibi suggested.

Kajal's teeth pierced her delicate skin, and the iron tang of blood filled her mouth. She was momentarily possessed by the urge to walk up to the woman and smack her rice bowl away, if only to see that sneer wiped from her face.

You have no idea what I can do to you.

The corner of her mouth quirked at the thought. It was satisfying in a way few things were lately, encouraging her to push beyond the realm of daydream.

She was about to take a step forward when she heard a thin, high whine, like wind blowing through a crevice. Gurveer Bibi didn't seem to hear it, still clutching her spoon like a battle-axe.

She's not worth it.

Kajal shook her head and led the dog outside. The sun was already fixing its eye on Kinara, promising a humid morning of damp skin and frizzing hair. The strange whine died down, as did her anger, leaving her tired in its wake.

Kajal spat the blood from her mouth. "Half-dead wretch." She narrowed her eyes at the dog. "You *don't* have fleas, do you?"

The dog gave a tentative wag of its tail.

"Reassuring, thank you."

But not even Gurveer Bibi could fully dampen her burgeoning hope. Kajal made for the fields with a somewhat lighter step, pursued by the padding of large paws on the dirt road.

Her attention strayed to the northern woodland. A pillar of smoke was coiling toward the sky, and she wasn't surprised to see a cluster of curious townspeople gathered at the tree line. The travelers were nowhere to be seen.

A few of those gathered frowned at Kajal and the dog. She lowered her head and walked faster.

"Irya," Farmer Abhay greeted when she arrived. He was leaning his weight on a plow as he surveyed the field. It was the one closest to town, and Kajal appreciated the short commute from the boardinghouse. A camel walked in circles around the stone well that pushed out water to irrigate the crops while Abhay's two small children ran between its legs. "You're late."

She glanced at the sun's position. "I'm on time."

He scowled, his sun-leathered face framed by deep lines. "Just find an empty row."

Harvesting and planting greens was repetitive work. Her worn leather slippers filled with soil as she transferred ripened greens to her small handcart and reached into the seed bag at her waist to replace them. Sometimes, the motion made the scars on her back ache. Today, she was slower than usual, preoccupied by the sight of the dog sitting silent and watchful at the edge of the field, amber eyes glowing faintly like twin stars.

It also didn't help that two farmhands behind her were chatting in low, solemn voices.

"It's a bad sign," one of them said. "A *warning*. I'm telling you, it's only a matter of time until we're hit. Did you hear about Jahar? Entire crop ruined. All that rye rotted overnight."

"I doubt it was that fast."

"That's what they said. Had to burn the whole field." He spat. "This must be our punishment finally come for allowing a usurper to sit on the throne. We've failed our dharma."

The other farmhand hissed at him to be quiet. "It's not dharma. It's a *curse*. Why else do you think the Vadhia are crawling all over, looking for those who cast it?"

Kajal grimaced. Anu Bakshi, the Usurper King—the moniker whispered only by those who despised him, or the very brave—had been ruling Dharati ever since she could remember. Those he had invited into his personal army were called the Vadhia, and did not operate in the same manner as the Dharatian military, though both fell under Bakshi's control. The Vadhia were fewer, elite, loyal.

And they had no qualms enforcing Bakshi's rule with cruelty. In recent years, Kajal had seen homesteads burned and would-be rebels hanged from trees. But in these last few months, with the blight growing worse by the day, the Vadhia had been given permission to fight back in whatever ways they could—specifically, eradicating supposed witches.

To be suspected of being a witch meant trials and torture, or banishment at best. Nowadays, the claim was as good as a death sentence.

Kajal struggled to drown out the men's gossip. The farmhand in the row beside hers paused to wipe sweat from his forehead, his rumaal stained with it. He nodded to the dog by the trees. "He yours?"

She looked around, as if he could possibly be talking to anyone else. When she realized she'd have to indulge him with a reply, she cleared her throat. "A stray. I guess he grew attached to me."

"Huh. Can't see why."

Kajal pursed her lips at the gibe.

"You named him yet?"

She supposed her creation did deserve a name. "Kutaa."

The man scoffed. "You named the dog *Dog*?" He stared at the animal a bit longer, frowning.

The dog stared back, hackles rising as if sensing danger. It made the nape of Kajal's own neck tingle unpleasantly.

Eventually, the farmhand shrugged and returned to harvesting.

She shouldn't have brought the dog with her; he was drawing too much attention. Dogs had never been popular in Dharati to begin with, as they were considered pests who haunted cremation grounds for bodies to scavenge (which *was* where she had found him, but as someone who'd spent a good deal of time near cremation grounds herself, she hadn't thought much of it).

Even Gurveer Bibi knew something was wrong with him. What if the woman tried to get Kajal in trouble? Never mind that she hadn't actually *done* anything, besides some light thieving here and there.

But Kajal knew from experience that those like Gurveer Bibi needed little provocation to pounce. That it was easier for people to point at and blame outside forces for their troubles.

She remembered the man in Siphar, ready to put a torch to her and Lasya's bodies. But the fury in his eyes had been more than understandable if what he'd said was true. If she had really—

If she had—

The corner of her vision flickered. Her chest tightened, cutting off her breath. A frisson of cold swept over her, despite the blazing sunshine.

Then she heard it: the same noise from the boardinghouse, a thin, high whine.

Slowly, Kajal turned.

A girl who cast no shadow stood beyond the field. Her white dress and black hair fluttered in a nonexistent wind, her feet hovering a few inches from the ground. She stared at Kajal with eyes red as cinnabar, so utterly and inhumanly still.

Those eyes used to be dark and warm. That flat, pale mouth used to always be curled up in a smile. That stiff, unmoving body used to be in constant motion, either swaying to music Kajal couldn't hear or practicing mudras or cutting up herbs.

"No," Kajal whispered.

No, I still have time. I thought I had more time—

The bhuta that was once her sister stared without recognition, without emotion. The whine climbed higher, louder, worming its way into Kajal's brain. It made her insides shiver and her knees weaken; it made the center of her forehead burn.

"Behan, please be careful," Lasya said, nervously twirling the copper ring on her pinkie finger. "We don't know what this will do."

"I'll figure it out," Kajal insisted. "This is me we're talking about. It'll work."

"What if it doesn't? What do we do then?"

A hand on her arm made her jump. One blink and the bhuta was gone, as were the cold and the whining drone.

"If you're getting heat sick, go sit in the shade," the farmhand said. "If you faint, I'm not going to move you."

Kajal scanned the field, but Lasya was gone.

"This isn't . . . This can't be right," she stammered.

According to the Meghanis' findings, bhutas didn't form until at least six months after death. She still had a few weeks until that marker, so why had her sister begun to haunt her already? Was she truly that angry, that desperate for Kajal to make good on her promise?

The blight. Had the tainting of Dharati's soil caused the bhuta to come early? Or perhaps Kajal really was heat sick and had imagined the whole thing. But Kutaa was also staring at the spot where the bhuta had appeared, ears at attention.

Farmer Abhay whistled sharply. "Irya! No dawdling!"

She forced herself to continue harvesting, ignoring the persistent thrum of dread under her skin. Telling herself what she'd seen wasn't real. Couldn't be real.

Pushing away every thought as she had grown so adept at doing these last few months, lest she end up back on the floor.

When the sun hit its zenith, Farmer Abhay called everyone into the shade. Kajal sat under a teak tree, tensing every time its leaves rustled, whisper-like, above her head. Kutaa lay down beside her and watched her tear the flatbread she'd been handed into pieces. She held a piece out to him, but the dog turned his head away.

"That's all right." Kajal scratched him behind the ears, which he seemed to enjoy. "I can't eat either."

She was staring at the spot where she'd seen Lasya when movement on the town's main road, which ran parallel to the field, caught her attention. A few men were running in the direction of the boardinghouse.

Gurveer Bibi's sons.

"Did something happen?" a farmhand murmured.

Kajal's uneasiness sharpened on the whetstone of her lingering dread. Dropping the remains of her flatbread, she approached the edge of the field.

Her gut twisted at the sight of people hovering at the entrance of the boardinghouse down the way. The throng parted at the arrival of the town's medicine man, who hurried through the front door and nearly collided into a woman on her way out. Kajal caught a brief glimpse of the woman's clothes before she disappeared into the crowd. One of the travelers.

"What's going on?" Kajal mused out loud.

An older auntie on her way to join the nosy onlookers glanced at her, tsking at Kajal's dirty clothes and the equally dirty dog behind her.

"You didn't hear? Gurveer Bibi is dead."

Chapter Four

"HEART FAILURE," THE medicine man claimed. "Found her twisted up with a ghastly look on her face, clutching at her chest."

Kajal kept her own face carefully blank as they carried the body out, covered in a sheet that did little to hide the strange contortions of its limbs. But under Kajal's blankness was a howling panic, clawing up her insides and rattling the bars of her ribs.

Once, in a village she and Lasya had passed through, a young man had been carrying buckets of milk when he'd dropped like a stone in the street. The milk had seeped into the dirt as he writhed and choked on nothing, scrabbling at his chest while his mouth foamed.

Kajal had insisted on staying long enough to learn what had caused it, much to Lasya's annoyance. Apparently, the young man had had a long-standing feud with a hunter who'd disappeared months before. Likely attacked by a rakshasa, the hunter was eventually found mauled and half buried in a ravine. But his body had been there long enough to form a bhuta, intent on taking the lives of those who had wronged him. If the villagers hadn't burned the body to release his spirit, the wraith would have grown stronger with each kill until it became a permanent fixture of the village, like a particularly murderous tree or building.

But according to the Meghanis, bhutas stayed within a couple miles of where their mortal forms had perished. There was no way Lasya's bhuta could have ended up *here*, so far from Siphar. And beyond that, there was no reason for the bhuta to target Gurveer Bibi, whom her sister had never met.

But Kajal had always considered herself above believing in coincidences.

"That girl stays at the boardinghouse, doesn't she?" A couple of farmhands had wandered over from the field; the one muttering was the same one who'd implied the blight was the work of witches. "She didn't used to have a dog. Did you see its eyes?"

"Do you see *her* eyes? Swear they glow red in the light."

A memory emerged, one she had tried to suppress but that nonetheless surfaced in her nightmares. A swinging noose, and a woman screaming for help, crying that she had done nothing wrong. The Vadhia standing around in their blue-and-marigold uniforms, brass pips gleaming at their collars.

Smiling.

Kajal's heart beat fast and hard against her breastbone. She had planned to remain in Kinara a bit longer, as she would need money to buy supplies for Lasya's resurrection and to arrange transport to her body. But she knew all too well what would happen if she stayed: the glares, the rumors, the suspicion. No good would come from it.

The boardinghouse was crawling with activity, and the farmer would harangue her if she didn't finish her row, leaving her little choice but to slink back to the fields. She reluctantly slipped into her routine of pulling up greens and dropping new seeds in their place, repeating to herself that she just needed to lie low until nightfall, then she'd grab her things and disappear into the dark.

But a sudden realization froze her in place, her hand wrapped around a stalk. She was lucky the people of Kinara didn't recognize a bhuta attack when they saw one, but if those travelers really were demon hunters, they surely would.

And if they had heard about her misdeeds in Siphar—a concern gnawing at her since last night—then she already had a target looming over her.

"Hey." Farmer Abhay snapped his fingers at her as he passed. "What'd I tell you about dawdling?"

She jerked. Her fingers spasmed around the stalk, and she pulled the mustard greens from their earthen bed.

At first, she didn't understand what she was seeing. What she was holding. The green veins of the plant had been overtaken with black, like a series of polluted rivers. A foul smell emanated from within the wide leaves, smoky and sweetly rotten.

Kajal dropped it and stumbled backward. The farmhand in the next row chuckled.

"Found another spider?" he teased. Then his eyes landed on the fallen plant and widened.

"Blight," he rasped. Then louder: *"Blight!"*

Kajal backed farther away as the other farmhands descended in a flurry of curses and cries. She stared at the field—at the spots of black beginning to wend through the rows—and wondered if there was anyone in this world with worse luck than her.

She ran. Leaving so abruptly was a foolish idea, but staying here was even more so.

She had to leave—now.

A bhuta attack and blight. Perhaps Kinara truly was cursed.

Or maybe Kajal was the only cursed thing here.

One of Gurveer Bibi's sons, who in Kajal's experience did little more than pick his nose and leer at women, seemed to have taken it upon himself to oversee the boardinghouse. She could hear him barking orders in the kitchen, which meant he wasn't around to say anything about Kutaa, who trailed her like a shadow as she slipped up to her room. Outside, the noise was growing, the alarmed commotion from the field making its way into town.

Kajal hastily washed her hands and packed her meager belongings. They didn't amount to much: a knife, a change of clothes, a small pouch of herbs that was a pitiful reminder of Lasya's beloved spice box.

And, of course, Kajal's notebook. But when she lifted the pillow to grab it, her heart plummeted.

It was gone.

She held the pillow in one clammy hand, at a loss. Her mind—usually a chaotic storm of chattering thoughts and colorful ideas that, yes, fine, maybe weren't *all* winners—had ground to a standstill. This couldn't be happening.

Who—?

The demon hunters.

Or, rather, the one she had seen slip out of the boardinghouse earlier.

"Oh, no no no," Kajal breathed, smooshing the pillow between her fists. "You're not getting me that easily." If anyone read even a page of that notebook, it would mean a short trip to the noose.

She threw her pack over her shoulder and, with Kutaa at her heels, bounded down the stairs as the furor grew outside. When she reached the door, she immediately saw why.

Agitated farmhands and fearful townsfolk had congregated near the boardinghouse. And there, at the center of their irate storm, were two young women—including the traveler-perhaps-demon-hunter who'd likely stolen her notebook.

Heat prickled along Kajal's skin. Before she could decide if she should hurry up and find where the woman's belongings were stashed or just run for the town's outskirts, someone grabbed her by the elbow.

"Got her," grunted Gurveer Bibi's son, the one who'd been in the kitchen. He was a hulking thing; he held a bottle of fermented rice wine in his right hand while his left one was an unmovable clamp on her arm. He dragged her through the crowd, ignoring Kutaa's warning growls.

Kajal stumbled as he pushed her toward the women. In addition to the traveler she was the only other female farmhand, an unmarried girl who socialized even less than Kajal did. She shook under the town's glares, ashen and unsure.

The traveler-perhaps-demon-hunter merely seemed bewildered, blinking and looking around with something like amusement in the upward tick of her mouth. Her brown hair was long enough to keep in a braid, and a silver stud glinted at her left nostril. Her gaze landed on Kajal, who stiffened, but the girl only raised her eyebrows, as if to ask *What is happening here?*

Don't look at me like I'm your conspirator, Kajal wanted to snap. This was the *last* thing she had wanted to happen, especially if this girl had Kajal's notebook and decided to use it as her escape ticket.

Sure enough, that's when the blaming started.

"One of you cursed our town!" a woman yelled. "First, the animal in the woods. Then, the fields. Our *crops*." Some of the townspeople murmured worriedly; those crops were a considerable source of income for Kinara. "Not to mention Gurveer Bibi dying so suddenly when the medicine man claimed she was healthy. It can't be a coincidence."

The son who'd grabbed Kajal curled his upper lip at her. She fought to remember his name—Sandeep? Gurdeep? Gurveer Bibi's two other sons flanked him, one as brutally large as Gurdeep(?), the other tall and stringy.

Doesn't matter, she told herself while her eyes flitted around, trying to find the best escape route. Maybe Kutaa could cause a distraction. Maybe—

Farmer Abhay leveled a coarse finger at the traveler. "You and that friend of yours arrived just before all this happened."

"That's true," the traveler said brightly.

"So you're admitting to having something to do with this?"

The girl made a face that Kajal would have snorted at in any other circumstance. "Now, that's quite the leap in logic, don't you think? My friend and I put down that diseased buck. We did you a favor."

"Just listen to the way she talks back," hissed an older woman in the crowd. "Impudent. Disrespectful."

Kajal pressed her lips together while sweat soaked her underarms. Kutaa prowled the fringes of the crowd, whining.

Farmer Abhay looked like he wanted to close the distance and strike the traveler across the face. "For all we know, *you're* the ones who cursed that buck in the first place." Murmurs of assent followed. "You and your *friend* could be rakshasas in disguise, come here under orders from the demon lord to spread the blight!"

The crowd gasped at the idea, most of them taking a couple steps back—including the other accused girl.

The traveler burst out laughing. Kajal's jaw dropped.

"That's a good one," the young woman giggled.

"She doesn't deny it!"

"Quick, find her accomplice!"

The traveler stopped laughing as members of the town watch moved forward. "Wait, what's happening? You really believe that?"

Of course they do, Kajal thought bitterly. *They're nothing but superstitious fools.*

The wide-eyed farmhand had, smartly, taken the opportunity to flee into the crowd while everyone's ire was directed at the stranger. This was the distraction Kajal had been hoping for; even Kutaa was waiting for her with his head down and muscles bunched. But then she thought of her notebook, her months and months of research—and a possible lead for the Vadhia if this girl decided to implicate her after all.

They can't prove it was you if you're not here.

She could make it to the edge of town and be on her way in the time it took the town watch to arrest the travelers. Kajal shuffled farther from the woman, turning on her heel—about to walk away like she always did, leaving others to their fate while she defied hers.

But in her mind burned the afterimage of a swinging noose and an echo of a helpless woman's screams.

Kajal had done nothing to stop it. There was nothing she *could* have done, not when she followed only one rule in this world: *Survive.*

Lasya would have done something then. And Lasya would have done something now, if she were here.

If Kajal hadn't . . .

She clenched her jaw and swallowed hard before turning back and blurting, "That's not how the blight works."

The crowd, including the advancing town watch and the bemused traveler, swiveled their fevered eyes to her.

"Um," she croaked under their stares. "So, the thing is . . . even if rakshasas *could* take on a human appearance, there's been no proof so far that they have the ability to spread the blight." When no one moved or made a sound, she kept going in a slightly stronger voice, reaching for the comfort of factual evidence. "The pattern of blight is unpredictable, yes, but most of what's been reported in the surrounding area has been in places with a *decreased* rakshasa presence. It's only after the discovery of blight that the number of rakshasas increases. It seems strains of blight tend to lure demons to those places, which is likely how the correlation came about, but rakshasas themselves are not the cause. If anything, it's the buck that caused the blight to form, which means the blight can spread through *animals*, not humans, or curses, or whatever nonsense you believe—"

Glass shattered on the ground near her feet. Kajal flinched.

"You."

Gurdeep—she was fairly certain it was Gurdeep—took a swaying step forward. His dark eyes were bloodshot, his mouth set in a grimace of grief. He flexed the hand that had thrown his wine bottle.

"My mother hated you," he muttered, coming closer while the others got out of his way. How had she not realized until now how large he was? He was built for farmwork, all broad shoulders and thick hands that could easily wrap around her neck and break it.

"I saw the way you talked back to her, just like this, thinking you're so much better'n the rest of us. She should've smacked you around, taught you some respect." Gurdeep laughed, off-kilter. "I bet it was you. All the stress you gave her wore down her heart. You *killed* her."

You killed her.

Kajal winced.

Gurdeep's eyes widened at her reaction.

"No . . . No, you think you're too clever for that, don't you? Was it poison? Did you poison my mother?"

"*What?* I didn't—"

"Liar!" he screamed before rushing her.

Kajal was too shocked to do anything but let him crash into her. She grunted as her elbow smacked the dirt road, a nauseating pain shooting down her arm.

Gurdeep huffed like a bull above her, grabbing her face and knocking her head against the ground. Her vision blackened. No one came to help.

"You'll pay for it," he seethed, his other hand finding her throat and squeezing. "Evil thing. I'll kill y—"

He let go with a shout. Wasting no time, Kajal rolled over and crawled away.

"Get the dog!" someone yelled.

"Kill the filthy mongrel!"

She raised her head. Kutaa had sunken his teeth into Gurdeep's shoulder.

"Stop!" Kajal cried hoarsely. "Kutaa, *stop!*"

She didn't think the dog would listen, but he let go and backed off with blood on his muzzle. Gurdeep kept hollering as he pawed at the bite mark.

Good. She wanted him to hurt. She wanted him to bleed, to feel even a fraction of the fear he had made her feel. An unnerving satisfaction bloomed within her.

Gurdeep pierced her with murderous eyes. But when he launched at her again, he seemed to slow, even the dust particles in the air stopping middrift.

A high, piercing whine filled her ears.

No.

A flutter of white, the low whisper of a voice she had once known and loved. Lasya stood behind Gurdeep, preternaturally still against the wind that accompanied her. It smelled of damp soil and rotten fruit, of something the earth harbored deep within its stomach, masticated and fermented.

Lasya's eyes glinted red as she stared at Kajal. The whisper and the whine grew louder, louder, until they vibrated against Kajal's bones and made her wish for death after all.

Find me, she thought she heard in the din. *Kill me.*

Gurdeep rocked back with a strangled cry and clutched his chest. His mouth opened and closed, trying desperately to suck in air, while his face purpled and his eyes rolled until only the whites were visible. His brothers grabbed his shoulders to steady him as his large frame shuddered and jerked, frothy blood leaking from his mouth. Then, at last, he lay unmoving.

The silence rang as loud as his screams. Kajal tangled her fingers in Kutaa's long, soft fur, unable to move, her knees aching on the dirt road.

"D-Dakini," someone whispered in the shocked hush that had fallen over the crowd. "*Witch.*"

Kajal barely heard the accusation. She couldn't tear her eyes off Gurdeep's body, Lasya's voice—the one she had been so scared to forget—echoing through her with its terrible request.

A mother and son, only a few hours apart, both preceded by her sister's ghost. Kajal couldn't deny any longer that Lasya had become a bhuta well before she should have.

One that was already starved for power.

Chapter Five

IT WASN'T HER first time in a jail, and it likely wouldn't be her last.

Kajal, reeling from the attack, didn't even put up a fight when members of the town watch grabbed her. Kutaa snapped his jaws, but one sharp word from her and the dog's ears flattened before he turned and ran. Despite present circumstances, Kajal brimmed with curiosity over how well he took her orders.

Law enforcement was tricky in rural Dharati. Unlike the bigger cities' use of magistrates, most towns and villages were left to look after themselves. Many had developed their own systems, such as Kinara's town watch, which consisted of dutiful citizens. They maintained small jails like the one she was hauled to, buildings of white brick with a couple barred-off cells.

"You don't have any proof," she argued as she was pushed into a cell. She knew it was pointless, but that wouldn't stop her from trying. "How could I have possibly killed him without a weapon? It wasn't me!"

"We all saw what happened," a town watch member retorted, a man with a glossy beard. "Gurdeep died right after he touched you. Not to mention you sicced that unnatural mutt of yours on him."

"Dakini," said the other, touching his forehead and flicking his fingers away. It was the same word flung at her in Siphar, the same accusation she couldn't seem to shake no matter where her feet took her.

Claiming that a human woman was a dakini, a type of rakshasa, was not a casual offense. It implied there was something *wrong* with her—even if she was merely widowed, single, or too smart for her own good. These women were thought to have been reincarnated from other types of rakshasas, or else had faced neglect and violence in their past lives and carried their hatred into a new one.

While it was commonplace for people to adorn their doors with chilis, neem leaves, and pouches of rock salt to ward off the evil eye dakinis were said to cast, these superstitions had strengthened in the last few decades. Over time, *dakini* had become synonymous with *witch*.

"It was *your* row where they found the blight," the bearded man went on. "All of Kinara's misfortunes can be traced back to you."

A pit yawned open in Kajal's stomach, where all her blackest thoughts went to calcify. This man believed what he was saying. He was willing to place the town's problems on her shoulders, to punish her as a means of fulfilling his dharma.

Because girls like her, who knew too much and conformed too little, must be full of darkness.

When the two men left to discuss her punishment with the rest of the town watch, Kajal paced the cell's straw-lined floor, rubbing the spot between her eyebrows. She ran into the wall more than once; the cell was cramped, and there were no windows to provide light. Kajal heard Kutaa's distant howl and cursed at him to be quiet.

Calm down. You can figure a way out of this. She had a feeling that whatever punishment they settled on, it would be enacted quickly. *Think, think.*

In the past, depending on the severity of her crime—theft, mostly—she had gotten away with whatever she had done by performing an ordeal. They varied wherever she went; in one instance, she had been weighed twice on a balance scale, and when she had weighed less the second time (thanks to the rock she'd wiggled from her sleeve when no one was looking), she was declared innocent. In another instance, she'd had to stay underwater while an arrow was fired into the lake and someone ran in to retrieve it, only allowed to come up for air once the arrow had been brought back (and the boy had taken his sweet time with it too).

This, though? Two people dying the same way, so close together? Blight running through their precious crops? She'd be lucky to receive an ordeal at all. Especially if any of the Vadhia were nearby and caught wind of the incident.

Keep going. The sweat had dried on her skin, leaving it itchy and tight. *I have to . . .*

But she was already too late.

"How did this happen?" she whispered to no one, the shape of her voice too large for such a small enclosure. "Lasya . . ."

The blackness around her was oppressive, thick, as suffocating as deep water. She kept pacing, four steps, then turn, four steps, then turn, if only to hear something amid all that silence. It wasn't enough, so she began to hum.

It was the song she'd hum when Lasya was upset, when they were bored, or simply if her sister requested it. *Lotus Blossom*—the title begrudgingly given after days of Lasya pestering her to name it. The melody was as familiar as the sound of her own name, the frame of her bones, something that had long been part of her.

Caught up in the notes, it took a moment for Kajal to realize there was a second set of footsteps.

Kajal froze. The footsteps stopped as well. She didn't move even as a sigh of cold air swept over her, the space between her shoulder blades prickling.

In the heart of the darkness came a flutter of white, a flash of red eyes.

Kajal stumbled into the wall. There was nothing in this cell save herself, some straw, and a few insects. But it was no longer silent. A whisper blew into one ear and then the other, breathing down the nape of her neck.

Kill me. Kill me.

"What does that mean?" Kajal croaked. "Lasya—"

She jumped when the door to the building opened. The whispers scattered, leaving her shaken and disoriented.

Kajal had expected someone from the town watch to return and reveal her sentence. She was surprised to find the two travelers instead. The young man held a torch, its flickering glow playing with the shadows of their clothes and faces, threading their dark hair with red.

The travelers approached her cell slowly, as if afraid she would turn into a snake and slither through the bars. *If only*. Kajal eyed the torch, helplessly thrown back to that day in the coffin, the chill of Lasya's body, digging in the dirt until her hands cracked and bled.

If they were demon hunters, then today was all the proof they needed.

"They say your name is Irya," said the young man—boy, really. Both looked barely older than Kajal. The boy had a prominent nose, and his hair fell in a swoop across his forehead. He had no adornments save for the tip of a faded tattoo peeking from his collar. "But I doubt that's true."

She glanced at the girl, who winked in a way Kajal found overly familiar, despite their recently shared injustice. "No. It's Kajal." She had grown used to throwing out false names since Siphar, but there was no use pretending in her current situation.

"Kajal." The boy said it like a bitter seed caught between his teeth. "No family name?"

"Why? You planning to write up a marriage contract?"

If Lasya were here, she would have done all the talking. Those were their roles: Lasya, the negotiator; Kajal, the thief. Without her sister's calming voice and pleasant words, Kajal was left to defend herself with nothing but nails sharpened on threats and insults.

The boy's mouth grew pinched, but the girl laughed. "I need to thank you for intervening earlier," she said, her tone considerably lighter than her partner's. "Even though it led to this."

"I don't want your thanks," Kajal spat. "I wasn't doing it for you. Is that why you came to gawk at me?"

"Not the sole reason. Want to hazard a guess as to the other?"

Kajal smiled. It was not a nice smile. "I think I'll leave the explaining to you."

"Right." The girl smacked her hand against the boy's chest, making him grunt. "The two of us heard about strange happenings in Siphar. A collapsed mine, dead miners, an aga ghora . . . and two sisters who'd died, only for one of them to come back to life and run off with the other's body."

The blood drained from Kajal's face.

"And now this," the girl went on, gesturing to the wall and the town beyond it. "Classic signs of a bhuta attack."

"Then . . . you *are* demon hunters."

"What?" the boy said. "Hardly." He looked down at himself, as if wondering what about his appearance had given her that impression. Even the girl seemed strangely offended.

Kajal was growing more confused. "If you're not demon hunters, then why are you here? Why did you follow me?" *Why did you take my notebook?*

"Dead girls don't come back to life every day," the boy answered.

"I wasn't *dead*. Siphar's medicine woman was wrong."

"Uh-huh. But your sister is dead. The bhuta is her, isn't it?"

Kajal pressed her lips together.

"We overheard the town watch," the girl said. "They're going to give you an ordeal in the morning."

That didn't sound so bad. She had survived ordeals before. She could do it again.

"An ordeal of poison," the boy added.

Never mind. *No one* survived an ordeal of poison; even walking weaponless into a battlefield seemed less of a risk.

Seeing the panic on her face, the girl sighed. "We might be able to help, but you have to be honest. Is the bhuta your sister? Did you manipulate her into killing those two?"

"Why should I be honest with you? I have no idea who you are or what you want."

Both of them smiled then, eerie in the torchlight.

"Because if we like your answer, we'll get you out of here," the girl said.

Kajal took another look at the two standing before her, attempting to suss out the lie.

"I'm Sezal," the girl said. She nudged the boy's side until he muttered, "Vivaan."

"I don't care about your names. I care about your motivation."

"Answer our questions, and we'll tell you more."

Kajal breathed out sharply. "Yes, the bhuta is my sister." Her fingertips twitched at the admission, unable to take it back. "But I didn't make her kill them. Not intentionally. She . . ." Another icy draft blew on the nape of her neck. "The bhuta formed sooner than it was supposed to."

"And somehow followed you here," Vivaan finished. "Were the six miners also because of your sister?"

Kajal curled her hands into fists. "No. That was just a cave-in. That was how Lasya . . . How she . . ."

Vivaan gave a short hum, as if he found the subject of her sister's demise trivial. He and Sezal shared a silent conversation until Sezal dipped her chin.

"We'll get you out of Kinara," Vivaan said at last. "But in return, you'll have to do something for us."

Kajal had learned from an early age that nothing was free—unless it was stolen. She leaned against the bars and crossed her arms, pretending at nonchalance. "Go on."

"Sezal and I have been hired by group of concerned citizens who want to do something about the current state of Dharati."

This, she was not expecting. "What's that supposed to mean?"

"You know what it means," Vivaan said darkly. "The Usurper."

When the warlord Anu Bakshi had made a campaign across Dharati, he'd amassed jaded and incensed citizens into his army before storming the capital—notably those from the wealthier districts who had opposed the then-king's mandates to cease the hunting and killing of rakshasas. Bakshi had killed the king, and when the royal battalion marched against his army, the crown prince had also been slaughtered.

Or at least, that's what Kajal had been told when she was young. She had been born and raised under Anu Bakshi's rule and didn't have a proper comparison to what their country had been like before. All she had to go on were the mutterings of the farmhands, or news broadsheets in the more affluent towns she passed through, which painted Bakshi as some sort of savior. Ironic, considering there were more rakshasas now than ever.

"So you're rebels," she guessed. "You want to depose Bakshi?"

Vivaan quickly looked to the door while Sezal grinned. "That's the heart of it," she agreed.

"Why?"

"Why?" Vivaan whirled back to her, thick eyebrows lowered. "Have you not been paying attention? The yaksha deities have run out of patience. They're furious at all the blood Bakshi's spilled on their soil. It's poisoned our land."

"You think he's responsible for the blight?"

"Bakshi *is* the blight. This imbalance started with him and will end when he's no longer on the throne."

Kajal stared at the twisting shadows on the wall as she thought it over. It was not exactly a secret that Bakshi was corrupt, but it felt so far away from her, inconsequential.

"What do you want *me* to do about it?" she asked at last.

Another silent conversation passed between Vivaan and Sezal. Vivaan then reached inside his shirt. What he pulled out made Kajal's eye twitch.

Sometimes I hate being right.

"Judging from the dog the town watch is trying to catch and what we've read here," he said, waving her battered notebook around, "you've had some success with your experiments."

She ran her tongue over her teeth; her mouth was so dry. "I've never seen that before in my life."

"Oh?" Vivaan flipped through the notebook, turning stained pages crowded with her uneven handwriting. "There's plenty of notes about bhutas. And . . ." He pointed at one of her doodles. "What's this supposed to be? Excrement?"

"That's Raja Hiss," she muttered in affront.

Vivaan smirked. "What we found most interesting are your theories about resurrection."

"You've done it, haven't you?" Sezal whispered. "You brought that dog back to life."

Kajal should have been horrified, unnerved, panicked. If the Vadhia were to find her with that notebook, she'd be executed on the spot. But brighter than her panic was a flash of unfamiliar flattery; Kajal was pleased that someone had finally acknowledged her work.

"We have a contact at the Ayurvedic University in Suraj," Sezal went on. "If you agree to help us, we'll take you there. You'll have access to whatever resources you need to continue your experiments."

Ayurveda was an ancient practice, the knowledge passed down from mothers and fathers to their children and then their grandchildren, from one town's physician to the next. There were also the Ayurvedic universities—one in Suraj, one in Malhir—where scholars learned to apply that knowledge for modern use. But much like with the Usurper King, the idea of them had always been distant, impossible for someone like her.

"Why would I agree to help your mission if I don't know what it is?" Kajal countered. The rebels obviously wanted her to resurrect someone, but she needed to hear it in their own words.

This time it was Sezal's eyes that darted to the door. "We shouldn't explain it here. Don't know who might be listening."

Kajal could *smell* the lie. "Then no deal."

Vivaan scoffed. "Fine." He dangled the notebook from his fingers. "Then I guess we'll give this over to the Vadhia who've been trailing you."

The entire cell seemed to contain Kajal's heartbeat, frantic and wild, pressing in on all sides. "What?"

"We're not the only ones who heard about the mishap in Siphar," Vivaan said. "You're lucky we tracked you down before *they* did. They'd be more than interested in what you've been up to."

In her mind echoed the memory of a woman's screams as the Vadhia rubbed chilis into her eyes, binding them with cloth to protect against the evil eye. Stirring up suspicion around the woman's singing and suggesting she was casting spells with her voice.

Whispering in villagers' ears that Dharati was being devoured by blight for a reason. That cutting off that beguiling voice with a noose would fix it.

Whatever Sezal saw in Kajal's expression made her put a placating hand on Vivaan's arm. "We'll make the deal sweeter. You're planning to revive your sister, aren't you? After you make good on your part of the bargain, we'll bring your sister's body to the university."

One of the reasons Kajal had stayed this long in Kinara was her unwillingness to travel alone. Following the belief that dakinis lured travelers off roads to eat their flesh, the Vadhia had shown no restraint in interrogating women who journeyed on their own. On the trek from Siphar to Kinara, more than one tree she'd passed had been decorated with swaying upside-down bodies, their eyes bound and their throats slit, blood nourishing the ground below like an offering.

Kajal touched her throat. If she agreed to this, not only would she have resources supplied to her for free, but she could avoid wandering through blighted Vadhia-infested lands to retrieve Lasya.

It was a gamble. A dog was one thing; humans, another. Considering that Kutaa—as beautiful and perfect as he was—didn't have the ability to eat, it would be beneficial to practice on a person before attempting to bring back Lasya. And if she fulfilled the rebels' wish, the only condition on which her freedom depended, then she could finish what she had started.

The bhuta would be gone. She would be reunited with her sister.

Everything could return to how it used to be.

Kutaa howled outside the jail. Kajal rolled her shoulders back, settling into the idea, glimpsing the first move of a new game where she would inevitably end up the winner.

Meeting the rebels' gazes, she grinned.

"On one condition," she said. "The dog comes with me."

Chapter Six

EARLY THE NEXT morning, she was given her last meal.

It was the same thing she'd made for herself at the boardinghouse: a simple cracked wheat porridge. Scooping it up with her fingers and shoving the mush into her mouth, she tried not to focus on the blandness or the texture, tried to appreciate that they had given her anything at all.

She would need all her energy if she was going to get out of this alive.

Kajal shut her eyes and thought wistfully of her sister's rice porridge, the kind she would make on chilly mornings. Lasya would add as much jaggery as she was willing to part with from her traveling spice box, made from palm sap and coveted like gold.

Her sister had always been so protective of her spices and herbs. One time, Kajal had taken a dash too much asafoetida to use in an experiment, and Lasya had been drawn to tears.

"These herbs are important!" Lasya had admonished. "They have to be in the right quantity to work with our specific constitutions. What if I run out? I don't want you getting sick, behan." While Lasya keenly followed the practice of Ayurveda when it came to preparing food, Kajal followed the practice as it applied to the human physique, learning about the tissues and channels of the body.

Kajal had rolled her eyes. "I'm not so weak that I'd keel over from an asafoetida deficiency."

Lasya pinched her hard in reply, spurring Kajal to take even more asafoetida in retribution, despite already having enough for her experiment.

For two miserable days, Lasya had given her the silent treatment. But, like they always did, they'd apologized and moved on. Forgiving each other had been easy, and a necessity; after all, they had no one else in this world save each other. Even death couldn't stop her sister from finding ways to stay by her side.

Kajal swallowed the sticky memory with difficulty. Lasya had believed in her, had indulged her boastfulness, and in the end, that very boastfulness had ruined everything.

"Lasya?" she whispered, ignoring the way her voice trembled. "Are you . . . there?"

Will you be able to forgive me this time?

There was no answer. She was still listening futilely when the town watch returned to collect her.

Her eyes watered when she stepped into the hazy sunshine, but after a minute of walking, they cleared enough that she could make out the shrine ahead. It was nearly the size of a building, carved from stone upon a plinth and washed red in the light of dawn. Three tall, pitted figures were distinguishable despite the years and the elements wearing them down: the Serpent, with its wings; the Elephant, with its crown of briar and bone; the Tortoise, with a banyan tree sprouting from its shell. The three yaksha deities, who'd made their home in the heavenly realm of Svarga after blessing the bedrock of Dharati.

The townsfolk had already gathered to witness her ordeal. Fear was as bright as a flesh-eating fire as they wept and pleaded and prostrated themselves before the shrine, begging for the yakshas to free them of blight and curses. Women had brought offerings of flowers, bowls of milk, and waxy red pomegranates heaped like a pile of misshapen hearts.

Kajal was forced to stand under the statues' blank stares, the town watch on either side. A couple hunters held bows with loosely nocked arrows, ready to release at her slightest misbehavior. A bit overkill, in her opinion.

Then again, they suspected her of witchery. She supposed she should consider herself lucky that this was the extent of it so far.

The townspeople backed away at her appearance. Gurveer Bibi's remaining sons glared at her with a loathing so intense it could have shunted her straight into the ground.

Vivaan and Sezal hadn't told her the details of their plan, only that they would come for her once she'd been taken from the jail, since the town watch had been posted to guard it all night. She searched the crowd, but there was no sign of them. She could hear Kutaa's muffled whines, though; someone must have finally captured him.

There was a thought nagging at her, but she wasn't sure what it was until she took a deep breath and realized: There was no smoke coming from the cremation grounds. They hadn't burned Gurveer Bibi's or Gurdeep's bodies.

Strange. What were they waiting for?

"No priests have wandered through here in a while," a farmhand was muttering. "No offerings have been given."

"We should have tended the land better."

"There's no fixing this," a woman proclaimed. "Everywhere the blight touches is ruined beyond repair. Just look at the Harama Plain."

At the name, many in the crowd shuddered and touched the centers of their foreheads before flicking their fingers, a warding sign to open their third eye against evil. The Harama Plain was the no-man's-land in the center of Dharati, where bhutas of soldiers felled by Bakshi prowled. Some thought it might be where the blight originated. But, unable to investigate the area without being torn to shreds, no one could definitively prove it.

A middle-aged woman with silver in her hair stepped forward.

"There *is* a way to fix this," she said, her voice commanding attention. "When we travel to the city, we hear tales of the blight. Of patches of land that are sick and withering because the yakshas have withdrawn their blessing."

She gestured up at the shrine. Several people fell to their knees and prostrated themselves again, as if that would do anything other than dirty their trousers.

"It's because we've allowed the rakshasas and their minions to have their way," the silver-haired woman went on. "The blight lets them breed, then spread their influence into our own communities!"

"I already told you that's nonsense," Kajal muttered as the crowd gasped, and the guard next to her shoved her to be quiet. Again, she cast her gaze around for Vivaan and Sezal. Had they been hit with second thoughts and left without her? Had they decided the bhuta was too much of a threat?

"We have no yaksha deities to fall back on, no divinely appointed asura and deva to aid us," the woman said. "The only way to remove this demonic energy is to cull those who strengthen it." She gave Kajal a pointed look. "Only then can balance be restored to our land."

Kajal swayed on her feet at the words, so similar to what the Vadhia had said before they'd hanged the singing woman. The same words they'd been spreading throughout Dharati for months.

These people wanted an easy solution to the challenges they faced that were beyond their control. They were terrified, and Kajal was their scapegoat.

You could show them true terror.

The eyes of the yaksha deity statues were heavy upon her, like a hand laid on the crown of her head. But this watchfulness wasn't coming from pitted stone—it was coming from the bhuta, a prickly sensation at the edge of her awareness. White fluttered in the corner of her eye, and she flinched before realizing it was just someone's dupatta stirred by the wind.

The silver-haired woman approached Kajal with a small jar in her hand, its glass a cheap, cloudy green.

"Irya, you've been found suspect in the deaths of two of our people, as well as in the presence of blight in our fields," the woman intoned. "You're believed to be a witch who placed curses on this town. Are you innocent, or guilty?"

These speeches varied from town to town, but Kajal knew the gist of what they wanted to hear. "I'm innocent, because I didn't kill them," she said. It wasn't *not* the truth. "And I have nothing to do with the blight. Or curses. Which, if you recall I mentioned before, aren't real—"

"She lies," hissed the man on her right. "There was a blighted animal in the woodland. She brought it here the same day that mongrel showed up!"

A murmur ran through the crowd. Gurveer Bibi's sons scowled harder, if possible.

"Amma's and Gurdeep's bodies are missing," the larger of the two growled. "She must have ordered that beast of hers to feast on them!"

Missing? Kajal frowned, and the crowd grew even rowdier, jeering at her and warding off the evil eye.

"The ordeal of poison will reveal if you truly are innocent," the silver-haired woman continued. "If you live, you will leave Kinara with your life. If you die, it'll be a punishment fitting for your crimes."

"I had to piss on straw last night," Kajal said. "Surely that's punishment enough."

A startled laugh from the crowd was immediately hushed.

Without another word, the woman passed her the jar. The glass was cool against her skin, her fingertips finding small imperfections in its bubbles and folds. Kajal loosened her grip in the hopes it would fall and shatter.

But the woman cupped her hands around Kajal's, digging between tendons as she pushed the jar toward Kajal's mouth.

She should have conditioned herself to resist poisons. She should have ingested small amounts of madar and datura every morning, sprinkled an arandi seed or two on her tasteless porridge.

Where are they? she thought furiously. Her lips were dry and cracked, longing for water and instead about to be wetted with toxin.

The glass had just touched her bottom lip when a coarse scream resounded over Kinara, so loud it vibrated though the jar. The people in the crowd echoed that scream with their own as a large shadow swooped over them.

The shadow belonged to a massive bird bristling with sharp feathers, and wings that stirred dust into the air with every flap. It sported a head similar to a vulture's, and its underside was covered in thick scales. Curved talons sprouted from its feet like sinister smiles. It circled the town and screeched again, the sound reverberating down the valley.

A sakela pachi. A slow grin spread across Kajal's face while the crowd panicked and dispersed. The hunters let their arrows fly, but they only knocked harmlessly against the demon's keratin plating.

Using the commotion to her advantage, Kajal hurled the jar at the shrine behind her. The glass shattered against the Elephant, and the poison dripped down its stone trunk.

"This is the dakini's doing!" someone cried.

Two pairs of hands grabbed her. But it wasn't the rebels; it was Gurveer Bibi's sons.

"Ah," she said as her heart gave a sickening thump. "So, this probably looks bad—"

She broke off with a gasp as they dragged her from the shrine. One fisted a hand in her hair, and pain lit across her scalp. Kajal fought back, stomping on the insteps of their feet, but it only enraged them more. They shook her and bruised her, spitting vile curses and names.

A sharp whistle broke through the screeches of the sakela pachi. Kajal despaired, thinking that the bhuta had appeared, that Lasya had also decided to make her pay—but it was the rebels riding toward her on horseback.

"Get away from her!" Sezal shouted.

Too invested in their vengeance, Gurveer Bibi's sons didn't listen.

Sezal pulled on her horse's reins, and the brown gelding reared with flailing hooves, which caught the bigger son in the chest and sent him flying. Rattled, the smaller one ran to help him.

Kajal coughed and choked on dust as Vivaan dismounted and hauled her to her feet.

"My dog!" She pointed to the building where she'd heard Kutaa's whining.

Vivaan swore and ran toward it.

Sezal reached down. "Come on!"

Kajal took her hand and scrambled up behind her on the gelding, her clumsy efforts making the horse step nervously sideways. Then again, it may have been reacting to the bird demon circling above.

"How did you manage this?" Kajal demanded over the uproar.

"What, you think we're able to summon rakshasas at will? We just know what it takes to lure them out."

The lack of pyre smoke suddenly made sense. "You took the bodies."

Sezal gestured at one of the taller buildings nearby. Kajal watched the rakshasa land on the flat roof in a great pile of feathers and scales, its beak yawning open.

It tore into what was undoubtedly Gurveer Bibi and Gurdeep. A severed arm sailed over the edge and plummeted limply to the ground.

"It's not elegant, but it got the job done," Sezal said.

"Rakshasas grow stronger when they eat the dead," Kajal reminded her.

"Yes." Sezal's smile fell. "But despite what these people believe about rakshasas, most don't go after humans or eat live ones. The sakela pachi should fly off once it's had its meal."

Vivaan returned, Kutaa at his heels. The dog let out a deep bark at the sight of Kajal.

"Let's go," Vivaan said once he'd swung up onto his own horse.

Kajal held on to Sezal as they rode for the town's perimeter. She worried Kutaa wouldn't be able to keep up with the horses, but if anything, being undead made him faster, as if he were no longer hindered by the normal limitations of his body.

Kajal hoped Sezal was right about the sakela pachi. She worked closely with death and did not shrink from it, but that didn't mean she wanted the townspeople to become a rakshasa's victims.

Are you sure about that?

She shoved the thought away, as well as her faint misgiving at the rebels' methods. They were her best chance of safely getting Lasya's body back. In the meantime, she just had to continue what she'd been trying to do all these months: keep her head down and avoid suspicion.

Easier said than done.

Chapter Seven

LASYA HAD ALWAYS been better at making friends than Kajal.

They had barely passed infancy when their parents died of illness. For the next seven years, they were passed around the village, reared more out of obligation than fondness.

With no family, no home, and nowhere to belong, they had chosen to wander instead. From town to town, village to village, poking their heads into other peoples' houses and asking for a bit of food as payment for work. Some had taken pity—*You poor girls, I can see your ribs! Come, I'll make you cha*—and some had merely sniffed and pointed out what needed to be done. Sweeping, cleaning, farming, feeding the cows, milking the cows, herding the cows inside when a monsoon sat crouched on the horizon.

The truly destitute had nothing to pay them with other than a corner in their shacks to sleep in. There had been many nights Kajal had slept tangled up with Lasya, each complaining about the other's snoring, both their stomachs grumbling, Kajal miserable and Lasya calm.

That calmness, as well as the tiny smile she constantly wore, was what had made her sister so approachable. People were drawn to her, ignoring Kajal's glower in favor of Lasya's ringing laugh. They had gotten away with so much because of that laugh.

Now Lasya was dragging others with her to the grave. As if she were lonely. As if she still so badly wanted to make friends.

Despite the afternoon sun beating down on her and the rebels as they rode from Kinara, Kajal shuddered. Sezal turned her head with some concern.

"Are you sure you weren't hurt this morning?" the girl asked.

"It's not that," Kajal muttered. She could have penned a list of everything that was wrong—it was too bright out, her thighs hurt from riding, the sway of Sezal's horse was making her nauseous, the sattu ladoo she'd eaten an hour ago was barely enough to sate her hunger—but getting manhandled by Gurveer Bibi's sons was not on it.

Sezal waited for her to continue. When she didn't, the rebel girl shrugged and turned back around.

They were a good dozen miles from Kinara already, avoiding the main roads and the distant villages in case news from Kinara had spread. The gentle forestland had evened out into flat plains of scrub and gnarled trees. The sky was unimaginably large and blue, with no hills or mountains to break up its expanse.

It made Kajal feel too exposed. Too seen. On the other hand, they would have plenty of warning should rakshasas or soldiers turn up.

"You made up that story about the Vadhia trailing me just to scare me, didn't you?" she asked of Vivaan, who rode ahead. Kutaa trotted beside them, fur rippling with his movements. "Either way, I'd like my notebook back."

Vivaan silently assessed her, as if she were a particularly complicated knot for him to unravel.

"I didn't make it up," he said at last. "We just found you first."

Kajal's stomach writhed. "Well, I agreed to help you—still waiting to get more details on that, by the way—so . . . notebook?"

"No."

"Why not?" It was nearly a whine.

"You know the concept of leverage, don't you?"

"All right, all right," Sezal interjected. "Kajal, we'll return your notebook once you fulfill your part in this. We'll tell you what that is when we make camp."

"Which will be . . . ?"

"A few more hours."

Kajal held in a groan. Sezal reached back to pat her thigh.

"I'll give you some chamomile when we stop," Sezal said. "Helps with muscle cramps."

She tried to parse out any hidden motives, but the girl seemed sincere enough. Kajal was used to people handing things to Lasya and overlooking her completely, relying on her sister to hand her half of whatever she received.

Being on the receiving end of something for a change was strangely awkward. She had no idea what to say, so she chose not to say anything.

The sun was on its way to setting when they spotted the priest. He was making a slow yet steady trek north, en route to cross them as they journeyed south.

Vivaan cast a questioning glance at Sezal, who shook her head. They didn't alter their path, meaning they saw no threat from the lone wandering priest. Still, Kajal kept her gaze down.

When he was close enough, Kajal furtively took in his features. He was not old, exactly, but a far throw from young, with wrinkles set deep on either side of his mouth, and brown skin dark and weathered from years of traveling. He wore traditional robes of saffron, with a sash across his shoulder and chest, ripped at their hems, and a wide-brimmed hat. Whereas the sun had deepened his color, it had leached the vibrancy from his clothing.

Kajal had roamed Dharati long enough to have had several run-ins with pujaris. The wandering priests went from shrine to shrine—in towns and in the wild alike—to give offerings and pray. This, supposedly, helped the elements of nature stay on course.

Although Kajal would walk faster at the sight of them, Lasya would slow down and reach into her bag. *We have little enough as it is,* Kajal would mutter.

Lasya would nudge her in reprimand. *Which means we shouldn't risk angering anyone, yaksha or otherwise.*

The pujaris were always appreciative no matter the offering or its size. Even when Kajal was on her own and gave them only a crumb of what she could spare, they would smile and bow.

This pujari walked steadily through the grass, his long walking stick helping pull him along. He raised his head and peered at them from under his straw hat. His mouth split in an uneven grin above his straggly beard.

"Greetings," he called in a croaking voice. "Do you have puja?"

The rebels reined in their horses. Despite the tension in her shoulders, Kajal automatically reached for the pack she no longer had.

"We've got it," Sezal assured her, rooting through her saddlebags. Vivaan did the same.

Kutaa's eyes never left the bent form of the priest. The pujari whistled at Kutaa, but the dog only twitched one ear.

The whistle wound Kajal's shoulders tighter. For a moment, she was back in Kinara's fields harvesting greens, staring at Lasya's motionless bhuta, that high whine an omen of death. Goosebumps pebbled her skin.

Sezal and Vivaan each gave the priest a sattu ladoo. Kajal watched in mild dismay as the small balls of millet mixed with turmeric and salt disappeared into the pujari's battered bag; she had been hoping to sneak another when Sezal wasn't paying attention.

The pujari bowed low, hands pressed together against his forehead, showing off the sarbloh bangle on his wrist. The iron bracelets were worn by most people in Dharati not only as a determent to rakshasas, but as a symbol that they belonged to the cyclical nature of the world—the wheel of dharma—and were mere specks within a wider cosmos.

Vivaan and Sezal didn't wear them. Kajal wrapped a hand around her own bare wrist; she and Lasya had never worn them either. But Lasya had never taken off the small copper ring Kajal had once gifted her, a paltry substitution that had nonetheless delighted her.

Realizing the priest's eyes had settled on her, Kajal stiffened. His jaw worked before he opened his mouth and clacked his teeth together in a strange pattern. Kutaa's ears went flat.

It was then she saw the dark tendril creeping toward the pujari's left eye.

"Go," Kajal whispered to Sezal. *"Now."*

To their credit, Sezal and Vivaan didn't hesitate and urged their horses onward. Once they were far enough away, Vivaan asked, "What's going on?"

"Blight."

Vivaan swore, and Sezal nearly turned to look over her shoulder before stopping herself. "Are you sure?" Sezal demanded. "I thought you said it couldn't affect humans?"

"I said it hasn't been known to spread through humans, but . . ." Kajal tried not to visualize the inky stain near the priest's eye. "Maybe that's changing."

"Then shouldn't we do something?" Sezal asked.

But there was only one way to deal with a blighted thing, and killing a pujari was beyond sacrilegious.

It had been disturbing enough for Kajal to see the blight infect an animal. To see it infect a human—even worse, a *priest*—made it feel like the world was beginning to deteriorate all around her. If she didn't get Lasya's body soon, her sister might deteriorate along with it.

Kajal pressed her fingertips to her forehead, rubbing them in a small circle between her eyebrows. She glared determinedly forward even as she felt the priest's gaze on her back, the clicking of his teeth echoing in her ears.

+✦+

They rode well into dusk, forcing the horses on even as the earth bruised black and blue with evening. When they finally stopped, it was in a grove of almond trees.

Kajal staggered from Sezal's horse and plopped to the ground as the other two prepared camp, murmuring to each other in grave tones. Kutaa sat beside her, showing no signs of weariness whatsoever. She marveled at it, at *him*, at what she had accomplished. Already her blood was fizzing with the potential of what she could do at the university.

Kajal idly petted him while Vivaan methodically brushed down the horses and Sezal gathered fallen almonds, tossing them in a small pot to soak. A memory came to her, unbidden: Lasya reaching for a bitter almond, and Kajal batting her hand away.

"Those are poisonous," Kajal had scolded. "If you want to eat them, take the skins off first."

"You think I don't know that?" Lasya had plucked the almond drupe from the tree, peeling away its hull. "Almond oil is good for the skin. But also"—her sister had smiled wryly—"we need to be prepared for anything, right? As much as I hate the thought."

Now Kajal waited to make sure the rebels weren't turned in her direction and slipped a generous handful of fallen almonds into her pocket.

Just in case.

Kajal then leaned in closer to Kutaa and whispered in his fuzzy ear, "Just how much can you understand me?"

He turned to look at her, and giddy curiosity held her in its grip. It was difficult to say whether he'd been an unusually intelligent dog in life, or if there was some singular connection they shared—the obedience of a creation to its creator.

She wanted to test his limits. "Can you retrieve my notebook?"

Kutaa sat unmoving, and she worried he couldn't understand after all. Then he gave a brief yawn, stretched, and padded silently over to the saddlebags. Kajal sat with her hands pressed to her cheeks, unable to believe this was actually working.

As he nosed through the bags, Kajal cleared her throat to gain the rebels' attention. "Back in Kinara, you said the two of you were hired by a group of . . . What did you call them? 'Concerned citizens'?"

"They call themselves the Insurrectionists," Vivaan said.

"I suggested the Rowdy Renegades, but it didn't take." Sezal threw an almond at Vivaan, which hit the back of his head.

He rubbed at the spot. "It's not a joke."

Kutaa was still searching. "How did you come to be Insurrectionists, then?" Kajal asked.

"We sort of fell into it," Sezal answered. "Heard some mumblings that interested us, and followed them to the so—"

She'd turned to her saddlebags, only to find Kutaa in the process of dragging out Kajal's notebook. Caught in the act, the dog froze.

"Uh," Kajal said. "Aha. Hmm. Weird."

Vivaan flashed her an annoyed look and went to take the notebook from the dog's mouth, playing a short game of tug-of-war until Kutaa reluctantly let go.

Kajal braced herself for their anger, or even their fists. Instead, Sezal reined in her laughter and dug through her bag for a small pouch, which she handed to Kajal. Inside were dried chamomile flowers. Kajal hesitated before Sezal made a gesture to go ahead and take some, despite what had just happened.

Kajal chewed on two, the flavor cloying on her tongue, and stretched out her legs. "One would think the yaksha deities would do something about fixing the land, instead of leaving it to the common folk," she said before they could decide they were actually mad at her.

"Such is the way with gods, I suppose." Sezal took the pouch back and crunched on a flower. "That's why we're tasked with fulfilling dharma, after all."

"So you believe you're acting under some divine purpose?"

Sezal inhaled wrong and started coughing around her laughter. Vivaan handed her a waterskin.

"*Some* of us do," she said after a few sips, waggling her eyebrows in Vivaan's direction. He rolled his eyes and gave Kajal a sattu ladoo. Kutaa, who'd come to sit by Kajal again, sniffed it. "But really, this goes beyond something as abstract as divine purpose."

Night had properly fallen. As Kajal ate her ladoo, ghost lights drifted through the field. They were an ethereal blue, tiny flames surrounded by balls of radiance. It was said they were the spirits of children who turned into benevolent yakshas once they passed from the mortal world.

Kajal held out a hand, and one of the ghost lights drifted close. The little ball floated a few inches above her palm and bathed her skin in pale sapphire before darting off into the dark again.

Those who lived in heavily populated areas hardly came into contact with the yakshas and rakshasas of their realm, and the supernatural could only be understood through stories. This was even truer of the mystical demon and heavenly races of the other planes, who hadn't been seen in many years. All the humans had were fanciful depictions from myth, such as the celestial apsaras, who danced among the stars, and the fearsome danavas, who could beguile others with illusions.

But in the country, nature was wild and unpredictable, and there was no telling what you could run into. Since the rebels didn't seem fazed by the ghost lights, they'd likely traveled as much as Kajal had. They certainly knew a lot more than the average citizen.

"You've stalled long enough," Kajal said once the ghost lights had moved on. "Tell me what role I'm playing in this production of yours."

Vivaan had lit his chillum. The scent of earthy tobacco drifted from its smoke. "We may as well," he agreed, though he didn't sound happy about it. "Considering we'll reach it tomorrow."

"It?"

"There's a place we need to visit before we head to Suraj," Sezal explained. "Something we need to get."

"Stop being cryptic. Just say it."

"After the Usurper King murdered the royal family to claim the throne," Vivaan said, "Crown Prince Advaith marched from Malhir to confront Bakshi's army. They clashed on the Harama Plain, between Malhir and Suraj. A thousand soldiers were left on that battlefield to be claimed by the earth, and they remain there to this day. Including Crown Prince Advaith."

He took a long draw from his chillum, his next words wreathed in smoke.

"We want you to find his body and revive him."

Kajal's stomach turned over so fast and suddenly it sent needles through her limbs.

She had heard of the Harama Plain—everyone had. Mostly, that no one dared approach it, that merchants and travelers went far out of their way to avoid coming close. Those who were unfortunate enough to not heed the warnings perished at the hands of the thousand bhutas left by the soldiers' corpses. Not even the famed Meghani demon hunters had been able to exorcise them, although they had the unique privilege of having survived the encounter.

"You— What?" She looked between them. "I can't have heard you right. You want me to stroll onto a battlefield crawling with bhutas and revive a dead prince?"

"To put it in simpler terms, yes," Sezal said.

Reviving a dog was one thing and reviving a human was another, but avoiding a thousand bhutas intent on ripping her apart to dig up a corpse? That was on an entirely different plane of existence.

No wonder they hadn't told her the plan from the start. If they had, she would have happily undergone the ordeal of poison instead.

"You won't be alone," Sezal added quickly. "Me and Vaan will go with you."

"We're just three people," Kajal argued. "Researchers have gone to study the Harama Plain, and none came back. Even other rakshasas stay away from it."

"We aren't researchers." Sezal patted her talwar sheath. "We can take on a few ghosts. And besides, you have a bhuta of your own. Maybe you'll be immune to them."

Kajal hadn't seen or sensed the bhuta since that morning, but that was beside the point. A weak laugh escaped her. "You really think this is going to work? Be honest with me. And what do you think reviving the crown prince will do?"

Vivaan set down his chillum with the slow deliberation of someone who'd rather chuck it at her head. "He's the rightful ruler of Dharati."

"So? What does that have to do with these rebel leaders of yours? Who are they, anyway?"

"A wealthy and influential family originally from the capital, distantly related to the late king," Sezal answered. "But the Sodhis lost power when Bakshi killed the royal family, and they moved out of Malhir several years ago. Not only do they despise him, they believe he ties into this blight problem." She circled her finger in the air to indicate the land surrounding them. "That things won't go back to normal until he's dethroned."

It sounded too clean, too optimistic. Especially if there was a noble family ready to claim power for themselves once the Usurper was gone, exchanging one autocrat for another.

"If the blight is the response to Bakshi usurping the throne, then the prince reclaiming the throne will end it," Vivaan went on. "The Sodhis will use their wealth and influence to supply him with a new army to do just that."

"In exchange for more power, I bet. Have you ever thought that maybe Dharati doesn't need a king at all? Why not get creative, think of another way to run things?"

"It's not that simple," Vivaan said in a low voice. "You don't understand."

"Then why don't you enlighten me?"

Vivaan stayed quiet, hands fisted in his lap. Sezal's brazen smile died.

"Before we can think about our future, we need to eliminate the present danger," Sezal said softly. "This is our best way of doing so. I understand we're asking a lot, but you did agree to help us." She glanced at the bag where Kutaa had found her notebook, the threat unspoken.

Kajal slowly took another bite of her ladoo. It fought with the leftover taste of chamomile, bitter and sweet at once.

"All right," she said after she swallowed. "But if I die and become a bhuta myself, I'm going to haunt you forever."

The rebels let out twin sighs of relief, and Vivaan eased his hand away from his talwar. For a moment, she wondered if giving her acceptance had meant keeping her life.

The rebels had bedrolls, and though it wasn't too cold, Kajal missed her sagging charpoy at the boardinghouse. Sezal noticed her eyeing a bedroll and shook it out.

"You can have it if you want," the girl said.

Kajal could count on one hand the number of times that someone had willingly given her something without compensation, and the chamomile and bedroll made up two of them. "I . . . No, that's all right." She shifted, suddenly and deeply uncomfortable. "Kutaa's warm."

"Suit yourself."

Kutaa *was* warm, and had no problem with her curling up against him. He laid his head between his two large forepaws, his amber eyes staring off at nothing. She hadn't had him long enough to tell if he actually slept or if he only stayed very, very still.

The night was heavy with stars and the distant sounds of creatures. An owl crooned nearby, and the grass rustled. The rebels' breaths turned deep, as if tomorrow weren't a matter of life or death. As if their faith shielded them from the ugly truths they didn't want to acknowledge. And from Kajal's experience, blind faith was more dangerous than any experiment she had conducted.

Forget this.

She wasn't going to be fodder for the rebels. Kajal got up as quietly as she could, Kutaa following with a confused tilt to his head. The saddlebags were too close to where Sezal and Vivaan were sleeping; she couldn't risk waking them to get her notebook or steal their supplies.

Rakshasas, the Vadhia, starvation—all were better alternatives to a thousand bhutas.

She turned east and started walking. Before she could get more than a dozen steps, something nudged the edge of her mind, an uncomfortable awareness. Kutaa felt it too, his fur bristling and his fangs pearlescent in the starlight. Following its silent call, she looked north.

There was a shadowy shape in the darkness, stumbling toward them through the tall grass. Its movements were ungainly. Wrong.

Even from here, Kajal heard the clicking of its teeth.

She reached for her knife before remembering it had been left behind in Kinara. Her legs locked in place, eyes darting between the figure, the rebels, and the eastern expanse.

The taste of chamomile lingered in the back of her throat.

Damn it.

"Wake up," Kajal hissed, stumbling toward the rebels. *"Wake up!"*

Sezal stirred and rubbed her eyes with a vague mumble. Vivaan was quicker to respond, sitting up and reaching for his talwar. "What is it?"

Kajal pointed, and Vivaan cursed. Sezal, finally realizing something was wrong, unsheathed her sword. Side by side, the talwars gleamed like ivory tusks. Kajal, armed with nothing but a dog and a handful of bitter almonds, got out of their way.

The pujari had lost his hat and his walking stick. When he shambled closer, Kajal could faintly make out more dark markings across his haggard face.

It had spread so quickly. Too quickly.

"We want no trouble," Vivaan called out. "Turn away."

There was no bartering with something like this, infected by blight and driven by animal instinct. Kajal could sense him, *smell* him from here, a smoky rot that turned the air thick and putrid.

The pujari let out a creaking, groaning noise. Kajal realized a heartbeat later it was a laugh. Kutaa answered with a growl.

And then came a sound that was becoming increasingly familiar: a high whine. The hair on her arms stood on end.

"Stay there, Kajal," Sezal warned, ignoring the sound entirely. The girl advanced toward the pujari, sword tip pointed at his chest. "We'll handle this."

A flutter of white, as pale as the moon above their heads—as pale as a funeral dress.

Kajal slowly turned and met her sister's empty gaze. Lasya's face was blank, shadowed, eyes flashing red like distant planets against the backdrop of the night sky.

No—this wasn't her sister. Not really. Just a specter Kajal had made with her own selfish desires.

"Lasya," Kajal whispered anyway. "Don't. No more."

The rebels made no sign that they could see or hear Lasya. As Vivaan ran at the shambling priest, the whine in Kajal's ears swelled, and she clapped her hands over her ears.

Kill me, the whispers breathed against her skin. *Kill me!*

"You're already dead," she choked out.

Unless her sister was begging Kajal to end this. To burn her to ashes and free her spirit.

No, Kajal thought. *I can fix this. I can—*

Vivaan carved a gash through the priest's robes to the stained skin beyond. The pujari's breath rattled while his hands attempted to claw at Vivaan's face.

Sezal jumped in. Her talwar flashed as it bit through the priest's neck. His head fell heavily to the grass, arterial blood spraying upward, while the body kept reaching for Vivaan like some grotesque puppet. With a quick motion, Vivaan cut the hands off the pujari's arms, then stabbed him through the heart.

The whine in Kajal's ears died. The place where the bhuta had stood was empty.

Kajal was halfway through a sigh when the cold claimed her. She gasped and fell to one knee, clutching her throat. The bhuta loomed over her, red eyes shining down—into her core, her soul—while phantom fingers choked off her breath.

"Kajal!"

The pressure disappeared, along with the bhuta.

Kajal took in a heaving gasp and coughed as Kutaa nosed at her in concern.

Sezal knelt before her, talwar wet with blood. "Are you all right? What happened?"

"The . . . bhuta." She couldn't account for the rise of hot shame in her stomach, couldn't meet Sezal's eyes. Vivaan wiped his blade clean, glancing between the dismembered heap of the priest's body and Kajal as if he couldn't decide which was worse.

"I didn't . . ." Kajal swallowed, trembling. "I-If it took another life, it would grow stronger. But . . ."

But the rebels had killed the pujari before Lasya could. Lasya, who had always graciously offered puja to the priests and smiled respectfully as they passed.

A shudder racked her. Kajal wondered if there would be bruises on her neck, physical proof of Lasya's violence.

She forced herself to meet Vivaan's assessing gaze. "Even after seeing what a bhuta can do, you still want to go to the Harama Plain?"

"We have to." Vivaan sheathed his talwar. "Clean your sword, Sezal. We can't risk blight." Sezal hastily searched for a rag. "We need to move. It'll be a risk to the horses, but the moon is bright enough we can probably ride through the rest of the night."

Kajal heard what he didn't say: that they needed to get her and the crown prince to the university before something like this happened again. She thought of all the promise and potential that waited for her there. Lasya's body lying in the shadow of the eastern mountains.

If she survived tomorrow, if she succeeded in bringing back the crown prince, she would be one step closer to saving Lasya. To saving them both.

Then finally, finally, she could ask for Lasya's forgiveness.

They packed up in silence, Sezal keeping the soaked almonds to peel and eat as they rode. Vivaan did something to the priest that Kajal couldn't make out, too preoccupied with trying to mount the horse on jellied legs and a sleep-deprived body.

As they once more headed south, light flickered behind them. Kajal turned and watched flames consume the pujari's body, their orange tongues licking toward the dark sky as if to taste the heavens.

Chapter Eight

IT WAS EASIER to think of the rebels' plan as something she'd dreamed up in the night. But as the sky lightened and her two companions' moods remained bleak, Kajal had the uneasy realization that they truly did intend to travel to the Harama Plain.

Beside them, Kutaa matched the horses' long strides. When they passed some fig trees, he briefly stopped to sniff at the fallen fruit, split and bloated from the previous day's sun.

Sezal reached for the laden branches and plucked a few, handing one to Kajal. The figs were small and purple, sticky and sweet on the inside. Kajal savored the honey-like flavor that replaced the sour taste of fear in her mouth.

"You and your sweets," Lasya had once scolded after they had attended a town festival. "How many jalebis have you had?"

Kajal, lying on her back at the onset of a stomachache, had weakly reached for the last syrupy jalebi she'd pilfered from a cart. "Not enough."

A piece of fig stuck in her throat, making her choke.

"Are you sure you're ready for this?" Vivaan asked, mistaking her undignified noise for panic. "Because if not—"

Kajal swallowed hard, forcing the fig and thoughts of Lasya down. "That's not it. I was . . . thinking about wasps."

"Wasps?"

Kajal held up her half-eaten fig, revealing the seeded pulp inside. "I read in a book that female wasps pollinate figs by crawling inside and laying eggs. Once the larvae burrow out, the female wasp dies and gets absorbed into the fig. Interesting, right?"

Sezal paused with her own fig held to her mouth, eyes round with horror. Vivaan grimly studied the bite he'd already taken from his. Kajal took another juicy mouthful and chewed noisily to disguise the nerves humming through her.

The closer they came to the battle site, the more signs of human life dwindled. They passed an abandoned village with dilapidated buildings, roads and homes reclaimed by nature.

And blight. Black ooze dripped from trees, marking patches of barren ground, eating away at a withered field of wheat like a desperate mouth in winter. When the wind blew in their direction, it carried the scent of char and rot.

"It appears so randomly," Kajal murmured, more to herself than the others.

"Those at the university believe it shows up in places where the rakshasas' energy surpasses that of the yakshas," Vivaan said.

"There's been no evidence to suggest rakshasas spread it," she reminded him.

"That might be, but you can't deny they're growing in number—growing *stronger*—because of it."

That, unfortunately, Kajal could not refute.

Sezal eyed the ruined wheat field as they passed a half-collapsed barn. "Do you think the blight not only makes rakshasas stronger, but bhutas too? Is that how your sister is able to stay with you, Kajal?"

Kajal furrowed her brow; she hadn't thought of that before. "Why ask me? I'm no bhuta expert. I still have no idea how you think we can evade a thousand of them."

"I may not be an expert either, but I know a thing or two." Vivaan's face lifted from its usual dour expression, making him appear younger—as if he shared her curiosity, her thirst for knowledge. "Since bhutas lack human sensation, they're drawn to things like loud noises, hard breathing, strong emotion."

Strong emotion. Anger and fear certainly seemed to be what drew Lasya to Kajal.

Kajal was feeling even less confident, if possible. "Are you saying we have to hold our breath and not make a sound?"

Vivaan tsked. "Nothing so extreme as that. We can slip by them so long as we're quiet."

"Bold words coming from someone who claimed he's not a bhuta expert," Kajal said. "These soldiers have been here for two decades, feasting on hapless travelers. They'll be strong."

"Then don't disturb them."

Kajal scoffed. "The bodies are buried. Of course we'll be disturbing them." Part of the yaksha deities' blessing ensured that if a body was left uncovered, the earth would eventually claim it. "At least that means this prince of yours has likely maintained all his . . . princely assets."

Sezal held back a snort while one Vivaan's eyes twitched.

The temperature dropped considerably, and Kajal shuddered. The sky overhead was a somber gray, the field before them a ragged span of murky grassland and scraggly trees.

Beyond the trees, the ground gave way to acres of mud and dirt where nothing grew. At first, Kajal thought it was more blight, the biggest stretch of it she'd ever seen. But it wasn't the same peculiar black substance as before, merely a churned-up field long since watered with blood.

The horses refused to keep going and tossed their heads in distress. Vivaan dismounted and spoke to his horse in a gentle voice, petting the space between its eyes, while Sezal helped Kajal down. Kajal took a few cautious steps forward, Kutaa at her heels.

The Harama Plain was massive. She could easily believe that two armies had clashed here, could see how the act of dragging the bodies away afterward would have been impossible. Mounds of earth studded the barren field where the bodies had been abandoned—rows and rows of barrows.

There were so many. How were they supposed to know which grave held the crown prince?

Vivaan stepped up beside her. "I can feel them."

She could too. Cold clamped around her like a vise, but instead of a whine, there were dozens of soft whispers. Shadows drifted across the expanse. Behind her, Kutaa flattened his ears.

"How are we going to do this?" Kajal whispered. "Do you even know what the crown prince looks like?"

"I do. There are portraits in Malhir." Vivaan's hand drifted to the fading tattoo that peeked out from his collar. This close, Kajal could make out a mandala-like design. "Search for a soldier decked in the most expensive armor, one with the royal crest on it. Beyond that . . . we'll just have to work quickly."

Kajal chewed the inside of her cheek. *This is absurd.* Although a newly formed bhuta typically hunted the people who'd wronged them in life, Kajal suspected these soldiers needed little reason to pounce on anyone who tampered with their resting place. What if she died before she could fulfill her promise to Lasya?

Then again, the rebels handing her over to the Vadhia with her notebook was an equally fatal alternative.

With that bitter thought, Kajal braced herself and walked onto the battlefield. The ground beneath her slippers was soft and springy, the air scented with stale blood. Despite Dharati's superstitions that dogs prowled in unsavory places, Kutaa hesitated at the edge of the field. "Stay there,"

Kajal whispered. He whined but obeyed, restlessly pacing back and forth.

She'd barely made it a dozen steps when a white wraithlike form materialized in the corner of her eye. Immediately, she came to a stop as it swayed in her periphery. She sensed it like the approaching heat of a fire, an instinctual danger.

"I see it too," Sezal whispered just behind her. "I thought bhutas were invisible."

"The stronger they are, the more corporeal they become," Vivaan answered softly.

And if they could all see this one, it was well on its way to reaching that state.

Kajal held her breath. The bhuta swayed closer, its whispers rasping like steel against steel. Kajal stared straight ahead, the hairs along her arms standing on end.

Eventually, it moved on, wavering through the air like mere tendrils of smoke. Kajal shakily let out her breath.

Vivaan grasped her elbow while Sezal put a hand on her back. "That's it," he encouraged. "Just ignore them."

The farther they went, the colder it grew. The rebels had left their cloaks with the horses, but at least their salwar kameezes were made of thicker fabric than Kajal's kurta and trousers. She resisted the urge to rub warmth into her arms, afraid the sound or friction would draw attention. The whispers rose and softened like a tide; when they got too loud, the three of them paused, waiting for the din to die down again before resuming their slow trek.

A scream pierced the air. Kajal's limbs locked in place, and the rebels reached for their weapons. But they couldn't find the source of the scream, could only flinch as it howled past them again.

Something moved to their right. The outline of a soldier staggering, with a weapon in his side, gargling on blood as he fell in the exact spot where a barrow stood.

They remember, Kajal thought, bile searing her throat. *They're trapped here in their death throes.* Like a wasp in a fig, deteriorating until only its essence remained.

Did Lasya remember her death this way? Was her bhuta constantly in pain, reliving what had happened?

Kajal's hands shook. A murmur brushed against the back of her neck—shapeless, wordless, but its intent unmistakable:

Get out.

They were not welcome here. The longer they lingered, the more bhutas would be alerted to their presence. Maybe even mistake them as enemy soldiers.

"Split up," Kajal suggested.

The rebels went in opposite directions, careful to not make noise as they dug through the mounds. Kajal continued straight ahead, the crunch of her slippers on grave soil roaring in her ears like a landslide.

Shadows flickered on either side of her. Her breathing was already unsteady, but there were other rattling breaths behind her, practically panting in her hair. Kajal whirled around, but no one was there. A distant wail swept across the burial mounds before cutting off violently.

Hurry.

Kajal knelt before a barrow and tore at the compacted dirt. It gathered under her nails and in the lines of her palms as it gave way. Part of her expected to see something horrifying, a decaying corpse with gray, diseased flesh.

But the yaksha-blessed earth had done its job preserving the fallen soldier. The face under his slanted helmet was ashen, twisted in agony. Old, brown blood stained his armor and lips. Kajal recalled prayers for the dead recited by pujaris, and considered for half a second whether she should voice one.

Hurry.

Kajal stepped over a rusted shield and dug through two more mounds, shoulders tensing every time a scream or shout or clash of steel rang across the field. Sezal and Vivaan worked quietly and quickly, often scanning their surroundings like paranoid cart vendors on the lookout for thieves. The bodies she discovered here were much the same as the first: gray, bloody, in the midst of some terrible pain. None of them wore armor suitable for a crown prince.

The whispers were now in her ear. Ice crawled along her spine, freezing her in place. If she moved too fast, she felt the faint touch of hands on her arms, encircling her wrists. It was all too easy to imagine a thousand bhutas grabbing hold of her, ripping her limbs from her body. Stopping her heart. Dragging her down into the earth with them.

Their fingers fitting to the bruises Lasya had left around her throat.

She couldn't swallow, could barely get a breath in. The building tension around her was sharp and brittle, a low drone of anger that had dread pooling in her gut.

She shut her eyes even as those phantom hands touched her, grasping, taunting. Her heart was lodged in her throat, blood rushing through her head.

It took her a moment to realize she had started humming.

The notes were trembling and barely formed, a gentle vibration in her throat. The song was simple yet familiar. A comfort from a past life.

Lotus Blossom.

It had the same effect on her it always had. Her body began to relax, her heartbeat slowed, and the hands of the bhutas gradually let go.

Kajal opened her eyes.

A small white butterfly fluttered before her. She stared at it and wondered if this was another trick. It was too bright and too lively for a place like this.

Kajal stretched out a hand. The butterfly perched on her finger, flapping its wings—once, twice—before taking off in the direction she had been walking.

Kajal followed. The soldiers' dying cries slipped off her like water, and if the bhutas were gathered behind her in a resentful wave, she didn't notice. She kept her eyes fixed on the white butterfly, wanting to see where it would lead her.

Eventually, it landed on a barrow. Its wings quivered when Kajal crouched down, and it took flight when she reached for it again.

Slowly, as if moving through a dream, she broke through the thick layer of dirt that covered the body. The bhutas drew closer, as if they, too, were curious.

Once the soil had been shifted, Kajal found a helmet made of bronze, with a chain-mail curtain. This was certainly different. Carefully, she pried the helmet off to study the corpse's face beneath.

He was dirty and bloodied, like the rest, but he wore an expression of serenity, like he hadn't fought his death at all. His hair was thick and black, ending in loose curls at his neck, and his lashes were surprisingly long. Kajal stared at his bloodless lips, the elegant arches of his eyebrows. Although his head was tilted to one side, his right arm outstretched in the same direction, the ground beside him was empty. She examined the spot until she grew dizzy, then forced herself to study him further.

His armor was similar to the other soldiers', a green-and-gold chilta hazar masha, layers of fabric studded with small nails. But whereas the others' coats were lined with brass, this one was properly gilded. Not only that, but his chestplate was emblazoned with two suns intersecting. The royal crest.

She had found him.

Kajal stood to get the rebels' attention. But as she waved her arms over her head, an icy hand grabbed her wrist.

The prince's face appeared before hers, eyes blazing red.

Kajal screamed.

The sound carried across the field, stirring the shadows and making the whispers rise into wails. Kajal fought against the prince's bhuta as it flickered from shadow to bloody specter. Although the prince's body lay in serene acceptance, his bhuta bared its teeth in fury. It twisted her arm and she was sent crashing to her knees, pain ripping through her shoulder.

Vivaan and Sezal called her name. *Idiots,* she wanted to snarl. *Don't rile them up more!*

The prince's bhuta abruptly let her go. Kajal fell onto the barrow as it screeched in displeasure, the sound so inhuman it set her teeth on edge.

Lasya held the prince's bhuta by the throat. Her sister's face was emotionless, her kameez fluttering around her.

Sezal, out of breath and drenched in sweat, knelt beside Kajal with her eyes widely fixed on the prince's specter. "What is—?"

"Lasya," Kajal gasped. "She's here."

Vivaan fell to his knees on her other side, staring at the corpse's face with his mouth agape. "This— This is him! You found him!" Vivaan frantically clawed at the remaining dirt. "Hurry!"

Kajal helped the other two break through the rest of the mound. Vivaan grunted as he dragged the prince out. While the rebels took off his heavy armor, Kajal looked over her shoulder at the chaos behind them. Lasya and the prince's bhuta were fighting for dominance, an odd dance of ghostly limbs. The horde of other bhutas had inched closer, roiling and murmuring like an approaching thunderstorm.

Vivaan lifted the prince's body into his arms, gilded armor scattered on the ground. "Run!"

Sezal pushed Kajal in front of her. Kajal's ears were filled with howls of rage, and a high whine wormed through her skull. The ground shook, and the two of them stumbled into each other while Vivaan tore on ahead.

Sezal screamed as giant gouge marks erupted on either side of them. Kajal leapt away when the ground split open under her feet, as if a massive claw had parted the earth as easily as a cat shredding fabric.

Kutaa barked madly at the edge of the field. Kajal grabbed Sezal's arm and forced her to run faster. Their clothes tore on invisible blades, and Vivaan tripped and nearly fell, blood spurting from his leg.

Kajal wasn't quick enough to evade the next gouge. The earth broke open underneath her, and she plummeted. She barely caught herself on the ledge, hands scrambling for purchase. She opened her mouth to call for Sezal, but she choked on dirt as ghostly hands grabbed her ankles and tried to drag her under.

"Kajal!" Sezal took her by the wrists and pulled. The bhutas pulled harder, whispering and groaning and tightening their hold as pain lanced through both her ankles. Kajal cried out and flailed her legs to dislodge them, slipping down farther.

I won't let you take me, she thought. Furious, crimson-edged intent spiked through her.

The bhutas suddenly shrank away. With Sezal's help, Kajal crawled up and out.

Kutaa was still barking when they finally stumbled onto the grass. The horses fought against their restraints, eyes rolling in terror. Vivaan threw the prince's body over the back of his gelding.

Once Kajal was in the saddle behind Sezal, the horses bolted. Kajal looked over her shoulder, but she couldn't see Lasya anymore, or hear her bhuta's whine.

"Thank you," she whispered, the wind eating her words.

They didn't stop until the horses were exhausted, Vivaan panting almost as hard as his gelding, and the horseflesh under Kajal's legs damp with sweat.

Kajal slid out of the saddle with boneless legs so the horses could drink from a nearby brook. She sprawled on her back in the grass, and Kutaa worriedly sniffed her face. She pushed him gently away, muttering that she was fine.

All three of them were covered in cuts and tears from the bhutas' attacks. Sezal's sleeve, torn and drooping, was hardened with drying blood from a wound beneath. For the first time, Kajal noticed a tattoo similar to Vivaan's on her arm. Following her gaze, Sezal covered the wound with her hand and went rooting for a bandage.

"I'll admit," Vivaan said once they'd calmed down, "it wasn't the best plan."

Kajal coughed out a laugh and threw an arm over her eyes. "Piss off."

"I saw the prince's bhuta," Sezal said quietly. "He must have . . . Will it follow us, the way your sister follows you?"

"I don't know." What Kajal had learned about bhutas from the Meghanis' essays fit the wraiths they'd encountered at the Harama Plain; it was only Lasya's case that deviated. "It's unlikely."

Vivaan carefully pulled the body from his horse and laid it on the ground. "If it does, all the more reason to revive him as soon as possible." He reached out as if to touch the prince's cheek, then curled his fingers against his palm. Kajal sat up and crawled closer.

The crown prince of Dharati, Advaith Thakar. Without his armor, he seemed smaller, younger, perhaps around her age. His dirt-smudged skin had retained some of its color. If it weren't for his unnatural stillness and his blue-tinted lips, he could have been sleeping.

"He's pretty," Kajal said. "For a corpse."

Vivaan arched an eyebrow. "He'll be prettier once he's alive."

Kajal lifted one of the prince's arms. It was already growing stiff. Some of her lingering shakiness abated as purpose recentered her. Rebellion and politics were rich people problems—she knew nothing about those things.

But this—death, corpses, decomposition—*this* she knew.

"Do you have a bag large enough for him?" Kajal asked, and they nodded. "Get it out. We need to pack him inside with soil to preserve him."

Vivaan frowned at the command, but Sezal moved to follow.

Kajal glanced at the saddlebag where her notebook was hidden away. Soon, she would learn whether or not she could fully resurrect a human. If she couldn't, there would be a lot more to worry about than bruised pride.

Chapter Nine

KAJAL FIRST GAZED upon the Ayurvedic University of Suraj with dry, bloodshot eyes.

Squinting in the dusk light, she could make out buildings of sandstone topped with dark domes, sparkling gaily as if there were no such thing as monster attacks in the middle of the night or a battlefield full of malicious spirits. The complex was crouched on a promontory overlooking a lake to the north, like an enormous beast. To the west, slightly beyond the promontory, lay the sprawling city of Suraj.

Sezal breathed out in relief. "We made it."

"It's beautiful," Kajal said.

Kutaa trotted between the horses. Both rebels had changed out of their bloody, torn clothing, and Sezal had let Kajal borrow one of her kameezes. It was loose on her, but the fabric was more durable than what she was used to and even had an embroidered hem, so she couldn't complain.

"It used to be a fort," Vivaan explained, the prince's body slung across the saddle before him. With the dirt packed inside the bag, it was difficult to tell that a corpse hid within. "Suraj is the second-largest city in Dharati, almost a mirror of the capital."

Kajal had heard that somewhere before, how Malhir greeted the sun in the east and Suraj bid it goodbye in the west. The City of Sunrise and the City of Sunset.

"Members of the royal household would come and stay here," Vivaan went on. Since claiming the prince's body, he'd been in a somewhat better mood, and his usual aloofness melted away into a scholar's fascination. "They constructed a palace connected to the fort. Many queens would come and stay here while the kings stayed in Malhir."

"Don't blame them," Sezal said with a smirk.

"Of course, it's changed since then." Vivaan gestured up at the promontory. "The royal line ceased to be, and instead of reverting it back to a fort, Bakshi made it a university."

Kajal sputtered. "*Bakshi* founded the university?"

"Unfortunately." His face reverted from open and calm to shuttered and solemn. "Over the last few years, he's been heavily invested in the work of scholars, healers, and lorists."

"But Bakshi controls the Vadhia, and the Vadhia have been targeting people with those skills."

"Those they've accused of witchcraft use methods like divination and stargazing, or 'ambiguous' healing practices. Bakshi set up the universities to steer people *away* from the mystical and to embrace the methodical." Vivaan shrugged. "Don't ask me to explain his reasoning."

A fire scorched up Kajal's throat. "But the people the Vadhia are accusing are too poor to go to the universities!"

The medicine men and women Kajal encountered had inherited their knowledge: which herbs worked best for certain illnesses, how to activate specific chakras, and even what kind of tea could knock someone out. Ayurveda was founded in healing, balance, and harmony, the gateway between humans and the universe.

As much as she appreciated the methodical, these were still Dharati's traditions. She hadn't realized the Ayurvedic universities had been created to quash that tradition instead of bolstering it. The idea sat in her like a thorn.

"And we're just going to ride up to the gates of an institution Bakshi owns?"

"Of course not. We're sneaking in." Vivaan cast her a sideways glance. "Is that a problem?"

"Nope. I love sneaking. Sneaking is the best." Besides, she'd rather not deal with guards. No doubt they were used to new students who arrived fresh and bright-eyed, pockets jangling with coin and wearing new shoes that weren't nearly worn through the soles.

"At least Bakshi's never visited," Sezal said. "He never even renovated the old palace."

"Do you think he might?" Kajal asked, queasy at the thought. Where Bakshi went, the Vadhia would surely follow. "Visit, I mean."

"If he does, he'll get a knife in the back for his trouble," Vivaan muttered.

The sun sank as they rode closer to the promontory. Curving stairs wrapped around tall minars topped with open-arched pillars and black domes. There was a macabre quality to the towers' structure, reminding Kajal of spinal columns.

They passed teak and neem trees growing along either side of the road, which led to wrought iron gates. The guards posted weren't dressed in the green of Dharatian soldiers or the blue and marigold of the Vadhia; their livery was black and gold, matching the colors of the flags that waved from the parapet high above.

"Don't let the different colors fool you," Sezal said when they turned their horses west, ignoring the road and the gate. "Bakshi may not visit, but he has this place under his thumb."

Sezal pointed ahead, and it was only then that Kajal spotted the noose. It was made of thick hemp rope and dangled from the bough of a neem tree like an uncoiled snake.

She jerked away as if scalded. "Bakshi is hanging students?"

"No. At least none yet," Sezal answered. "But there were a couple of professors who taught and practiced occult subjects. Bakshi considered them 'a threat to progress and their fellow man,' so . . ." Sezal didn't need to finish.

A frenetic laugh resounded through Kajal's head. *This* was the place in which she was supposed to run her experiments? Her breaths shortened, and she could have sworn she smelled a hint of pyre smoke and ash.

They waited until a few hours after moonrise before hiking up the hill toward the university. They approached the wall from the north, where the promontory overlooked the lake, almost directly opposite the entry gate. Kajal's gaze darted around, but there were no sentries or guards that she could see.

"You're not planning to scale this, are you?" Kajal asked, pointing up at the wall. "I'm good at climbing trees, but this is a bit too vertical for me."

In response, Sezal rapped her knuckles against the stone. They stood silent, Kajal worrying at her lower lip while Vivaan glared at her, daring her to say anything else. Just as she was about to break, a square-shaped segment of the wall pushed outward.

Kajal stumbled back as a hand reached out of the gap and made a "Come here" gesture.

"A little help, please?" came a voice from behind the stone.

Vivaan seemed unwilling to let go of the prince's body, so Sezal hurried forward and pulled the wall segment out farther. From the other side emerged a young woman.

"I underestimated how heavy that was," she panted, wiping her wrist against her temple.

Kajal assessed the young woman as she stepped into the moonlight. She was at most a decade older than Kajal, her round face pretty and her small mouth offset by a pair of large brown eyes behind a pair of glasses. Her hair was piled in a bun, and she wore a simple blue kurti and white churidar over her full-figured body.

"Jasmeet," Sezal said in greeting. "I'm glad you saw our signal."

Earlier, when they'd settled in the field to wait for nightfall, Vivaan had lit a torch and held it up for five seconds, explaining to Kajal that their contact climbed one of the towers every sundown.

"I've told you, it's *Jassi*," the young woman admonished. She then beamed at Kajal. "Behan, you're here!"

Kajal stiffened. No one had ever called her *behan* except for Lasya.

Sezal put a hand on Kajal's shoulder. "Meet your new sister, Professor Jasmeet." She loudly whispered to Jassi, "Don't let her shyness fool you. There's a devious mind behind it."

The professor laughed. "Good! The more devious, the better. Especially if she's being roped into all this." She dipped her chin at Kajal. "As you've likely surmised, you'll be pretending to be my baby sister during your stay. My real sister lives in Malhir, and she's never visited, so no one knows what she looks like. That means I'll be calling you Nishaa in public."

"I'm *not* calling you 'didi.' " Kajal would only ever use that word for Lasya.

"You don't have to. I know I'm your elder and a professor, but considering our situation, you can call me Jassi. I hate being called Jasmeet, anyway. Feels too formal."

"I'll keep it in mind." Kutaa nudged her thigh, and Kajal placed a clammy palm on his head. "My name is Kajal."

"Kajal," Jassi repeated before turning to the dog. "And who's this?"

"Kutaa. My dog."

"He's very handsome."

Kajal had no idea what to say to that.

"We think we know how to move forward now," Sezal said after an awkward silence.

"Ah." The professor studied Kutaa again, who wagged his tail once. Her eyes and smile widened. "I see. Do you mind if I—?"

"Let's get inside first," Vivaan said testily.

"Oh, yes. Good idea."

They squeezed through the wall's opening and pulled the stone back into place. On the other side they were plunged into the shadow of a tall sandstone building directly before them. Vivaan held the bag closer to his chest while they crept forward, following Jassi as she quietly unlocked the building's front doors and ushered them through. With the doors shut behind them, Kajal could finally take a full breath.

"There aren't any guards in the buildings, are there?" Sezal asked in a hushed tone as they ascended a flight of stairs.

"Not this one, no," Jassi whispered back.

"What is this place?" Kajal asked.

"It's where the laboratories are. Some classes are held here, but it's mostly reserved for private study, or for the professors and visiting experts who require them."

At the end of a corridor, Jassi opened a wooden door with iron studs and beckoned them in.

Excitement skittered across Kajal's skin and made her shiver.

The room was three times the size of her room at the boardinghouse, and instead of windows, the walls were adorned with oil lanterns. Their light fell across two tables, one empty and the other filled with equipment and tools, from pliers and forceps to glass jars and tins full of herbs. Several sizes of mortars and pestles rested in a small box, beside another containing powdered graphite. Sheaves of parchment stood ready under the weight of pens and charcoal pencils.

"This is my private laboratory, but I'm handing it over to you," Jassi explained. "For the time being, anyway."

Kajal, admiring the layout, did a double take. A fully stocked, dedicated place to work was something she had only ever dreamed of. Even though Jassi was doing it for the rebels, it was nonetheless a momentous offering, a gift she couldn't possibly repay in this life or the next.

The words that eventually escaped Kajal were hoarse. "Thank . . . Thank you."

"Don't worry about it. It'll at least give you some space to think." Jassi winked. "And the best part: The door locks." Kajal forced a small laugh.

Vivaan carefully laid the bag on the empty table while Jassi knelt and inspected Kutaa's teeth, eyes, and pulse. He sat calmly through it all, only giving the occasional flick of his fluffy ears.

"In*cred*ible." Jassi's glasses glinted in the lanterns' flames. "You really revived him?"

Kajal crossed her arms. "He wouldn't be here otherwise."

"Of course, of course." Jassi lifted one of the dog's large paws. "Does he have all the same functions he had in life?"

"No." It pained her to admit it. "He doesn't eat, and I don't think he sleeps."

Vivaan scowled at hearing this bit of information for the first time, but Jassi hummed in thought. "I'm sure we can figure out how to adjust your process and restore the prince to full working order," she said.

"See, this is working out great," Sezal said cheerily.

"As long as you don't forget your part of the deal," Kajal stressed. "Also, I'll be needing my notebook back."

Jassi looked up from rubbing Kutaa's ears. "What deal?"

Kajal would have rather leapt from the university's tallest building than explain Lasya again. Sezal, taking pity, did it for her. By the time she was done, Jassi regarded Kajal in a new way she didn't like.

"Oh," the professor breathed. "Oh, Kajal, I'm so sorry."

Kajal was about to rattle apart with discomfort until Vivaan stepped forward and pulled them back to the matter at hand.

"Any measurements or information you need from your notebook you can copy here," he said. "We'll keep it safe until it's time to perform the resurrection." Kajal's mouth twisted, knowing *keep it safe* really meant *keep you in line*. "I assume I don't have to remind you both that what we discuss and what we do is confidential. If word gets out about His Highness's body, or its location—"

Jassi waved a hand through the air. "You'll put my head on a spike? Weigh me down with rocks and toss me in the lake?"

Sezal snorted, and Vivaan rolled his eyes. "So long as you understand." He waited for Kajal to agree, which she did quietly.

"The fact that you were able to revive the dog is a miracle in itself," Sezal added. "We have full confidence that with the right support"—she nodded to Jassi—"you'll be able to accomplish this."

"The Sodhis wanted me to try my hand at it, but I couldn't reanimate so much as a fly," Jassi said. "To bring such a big dog like this back to life? You're amazing."

Just like when the rebels had found her in the cell in Kinara, Kajal's chest swelled with pride. The fact that someone, anyone—even rebels with goals far removed from hers—had looked upon her work and found it awe-inducing was immensely satisfying.

"I want to take a better look," Kajal said, bolstered.

Vivaan stepped aside so she could untie the strings at the top of the bag. Behind her, Jassi speculated about whether they should store the body in the university's ice cellars belowground, where they kept cadavers used for anatomy classes, the intense cold having proven effective at staving off rakshasa interest.

"That won't be necessary," Kajal said. "The soil will keep him in stasis."

Kajal peeled back the canvas and carefully brushed the dirt from the prince's face. Jassi's hand flew to her mouth.

"You actually did it," she whispered. "You found him."

"What, did you think we hauled a sack of rice here?" Sezal demanded. "It wasn't exactly a pleasant stroll through a garden. I'll be having nightmares for a year."

Kajal remained silent while she inspected the prince's body, taking note of the injuries he'd sustained in battle. She stared at his face and tried not to think of his bhuta, both thankful and puzzled that it hadn't followed them like Lasya's did. After seeing what she needed, she covered him back up.

She made a "Gimme" motion at Vivaan, who reluctantly handed over her notebook. She flipped through it with a fond smile, delighting in its familiar weight and its sweet scent. "I'll need zinc, limestone, and gotu kola, for starters. And plenty of salt."

"That's all doable," Jassi said.

"Getting the components will be the easy part," Kajal agreed. "The challenge comes in putting them together and activating his chakras the right way. Since I can't tell what his specific dosha balance is, it'll be a bit of a gamble." When the doshas were in harmony, there was health. When unbalanced, there was disease—much like the blight. Achieving that harmony had been Lasya's strength, though, not hers.

"I don't think we have to worry about deteriorating tissues or brain damage." Kajal glanced at Kutaa. "But he may not be quite the same as he was in life."

Vivaan frowned at the bag. "We need to do whatever it takes," he said softly.

His conviction aside, Kajal couldn't help but wonder how the prince would react to being forced into life after death.

"We lose this opportunity, we lose everything," Vivaan told her. "Once you're ready, Jassi and Sezal and I will assist you, so don't get any ideas about doing this on your own. We don't want His Highness ending up like that one." He nodded in Kutaa's direction. "Remember that one mistake could cost us. *Everything* must go perfectly."

Her mistakes had already cost her plenty. But seeing the shades of desperation on Vivaan's face, the tightness in Sezal's eyes, the sober line of Jassi's mouth, she knew that meant nothing to them. They had their sights set on something much bigger than one girl and her dead sister. They cared about far more than themselves.

She wondered what that was like.

Jassi and Kajal saw the rebels off at the wall. Vivaan and Sezal would stay in the city and collect some of the ingredients on Kajal's list. Sezal flashed Kajal one last reassuring smile, and Vivaan gave her a grave nod before they slid the stone back into place.

"I'm pretty familiar with the guard rotations, so we should be in the clear to get back to my flat," Jassi said. "Just stick close to me."

Outside the laboratory building was a hexagonal courtyard with a fountain at its center, surrounded by narrow channels of water lined with blue-veined marble. On the opposite side of a large archway stood a squat building with embossed silver-leaf doors and topped with a fat, pear-like roof. The design on the doors was sinuous and streaked with turquoise. A Serpent temple.

Next to it was another sandstone building, easily four stories or more, interspersed with latticework windows and engrailed arches. Jassi led Kajal toward it as they stuck to the shadows, Kutaa silent at their heels.

"The Serpent Court is reserved for student housing," Jassi explained quietly. "But the junior professors also have flats here. Mine's on the top floor."

Kajal found it hard to believe. A building as nice as this one, and people actually *lived* in it? Students, no less?

"How did you end up in this little group?" Kajal asked.

"If you're looking for an exciting story, I'll have to disappoint you. One of the Sodhis' children attends the university. When their parents came to visit the school, they approached me to ask if I would be interested in conducting some experiments for them. I agreed."

"What about Bakshi?"

"Oh, I hate the bastard. If I can help the Sodhis depose him, I figure that'll be my life's dharma." Jassi fiddled with her iron bangle. "One step at a time."

"I thought . . ." Kajal hesitated, but Jassi indicated for her to go on. "I thought being a professor, you wouldn't have to worry about money."

Jassi fought not to laugh. "You'd be surprised. Most of the university's finances go into funding experiments and research. And my sister and my father are dependent on me."

"Is this the sister I'm pretending to be?"

Jassi's expression softened. "She's much younger than me, and our father can't work anymore because he's ill." There was a long pause. "So I send money home often. I don't get to visit much, but when I do, I always make sure I have a present for Nishaa. If I don't, I get an earful. Sometimes a light beating."

Kajal gave a smile, but it wavered and fell. Her eyes stung thinking about all the moments Lasya had snuck little gifts into her hands—ladoos or glass beads or pretty stones she'd found while walking.

She was abruptly snatched from her reminiscing when a hand grabbed her shoulder. It spun her around, and she despaired that the prince's bhuta had followed them after all.

Instead, she came face to face with a soldier.

Kajal's mouth hung open, but nothing came out. Her mind, the thing she relied on most, ground to a halt as her eyes darted around his uniform of blue and marigold.

The Vadhia.

"What are you doing out past curfew?" the soldier demanded. Although his voice was deep, he seemed around Vivaan's and Sezal's age. His black hair was glossy, like he oiled it every night. "Answer me."

A snake coiled around Kajal's chest and squeezed, turning her breaths fast and shallow. Her sight darkened, and she heard Kutaa growl behind her.

Heard the creak of a woman swinging from a tree branch.

Heard the sharp, echoing snap of bone.

The air turned brittle and cold. Where the soldier touched her felt like death itself, rotting and diseased, a blight of her own making.

And then came the whine. High, droning, unceasing.

"N-No," she whispered. "I—"

The hand was wrenched off her. Jassi stood between her and the Vadhia, holding the latter's wrist.

"I'm sorry, Jagvir," the professor said. "My little sister arrived today, and she was too excited to sleep. She wanted to see my laboratory."

The soldier frowned, peering over her shoulder at Kajal. "Sister?"

"Nishaa. She came all the way from Malhir." Jassi looked over her shoulder with a smile. "You're not used to traveling so far, are you?" she asked Kajal.

Kajal knew she was supposed to speak. But her mouth moved without sound, too focused on the whine that burrowed into her, growing louder the harder her heart pounded.

Don't, she pleaded to Lasya. *I can handle this. I can . . .*

Kill him. I can kill him, if I have to.

She thought about grabbing the soldier's head and smashing it against the cobblestones. She thought about drowning him in the fountain while he struggled, bubbles rising from his mouth until he stilled. It would be better if *she* took his life, like the rebels with the pujari, if that meant she could prevent the bhuta from getting stronger. Spare Lasya another murder.

Gradually, the terror that had caught her in its stranglehold loosened, replaced with sickening satisfaction. The whine faded away.

"Right," she said hoarsely. "But I'm . . . I'm pretty tired now."

The soldier, Jagvir, slid his icy gaze past her. "What's that animal with you?"

Jassi's laugh was mild. "What, you haven't seen a dog before? He's my sister's. Follows her everywhere. It's adorable."

He made a face, like Kutaa was anything but adorable. "It's past curfew, Professor Jasmeet."

"I know, I know. I'm sorry. It won't happen again."

"It better not." His hand drifted to his belt. Kajal's eyesight strained in the darkness to make out the nautilus shape of a leather whip curled there.

The scars on her back throbbed.

Jassi gently steered Kajal toward the dormitories. Kajal managed to get up a couple flights of stairs before her wobbling knees gave out.

Jassi knelt beside her. "I'm so sorry. I should have been paying better attention—"

"There are *Vadhia* here?" She knew the university was Bakshi's, but she hadn't expected his soldiers to bother themselves with it if he never came.

"They sometimes use the soldiers' housing as a way station, and they technically outrank the university guards." Jassi shook her head. "I think Jagvir's in a particularly bad mood since he just got off the road yesterday. He was on some mission that didn't go well."

We're not the only ones who heard about the mishap in Siphar, Vivaan had told her.

"A lot of us don't like it either," Jassi said when Kajal shuddered. "But as long as we lie low, they shouldn't bother us."

Lie low. How was that possible when she had a prince to resurrect and her sister's bhuta haunting her, already on the hunt for its next victim? She had managed to stave off the bhuta this time, but there was no telling if she could do it again.

She reached up and touched her neck, sore where the bhuta had choked her on the road. She thought about how it must feel to have a rope digging into her flesh instead, and hoped news of her misdeeds in Kinara didn't travel south.

Chapter Ten

THE BANGING OF fists against wood echoed through the desolate dark. The ungiving surface above her stung her palms with splinters and sent numbing vibrations down her arms. Her breaths filled the cramped space with the frightened pitch of a trapped animal.

Kajal pounded harder, desperate to break free. *Lasya*. She had to get to Lasya. She had to bury her deep beneath the earth's surface as if she were nothing but a sprouted root ready to grow and ripen into something once again living.

Smoke leaked through the gaps in her coffin. The first hint of heat nipped her skin, flames crackling while she kept knocking against the lid as hard as she could.

Something took hold of her arm. Like the bhutas that had clawed at her ankles, wanting to drag her down into the earth, down and down until—

With a scream, she was pulled from the coffin, from the darkness, from the smoke and heat. Her eyes flew open.

She stared up at a ceiling she didn't recognize. She turned her head and found Kutaa, his jaws around her forearm in a soft bite. Seeing she was awake, he let go and backed away, ears turned toward the central room of Jassi's flat.

Last night returned to her in a rush. She had been led here, nerves jangling, to find there wasn't only a bed waiting for her, but a whole room.

The floor and walls were dark, the bed frame, like the table and desk, made of rosewood. There was also a trunk for clothes, though she had nothing to store in it.

Someone was knocking at the door. Kajal cursed and struggled against the sheet she'd gotten tangled in. Warm sunlight slanted across her legs; she briefly wondered if that was what had inspired the flames in her dream.

"Coming!" she croaked. Thankfully, she was already dressed, too paranoid to sleep in her underthings in case she had to flee during the night.

She lurched into the central room. A rug of green and gold was spread over the floor, and a round table with two chairs was situated at the window, stained with cup rings. There was also a desk against the left wall, covered in papers and books dragged from what was now Kajal's room and what she suspected was formerly an office. Through a door on the right was Jassi's bedroom, the bed unmade, the professor gone.

Kutaa stood braced in the middle of the room as Kajal flung the front door open wide. The person on the other side jumped, hand held up to knock again. They were about her age—a student, she guessed—dressed in a colorful embroidered kurta of blue and green. Their hair fell in a straight sheet to their shoulders, and their aquiline nose glinted with a gold septum piercing.

"Finally," the student said. "I didn't think you'd still be asleep."

Kajal was about to demand what else she'd be doing so early in the morning, but the sunlight coming through the window indicated it must be closer to noon. Considering how little sleep she'd gotten the previous two nights, she supposed that was fair.

Kajal scratched her scalp, grimacing at the tangles in her hair. "Where's Pro— Jassi?"

The student smirked. "You don't have to pretend in front of me. I know about the Insurrectionists."

Kajal stopped trying to undo a particularly gnarled knot and gave the student another once-over. "You do?"

"I'm the youngest child of the Sodhi family." When Kajal made no sign of recognition, the student put their hands on their hips. "Really? No one explained any of this to you?"

Then it clicked. "Ah, the nobles, right? The ones who want to depose Bakshi?"

"Say it a little louder. I don't think the students on the next floor heard you." They crossed their arms and leaned their long, lanky body against the door frame. "But yes. Part of the reason my parents ultimately agreed to send me here was to 'keep an eye on things.'" They rolled said eyes, which were the light brown of cinnamon bark. "Never mind the only things I want to keep my eye on are books. Anyway, Professor Jassi told me about you this morning."

"Where is she?"

"She has classes and got roped into some meetings, the latter of which was definitely code for 'I need to go see a guy about some stuff.' Supplies for you, most likely. She apologizes and says she'll meet up with you later. In the meantime, I'm supposed to show you around. At least until I have— Oh!"

Their voice strangled at the end, and Kajal immediately saw why: Kutaa had stalked to the door.

"I was told you had a guard dog, but I've never seen one so big." The student extended a hand. Kutaa sniffed their thin fingers and protruding knuckles before he wagged his tail in acceptance. Emboldened, the student patted Kutaa's head. "Who do we have here?"

"Kutaa."

The student raised both eyebrows but didn't comment. "I'm Dalbir. Please don't refer to me as 'he' or 'she.'"

"I'm Kajal. Or Nishaa, I suppose. 'She' and 'her' are fine."

Dalbir gave the dog one final pat and glanced meaningfully at Kajal's hair. "I'll give you a moment to clean up. When you're ready, meet me in the hall. I'll bring you to the commissary."

Kajal closed the door and turned to Kutaa. "You have to stay here until I come back. I don't want to draw any more attention to myself." Kutaa gave a single wag of his tail, which she took as consent.

Once Kajal had tamed her hair, brushed her teeth with neem leaves, and unsuccessfully tried to straighten the wrinkles in her clothing, she followed Dalbir out. It was surprisingly noisy in the dormitories. They passed a couple girls fighting over a hair clip, someone calling down the stairs to their friend below, and a student sweeping their floor while singing off-key.

"Quiet hours don't start until late afternoon," Dalbir explained. "A lot of students go to the library to get work done during the day."

Her heart fluttered. "There's a library?"

"Of course. This is a university, what did you expect?"

She really didn't know. The only schools she'd encountered were small, with no-nonsense teachers and cramped classrooms and a yard for calling attendance. Where the children almost always wore simple uniforms and were required to keep their hair and nails at appropriate lengths. Kajal had wanted to attend one until she learned teachers hit students' palms with a stick if they gave wrong answers. Being here was wholly outside of her experience, and a hefty dose of trepidation was mixed in with her excitement.

Now that it was daytime, she took care to observe her surroundings, the same way she had when she and Lasya went somewhere new. Jassi's flat was on the top floor, and there were windows she could crawl through to climb onto the roof. Down on the first floor were archways that seemed good for hiding behind, and if worse came to worst, there were plenty of students she could grab and threaten. A chokehold would work well enough, but a knife would be even better.

"How long do students attend the university for?" Kajal asked as they crossed the Serpent Court, the air already congested with incense from the temple.

"The average is three years or so. But it depends on how quickly you can find an advisor who'll help you transition into a profession."

They passed under the archway and into the university's central courtyard. It was bustling with people, some lounging before a star-shaped pool with a marble fountain, others hurrying between buildings. One of the pavilions had its curtains drawn, affording a view of a professor leading a sleepy group of students through guided meditation.

Like the Serpent Court, the central courtyard was hexagonal in shape, and there were two additional courts to the west and north. Above each gate loomed a stone statue of one of the yaksha deities: the Elephant, the Tortoise, and the Serpent.

Kajal went to sneak a glimpse through the Tortoise archway, but Dalbir grabbed the back of her shirt.

"That's the housing for the senior professors, staff, and guards," Dalbir explained. "We're not allowed in unless the temple is open for a special occasion."

The warning came too late. Kajal had already noticed the whipping post at the far end of the courtyard.

Her blood turned to rime along her veins. She stared numbly at the post, elevated on a wooden platform, until her vision blurred.

There was no limit to the number of punishments for someone like her. She had stolen more times than she could count. She had punched a merchant's son for touching her sister. She had broken the window of a sweets shop because they refused to sell her Lasya's favorite kind of burfi, on account of her dirty face and shoeless feet.

But the post—that had been for raking her nails down a soldier's face.

She still carried a couple of raised scars along her ribs and between her shoulder blades where buckskin leather had bit her skin. Because the one who had whipped her had not held back on account of her being young or a girl; because they had wanted not only to teach her a lesson but to give a warning to everyone who'd watched and done nothing.

Do not oppose us.

Her body was a jumble of sensory memories. Sun flashing on teeth, and the brass pips of a blue-and-marigold uniform. A trickle of blood down her spine. Lasya sobbing, begging them to stop.

Dalbir followed her gaze. "The Vadhia built that after a professor was overheard bad-mouthing Bakshi."

It was a struggle to speak. "They whipped a *professor*?"

"They've done a lot worse."

The noose. Any feeling that had begun to return to her in increments fizzled back to numbness.

"Apparently, it was to 'dissuade others from following the same sentiment.'" Dalbir shook their head in disgust. "Come on. We shouldn't linger here."

A distant whistle blew past Kajal's ears. She hurried after Dalbir, putting distance between them and the post.

They passed under the statue of the Elephant and into a courtyard flanked by two towering minars. Colonnades gave way to latticed marble windows in a glimmering sandstone building that loomed above a small temple.

Kajal noticed a blocked-off archway behind it. "What's that for?"

"It leads to the old palace. Nobody uses it, and we're not allowed inside." Clearly uninterested, Dalbir ushered her down a stone pathway that led to a squat side building. "The majority of classes are held here, but the commissary is this way."

The commissary was littered with tables and floor cushions on thick rugs. Students' chatter filled every nook and cranny, making Kajal's shoulders tighten. She kept imagining that their eyes were fixed on her.

"I don't have any money," Kajal admitted. Living as she had, not much embarrassed her, but the way Dalbir peered at her now made her flush.

"Students and professors don't pay for food," they explained. "You take a plate, and the servers hand you whatever you want, but you have to clean the plate yourself at the wash station before you return it."

She didn't have to pay for food? It seemed far too good to be true. Under Dalbir's encouragement, Kajal grabbed a couple of rolled-up rotis slathered with ghee, feeling odd in her own skin.

She paused when she saw a knife on the other side of the counter. It wouldn't take much to distract the server and grab it. Her fingers twitched, envisioning the Vadhia she'd run into last night. The whip coiled at his belt. The post. The noose.

As she was about to make her move, a bell tolled a deep tune somewhere close by. Dalbir rearranged the bag slung over their shoulder.

"You have a class?" Kajal guessed.

"Mythic History. I'm studying to be a lorist. I trust you remember the way to Professor Jassi's flat?"

She didn't want to go back to Jassi's flat. She wanted to explore, to poke and prod and discover, to pretend she was just another student. But she doubted she could blend in so easily; the university's rules were completely foreign to her. Also, she didn't like the idea of walking through the grounds alone while that soldier was here.

Taking a bite of roti before someone decided she couldn't have it after all, she gestured with the other toward the door. "Can I see the classrooms first?"

Dalbir allowed her to follow them to the main building. She licked the ghee that rolled down her wrist as they trotted through long hallways that sported vaulted ceilings and were flanked with frescoes and marble relief panels.

Up a flight of stairs, students her age streamed by like schools of fish, the ruckus even more intense than in the commissary. Dalbir led her to a pear-shaped archway, beyond which was a room situated with tiered benches facing a wall covered in a dusty blackboard. It smelled of parchment and dust, the air buzzing with murmurs.

"There, you've seen it," Dalbir said. "Happy?"

Figuring she had some time until Jassi returned with supplies, Kajal ignored Dalbir and made her way to the bench farthest back. Dalbir sighed and followed her. She had no materials—no paper, no pen, no way of taking notes—and she gazed longingly at the sheaves of parchment the students had, missing her captive notebook.

As she was sliding into an empty spot, she accidentally knocked into the girl sitting in the row ahead. The girl rocked forward with a great deal more force than Kajal suspected she'd hit her with, and her pen spilled a slash of ink across her parchment.

The girl whirled around with murder in her dark eyes. Kajal was alarmed by how beautiful she was, her dark bronze skin smooth as nacre and her heart-shaped face framed by curly reddish-brown hair. The two girls on either side of her—sisters, if their similar features were anything to go by—gasped in unison.

"Well?" the beautiful girl said in a low voice after a moment of strained silence. "Aren't you going to apologize?"

Kajal had run into a wide variety of people during her travels, both with Lasya and on her own. She immediately knew what sort of person this girl was—the spoiled upstart, the cherished daughter who walked through the world with the confidence of one who would inherit more than they were worth.

A smile bloomed on Kajal's face. "I was going to, but now I don't think I will."

Dalbir groaned, and the girl's friends gaped. They were beginning to draw attention from the other students.

The beautiful girl narrowed her eyes. "Excuse me?"

"Forced apologies are meaningless. Although I suppose you're used to hearing empty words."

Before the girl could form any sort of retort, a middle-aged man walked into the classroom. The students shot to their feet until the professor gestured at them to sit. Dalbir took the opportunity to shove Kajal farther down the bench, away from the trio of girls.

"What was *that*?" Dalbir hissed. "First you barge your way into a class you're not enrolled in, then you make enemies with the university's top student?"

Kajal's smile soured. "Top student? *Her?*"

"Yes! All the professors and students love Vritika. You'll only paint a target on your back if you get on her bad side." Dalbir shook their head, rummaging through their bag for a piece of parchment and a pen. "Then again, you've probably already done that. You should have just apologized."

Kajal sneered. She had survived far worse than one stuffy girl who didn't like being told no. She'd had entire towns out for her blood.

The professor stood before the blackboard. His mustache was heavily streaked with silver, matching the gray turban he wore. He tapped a piece of chalk against the blackboard to get everyone's attention.

"Good afternoon, class."

The students responded in a chorus of "Good afternoon, Professor Manraj."

"Who remembers what we discussed earlier this week? Arjun?"

A boy stood. "We began to cover the three planes."

"Which are collectively called . . . ?"

"The Brahimada."

"Good." Professor Manraj nodded, and the student sat with a pleased smile. "Also known as the Universal Divide." He drew three lines on the board, one on top of the other. "Who knows their names and their order?"

Kajal wasn't at all surprised when Vritika stood to answer. "The highest level is Svarga, the heavenly plane, where the yaksha deities and their subordinates dwell. There, one can find both elemental spirits and celestial races, like the musical gandharvas. Under Svarga is Martya, the mortal plane, which *we* inhabit alongside yakshas and rakshasas that maintain the land. Below that is Patala, or the underworld, where divine races such as the nagas convene and are ruled over by the demon lord Dukha."

Professor Manraj labeled each level as Vritika spoke. When she sat, he wrote *Brahimada* under the sketch. "Very good. The entire structure of our universe depends on the balance of each of these planes, both the light and the dark, the good and the bad, and everything in between. Too much of one will inevitably cause harm. For example, poisons taken in large quantities lead to death, but taken in smaller doses, they can be useful in medicinal applications.

"This is why humans are expected to maintain dharma, as upholding these duties helps stabilize Martya. We leave offerings at the shrines, we go out of our way to preserve nature, and we have priests devoted to delivering our prayers."

Recalling the pujari who had been consumed by blight, Kajal grimaced.

"Of course, the rakshasas are also a part of this natural flow of the universe," the professor went on, pointing to the level of Patala. "Their darker energy, tamas, balances out the lighter energy of the yakshas, called sattva—and both convene with our mortal energy, rajas. But while we are often divided by these three energies, nothing is ever truly sattvic, rajasic, or tamasic. They all course through us in varying levels, which further helps us achieve that sought-after balance."

He turned and added a couple of shaky humanlike drawings beside the planes. The class stifled their laughter, and Professor Manraj grinned. "Yes, yes, my art is quite bad. But these two figures, the asura and the deva, are the best examples of this interplay of energies."

Dalbir straightened beside Kajal. The movement caught the professor's attention, which then shifted to Kajal.

"Ah, we have a new face today. Perhaps you can share what you know about this topic."

Kajal had hoped the professor would ignore the stranger who wasn't supposed to be in his classroom, but no such luck. The students stared at her, waiting, and a nauseating force went through her. For a moment she forgot how to breathe.

It wasn't until Dalbir elbowed her that she reluctantly got to her feet. "I . . ." She eyed the blackboard, the stick-figure drawings.

It wasn't as if she hadn't heard tales over the years of the asura and deva. Of their greatness and their follies, their divine powers and celestial weapons, the way they could stop wars as easily as they could start them. But it was difficult to picture Dharati having guardians when contemplating the current state of things.

The crowd at her ordeal of poison had been riled at the idea of being abandoned by their fabled protectors, convinced that taking their ire out on a witch would be enough to undo years of corrosion.

When she remained silent, a soft snort came from Vritika. Kajal clenched her jaw.

"Not to worry," the professor said. He gestured for Kajal to sit again, which she did with little grace. "According to lore, the asura and deva are the ambassadors of the rakshasas and yakshas, respectively, and our strongest links to Patala and Svarga. They are said to be human, but also *more*. Only they have the ability to maintain the gateways to these other planes." He drew connecting lines between the stick figures and the planes. "Together, they preserve the balance of the Brahimada."

He paused, chalk dust falling from his fingers. "However, these last several years the balance seems to have shifted to tamasic energy. With a lack of the yakshas' sattva, more crops are failing, and more rakshasas prowl the land."

His words sent an uncomfortable hush through the room at what he was deliberately not saying: *blight*. Kajal doubted the Usurper King wanted students in the university he'd founded to be reminded of the tidal wave of decay stealing through the country during his rule. Not without attributing it to witches, at least. With the threat of the whipping post out in the open, everyone had to tread carefully.

One of Vritika's friends stood. "Professor, do you believe the asura and deva actually exist?"

Professor Manraj put the chalk down and wiped his hands. "That's been the subject of much debate, as we have both historic records of people claiming to be them as well as stories of their accomplishments that are clearly exaggerated. Personally, I like to believe they once existed."

"Then does that mean we no longer have an asura and a deva? Are they not working together as they should, or have they abandoned Martya? Are the yaksha deities and the demon lord fighting?"

"All good questions, Siddhi. Each could be a possibility."

"Or perhaps the asura is merely doing what they do best," said the other sister without bothering to stand up. "Being evil."

"Riddhi," Siddhi admonished.

"Well, that's a rather excessive statement," Professor Manraj said in a diplomatic tone. "The asura isn't *evil*. They are merely the bridge between the other two realms and Patala; a wielder of tamas."

"But isn't tamasic energy the reason why the blight is spreading so far?" the girl pressed.

Professor Manraj sighed. "That is one theory, yes. This is the infuriating part of dwelling in Martya, where we have no control or insight over such matters. We are always at the mercy of the deities, with little in terms of answers."

He spread his arms out. "Which is partly why this university exists. We must figure out how to navigate our world without relying on the divine. That is why each of you is here, is it not?"

The students nodded. Kajal clasped her hands tight in her lap until the knuckles turned white as bone. She thought of the black stains on the pujari's face, the echo of his clicking teeth. Of the desolation of the Harama Plain and the sheer number of soldiers that had fallen to Bakshi's greed. Of the women tortured and tried for the simple crime of living.

Of the body lying in the laboratory, waiting for her to revive it.

Vivaan and Sezal believed restoring Advaith to the throne would get rid of the blight. But would that be enough? Or would it only continue to pollute the whole of their realm, and her sister along with it?

Chapter Eleven

"I APOLOGIZE FOR not showing you around this morning," Jassi said when she met with Kajal in the laboratory later. "Did you have any trouble?"

"No. Dalbir helped." Kajal decided not to mention she had stolen into a class.

But Jassi's smile was knowing. Had Dalbir snitched? She made a note to drop a beetle into their bag later when they weren't looking.

"Try not to antagonize the students during your stay," Jassi said. "The others want you to be discreet. That means no more sneaking into classrooms or getting into fights." Kajal made a face, and Jassi laughed. "I know, I know. But trust me when I say that Vritika is far more than she seems."

"You're taking *her* side?"

"I'm taking no one's side. In any other situation I would suggest the two of you become friends."

Kajal thought she'd rather make friends with a scorpion.

"Besides, she comes from an influential family of demon hunters," Jassi said. Kajal couldn't picture someone like Vritika wielding a crossbow with priest-blessed bolts. "That's why she's here, actually—to learn more about tamas and the blight. The Meghanis have already done some studies, but—"

"She's from the *Meghani* family?" Kajal interrupted, aghast.

"She is indeed. Their second-youngest child, I believe. So she's out to prove herself." Jassi gave her another of those discerning smiles. "Like you."

Heat touched Kajal's face, but she told herself it was outrage for Vritika's existence in general, and in particular that she was part of the family Kajal had relied on for research all these months.

Research. The heat instantly drained back out of her.

The Meghanis, outside of investigating the Harama Plain, were also credited with discovering a method of bhuta exorcism for when the body could not be found and burned. Since a warped soul could not travel to the underworld on its own, they trapped the bhuta within an array of iron or burned turmeric, then recited atma shanti mantras until the soul was forcefully guided to Patala to face retribution, rebirth, or reward.

If Vritika found out about Lasya and performed an exorcism, Kajal would lose her sister's soul to the cycle of reincarnation.

"What's wrong?" Jassi asked.

Kajal wiped her face of emotion. "Nothing." Pushing her dread down, she helped Jassi sort through the package she'd brought from the city.

The rebels had been able to get the limestone and zinc, and Jassi had taken herbs from the university's supply. Kajal cataloged her new inventory while the body of the crown prince lay behind her, the slab of limestone now resting between him and the table. She found herself peering back at him, as if already expecting him to move and speak.

Avoiding Jassi's eyes, Kajal plunked some zinc into a mortar. "I was thinking it would be best if I was the only one who had the key to the laboratory."

"Oh?"

"Yes. Um." Her pulse jumped at her wrist, and she covered it with a hand. "I'll need a private space to work. And I . . . I'd like to keep my procedure a secret. So that it doesn't fall into the wrong hands."

While that was technically true, she also wanted to secure her usefulness to the rebels so they'd uphold their end of the bargain and not turn her over to the Vadhia. Even if they did have her notes, getting rid of her would set them back weeks, months, maybe years.

Jassi looked a little hurt, like Kajal was insinuating *she* might be the "wrong hands."

"Sorry. I—"

"Don't be sorry," Jassi said, uncharacteristically stern. "We're often conditioned to apologize for the things we need. You need privacy, and you have a good point about keeping this a secret." She handed over the key. "You're not being a burden, Kajal."

Kajal stared at her blankly, the silver key heavy in her palm. She slowly closed her fingers around it and murmured a quiet thanks.

She stayed behind when Jassi left to grade papers in the library. While the rebels wouldn't return her notebook until it was time to carry out the experiment, she recalled most of her measurements and had little trouble writing them out. She even redrew Raja Hiss, adding a little talwar that he held with his tail. Then, feeling restless, she started preparing the ingredients.

She ignored her stomach when it cramped with hunger, too focused on grinding up the zinc with a mortar and pestle and pressing it into pellets. Her reluctance to leave her project half finished was only offset by her uneasy awareness of the body behind her. She could *sense* it, like low-hanging clouds that brought pressure to the air before a monsoon.

Hours flew by until curfew drew near. She got up and, in the process of stretching muscles sore with neglect, spotted a scalpel among the laboratory's tools. The blade was small yet precise, its tip gleaming. Thinking of the lost opportunity to grab a knife in the commissary, Kajal slipped the scalpel into the waistband of her salwar.

"You saw nothing," she told the prince's corpse.

She covered her notes and blew out the lanterns. As she was turning the key in the lock after closing the door behind her, a familiar voice made her start.

"What are you doing?"

Vritika stood in the hallway, a canvas bag that bulged with books slung over one shoulder. She was flanked on either side by her friends, the two sisters, who had been so indignant on her behalf earlier.

Kajal held up the key. "Locking up?"

"That laboratory belongs to Professor Jassi, and she doesn't give students access to it. Not even those she's advising." From Vritika's tone, it seemed like a sore spot Kajal was tempted to poke.

"Doesn't give access to *you*, sure." Kajal swung the key around one finger by its circular bow. "But it's mine now."

The sisters scoffed, but genuine shock flitted across Vritika's face. "What are you talking about? We're only first-years. We're not allowed to have laboratories until our third year!"

"I'm not a first-year. I'm not a student at all, actually. Jassi is my sister, and she gave it to me for private research." Kajal was used to falsehoods, but this one tasted acerbic in her mouth.

Vritika's hand tightened on her bag strap. The other two looked disbelievingly back and forth between their leader and Kajal.

"*You're* Professor Jassi's sister?" If Kajal didn't know any better, she'd say Vritika was offended by the notion. "You don't look much alike." Not knowing how much freedom she had to invent her backstory, Kajal merely shrugged. "I see. So it's not deserved, it's merely bias."

A member of the Meghani family should be no stranger to bias, but Kajal was stunned by the attitude. There was blatant jealousy in her voice, but also something else—something very much like dismay.

It reminded her of crying in Lasya's lap, howling at how unfair it was that other children got to be normal, got to attend school and eat three times a day, and not have to worry about finding new clothes.

Kajal shrugged again. "That's just the way it is."

The flash of rage and distress in Vritika's eyes sparked an unspoken desire within Kajal. People like Vritika were always handed things. Kajal wanted to luxuriate in the feeling of having something Vritika didn't and so obviously wanted.

The line of Vritika's mouth thinned. One of the sisters—Siddhi, the one who had asked Professor Manraj all those questions in class—noticed and wrapped an arm around Vritika's shoulders. The other stepped forward.

"You're lying," she blurted. "I bet you stole that key."

"You can ask Jassi if you don't believe me." Kajal pocketed it. "Anyway, I have more important things to do than stand here and argue."

"Right." The girl crossed her arms, but the gesture seemed more defensive than imperious. "You didn't even know who the asura and deva were."

"That's not— What's that supposed to mean?"

"It means that even if you *were* a student here, you'd be an abysmal one." The girl smiled, like every wound she gave Kajal was a bandage for her own. "Better get reading if you want to catch up, dakini."

Kajal had been about to take Jassi's advice and walk away, but the last word sent a red-hot flash through her. She reached up to grab the braid resting heavy on her shoulder.

Rakshasa dakinis wore their dark hair in a plait, which they used as an extra limb to do their bidding. Usually as a means to drain blood from their victims. With the Vadhia looking for any excuse to pounce, Kajal had taken to wearing her hair down or tied with a simple cord. But she had unthinkingly braided it in its usual style after Dalbir had woken her this morning.

The accusation should have been nothing new. Even before the rise of the Vadhia, she and Lasya had been suspected of witchcraft. She remembered clearly, too clearly, a rock flying from the hand of a superstitious villager and hitting Lasya's temple. She remembered facing the people of Kinara as they touched their foreheads and flicked their fingers to ward against the evil eye.

But this . . . this felt different. *She* felt different.

Kajal slowly turned back around. The scalpel she'd tucked into her salwar was a brand against her skin.

"Riddhi," Vritika snapped. "You know what the Vadhia are using that word for."

Siddhi's gaze darted around as if a soldier might be hiding along the hallway, but Riddhi didn't seem sorry in the least.

"Yes," Riddhi agreed. "Which is why I said it. I've met girls like her. I know exactly what they are."

Kajal met her piercing stare until the stone around them began to hum. It vibrated under Kajal's feet, into the roots of her teeth.

Then the whine started.

It broke the shell of Kajal's fury, making her gasp. The whine was faint, like the drone of a faraway insect, but in her mind's eye was Gurdeep's face frozen in rictus horror.

Cold swept across her body even as sweat dotted her forehead. A whisper breathed against the back of her neck.

Kill me.

For a second, she met Vritika's dark eyes, which narrowed in confusion.

Kajal ran. One of the girls called something behind her, but the voice couldn't penetrate the escalating whine in her head. Kajal slapped her hands over her ears and bounced off the walls all the way down the corkscrew stairs, but it did nothing to drown it out.

"Lasya, don't," Kajal panted. "Please, if you love me, don't!"

She burst out into the cool night air. The whine died to nothing, but it left her shaking and feverish. The students and staff who passed her gave her funny looks, but she hardly noticed.

Kajal strained to hear any screams from above. All was quiet. Lasya hadn't struck. Kajal had gotten away in time, or perhaps her pleading had stopped the bhuta from striking. She slumped against the side of the building with relief.

Then the pain descended.

It wrapped around her neck and *squeezed*, her bones just on the verge of cracking. She clawed at her throat, mouth working soundlessly, body convulsing against cool stone. She dropped to her knees as her lungs burned, her chest so tight she thought it would burst open and spill blood and organs across the courtyard.

Days seemed to pass until it lifted. Kajal coughed and sucked in air, shivering hard enough to rattle her teeth. The backlash had been even more intense than before. She reached for her neck and was horrified at the raised lines of scratches along her skin.

I should have let the girl die, Kajal thought. At this rate, another death—hers or someone else's—was a matter of when, not if.

But with a Meghani here, it could be traced back to her. Could lead to Lasya's exorcism.

Could help the Vadhia finally track her down.

Every hour she wasted was another hour rumors could start circulating. And if Lasya was already this powerful, how long would it take before Kajal ended up dead by her sister's hand?

She pressed her forehead against the stone wall and tried to think. The rebels would only bring her Lasya's body once she had revived the prince to their satisfaction, and she likely needed a little more time in order to get the method exactly right. Yet stronger than her rationality was the return of her rage.

Even if you were *a student here, you'd be an abysmal one.*

She bared her teeth.

Forget the rebels. She was resurrecting Advaith *tonight.*

She went to the flat to stuff some pillows under her blanket to make it look like she'd turned in early. Then she collected Kutaa and locked them both in the laboratory.

"You'll help me, right?" she whispered, ruffling his fur. He gave a low woof.

She was thankful for her long hours spent here earlier, though she still had some work to do. Once the components were prepared and everything was assembled, Kajal stared at the bag laid out on the table, above the slab of limestone. The scratches on her neck burned with urgency.

Ideally, she would have tested it first to make sure her measurements were correct, to determine if anything was missing or needed to be adjusted to ensure no mistakes. But Riddhi's words had laid a challenge at her feet—one she was more than capable of meeting.

Kajal untied the bag and let the earth packed inside spill onto the floor. Kutaa sat and watched with keen, glowing eyes as she pulled the bag completely away. All that was left was the prince, dirty and grimy and very much dead.

She carried over the basin of water from the corner. "Sorry about this, Your Highness."

Kajal was not a stranger to nakedness. Living the way she had, she couldn't help but see things. Nonetheless, peeling the clothes off a dead body was a new and unpleasant experience, a foreign mixture of discomfort and disgust. There was clotted, dried blood that made the fabric stick to his skin in places, and Kajal had to stare up at the ceiling muttering curses as she shimmied the trousers past his hips.

He looked even more like a cadaver then. It didn't help that there were twin wounds in his abdomen, old and red, where some sort of weapon—Bakshi's, no doubt—had punctured his armor and delivered the fatal blow. They were strangely symmetrical, the skin jagged around the edges where the weapon had caught his flesh on the way out.

Already light-headed, Kajal did her best to scrub off the dirt and blood. She wiped a wet cloth down his arms and across his shoulders, being extra careful when she cleaned his face. His serene expression calmed her.

When she moved the cloth to his chest, she paused. He was wearing a pendant on a thin chain around his neck. It was a rectangle of pale amber, artlessly forged. Preserved inside was a single lotus petal, its pink shade warped by the amber's hue.

She had expected royalty to wear fine jewelry of diamonds and rubies and gold. Why would a crown prince wear something this ugly?

Kajal slipped it off and set it on the worktable before returning to her task. Other than the necklace, he also wore a sarbloh bangle, which she decided to leave on; the pure iron might help with the conducting of his energies.

Once the wounds in his abdomen were washed, she sutured them closed, afraid they would bleed as soon as he woke, depending on how quickly his circulation kicked in. She stared at the ceiling again with gritted teeth in order to clean the last bits of him and, when she was done, covered his lower body with the cloth. Kajal pushed the basin away and looked at the prince.

Please, she thought, rubbing her thumb against the finger where that butterfly had perched. *Please work.*

It had to.

Heart in her throat, Kajal collected the zinc pellets. She wrenched the prince's jaw open and stuffed the pellets into his mouth. She used the pestle to push them down as far as she could, grimacing despite knowing full well he couldn't feel it.

Kutaa followed her every movement as she slathered salt over the prince's skin. On top of this, she sprinkled goldenrod and gotu kola, and rubbed some into his teeth for good measure. Her mixture of adder's-tongue oil she used to anoint the junction points of the doshas, the ones that helped maintain Vata, Pitta, and Kapha in the body. Vata, for space and air. Pitta, for fire and water. Kapha, for water and earth.

Her racing pulse made her vision blacken at the edges. Kajal leaned against the table and caught her breath.

"Such a smart sister I have," Lasya cooed, pinching Kajal's cheek. "You can do anything, can't you?"

"Not anything," *a younger Kajal had grumbled, despite her pleased grin.*

"Anything. Once you put your mind to it, you'll accomplish it. I believe in you."

Kajal blinked away her tears. Inhaling deeply, she reached for the prince's body.

When she had brought Kutaa back to life, she had focused on only a couple of chakras, urging sentience and a heartbeat without considering everything else that made up a life. She had to do better this time.

Kajal settled a hand on the top of the prince's head. "Sahasrara, open." A distant hum of vitality ignited against her palm. She pressed a thumb to the center of his forehead. "Ajna, third eye, open." A pinpoint of energy swirled beneath her thumb pad.

She touched his throat, his navel, his hip, the inside of his thigh—her earlier discomfort overtaken by focus—making sure each chakra was connected and opened, that energy could flow through his channels. She paid special attention to the stomach, hoping it would allow him to eat again.

Damp with sweat, she touched his heart last. "Anahata, open."

The prince's body jerked.

Kajal pressed more firmly against Advaith's chest, salt granules digging into her palm as she directed the energy to surround the organ. The prince's body jerked again, limbs flopping like a fish on land. She bit back a cry as energy lashed painfully up her arm, settling around her with a faintly metallic smell, raising the fine hairs along her body.

The limestone groaned. Under her hand, wintry skin grew warm.

Kajal didn't dare let go. In her disorientation, she thought she saw flashes behind her eyelids, the landscape of unknown places, the faces of people she didn't recognize. Her heartbeat thundered in her ears, a brutal reminder that her life, too, could be taken away in an instant.

The next pulse of energy passed through the prince's chest and made him arch off the limestone, which cracked in two with a boom like crashing thunder.

His eyes flew open.

He and Kajal stared at each other for a breathless moment. Then he screamed and pushed her away. Kajal toppled to the floor as he thrashed and fell off the table.

Kutaa came to stand between Kajal and the prince, growling. Advaith snatched the fallen cloth to cover himself and pressed his back against the wall. Salt fell from his skin as if he had just emerged from sand.

"Who are you?" he demanded. His voice was rasping and breaking, whether from being dead nearly two decades or from her shoving the pestle down his throat, she wasn't sure. "Where am I?"

Kajal stood with hands held before her in a gesture of peace. Her body was weightless, her face overtaken with a dazed smile.

"I . . . I did it." Tears sprang to her eyes again. *"I did it!"*

She wanted to fall to the floor, wanted to sob, wanted to ride east to Lasya—blight and the Vadhia be damned. The only thing stopping her was the prince's bewildered horror. For someone who'd looked so tranquil in death, he had quite an expressive face in life.

"Did *what*?" he choked out, glancing between her and Kutaa. Still pitifully clutching the cloth to himself, his other hand went to his sutured wounds, which were trailing blood down his hip bone. "Where am I? Who are you?"

Kajal kept her hands raised. "Your Highness, there's no need to worry. I promise I'll explain everything. You're not in danger."

He froze at her words. Now that his eyes were open, she saw they were a warm, light brown, framed by those ridiculously long lashes. They widened as they regarded her.

"What did you call me?" he whispered.

"Your . . . Highness?" A hint of trepidation made Kajal's smile falter. Were his memories damaged? Did this mean Lasya's would be too? "You're the crown prince of Dharati." *Remember. You must.*

"Crown prince?" he repeated blankly, and her trepidation spiked into full-on panic.

"Isn't that you?" she demanded. "Aren't you Advaith Thakar?"

"Advaith? No, I . . ."

He shook his head, salt and grave soil falling from his hair.

"I'm not Advaith," he said. "I'm his brother."

Chapter Twelve

KAJAL FROZE WITH her arms held out before her, less a gesture to reassure the boy than to reject his words.

She blinked slowly. He blinked back just as slowly, like a cat.

"What," she rasped.

His face twisted in . . . fear? No, it was more nuanced than that. Something like regret, like he hadn't meant to speak it out loud.

"What did you say?" she demanded, mind sluggish with incomprehension and that ever-growing panic. Perhaps the process *had* damaged his memories, or his sense of self. But if so, then why come to this very specific, very unsettling admission?

"The prince didn't have a brother," she insisted. She lowered her arms and took a step forward. He didn't flinch, but his mouth tightened. The cloth he held was stained with the blood leaking from his abdomen. "You were identified as Advaith. You were wearing his armor."

Of course, when waking in a strange laboratory with a strange girl and an even stranger dog hovering over him, he might have instinctively lied to protect himself. But he shook his head again, lifting his eyes back to hers. They were nearly the same shade as the amber pendant she'd taken off him.

"My name is Tavinder," he said firmly. "And I want to know how I came to be here."

Kutaa maintained his position between them, unmoving, waiting for Kajal's order to attack or stand down. She let him stay exactly where he was.

"You're here because you were identified," she repeated. "As *Advaith*."

"*Who* identified me?" he asked. "Who even are you?"

"Does that mean you admit to being the crown prince?"

He leaned his head back until it met the wall with a low thunk. "Yakshas preserve me."

"Funny thing, that," she said. "They did. You died on the Harama Plain, which became a burial mound for you and your soldiers, a no-man's-land filled with bhutas. We found your body, one thing led to another, and now here you are."

His brow furrowed. He parted his chapped lips as if to tell her off, but then his gaze turned inward, unfocused.

"I died?" he whispered, more to himself than to her. His free hand went to his wounds, which were beginning to clot. Kajal made a mental note of that, and to check his circulation once he let her examine him. "I . . . died . . ."

"And I brought you back," she finished. "Feel free to applaud or sing my praises. Preferably both."

His confusion gave way to alarm. "That's not— No. *No*. If I'm . . . then Advaith is . . ."

Kutaa's fur bristled as the prince grew agitated, his chest heaving with panicked breaths as he wrestled with the idea of his own mortality. Kajal allowed herself a moment's satisfaction that his lungs were working well.

"You don't have to keep lying," she insisted. "I—"

"I'm not Advaith!" he yelled. "I don't know where he is. I—I have to—"

His gaze landed on the door. He darted straight for it.

Kutaa barked. Unthinking, Kajal launched herself at the prince and wrapped an arm around his neck, pressing down on the carotid artery. He stumbled and fell against the door, too startled to fight back. He could only grab her arm until he lost consciousness and slid to the floor in an ungainly sprawl.

Kutaa padded over and sniffed at the prince's hair before giving her a flat look.

"Mm," she agreed. "Could've gone better."

When Supposedly Not Advaith roused next, he jerked against the chair Kajal had hauled him onto. He flexed his arms against the rope she'd wrapped around his torso, binding him to the chair's back.

"What are you *doing*?" he demanded.

"What are *you* doing?"

"What am *I*—?" He fought harder against the rope. "Untie me!"

Kajal took the stone pestle from the table—the one she'd used to push zinc pellets down his throat—and smacked it against her palm in warning.

"What a commanding tone," she drawled. "Almost like an order from a prince, wouldn't you say?"

He let out a sound halfway between a growl and a frustrated sob. Then he noticed the bloodstained cloth on his lap. "Why am I naked?"

"I don't think you'd prefer to wear the outfit you died in." Using the pestle, she pointed at said outfit, caked in dirt and blood, on the floor. "But if you change your mind, let me know."

He grimaced at the pile of clothing, then dropped his chin to assess the wounds she'd sutured. When he'd been alive, they had been fatal. But resurrection was a form of healing, she guessed; and from her observations of Kutaa, there was a possibility of heightened strength and perseverance.

Her grip tightened on the pestle, glad that her scalpel was close by. If he did have revenant strength and broke free, she had to be ready.

He suddenly grew frantic again. "My necklace. Where is it?"

"What, this ugly thing?" She lifted the amber pendant, letting it swing like a pendulum. He eagerly followed its arc. "Don't worry, I don't want it."

"Then will you return it to me?"

Kajal hesitated. Thinking he might be more receptive if she granted his request, she warily stepped forward and slipped the chain over his tousled head, letting the pendant settle against his chest. He breathed out in relief.

"Let's try this again." Kajal backed away, pleased at the steadiness of her voice. "I'm Kajal. I resurrected you on behalf of an interested party. This is Kutaa, my undead dog." Kutaa whuffed softly. "Your turn."

"Undead . . . ?" He visibly forced himself to move on. "What do you mean by 'interested party'?"

"I'm going to leave that to them to explain. I'm only a freelancer." She leaned her hip against the table, smacking her palm lightly with the pestle again. "Your turn, I said."

"I already told you. My name is Tavinder Thakar. I'm . . ." His pause was a long, ringing silence that filled the laboratory with a tension she wouldn't need her scalpel to cut. "I'm the brother of Advaith Thakar, the crown prince of Dharati. His twin brother."

Kajal had become skilled at intuiting liars over the years, noting the way their eyes shifted, their bodies twitched, their foreheads beaded with sweat. But this boy merely sat and stared at her with steadfast determination, albeit threaded with unease.

She knew that body language too. It was the language of one who had been keeping a secret their whole life, only to have it unravel before their eyes.

Kajal's arm dropped to her side. "You're telling the truth."

The boy—Tavinder—grunted. "That's what I've been saying."

"I don't understand." *Twins,* she thought, mind spinning. "If Advaith had a brother, why keep it hidden? And why were you using his name and armor to fight against Bakshi's forces?"

He turned his head away with a clenched jaw. He'd seemed to have reached his limit.

"I guess it's not my business anyway," she muttered. She didn't belong in whatever world he came from, full of politicking and deception and wars and duty.

Tavinder licked his lips, their previous blue shade having ripened to pale pink. "I still don't understand why I'm here. *How* I'm here."

Kajal squatted so she was more on eye level with him. "What do you last remember?"

He took a few moments to think. His hair hung on either side of his face, in dire need of a wash. Despite that, he certainly had the bearing of a prince, or someone prince-adjacent. Something in his posture, his speech, his presence.

The only thing that marred the image—other than his being naked and bound to a chair—was that he kept his chin down. As if wanting to take up less space or avoid notice. Even Gurveer Bibi had spoken to her with her nose pointed skyward, convinced of her superiority.

Interesting.

"I remember putting on Advaith's armor," he whispered eventually. "And riding out to the Harama Plain. I remember fighting. Then . . ." He shook his head. "There are holes. I don't know what happened. But I remember pain."

He shuddered, goosebumps erupting over his arms. Kajal felt rather sorry for his current state, and that she hadn't thought to bring anything for him to wear. At the time, clothes had seemed the least of her problems.

Then it all crashed down on her.

She had succeeded in reviving a prince, but not the prince the rebels wanted. She had been so sure she could deliver Advaith to them come dawn and they would get her Lasya's body in return. But this *wasn't* Advaith.

Did that mean they wouldn't retrieve Lasya until they'd found and revived the real crown prince?

Kajal straightened and touched the scratches at her neck. *No*. She didn't have time for that, not with a Meghani and Vadhia soldiers at the university, and not with her sister's bhuta already hunting for her next victim.

She laughed, low and helpless.

"You didn't answer me," Tavinder pressed. "About why and how I'm here. About why you were searching for Advaith. Is he . . . Is he the one behind this?" Hope leapt into his eyes, and he looked around like his brother would materialize in front of him.

Kajal was getting tired of being the one to deliver bad news. "Advaith is dead. That's why we were searching for his body in the first place."

"De—" Tavinder's voice choked off, as if he were physically incapable of saying the word. He flexed his arms against the rope again. The chair creaked ominously.

"He can't be," Tavinder whispered. "You're mistaken. I went to fight for him so that he *wouldn't* die!"

"It seems like neither of us has the answers we want." She pinched the bridge of her nose, beneath where a headache was forming. "Look, I . . . I'm going to get you something to wear, maybe some food"—her stomach made an inquisitive noise—"but the situation right now is *very delicate*, and I need you to stay here. Stay," she repeated, holding her palm out toward him as if she were giving a command to Kutaa.

"He can't be dead," he kept mumbling, eyes wild.

Kajal made a silent gesture for Kutaa to follow her. "Stay," she said again, shutting the door on Tavinder's bewildered expression and locking it behind her.

✦✦✦

Hoping the dog's abilities were up to the challenge, Kajal told Kutaa to sneak ahead and sniff out any guards. She kept to the dark corners and slanted shadows of predawn, following the vague shape of Kutaa's tail as he led her through a winding path back to the dormitories.

Kajal's heartbeat didn't settle until she reached Jassi's flat. The professor was fast asleep, snoring, her body akimbo. Kajal made quick, silent work of Jassi's clothes trunk, but even her longest pair of salwar wouldn't be big enough for Tavinder.

Gathering her resolve, she tiptoed down a flight of stairs toward Dalbir's room, thankful they'd pointed it out yesterday. The crack under the door was dark, and when a disheveled Dalbir answered her quiet knock, there was a pillow crease on their cheek.

"I have an exam today," they muttered.

"Do you have a spare set of clothes I could borrow?"

Dalbir blinked owlishly. "What?"

"I spilled cha in my clothes trunk, and I don't have anything else to wear."

"*That's* what you're worried about at"—they leaned out to gauge the sky beyond their doorway—"five in the damn morning?"

"Couldn't sleep. Nightmares. I have this recurring one where I'm being chased by a giant festering foot with a hunk of bone sticking out the top, and I think it's trying to get me to scratch an itch on its sole—"

Dalbir interrupted her with a long sigh and disappeared into their room. They returned with a pair of dark-blue jodhpurs and a long green kurta.

"Don't stain them," Dalbir warned before firmly closing the door in her face.

Hugging the clothes to her chest, Kajal hurried back to the laboratory with Kutaa while the fringes of the sky tinged gray with light. Soon Jassi would wake, and Kajal would have to admit what she'd done. Would have to face the rebels.

Unless she found some way to spin this.

Her mind frantically sputtered with ideas, but as she strode toward the laboratory and reached for the key in her pocket, they fell and scattered like marbles.

The door was open. Where the knob and lock should have been was a ruin of broken wood, as if a fist had punched straight through.

"Shit." She ran into the laboratory, dropping the clothes at the sight of the empty chair, the frayed rope, the missing soldier's uniform.

So he'd discovered his revenant strength after all.

Kajal scanned the worktable to see if anything else had been taken. Her notes were still there, glaring accusingly up at her.

Oh Raja Hiss, we're really in it now.

Kutaa's hackles rose at her agitation. But while she turned in a tight, panicking circle, wondering where Tavinder could have possibly gone, the dog went to the bloodstained cloth and sniffed at it.

"Can you follow his scent?" she asked hopefully.

In answer, the dog ran through the door. Kajal's eyes were hot and itchy, her body buzzing with lack of sleep, but adrenaline spiked through her veins as she followed.

She couldn't let Tavinder escape. Couldn't let any of the Vadhia soldiers see him, in case they somehow recognized the former crown prince. There were portraits of him in Malhir, Vivaan had said. It was a possibility—one she couldn't risk.

The air was crisp, and her slippers slapped against the ground as she ran behind Kutaa. When she spotted a Vadhia uniform in the central courtyard, she quickly pulled herself and Kutaa into a niche. She palmed her scalpel, but the soldier passed by without noticing them.

Kutaa steered her through the Elephant Court, to the door that led to the old palace. The lock had been crushed by an impatient hand and now lay mangled on the ground. Kajal stuffed it into her pocket and followed Kutaa through the archway.

The hexagonal gardens of the royal quarters were both overgrown and dead, the water in the stained fountain long dried up. Along the perimeter were shrubs of still-blooming sky flower, purple stalks of fountain grass, and waxy red iresine bushes. Pandan leaves rustled together in a chorus of frenzied whispers.

Kutaa didn't falter as they brushed by the tangled, gnarled plants and into a series of long corridors full of marble relief panels and colorful murals. The paint was cracked and faded, depicting scenes of elemental spirits dancing in pastoral landscapes, of hulking daityas in armor, and of horned danavas crafting illusions in the sky. One showed a young woman riding a tiger demon, scimitar held out for battle. Another showed an antlered boy kneeling in the light coming from Svarga above him.

The corridors had been built in a zigzag shape—likely to slow down intruders and assassins—and Kajal was dizzy by the time she and Kutaa stumbled upon the back gardens. They were in the same state of overgrown neglect, with a wall covered in spiderwebbing ivy. Kutaa stopped at the base of it, whining.

"I'll go on ahead," she panted. "Stay here."

Kutaa restlessly paced while Kajal climbed the thick natural trellis. Some of the vines gave way under her hands, making her scrabble, but she'd had more than her fair share of launching herself over walls to escape precarious situations.

She perched at the top and caught her breath. There was just enough light now to reveal a figure running north.

"Idiot," she snarled once she dropped into the long grass. "Where's he even running to?"

His legs were longer than hers, and though she had the advantage of not being dead for nearly twenty years, he had that frightening new strength he shared with Kutaa. She had to put her head down and tap into the heated resource of her fear to spur her faster. Grass whipped at her legs as she descended the slope of the promontory with a speed that would have her falling ass over crown to the bottom if she lost even a sliver of control.

She must have made an awful lot of noise, or else Tavinder sensed her gaining on him, since he looked over his shoulder. She had no breath to curse him out or tell him to stop, but she made sure her expression screamed it for her.

The earth *shivered* under her feet. Kajal lost her balance and tripped forward, scraping an elbow against the ground. Something wrapped around both her ankles, just like the clawing, grasping bhutas on the Harama Plain. She twisted around and pulled out her scalpel, only to freeze at what she saw.

Roots had punctured through the earth and formed long, knobby hands. They encircled her ankles, holding her in place.

"What—?"

More roots slithered from the loosening soil, forming a head, the long, waving grass hanging from its skull in the likeness of hair. It stared at her with hollow eyes that wept dirt.

A yaksha.

She briefly stayed her hand. But Tavinder was getting away, and her future hinged on him. *Lasya's* future hinged on him.

Kajal lunged. She sliced and stabbed at the root hands, careful not to accidentally jab herself. The yaksha writhed, its roots groaning in pain. The spindly, strong fingers tightened briefly before she hacked one off and it twisted away. She kicked out of its hold and scrambled onward.

She couldn't stop to question why a yaksha, of all things, had attacked her. She thought she heard Tavinder swear as she once again gave chase, following him to the rise of a nearby hill.

The sun finally broke in the distance like the hint of yolk in a cracked egg. At first, Kajal thought that was what was distorting her vision, but then there was a flurry of disturbed air and she nearly tripped again in astonishment.

Butterflies flocked around her. Dozens of them, white and glowing, harmless yet trying desperately to get in her way. She batted at them, but they kept closing in, wings beating furiously at her skin and hair and clothes.

She knew the look of them, the feel of them. One of their kind had led her to what she'd thought was Advaith's body.

What is going on?

While Kajal tried to swat them away, the distance grew between her and Tavinder.

"I'm not going to hurt him!"

She didn't know what made her say it, why it felt like the only thing she *could* say. Almost reluctantly, some of the butterflies danced away while others continued their gentle battle. She picked up the pace, arriving at the base of the hill as Tavinder crested the top of it.

"Stop!" she yelled.

He did stop, but only to turn and fling his hand out toward her, a move halfway between offense and defense. More of those butterflies surrounded him in an aura of shimmering white.

And then she realized—it wasn't just the butterflies. As the sun climbed behind him, the honey of his eyes sharpened into something pale and inhuman, like the ghost lights that bobbed above the fields at night. The tips of his fingers became the pinpricks of faraway stars. His hair stirred and the ground hummed and the wind smelled of ancient, growing things.

He was a fixture on the hill, a statue of some ancient and revered soldier in his tattered and stained uniform. Like a reminder that war was not a thing of glory but instead a thing of mud, of churned earth and blood between teeth and anguished cries cutting through fog.

But as the sun limned the horizon and those butterflies swarmed around him, he transformed again into something wholly unreal. A deity who had stepped forth from their hidden realm to survey the mundane, a bringer of light after the long cold hours of nightfall, a fast and terrible star aimed at an already dying world. Mercy, and forgiveness, and justice.

Kajal believed in hard truths and blunt facts. She did not like the uncertainty of other worlds and empty words and the promise of an ending without a proper beginning.

And yet here she was, staring at a boy who should be dust, burning blue and white amid the dawn as if he had willed it into being.

And she—she was lampblack, a crimson stain splashed across a shrine, the first uneasy whiff of smoke in a dry and barren summer.

A low creature gazing upon a god and pleading to go unnoticed.

They stared at each other for she didn't know how long. Long enough for the sun to drench him, to throw him into silhouette. The butterflies at her shoulders stirred the hair at her neck.

"What . . ." Her voice failed her, and she had to try again. "Who are you?"

He lowered his arm, much like she had lowered hers in the laboratory when she'd sensed he could be reasoned with.

"I already told you." His voice floated down to her on beams of light, like wings skimming the surface of water. "My name is Tavinder Thakar. And I am the deva of Svarga."

Chapter Thirteen

ALTHOUGH THE GRASS under her was cool with dew, the sun rising at Kajal's back was a hot brand. She was thirsty, and her stomach cramped with nerves and hunger. But she didn't dare move, not when the boy sitting next to her fidgeted as if ready to take off at the slightest provocation.

The butterflies continued to flit around them. They were white specks in the corners of her eyes, like the squiggly spots she saw when she stood too fast after hours of reading. Kajal realized now the butterflies were yakshas. Sometimes one lit upon Tavinder's shoulders or hair in a delicate kiss before taking off again.

Kajal risked another glance at him. He was chewing enterprisingly on his lower lip, which was in danger of cracking open. He'd pulled the amber lotus pendant from under his ratty shirt and fiddled with it between his fingers, turning it over and over.

"Do they not allow semiprinces to wear proper jewelry?" she murmured.

He gave her a sidelong glare. His eyes were their usual warm brown again. "It's important to me."

"Did you make it?"

"No." He returned to surveying the city of Suraj, glittering in the early pink-streaked morning. The university perched above was like a patient vulture. "Someone made it for me."

She waited for him to elaborate. He did not. That was fair; they had known each other all of a few hours, and not on the best of terms.

But there was something she had to clear up.

"You claimed you're the deva," she said, and he tensed. "That's impossible."

"I assure you, it's possible," he said wryly. "Or do you need more proof?"

The yaksha that had grabbed her. The butterflies. The way he'd looked on the hill.

Kajal's mouth dried. She rubbed small circles on the center of her forehead as her thoughts returned to yesterday in Professor Manraj's class, hearing about role of the asura and the deva in maintaining peace and balance between the three planes. The possibility that the increase of rakshasas, of blight, was due to their negligence.

A dead deva could certainly cause that.

The blight. If the deva had been dead all this time, would his resurrection mean the blight would recede? Maybe the rebels were actually onto something.

"Does that mean the asura is Advaith?" she demanded.

Tavinder leaned away from her sudden interest. "Yes. The asura and deva are always born as twins. Identical in every way, save for their powers. When a pujari blessed us at our birth, he immediately sensed what we were."

"Is that why you were kept a secret?"

His mouth tightened. "No. Advaith was the first to be born, so he was made crown prince. My father was afraid of a succession crisis—never mind I never *wanted* to succeed him—and worried that if we ruled side by side, the people might be divided in their loyalty. So I remained hidden. If anything were to happen to Advaith, I would take his place."

"That seems . . . cruel."

"It's not like I didn't live my own life. Advaith and I frequently went on missions together. When only the asura was needed, I would have to pose as the crown prince, but that was rare."

"You fought in his armor because you were pretending to be him."

He nodded. "Advaith wanted to face Bakshi alongside me, but we couldn't risk it. Couldn't risk his life." The pendant glinted as he turned it toward the sun. "I guess it didn't matter in the end."

The words were flat and emotionless, like he couldn't bear to give them more than a fleeting thought.

"Yes," Kajal said. "And now Bakshi sits on the throne."

He wrapped a protective hand around the pendant. "Is this why your 'interested party' resurrected me?"

She raised her eyebrows. "I doubt they knew you and your brother were the deva and asura, but I guess that's a nice bonus."

"I won't do it. Not without Advaith."

"You—" Kajal reined in her irritation, kept her voice level. "You don't even know what *it* is."

"They thought I was Advaith and went out of their way to resurrect me. What else would they want other than to restore a legitimate heir to the throne and take it back from Bakshi? And for that matter, how *did* you resurrect me?"

"Ayurveda." It was the truth, sort of, though pared down considerably.

"Ayurveda," he repeated slowly. "There may be holes in my memory, but I don't remember Ayurveda having anything to do with magic."

"It doesn't," she said. "But our soil, our plants, and our minerals are all blessed with sattva. I simply used that natural energy to tap into your chakras. Speaking of which . . ."

She took his wrist. He tensed again but didn't jerk away. Under her fingers was a weak, fluttering pulse, the radial artery skittish against her skin.

"Your circulation is off," she muttered. "I'll see what I can do about that. How do you feel otherwise? Physically, I mean."

"I don't know. Fine? This kind of hurts." He pointed to the sutured wounds. "But not enough to kill me. Again."

"Are you tired after all that running?" She certainly was. She moved her fingers to his neck, the carotid jumping at her touch. "Thirsty? Hungry?"

Tavinder grabbed her wrist. "Who *are* you?"

Now it was his thumb pressed to her speeding pulse. She swallowed and avoided his gaze. "I told you—my name is Kajal. That's all you need to know."

"I don't think it is." His grip tightened. "You brought me back to life. No one knows how to do that, not even the yaksha deities or Lord Dukha."

"And you've asked them yourself, have you?" She huffed at his impatient frown. "I experimented. I tested until I got the result I wanted. That's it."

She would not bare her throat, nor would she try to make him bare his. She only wanted him to perceive her as a nonthreat. To get past his defenses enough that he would go along with the plan forming in her mind.

The rebels likely didn't know Advaith had a twin brother. If Kajal revealed the truth, they would no doubt turn over all of Dharati looking for the real crown prince.

Which would mean an even longer delay in getting Lasya's body. Lasya's punishment the night before had nearly killed her. Kajal wasn't sure how much time was left before everything that had made up her sister was gone and only a murderous wraith remained. How much time she herself had left.

"You were right," Kajal said, making her body and her voice smaller. "The interested party is a group of rebels who want your brother on the throne. I was in a difficult situation, and they got me out on the condition that I would bring Advaith back to them. If I didn't, then I'd be turned over to the Vadhia as a witch. Bakshi's personal army," she clarified at the confused tic of his eyebrow. "But you're not Advaith. Which means . . ."

She made sure her voice broke and widened her eyes in dawning fear, putting seventeen years' worth of lying to good use. "If they know I messed up, they'll expose me. I'll be *killed*."

Alarm replaced Tavinder's confusion. "What? But this isn't your fault. You didn't know I existed."

"That won't matter to them! I know too much, and—" She nearly let the fact of the bhuta slip, a true shiver going down her spine as the scratches on her neck burned. "You want to find Advaith. Believe me, I get it. In addition to getting me out of an ordeal, the rebels also promised to bring my sister to me, who's stuck in the east. Once they bring her here, we can find Advaith together. Then you and the Insurrectionists can carry out your plans, and I won't be fodder for the Vadhia."

He released her wrist. "You'll help me find my brother?"

"That's what I said. I didn't mess up your hearing, did I?" She leaned forward as if to check his ears, but he shooed her away. "You just have to do me a small, *tiny* favor until then. Which, honestly, isn't asking much considering I gave you the gift of a second life."

His expression hardened. "What favor?"

"Pretend to be Advaith."

Tavinder emitted a choked sound.

"Only until I get my sister back!" she said quickly. "Besides, you already come with the perfect excuse: You have holes in your memory. Anything they ask that you don't know the answer to, you can use that as an explanation. Then we'll get the real Advaith, and everyone will be reunited, and it'll be all sunshine and rainbows."

His face could have doubled as a storm cloud. She got a sudden premonition of unease.

"A lot of your plans rely on my cooperation," he said evenly.

Kajal was so used to people being at least a half step behind her that it threw her off to have someone match her stride for stride. The realization beat wings against her ribs, like she'd swallowed some of his butterflies.

Nonetheless, her cheek twitched in annoyance. "What do you want?"

"I want a day to explore the palace before you bring me to these rebels. If Advaith . . . If he really . . ." Tavinder swallowed. "I worry his disappearance might be tied to being the asura. I just need one day to try and figure out what happened."

His demands could have been worse. And loath as Kajal was to delay any further, a single day was preferable to however many it would take if the rebels learned she'd raised the wrong prince.

"Fine," she agreed. "As long as you make good on your end afterward."

He leaned his forehead against his palm. "I hate this."

She patted his knee. "It won't be for long." Then, to really drive it home: "The world has been out of balance. With the asura and deva's return, you can save a lot of people."

His eyes searched hers. But she didn't need to fake her disquiet, her need for these obstacles—Bakshi, the blight—to be dealt with by someone else, allowing her to focus on Lasya. Allowing them to return to a simple life together.

"How is the world out of balance?" he asked.

"I'll tell you on the way back."

He stood, disturbing the butterflies above his head. He held a hand out to her, which she ignored.

"He was supposed to be here," Tavinder said as she brushed dirt from her trousers. "Advaith. He was meant to stay in the royal quarters while I fought. We were going to meet on this hill when it was safe."

"Maybe he was taken somewhere else?"

"The guards were under orders not to move him." He turned to the university, walking ahead on long legs. "I need to check his room."

They walked in silence until his stomach let out a loud gurgle.

"Aha!" she cried. "You *are* hungry!"

His shoulders hunched. "Shut up."

"No, no, this is good! I'll need to run a couple of tests, but—I think I really did it. I pulled off a full resurrection." She laughed giddily, hands clasped together. "I should monitor what happens after you eat, and if you can defecate."

He sputtered. "Absolutely not!"

She barely held back her cackle. "Sorry, sorry. You'll have to forgive this humble servant her excitement, Your Highness."

He sighed, as if vying for patience. "Don't call me that."

"Most Esteemed and Holy Deva?"

"No."

"Then what do I call you? When we're not with the rebels, I mean."

"Tav is fine," he grumbled, walking faster.

She informed him of recent events while they walked, from Bakshi's rise to power to the spreading blight and retreating yakshas. His face was grim—well, grimmer—when she mentioned the Vadhia causing chaos in the countryside.

"Even if there *are* dakinis living in rural villages, they'd have nothing to do with the imbalance," he argued, reaching up to grasp his pendant. "Either Bakshi is a fool or he's leaning into superstitious fear to fuel his agenda."

"Why not both?" Kajal said.

Kutaa wagged his tail once Kajal and Tav had scrambled over the wall into the overgrown gardens. Kajal rubbed Kutaa's face until his fur fluffed out into a mane.

"Was this undead dog of yours one of your experiments?" Tav asked.

"He was my first success, although I botched a couple things."

"What happened to the cadavers before him?"

Remembering the chickens, she shuddered. "You don't want to know."

They made their way into the twisting corridors of the royal suites. Though she longed to drag Tav to Vivaan and Sezal right then and there, she needed Tav to cooperate, which meant a day of babysitting. But it wasn't too bad; she could at least observe him and refine any problems before resurrecting Lasya.

They entered a gallery with a convex ceiling covered in hundreds of tiny mirrors. Kajal blinked, and dozens of her blinked back. "I can't believe people used to live here. That *you* used to live here." A single gem from this place could pay for a whole village to be fed for a month.

Tav walked to the nearest wall and put his hand against a thin crack.

"It's our second home. Was." His fingertips paled as they pressed harder against the wall. "The state it's in . . . I've been dead for a long time, haven't I?"

His voice was hushed, wavering at the edges. Kajal wasn't sure what to say or if she should answer at all. He stood with his back to her, and her gaze traced the outline of his shoulder blades against his stained uniform.

Eventually, she said, "Nearly twenty years."

It came as a blow. The breath punched out of him, and he fisted his hand. After a long, silent moment, he turned to the corridor.

"This way," he said hollowly.

Kajal had never had a home. At least not one she could remember. She didn't know what it felt like to traipse down hallways she owned, or to enter rooms no one else was allowed to set foot in. She didn't understand what *homecoming* meant, the sensation of returning to a haven, her own private refuge. Nor did she understand what it would be like to see that home destroyed, neglected, empty of what had made it a haven in the first place.

Then again, perhaps she did. Maybe *homecoming* was returning from a day of work to whatever little hovel she and Lasya had found, to her sister's smile and the smell of something cooking. The emptiness of these rooms echoed the emptiness in her heart—her sister's smile frozen, her spices stale and unused.

A frisson of cold swept through her. She stopped walking as a thin sound started in her right ear and traveled toward the left, a nasal, discordant humming. A handprint formed within the dust on the wall, and then another.

Kajal's fingers turned numb, and the humming grew louder. She was used to desperation, so she let her thoughts turn unerringly toward it: thoughts of leaving Tav to handle the rebels himself while she grabbed what she needed from the laboratory, stole a horse, and rode east.

But she knew she'd be riding through a land of death traps. A land filled with not only disease and demons, but the Vadhia and the people they had convinced to turn on girls like her—girls who were angry, alone, and atypical.

"Are you all right?"

She jumped. Tav had walked ahead, but he'd stopped when he realized she wasn't following.

Kajal glanced at the wall, but the handprints were gone, as was the humming.

She cleared her throat and joined him. "Fine."

They were in one of the corridors lined with murals. The images spanning the walls on either side were similar in theme yet otherwise nothing alike. On the left was an aged painting of gilded doors thrown open amid a brilliant light, an indistinct human figure standing before them that cast a long shadow. In their hand they held a pole-like weapon that was topped with a disk of metal shaped like a sunburst. A sudarshana chakra.

On the right were doors of obsidian, revealing a billowing darkness and a figure before it about to be swallowed by silver-streaked clouds. They held a trishul, the trident's three prongs wickedly sharp.

The asura and deva are the ambassadors of the rakshasas and yakshas, respectively, and our strongest links to Patala and Svarga, Professor Manraj had explained. *Only they have the ability to maintain the gateways to these other planes. Together, they preserve the balance of the Brahimada.*

A couple of butterflies fluttered from the ceiling to land on Tav's shoulders, glowing wings beating slowly, like a resting heart.

"What is it like?" Kajal whispered. "Being the deva."

Tav wrenched his gaze from the deva's depiction, and she nearly bit her tongue. In the dim corridor, his eyes were even more uncanny, almost like Kutaa's, as if he could perceive things beyond the mortal world. She was about to tell him to ignore the question, that it didn't matter, but he spoke before she could.

"Strange," he answered quietly. "Although utterly natural. Maybe because we started training when we were so young. The yakshas came to guide me to Svarga, and the rakshasas guided Advaith to Patala. We each met the yaksha deities and Lord Dukha to pay our respects."

Kajal frowned. "Does that typically happen for the asura and deva?"

"I can't speak for other generations, but yes, I think so. They needed to instruct us on our duties."

A peculiar sort of envy bloomed through her. "And what were those duties? Anything like the stories?"

"Sometimes. Once, I was told to cleanse a lake that had been poisoned. Another time, there was a fight between the nagas and the garudas that Advaith and I broke up. Sometimes I led earth yakshas to farmsteads where the fields were failing, or healed villages infected with plague."

She turned to the mural on the right, her gaze tracing the shape of the obsidian doors. "And the asura's duties?"

He looked at her askance. "You can ask Advaith, once we've found him." He pointed at the deva's mural. "I tried to call for it, on the hill."

She followed the line of his finger to the disk of the sudarshana chakra.

"I spoke the mantra to summon it, but it didn't come," he clarified. "No matter where it is, it's supposed to materialize at my call." Tav flexed his hand. "So why didn't it?"

Kajal swallowed, tasting dust in the back of her throat. "First we locate your brother. Then your weapon." *But only when Lasya's breathing again.*

They silently moved down the corridors, having little in the way of light other than the butterflies that kept them company.

"What are they, anyway?" she asked.

"Messengers. Scouts. The yaksha deities gave them to me to help with my missions. I can understand them, but I don't think anyone else can. Advaith couldn't." One landed in his hair, and the hardness of his expression broke into something wistful and fond. "Some say they're the souls of those who meditated until they reached enlightenment. That once they fulfilled their dharma, they wished to be reborn as guides to others."

"I've heard that before," she said. She'd also heard that butterflies were a symbol of growth and reincarnation. It was fitting, then, that Tav was something that had been reborn.

Eventually, Tav stopped before a set of large engraved doors. He reached out as if to open them, then stopped.

"The chambers my parents used," he explained. His face crumpled with heavy emotion before he could leash it. "Sometimes Advaith or I would sleep here if we'd gotten into a fight."

"The two of you shared a room?"

"When we were children. Not because there wasn't space, but because we couldn't sleep without the other." He took a deep, steadying breath she could almost feel in her own lungs and moved down the hall. "We started using separate rooms at thirteen. They're over here."

He opened another set of double doors to reveal a wide bedroom beyond. It had no doubt been lavish once, the ceiling engraved and the walls' base molding made of solid gold. The bed was a large four-poster with gauzy, bug-eaten curtains, but the fabrics were rich and brocaded, speaking of unimaginable wealth. A heavy layer of dust had settled over everything, and clouds of it billowed with each footfall. Kutaa sneezed with a shake of his head.

Kajal's first instinct was to find a tool to chip away at the gilded wall panels. She only refrained from doing so because of Tav. That heavy, leaden realization had claimed him again, as if the cracks running through the old palace were mirrored in his chest.

"He's really . . ." His voice was strangled. "He's gone. They're all gone."

Kajal shifted awkwardly. She had no idea how to comfort a former prince who was coming to terms with his entire family being dead. Thankfully, Kutaa took the initiative and walked to Tav's side, leaning against him.

Tav looked down, startled. His eyes were bright and red-rimmed—*Tear ducts are working,* Kajal noted eagerly—and the hand he settled on the dog's head shook.

"This is Advaith's room," he said softly, as if not to disturb the stagnant, stale air. "After our mother passed away from fever, I'd sometimes come here when the night and my thoughts were too loud."

Kajal thought of her and Lasya huddling against the cold. How Lasya would sometimes whisper what she could remember of their parents, nothing but vague, blurred images in Kajal's mind.

"You said he was supposed to stay here while you fought," she said.

"Yes. There were soldiers stationed here, and he had Ranbir with him."

"Ranbir?"

"His personal guard. My father chose the most skilled warrior from his army. He even accompanied Advaith on some asura missions. But Advaith was worried about a human getting caught up in rakshasa affairs, so he granted him special protection. He imbued a gem with some of his power and fused it to Ranbir's forehead."

Kajal whistled. "I didn't know something like that was possible."

"Advaith was sometimes too innovative for his own good." Tav headed for a large desk. With a sweep of his hand, butterflies scattered around the room. "Ranbir was devoted. He wouldn't have let Advaith walk out of here. Something must have happened."

Kajal made for the bed. Kutaa sat and watched as she lifted one tasseled pillow and then another, folded the sheets back, lifted the padded mattress.

"You could help, you know." She pointed at the butterfly currently investigating under the bed. "*They're* helping."

Kutaa only sneezed in response.

Kajal and Tav took apart the room in silence. She found several books on poetry and statecraft on the shelves, as well as timeworn trinkets: a pile of rocks, a beaded bracelet, a wooden carving of a naga warrior. There was even a lock of dark hair in a small ruby-encrusted box, tied together with red string.

"Did he have a lover?" she asked, showing Tav the box.

"I don't think so. None that he told me about, anyway." He was in the process of organizing a pile of papers on the bed. "I found some correspondence between him and our father, as well as old drawings of his, but nothing that would indicate where he might have gone."

Kajal leaned over to peer at the drawings. They were quite good: One depicted a craggy mountainside with two indistinct figures lounging on a rock; another was undoubtedly the palace in Malhir; and another showed a landscape of tall, spindly trees above a lake, where a trident floated above its center.

She lingered on the trident, her gaze straying only when Tav laid down the last drawing. It was of a long, lazy stretch of river covered in a riot of lotus flowers.

For some reason, it made her breath catch. At Tav's sideways glance, she waved a hand before her face.

"Sorry," she coughed. "Dust."

He sat on the bed and returned to the drawing. His fingertips followed the river's gentle, serpentine curve, then reached for the pendant around his neck. That familiar, unspeakable grief made his eyes glisten, and Kajal had to look away.

"He was talented," she said.

"Yes," he murmured. "But these don't tell us what happened. I—"

As he stood, his eyes suddenly rolled to the back of his head, and his body crumpled to the floor.

"Tav!" Kajal knelt and rolled him over. He was already stirring with a groan, eyelids fluttering. She grabbed his arm and pressed two fingers to his wrist, counting the rhythm of his pulse. Then she pressed her ear to his chest to hear his heartbeat.

"Hawthorn or chickweed," she muttered with a snap of her fingers. "I *knew* I should have included one of those."

She jumped to her feet and was halfway across the room when he weakly called, "Where are you going?"

"What? Oh." Kajal looked between him and Kutaa. "You keep searching. I'll return soon."

He propped himself on an elbow. "No. You promised me one full day."

Kajal put a hand on her hip. "The rebels told me that if I made *one* mistake, they'd turn me over to the Vadhia." She was so practiced at lying that her body's only reaction was to accelerate her pulse a little. "Your circulation is completely off. You just *fainted*. I can't have you dropping dead again before the rebels even see you."

He sat up against the wall and ran a hand through his hair. "I don't think I want to work with these people if they're willing to do such a thing."

"Unfortunately, the family that backs them has the money you need to raise an army against Bakshi."

"Which family?"

"The Sodhis."

"They sound familiar . . ." He frowned. "I still don't like this."

"I get the feeling you don't like much of anything. Regardless, I'll need to gather some things to fix your circulation, and you need proper clothes and food. You *are* hungry, yes?" His stomach rumbled again, right on cue. "That's what I thought. Kutaa, bite him if he tries to run."

She hurried out the door before he could argue further.

Chapter Fourteen

KAJAL SLIPPED OUT of the old palace and into the Elephant Court, her mind foggy with element ratios and measurements for improved blood flow. Maybe if she—

"What are you doing?"

The voice pierced through her like a fishhook. The only time she'd heard it was in the dead of night, and it had made her want to drop everything and flee. She felt much the same now as the Vadhia soldier, Jagvir, paused on his way to the commissary to give her an impolite once-over.

She was bombarded with a muddle of sensation: cool glass under her fingers, the crack of leather, the smell of blood and blight.

"I . . . Walk," she mumbled, keeping her head down. "To stretch my legs."

"This early in the morning?" He took in her windblown hair and her dirt-strained trousers. His eyes were cutting and curious, like he was trying to put some thought together. "Where's that filthy scavenger of yours?"

In her mind she was strangling him, crushing his larynx with her thumbs. "S-Still asleep. Lazy."

He spent another long, intolerable moment staring at her. Kajal's hand drifted toward her scalpel.

"*There* you are."

An arm was slung around her shoulders. Kajal jumped and nearly stabbed Dalbir between the ribs.

"I went to Professor Jassi's flat to get you for breakfast, but she said you'd already gone to the commissary," Dalbir went on. Their tone was casual, their smile unfazed as they turned it on Jagvir. "I hear they have egg bhurji parathas. You should get them while they're fresh."

Jagvir lingered a second more, then exhaled a scoff before leaving.

Kajal leaned against the nearest sandstone wall. Her heart was beating so fast she thought it would turn to pulp. She caught a flutter of white and shut her eyes tight, humming *Lotus Blossom* until she calmed down.

"You all right?"

She opened her eyes. Dalbir stood before her with a vaguely concerned expression.

"I don't like the Vadhia," she muttered.

"Shocking. No one does." They crossed their arms. "Professor Jassi couldn't find you this morning and was worried."

"I wanted to stretch my legs."

"So I overheard." They arched one eyebrow. "What happened to those clothes you so rudely woke me for?"

"Uh . . . I was going to change into them after my walk." She decided a change in subject was in order. "Don't you have an exam today?"

"Not until this afternoon. And no, you cannot come with me."

"I wasn't planning on it. I'm going to wander the university grounds, see if I can find some ingredients for . . . for the experiment."

"I'll go with you. Show you around, make sure you don't get lost."

Kajal swallowed her immediate no. Despite their reactions to her antics on her first day, Dalbir didn't seem to hold it against her. And they *had* gotten rid of that soldier.

"Only if you know where I can find hawthorn or chickweed," she conceded.

Dalbir rubbed their chin. "Farmers sometimes plant hawthorn trees on their property for good luck, and to drive off wandering rakshasas. There's plenty of farms around, and I'm sure I've seen hawthorn trees north of the lake. You might also be able to find chickweed in the gardens."

"Then I'll look there."

The university was gradually stirring to life, a handful of groggy professors and yawning students on their way to breakfast or morning classes. The rising sun was already baking the paving stones, warming her tense shoulders.

"There's been talk about you, you know," Dalbir said after a passing student stared at Kajal.

"What sort of talk?" she asked warily.

"About your run-in with Vritika." Their septum piercing glinted above a grimace. "About how you refused to apologize, as if you were some foreign princess. Riddhi's been saying all sorts of nasty stuff too."

Kajal bristled. "What's her issue with me, anyway?"

"Rumor is that her and Siddhi's older brother was seduced by a dakini, and he ended up throwing himself off a cliff when the girl broke his heart. They come from a superstitious family and think he was bewitched. Now she's quick to point fingers at anyone who seems . . ." They paused with a pointed glance at her. "*Off.*"

"That's ridiculous."

"That's superstition. It's even more of a scandal considering who you're pretending to be." Their tone was far too smug for her liking. "I want it on record that I *did* warn you not to get on Vritika's bad side. The professors and students all adore her."

Kajal snorted. "I can't see why, other than that she's a Meghani."

"She's smart, and she assists the professors all the time. And she doesn't talk back."

"Right. She has her lackeys do that for her." Kajal peered at them sidelong. "You really care about what people think, don't you?"

"Of course I do. Isn't that natural? Besides," they said bitterly, "I have to behave."

The two of them walked through the open gates, their position on the promontory affording them a view of Suraj below. Smoke rose from long chimneys among the shimmering metallic roofs of temples. A long, wide thoroughfare broke the city into two sections, like opposite banks of a river. It seemed impossible that she and Tav had just been sitting on a hill looking at the same view.

Past the neem and teak trees were verdant gardens that gave way to a wide meadow. Beyond were rows of wheat that belonged to the local farms, and far to the north of that lay a stretch of rice paddies.

She couldn't help but wonder what would happen to all this growth if the blight came to Suraj. If they found Advaith's body and restored him as the asura, would the princes' powers be enough to stop it? Would their claim of legitimacy be enough to dethrone Bakshi?

That's not your problem, she reminded herself. *Focus on Lasya. Just one more day, and the bargain will be fulfilled.*

"Thanks for the excuse to get out, by the way." Dalbir's voice wedged into her thoughts. "I've only been here a month or so, and I've been too busy with coursework to explore."

"I thought you said you'd show me around?"

"I didn't say I'd be particularly good at it."

Kajal suppressed a laugh. She wasn't here to make friends or allies. She'd never had them before, and she didn't see the point in having them now.

Still, her inquisitiveness got the better of her. "Why do you want to be a lorist?"

Dalbir tucked their hands into their pockets as they made their way down the path. "Growing up, my tutors taught me things like philosophy and astronomy and herbology. But what I really love is myth, and how it's helped shape our society and beliefs—even our medicinal practices."

Dalbir had had the luxury of tutors, while she and Lasya had fought to get even one book to read. She made a note to search Dalbir's room later, in case there were any valuables they'd brought from home she could sell.

"Take the asura and deva, for example," they went on. "I find them fascinating."

Kajal caught herself before she stumbled. "What? Why?"

"There's so much mystery surrounding them! It's like what Professor Manraj said: They're somewhere between historical and mythical figures, and we're not sure what the exact truth is. Some would argue the lack of evidence is the basis for belief, while others *need* that evidence to better understand."

Kajal thought of the very real deva sitting in the dusty quarters of the old palace. "And what do you think?"

Dalbir grinned, exuding the same manic energy Kajal got when she was in the middle of an experiment. "What *I* think doesn't matter, because even if they only exist in the form of story, they still *exist*."

Kajal prudently remained silent. She didn't know how to tell them she was one for evidence, not belief. And, yakshas preserve her, what evidence she had.

"In fact, that's going to be my focus of study," Dalbir went on. "I want to write a book about them."

"About what, exactly?"

"Don't know yet. But that's one of the beautiful things about myths: They often don't relay something that actually happened. Rather, they give an impression of the time period in which they were made, and reflect the morals and beliefs of those who made them. Take, for instance, the myth of the yaksha deities ordering the deva to carry a single drop of water and to care for it no matter what. But the deva sees an animal dying of thirst and gives it the drop of water, which pleases the yaksha deities. It's just a lesson to be kind to animals, or those who are helpless."

Kajal wasn't sure if that was the lesson she'd take from it, but she nodded regardless.

"Anyway, when I heard about the university, I decided to visit and see if it was a good fit for me. But I'm the Sodhis' third child." Dalbir's smile soured. "They want me to be invested in their schemes like my siblings are, so I had to agree to spy on professors who are loyal to Bakshi." They let out an overdramatic sigh. "The things I do for knowledge."

"Tell me about it. I couldn't afford this place on my own."

"You have no family to support you?"

Kajal was impressed they could so bluntly ask a question most people would politely dance around. "Ah . . . no. I'm on my own."

"I'm envious."

"*You're* envious of *me*? You grew up in some lavish mansion while I've had to travel from place to place to get by."

"And it sounds incredible. Think of all the experiences you've had! The types of people you've met! All the things you must have learned!" Dalbir's hand fluttered through the air to take in the land around them. "Meanwhile, I got my kicks reading about adventures instead of having one. My parents would have a fit if I strayed more than half a mile from the estate. This is the farthest from home I've been."

Kajal barely resisted the urge to trip them. "Trust me, scrounging for money and food is *not* romantic. Nor is performing ordeals when the townspeople decide you're a little too strange for their liking."

"Well, now you *have* to tell me more. Did you ever run into rakshasas? What are villages like? How many ordeals have you been given?"

Kajal indulged their curiosity with only the barest details until they reached the base of the promontory and followed a stone path to the sprawling gardens. Bright-red shrubs melded into a geometric hedge pattern, and plots of colorful flowers waved gently in the wind, visited by fat bumblebees.

Dalbir's attention was stolen away by a plot of roped-off land reserved for experimental gardening. Kajal recognized a variety of Ayurvedic herbs, but there was no chickweed.

Remembering the farms, she left Dalbir to ponder some vines crawling over starter trellises and kept walking north, heading toward the wheat fields. A flare of victory rose in her at the sight of a hawthorn tree standing near the bank of a glittering lake, its leaves silvery green, its branches starting to sprout pink blossoms. Between the blossoms and leaves were the small red haws she needed.

She eagerly plucked them off and stuffed them into her pockets. She would grind them into a paste and have Tav consume it while she focused on his heart chakra. Then he'd be fit for an audience with the rebels.

The sudden disappearance of birdsong preceded the sound of rippling water. She froze, fingers pinched around another haw, straining to hear a sound in the ensuing silence. A moment later, the grass rustled. Her hand spasmed and the haw burst between her fingers, staining her skin red.

The breeze carried a whispering laugh to her ears.

"Little girl, what do you have there?"

A lithe figure rounded the tree, its movements sinuous. First came the sleek and beautiful face of a young woman, her hair dark and straight, falling past slim shoulders and bare arms dripping water. Her torso was wrapped in a leather bodice that hugged the curves of her waist.

But from that waist down, the young woman's features were those of a large, muscular snake.

Kajal stayed perfectly still as the nagi slithered toward her, keeping to the shade of the hawthorn tree. The nagi's eyes were black and lit with amusement, and there was a green undertone to her gray skin. The scales along her bottom half winked here and there where sunlight peeked through the branches.

When she got too close, Kajal lifted the hand stained with haw juice. "Stay back."

The nagi grinned, showing off sharp teeth. "So afraid. I won't hurt you."

Kajal licked her dry lips. The nagas were a demon race from Patala, the only ones who could travel between the planes through bodies of water. They were generally not considered malevolent; in fact, there were stories of nagas assisting the yakshas in eras long past.

But that didn't change the fact that they were venomous and bore fearsome strength. That even among the most peaceful were those prone to violence.

"What do you want?" Kajal demanded.

"Mm, nothing, nothing." The nagi slithered around to her other side, leaning in to sniff her. Kajal extended her stained hand, and the nagi leaned away with a sibilant laugh. "Is it not enough to be curious?"

"You shouldn't be here. Return to your home."

The nagi breathed in sharply. Then her tail curled around Kajal's feet, not quite touching. "What an interesting thing for you to say."

Sweat formed on Kajal's nape. She tried to take a step backward but nearly tripped over the nagi's tail. She glanced toward the gardens, but there was no sign of Dalbir.

The nagi sniffed her again. Her nose was flatter than a human's, the nostrils barely more than slits. "Oh, little girl, such darkness on you." Her teasing expression was gone, replaced with an even more distressing somberness. "It smells like death."

Kajal screwed her eyes shut as her breathing stuttered.

"Do you really think it'll work?" Lasya asked, crouching before the notes Kajal had written in the dirt.

"It will," Kajal insisted, indignant that Lasya, of all people, might be doubting her. "It has to."

Lasya hugged her arms around her knees. "This is dangerous, behan. You could get hurt if you strain yourself too much."

"I can handle it," Kajal said. "I can do anything, remember?"

A flash of light, dozens of hands clawing at the ground, Lasya's scream, the thundering crack of stone.

"Kajal?" Dalbir's distant call wrenched her back to the present.

"Wait there!" Kajal cried.

The nagi came in close, putting her face right up to Kajal's. The haw juice that stained her shaking hand would burn the nagi if she pressed it to her flesh, but Kajal made no move to do so.

"You tell me to return home," the nagi whispered in Kajal's ear, stirring the hairs that fell against her cheek. "You should listen to your own advice."

The nagi retreated, circling around the tree before slipping soundlessly into the lake.

Once the last inch of the nagi's tail disappeared into the water, Kajal dropped her arm and ran.

Chapter Fifteen

DALBIR ESCORTED KAJAL back to Jassi's empty flat, asking no fewer than five times if she was *sure* she was all right. Doing her best impression of someone who had not been inexplicably accosted by a nagi, Kajal assured them no fewer than five times that she was fine, just hungry.

As if she'd predicted this, the professor had left a plate of mathri on the table, the fried dough studded with cumin seeds. Kajal wasted no time shoving one into her mouth while trying not to leave crumbs on Jassi's rug.

Jassi had also left a small note under the plate: *Figured you're busy with lab work. Remember to eat!*

Kajal stopped midchew, the mathri turning ashy in her mouth.

You have to remember to eat when you get in these moods, Lasya had berated her on more than one occasion after Kajal had spent hours researching. *Look, the rotis I've made for you have gone cold.*

Kajal forced herself to swallow, then stuffed the rest of the mathri into her haw-filled pockets. She fled to the laboratory—the door was still broken, but it could at least swing shut—where she ground up the berries into a paste with a mortar and pestle.

"He's about a hundred and sixty pounds," she murmured, an estimation based on his stature and how difficult it had been getting him into that chair.

She scribbled the numbers in her notes. "And if a typical resting heart rate is under a hundred beats a minute . . ."

It was afternoon by the time she returned, jumpy and cotton-headed, to Advaith's room. It was empty. Kajal was about to panic when she noticed that another doorway down the hall had been opened. She stepped into a bedroom similar to Advaith's, but with a few notable differences.

For one, there were decorative swords along one wall, ranging from talwars with elaborate goldwork to shamshirs with animals engraved onto the blades. And while Advaith's shelves had held many books, these mostly held figurines of painted soldiers, yakshas, and rakshasas, as well as game boards for mancala and pachisi. The few books here were on military campaigns and ancient epics.

She made the logical leap that this was Tav's bedroom, partly because Tav himself lay in the middle of the floor, fast asleep. He must have worn himself out looking for clues; or maybe the emotional toll had caught up to him.

Kutaa, tucked against his side, blinked at Kajal in greeting. A few butterflies had stuck around to keep up the search.

Kajal crouched beside Tav and observed the slow rise and fall of his chest, the twitch of his long eyelashes. His lips were pale, almost blue. Even in sleep, his brow was furrowed, and she couldn't help but press her finger against the divot.

He woke with a start and grabbed her wrist. They stared at each other until the divot between Tav's eyebrows deepened.

"Were you . . . watching me sleep?" he asked hoarsely.

"Maybe." She reached into her pocket and drew out a slightly broken mathri. "Food?"

Tav sat up and snatched the offering. "You left me alone for hours, and you only brought mathri?"

Kajal snatched it right back. "You can sit there while I eat them all, then."

Tav sighed and held out his hand. Kajal returned the biscuit, and he munched on it without further complaint.

Kajal wrapped her arms around her legs. "I'm glad you can eat. Everything else feels more or less the same as it did before?"

"I think so. I'm cold, though."

"That'll be your circulation. I brought something to fix that. And clean clothes."

At his pointed glare, Kajal turned around while he changed into Dalbir's jodhpurs and kurta. "Not like I haven't already seen it," she mumbled—which, judging by the teakettle-sharp sound he made, did not help.

She crossed her arms as she studied one of his hand-painted figurines. It was of a dakini, the rakshasa kind, with a long, dark braid and a third, vertical eye upon her forehead. Kajal stared at it until her vision went hazy and her head started to pound. She knuckled at her temple, wanting dearly to fall into a dreamless sleep.

"Did you paint these yourself?" she asked.

"Yes. Advaith did a few of them, though." His voice got closer until he was standing beside her. Dalbir's clothes managed to fit, though the kurta strained at his shoulders. He picked up the dakini figurine with such care that Kajal wondered if it was one his brother had painted.

"You still plan on bringing me to these rebels of yours?" he asked.

"First thing tomorrow morning," Kajal confirmed.

He took a deep, shaking breath and set the figurine down. "Until we find my brother's body, I don't want them to know Advaith and I are the asura and deva."

"Why not?"

"It would be too dangerous. Especially with Bakshi's soldiers everywhere."

She thought of Jagvir and the whip at his belt. "Fair enough." Kajal turned to her supplies. "But in order for me to hand you over, you have to be whole and functional."

She uncorked the jar she'd stored the haw paste in and spread the paste over a mathri with a finger. The smell brought her back to the lakeside, reminding her of the sibilant laughter of the nagi, and a chill stole through her.

Tav wrinkled his nose when she presented the red-slathered mathri to him. "Really?"

"Pretend it's a fancy royal appetizer."

He reluctantly took it. "You remind me of the palace medicine man. He'd pour all sorts of vile concoctions down my throat when I was sick."

"I'll consider that a compliment." She made an impatient gesture. "Eat."

"This is *awful*," he choked out after his first bite, crumbs spilling into his lap. Even Kutaa leaned over to sniff at it only to jerk his head back like it had personally offended him. "These flavors do not go together."

"So sorry it's not to your refined taste, Most Brilliant and Cultured Highness."

He grumbled something along the lines of "Like to see *you* try it."

"Trust me, I've eaten worse. You ever bit into an apple that was complete mush and found half a worm waving back at you?"

"I . . . can't say that I have."

"Then enjoy your snack, Holiest Deva of the Refined Palate."

Kajal pressed two fingers to Tav's chest, above his heart chakra. She closed her eyes and focused on his heartbeat, the telltale sign of sattva running through every vein, muscle, and nerve.

"Anahata, open," she said.

Tav gasped as the force of the sattva flooded his chest, making it heave under her fingers. His heart pounded a hectic rhythm, the natural stimulant of the haws encouraging his blood to flow.

He doubled over and panted. Kutaa worriedly nosed at his face, and Tav grasped a handful of the dog's fur to steady himself.

"What . . ." Tav blinked hard and rapidly, like his vision had blackened. "What did you do?"

"What the medicine men and women do," she answered with a shrug.

"That wasn't just Ayurveda."

"Whatever you say." She lifted one of his hands. When he'd gripped her arm earlier, his fingers had been icy, but now his skin was warming. She laid a finger over his wrist above his iron bangle and counted his pulse.

His hand was larger than hers, and paler. The knuckles were jutting and the nails rounded. There were rough calluses along his finger pads and palm, as well as small silvery scars. She idly traced a triangular-shaped one along the base of one finger.

"Weapon training," he murmured. "Advaith dared me to flip and catch a dagger."

"I take it you didn't catch it?"

"Not by its hilt, no."

A faint smile flickered at his mouth. His lips had blushed to red, either from the haw paste or his improved blood flow. Kajal wondered at how such a tiny smile could soften such a dour face, which reminded her of how peaceful he'd looked while dead.

She dropped his hand like it had burned her. "Well, I think the haw paste did the trick. You might need to eat more at regular intervals, but— Oh no."

Blood was beginning to seep through Dalbir's kurta in the place where Tav's wounds lay. Tav pressed a hand to them, frowning not in pain but in confusion. So much for not staining Dalbir's clothes.

Kajal took the sheets from his bed and ripped them up for bandages. Together they wrapped them tight around his torso. By the time they were done, the bleeding had stopped.

"As the deva, I tend to heal faster," he explained.

"Fascinating." Her fingers itched to write it down. "Still, don't run around opening up the stitches I gave you until the wounds fully close."

He was about to answer when he was interrupted by one of his butterflies. It flitted around his head in agitation or excitement, and his eyes widened.

"Show me," he ordered.

The butterfly flew toward Tav's desk.

"I already checked there," Tav told it.

But the butterfly was insistent, flapping underneath the desk and toward one side.

Tav knelt down. "There's something . . ." After some fiddling, Kajal heard the slide of wood followed by Tav's hoarse laugh. "When did he have *this* installed?"

When he leaned back, a folded yellowed letter was in his hands. Kajal inched closer.

"What does it say?" she prompted.

Tav ripped open the wax seal. Kajal read over his shoulder:

I cannot sit around waiting. What good is all my training if not in preparation for the greatest threat we've faced? How am I to stay here, tucked away like a precious, breakable object, when my brother is out there fighting for the future of this country?

If you find this, something has gone wrong, though I tried my best to prevent it. If we are separated—whether in death or divide—know that I've chosen to do what I thought was right, no matter the price.

Tav—it is not your fight alone. It never has been, no matter what Baa-Ji said.

I'm sorry.

Kajal waited for Tav to react. He stayed on his knees, the paper trembling between his hands. After a minute of debate, she put a hand on his shoulder.

That seemed to rouse him, though he continued staring at the letter. "He . . . He followed me to the battlefield. Why? *Why?*"

He stood so abruptly that Kajal was almost knocked off her feet. The letter crumpled in his hand as his face twisted.

"The point of protecting him was to keep the heir alive!" he growled. "It was *my* fight. He didn't . . . He wasn't supposed to . . ."

His breaths came in great heaving gasps that were nearly sobs. Tav folded in on himself.

"He's dead," he whispered. "He's *dead*. Because of me."

Kajal's vision blurred. She was sitting in the dirt and grass outside Siphar, Lasya a warm presence at her side.

"I don't see any other way to do it," Kajal said. "Something must be done."

"What if it's supposed to be this way?" Lasya asked. "We shouldn't oppose the natural order of things."

"But that's what I'm good at," Kajal countered with a smirk.

Cracks in the earth, a hollow scream, Lasya's name caught in her throat.

She came back to herself with a violent shake. Tav was on his knees again, holding his head in his hands, making sounds like a wounded animal. She saw herself kneeling on kindling, refusing to accept the truth.

With gritted teeth, Kajal grabbed a fistful of Tav's hair and yanked. He stared up at her with glassy eyes. They cleared a little when she lightly slapped him.

"Stop it," she snapped. "Your brother's decisions are not your fault. His death is not on your hands." She thought of Lasya in the coffin, lips ticked up into a peaceful smile. "You want to do right by him? You find his body. But first, you make good on your end of our deal."

The day Tav had bargained for was up. She had to get Vivaan and Sezal on the road to Lasya.

"Tomorrow, we go to the rebels," Kajal continued. "Once they leave to fetch my sister . . . we'll search for your brother. And thanks to this letter, we know exactly where he is."

The marrow-deep terror of the Harama Plain was something she'd never wanted to repeat. But luck had never favored her; why would it start now?

His eyes focused a bit more. "But . . . You said that it was . . ."

"Immensely, extremely haunted? I did." Her fingers tightened in his hair. "So I hope for both our sakes you're not afraid of ghosts."

Kajal left Kutaa and the rest of the mathri with a silent, grieving Tav and went to find Jassi to set up the next stage of her plan. She only realized how late it had gotten when she slunk back into the Elephant Court. Past curfew, in fact.

Damn. She kept an eye out for wandering guards or soldiers as she picked out a careful path through the central courtyard, grateful for the burbling fountain that masked her footfalls. She was halfway across the Serpent Court when a sound made her freeze. But it wasn't a cry of alarm.

It was a giggle.

Kajal warily continued toward the dormitories, where lights were still burning through the windows. The lowest level was mostly dark, the moonlight making long shadows of the columns.

Another giggle, and then a much lower moan. Kajal realized what she was hearing at the exact moment that she passed an archway where two murky figures were entwined.

She was about to scurry off and hope they hadn't seen her when the figures jumped away from each other. One wore a uniform of blue and marigold.

"What are you doing?" the other figure demanded in an all-too-familiar voice. It was one of the sisters who followed Vritika. Kajal couldn't tell which in the gloom, but she could see the girl's shoulders were hunched.

The Vadhia soldier took a step into the moonlight. Kajal's stomach twisted viciously at the sight of oil-slick hair and a coiled whip. *Jagvir.*

"Were you skulking around Professor Jassi's laboratory again?" the girl asked. Her arms were crossed, and her eyes flitted everywhere, as if afraid of more people melting out of the shadows. "What is it you're doing in there? Does she even know you're out past curfew?"

"Again," the soldier added.

"Are we conveniently ignoring that you're out past curfew too?" Kajal retorted. "And what I do is none of your business. Why do you care so much?"

"I don't care about *you*. But if you make trouble for Professor Jassi—"

"Riddhi," Jagvir said sharply. "Drop it."

Riddhi flinched, and despite everything, resentment unspooled in Kajal's chest on the girl's behalf.

"Look," he said to Kajal, "I won't report you to the guards if you just go and forget this happened."

"Gladly." Kajal turned to do just that. Were the students not allowed to get involved with soldiers? She tucked that information away in case she needed it.

But Riddhi didn't know when to leave well enough alone. "You don't belong here," she called after Kajal. "Everyone enrolled in the university was accepted on honest terms, based on merit."

The world rained crimson. No merit? She had raised someone from the dead with her own two hands. She had chased knowledge however she could, whenever she could, the culmination of which would put Riddhi's own paltry experience to shame.

Seeing that the barb had landed, Riddhi laughed humorlessly. "You know it's true. If you're really Professor Jassi's sister, then why so many secrets? Why all the sneaking?" Her voice drew closer. "For all we know, you could be a backwater witch who enthralled Professor Jassi into thinking you're related. But I wasn't fooled by the dakini who bewitched my brother, and I won't be fooled by *you*."

The word *dakini* broke through the layer of Kajal's wrath and into her core, pinning her in place. The notion was absurd, but it didn't matter when a Vadhia soldier was standing in their presence. When Riddhi *knew* what it meant. Behind her, Jagvir shifted on his feet.

"Dakini?" he repeated.

Kajal fisted her hands to prevent them from straying to the scalpel hidden in her salwar. Although the night was cool, her clothes stuck to her skin with sweat.

That's when the humming started.

Kajal's breath caught. The faint, lilting hum seemed to come from everywhere.

Lotus Blossom. The song she had created for Lasya.

She nearly tripped in her haste to flee. Riddhi said something else, but Kajal couldn't hear it over the rising volume of the song, the soft lullaby gradually changing to something off-key, sinister.

No, no, no.

She scrambled up the flights of stairs, desperate to get as far away as possible. Once she reached the dim hallway leading to Jassi's flat, she made it only a few feet before the humming cut off.

Lasya hovered at the end of the hall. Her white dress floated around her, dark hair blowing in a nonexistent breeze. The silence emanating from her was absolute, suffocating.

Her eyes were completely red.

"Don't," Kajal whispered. "Lasya—"

She couldn't even scream as she dropped to the floor, writhing under the assault of a dozen knives piercing through skin and muscle, an unending torment. It was as if her veins were being slowly stripped from her body, her spinal fluid replaced with blistering fire.

She thought she'd known pain when she'd held her sister's lifeless face between her hands. But that was an anguish made from a cold, hollow substance, something she couldn't build armor for; this was made from guilt and punishment, the agony of her flesh reminding her over and over that she was alive and Lasya was not. That Lasya could continue bruising her, like testing fruit for its ripeness, until she split and burst.

Stop, stop, stop, she mentally cried. *Make it stop!*

At her pathetic pleading, the pain gradually leached away. She lay panting on the floor as tear tracks dried on her face and her heart settled into its regular rhythm. She pushed herself up, but Lasya was gone.

"Kajal?" came Jassi's voice from her bedroom when she finally managed to stumble through the front door. "Where have you been? You're out past curfew."

"I'm sorry," Kajal croaked. "Won't happen again."

Jassi walked out into the central room. "Dalbir said you two— Are you all right?"

Kajal swayed on her feet. "I . . ."

"Here, you should lie down."

Clammy and shaking, she allowed Jassi to lead her to bed. The hum still filled her ears like a promise.

She dozed in and out while Jassi came in to check on her. Kajal tried more than once to tell her about Tav, about Lasya, but the words were too heavy in her mouth. The echo of pain lingered in her bones. Asleep or awake, she was mired in the nagi's laughter, Lasya's hum, the word *dakini* shaped on Riddhi's lips.

A scream tore through the dormitories.

Kajal started awake. She staggered out the door and into the hallway, Jassi on her heels wearing oversized pajamas.

"I think it came from below." Jassi rushed for the stairs. Kajal lingered at the top, using the wall to help her stand.

After an eerie silence, a horrible wail echoed upward. Voices were raised in confusion and fear, students calling for the professors and guards.

The wailing dissolved into furious sobs. "Riddhi! *Riddhi!*"

"How did it happen?"

"What's that foam around her mouth?"

"I saw it, she suddenly spasmed and fell over!"

Kajal slid down the wall. Siddhi continued to cry out her sister's name, ignoring the students trying to soothe her. Vritika's voice was among them, thick with tears.

"What happened to her?" Jagvir was demanding. "I was just— Someone wake the soldiers!"

Kajal turned and vomited.

She coughed and shuddered on her knees, Siddhi's cries burrowing into her like nails. A sister, gone. Because of her. And now the Vadhia would be shaken like a kicked wasp's nest.

Kajal slapped a hand over her whimpering mouth.

Lasya had punished her and claimed a life anyway—a life connected to a demon hunter *and* a Vadhia soldier. Kajal was no longer strong enough to stop the bhuta from killing those around her, from pulling them both toward ruin.

No. No, she was so *close*.

She just had to get Tav to the rebels. She had to . . .

Find me, the bhuta whispered in her ear. *Find me.*

Kill me.

Chapter Sixteen

THE DORMITORIES WERE crawling with activity, the students too alarmed to return to bed. Had Riddhi's body been carried away? Were the Vadhia stalking the university grounds in search of answers?

Kajal's mind whirled with possible consequences. She fell into a tactile memory of glass at her lips, the whiff of sickly-sweet poison, the eyes of a furious town upon her.

The crack of a whip splitting skin.

After stumbling back to Jassi's flat, Kajal sat, dazed, at the table until Jassi came back in the early hours of morning. By then the dormitories had fallen silent, but the kind of silence that falls after the end of a booming sound: anticipatory and uneasy, preparing for the next. Disquiet was written in the line of the professor's mouth.

"A messenger's been sent to inform the family," Jassi said. "The Vadhia are on alert. Especially Jagvir. Vritika said it looked like a bhuta attack."

Kajal's flinch was damning. Jassi inhaled sharp enough to mimic a dagger between Kajal's ribs.

"Your sister's bhuta?"

"I didn't mean for it to happen!" Kajal stood, knocking the chair back. "Riddhi was out past curfew, and she was . . . she was so *mad*, and . . . I didn't want . . ."

The professor grasped her shoulders and shook her. "Breathe. Take a moment." Once Kajal had managed a few deep breaths, Jassi asked, "But why were *you* out past curfew? Where have you been?"

Kajal's face heated. Staring at the floor, she said slowly, like they were the last words she'd ever speak: "I revived the prince."

For a long while, Jassi said nothing. Eventually, the professor lifted Kajal's chin and met her eyes. Kajal forced herself to not look away, to stand her ground no matter how much of it had already crumbled beneath her.

"You're not lying," Jassi whispered. "Did it work?"

Kajal nodded.

"I . . . Kajal, I was supposed to assist you! Where is he? Why did you do it on your own?"

Kajal thought back to the hollow, aching fear of seeing the bhuta, the resonance of Lasya's lullaby mocking and cold.

"Time," Kajal said simply.

Jassi's fingers briefly dug into her shoulder. "Show me."

Tav was pacing the gardens while Kutaa sat and watched him. Jassi's gasp upon seeing him made Tav's hand dart to the hip where he'd once worn his sword. The two of them stared at each other, Tav with suspicion and Jassi with incredulity.

Then Jassi fell to one knee. Tav's alarm tripled, and Kajal would have laughed had she not been in the middle of a lengthy yet discreet panic attack.

"Your Highness," Jassi whispered. "Your *Majesty*. Welcome back."

Tav's lips parted, but no words left them.

Kajal cleared her throat pointedly.

"Right," he said. "Um. Thank you. Who are you?"

Advaith must have received the bulk of their deportment training. Kajal imagined the crown prince sitting with perfect posture on a cushion, being lectured on grace and conduct, while Tav was left to swing his sword at training dummies as a means of mediation.

"I'm a professor here at the university," Jassi answered, unaffected by his clumsiness, or else hiding her surprise fairly well. "Jasmeet Singh, but please feel free to call me Jassi. I'm a member of the Insurrectionists who have been working to bring down the tyrant Anu Bakshi and restore the true heir."

At those last words, Tav turned wan. White fluttered in the corner of Kajal's eye, and she nearly bolted, but it was only his butterflies hiding among the dead branches of the trees and bushes.

"He can eat," Kajal blurted before Jassi noticed them. "We tested it. All of his chakras were opened, and his bodily functions seem to be . . . functioning."

Tav silently mouthed *bodily functions* to himself.

Jassi gave Kajal a tired, shaky smile. "Well done."

Despite what had happened last night, Kajal's chest filled with bright, bubbling delight.

"Your Majesty," Jassi said, "I'm sure you're tired. If you follow us, we can tend to your needs; we could draw you a bath."

Tav shifted, no doubt feeling a keen need for that bath. "And in return, you want me to meet with these Insurrectionists."

"Just so."

Tav looked to Kajal. Not for counsel, but as one conspirator seeks out another. Any thoughts Kajal had briefly entertained about telling the rebels the truth had dissolved at the sound of screams echoing through the dormitories, the horror on Jassi's face.

If they knew this boy was not Advaith, had not received the same training and did not have the same destiny, they wouldn't rest until they found the real crown prince. But the bhuta had evolved into something Kajal could not control. They had to keep up the lie, at least until the rebels got Lasya's body.

Whatever showed on Kajal's face made Tav square his shoulders.

"Very well," he said, his tone changing to something more commanding. Perhaps he had shared Advaith's training after all. "Lead on."

"You know, when you asked for a change of clothes, you could have told me it was for a *prince*," Dalbir admonished Kajal. They had brought up more outfits while Tav took his bath. "I would have chosen something with more embroidery."

"He needs to avoid attention," Jassi reminded them. "Especially if we're entering Suraj."

Kajal greeted this news with a healthy blend of unease and anticipation. Unease at the prospect of explaining all this to Vivaan and Sezal, anticipation at getting on with her plans.

"Dalbir," Jassi said, "you'll be coming with us."

Kajal frowned. "Why?"

"My family *is* funding this entire operation," Dalbir reminded her. "Which means I have to report everything back to them. But honestly, this'll make for a great story. I'll throw in some embellishments if you like. Make you out to be a brilliant yet misunderstood eccentric." They gave a crooked grin. "Then again, that's not much of an exaggeration."

Kajal's scoff came out choked. She wondered if that meant reporting Riddhi's death too.

"Were you here?" she asked quietly. "When it happened?"

Dalbir glanced at the floor as if they could peer through stone to the spot where Riddhi must have collapsed. "I was already asleep, but the chaos woke me up. I didn't go out to check." They leaned against the wall, arms crossed. "The screams were enough to tell me what had happened."

Dalbir seemed unusually aloof until Kajal noticed the tension in their jaw. She understood; sometimes the best way to accept something was to distance yourself from it, almost to the point of indifference.

"I heard it might have been a stroke or heart failure, but that can't be right. Not in an otherwise healthy sixteen-year-old girl. Vritika's convinced it was a bhuta attack, and since she's a Meghani, I'm inclined to believe her. The Vadhia are too—they'll be searching for bodies the bhuta might belong to. Who knows, maybe the professors they hanged are finally seeking vengeance." Dalbir shook their head, hair swaying. "Good thing you got a head start on His Highness, huh?"

Kajal exchanged a nervous look with Jassi. She could tell the professor wanted to reveal the truth about the bhuta, but Kajal was sick of exposing her biggest mistake to others she barely knew.

Thankfully, that was when Tav emerged. Freshly clean, his hair fell in damp waves to his shoulders, and there was a faint shadow of stubble at his jaw that made Kajal long for her notebook. *Follicles unaffected; blood flow must have improved if it's able to feed the follicle root and promote new growth.*

Jassi and Dalbir stared at him. While Kutaa had an aura that wasn't *wrong*, exactly, but wasn't quite *right* either—even the townspeople in Kinara had picked up on that—Tav was indistinguishable from any other living boy his age. Whole. Human.

Well, mostly human. Kajal kept a lookout for those yaksha butterflies, worried they'd sneak into the flat and make Jassi even more paranoid than she seemed to be.

Tav was introduced to Dalbir and politely listened to what they had to say about the Sodhis' plans, but he kept sending Kajal glances that varied from wary to considering to beseeching. The latter was whenever Jassi would ask him a question he didn't want to answer.

"Let's save it for when everyone's together," Kajal interjected. "That way he doesn't have to repeat himself."

"Good point," Jassi said. "We've been up all night. We should all get some sleep before heading into the city this evening. You can take my bed, Your Majesty."

"There's no need. I'm fine out here."

"You don't feel tired?" Kajal asked, yearning to poke and prod at him again.

"I mean—yes, I think so. But I don't want to steal anyone's bed."

Kajal sighed through Jassi's silent bafflement. "Take my bed. Jassi and I can share. Hers is bigger."

Tav opened his mouth to argue, then thought better of it. "All right."

Once they were alone in Jassi's bedroom, Kajal didn't have to wait long before Jassi spoke the words she'd been dreading.

"Tell me exactly what happened with Riddhi."

Kajal swallowed, her throat dry. "I ran into her and Jagvir while coming back from the old palace. She said some things that made me angry, and that's when I felt her. Lasya."

Jassi's face tightened.

"I didn't mean for it to happen," Kajal whispered. "I resurrected the prince because the bhuta's getting stronger. I've been able to stop it before, but even though it lashed out at me when I tried to stop it this time, it made the kill anyway."

Although she was surrounded by death, she'd never wanted to be the cause of it. Yet it seemed that, in her presence, death was not merely a threat but something inevitable.

Such darkness on you, the nagi had whispered to her by the lake. *It smells like death.*

Jassi turned her gaze toward the bed as if questioning whether she felt safe sharing it with Kajal. "So that's why you did it. You're scared of your sister's bhuta."

Loath as Kajal was to agree, she was even more reluctant to admit that resurrecting Tav was largely to prove she could. "The longer I wait, the more powerful she'll become. As we've just seen."

The muscles of Jassi's jaw flexed. Then all her aggravation seemed to leave at once, loosening her shoulders and expression.

Kajal stiffened as a pair of arms came around her.

"You should have come to me," Jassi scolded, though her voice was gentle. "But I understand. I'm so sorry you're in this position, Kajal."

Kajal remained rigid and bewildered, locked within an embrace she'd done nothing to earn. For a moment, she remembered the way Lasya had held her, familiar and warm, her clothes smelling of the spices she loved. Remembered tucking her face against her sister's shoulder and letting Lasya rub her back with large, soothing circles.

Her eyes stung. With a shaky gasp, she broke out of Jassi's hold.

"It's fine," Kajal muttered. "Let's . . . Let's just sleep. We'll deal with it later."

But as Kajal lay there, with her back to Jassi and Kutaa on the floor below, her mind and her heart refused to settle. Her rest was uneasy and fragmented, conjuring images of a gnarled tree, a beaming trident, and a river blooming with wild lotus.

Suraj was brilliant at dusk.

Lanterns had been strung across the broad streets, and windows were filled with a warm glow. The beaten metal of temple roofs that gleamed under the sun now reflected the lamplight, as if hungry for radiance. Behind the buildings loomed the last of the day's light, throwing everything into a dance of shadow and flame. It truly was the City of Sunset.

Kajal hadn't been around this many people in a while, not even at the university. Kinara had been sparse compared to the pack and crush of Suraj. There were farmhands coming home after a long day in the fields, hawkers shouting about their goods, musicians with sitars and drums hoping to earn coin, urchins darting in and out to ply their swift trade with nimble fingers. There was a hazy smell to the air—smoke and steam and a hint of refuse—though from what she could see, the city was surprisingly clean.

Some Vadhia were supposedly stationed here. Every flash of yellow and blue made Kajal twitch as Jassi led the way through congested streets to where the rebels were staying. Dalbir, meanwhile, was having an excellent time taking in the sights, apart from the glances they spared for Tav.

The prince was wrapped and hooded in a long cloak. He walked with his head down, chewing on his lower lip. He'd barely said anything after they'd woken from their naps, maintaining a worrying distance.

Kajal could hardly remember the days after the accident in Siphar. There were only fragments of stumbling down dusty roads, empty and raw, an animal that had been gutted and bled dry.

After some debate, Kajal shifted to his side until their shoulders brushed. "I doubt anyone will recognize you here. You can look around if you want to."

He roused from his stupor. "I've been here often," Tav murmured back.

"Oh. Right." Kajal scratched her cheek. She wished Kutaa had come with them, but a dog of that size and demeanor would earn too many stares. "And it hasn't changed at all since you were here last?"

"There are more buildings, I think. And more people." His eyes snagged on a vendor, and he frowned.

It was the first real expression he'd made in hours, and Kajal had no idea what had caused it. There were always a number of street vendors in the larger cities, some of them so aggressive they would walk right up to you and try to shove their merchandise into your hands. One time, Lasya had been reduced to tears by a persistent vendor who wanted her to pay for the sesame candy he'd made her touch. Kajal still remembered the crunch his kneecap had made when she'd kicked it.

She was pulled from the memory when Dalbir clutched her sleeve.

"What's he doing?" they demanded.

Tav was marching purposefully to a wooden stall erected at the mouth of an alley. It appeared humble enough to Kajal, but as she rushed forward, she noticed it was covered in charms and papers. The charms were standard fare: bits of metal and wood in shapes of benevolent hands with eyes in the center to ward off rakshasas, innocuous enough the Vadhia wouldn't care. The papers were crowded with inked mantras for wellness and protection, as well as depictions of the three yaksha deities.

But one pile was full of drawings of a strange pair. One face was drawn with elegant lines and beautiful features, while the other bore exaggerated ugliness, a tongue poking out between sharp teeth and beady eyes under bushy brows.

"Hello, young sir, good evening," the vendor said. "Have you a need for warding amulets or charms?"

"What is this?" Tav pointed at the drawings.

"Young sir, that is the asura and deva! If you put up their likeness above your bed or over your door frame, they will help guard against malevolent spirits, rakshasas, and the evil eye."

Tav grabbed the top drawing and shook it in the man's face. "This isn't what the asura looks like! Why have you drawn him so hideously? What's wrong with you?"

The vendor recoiled. Kajal grabbed Tav's arm.

"It doesn't matter," she hissed in his ear. "I'm sure your brother is a lovely specimen, but *they* don't know that."

"Young sir, I-I'm not sure why you're upset," the vendor sniveled as he wrung his hands together. "The deva brings peace and wellness, while the asura brings chaos and war! It is only with the deva's influence that the asura can use their wicked ways for good."

Tav drew himself up, and Kajal sighed.

"The asura is not *wicked*," Tav spat. "Or ugly. Remove these and redo them!"

Jassi quickly grabbed Tav's other arm and steered him away. "He's had too much to drink," she told the vendor with an apologetic smile. Kajal and Dalbir hurried after.

Once they were out of earshot, Jassi dropped Tav's arm. "I'm sorry, but we couldn't risk a scene." She hesitated, clearly wanting to ask what had gotten him so riled, then merely shook her head. "We're close. Please be patient a little longer, Your Majesty."

Tav glared at the drawing he'd accidentally stolen. He balled it up and shoved it into his pocket.

The rebels were staying in what had to be the most dilapidated building in Suraj, a cramped honeycomb of rooms situated near a dyeing and textile factory. Acrid smoke and vinegary odors wafted through the chimneys in a constant stream.

As Jassi led them through the front doors and up a flight of creaking stairs, Kajal took up the rear with Tav.

"Is it true?" she asked softly. "That the asura isn't wicked."

"Of course. I know my brother best, and he was always good. Always looking out for others. These myths and stories people pass around only tell half-truths at best. Our powers may be different, but they're not opposite—they're complementary. We strengthen each other."

Kajal thought of Lasya's application of Ayurveda in food and her own application of Ayurveda in the body.

Jassi reached a door on the topmost level and gave two soft knocks, then two more after a short pause. The door opened, and they shuffled inside, everyone silently electing to keep their shoes on due to the filthy state of the floor.

Kajal lingered in the doorway, Tav behind her. From here, she could plainly see the confusion on Vivaan and Sezal's faces. They'd been in the middle of preparing dinner, judging from the flour on Sezal's hands and the low fire in the earthen cooking stove in the corner.

"Jassi," Vivaan greeted. "Has something happened?"

Kajal didn't hear Jassi's reply. She reached for Tav's wrist and squeezed hard.

"If you can't convince them, it's over," she whispered.

His expression hardened, turning his eyes a shade darker. Before he could speak, everyone angled toward the door—to Kajal and the person she was blocking.

Taking a deep breath, Kajal stepped fully into the room and allowed Tav to enter. He closed the door behind him and lowered his hood.

Kajal hadn't known what to expect. Stunned silence, perhaps, or questions lobbed at her about what she'd been thinking. She didn't anticipate the wrecked gasp from Vivaan, nor the way he immediately fell to both knees and lowered himself until his forehead touched the floor. Sezal followed at a slower pace, eyes widely fixated on Tav.

"My prince," Vivaan whispered. Kajal had never heard him like this, reverent and awed.

Tav's smooth mask was already cracking. She had known him only a day, and already Kajal could tell he wanted to squirm in discomfort like he had at Jassi's deference.

"There's no need for that," Tav said. At least his voice was unaffected, smooth and assured, likely the tone he'd once employed for the soldiers under his command. "Rise."

Sezal, realizing her hands were dirty, quietly cursed and searched for a cloth to wipe them. When Vivaan lifted his head, he looked as if nothing short of an earthquake could wrench his gaze from Tav.

"How did this happen?" Sezal demanded.

It was Jassi who stepped forward and explained. Kajal, hands clasped behind her back, attempted to appear as nonchalant as possible.

She steeled herself when the rebels turned to her. "We warned you not to do this on your own," Vivaan admonished darkly. "The number of things that could have gone wrong—"

"But it didn't go wrong," Kajal quickly said. "I've been evaluating him all day, and everything seems intact."

"Evaluating?" Tav murmured.

"But why do it without telling anyone?" Sezal pressed.

Kajal didn't answer. It was Jassi who said, "There was a bhuta attack."

Dalbir, who'd been silently watching, started. "So it *was* a bhuta? Then do you know where it came from?"

Kajal's mouth twisted before admitting, "It's mine. Or, rather, my sister's."

Now even Tav was staring at her. Here at last was the stunned silence she'd expected, and it made her pulse jump with every second it crawled on.

"That's why you learned this," Tav whispered, almost to himself. "Resurrection."

"Wait, so Riddhi was— That was *you*?" Dalbir demanded.

"Not *me*," Kajal argued. "I didn't *want* her to die!"

"Wait," Sezal interrupted, "a student is dead?"

"That's why I needed to resurrect the prince right away," Kajal half lied. "The sooner I achieve my end of this, the sooner you can fulfill your part of the bargain and I can get rid of the bhuta."

"If your sister's body is in the east, we can all go to the Sodhi estate and bring the prince with us," Sezal suggested. "It's somewhat south of Siphar."

Kajal ignored Tav's nervous look. "No," she insisted. "You have to bring Lasya here, to the university."

Vivaan's brow furrowed. "Why? It would be in your best interest to come with us."

Not when you'd turn right around once you realized you have the wrong prince, she thought.

"It's because of me." Tav clenched and unclenched his hands at his sides. "My memories. I . . . can't seem to remember very much from around the time I was killed. Only pieces here and there."

Vivaan swayed as if he were about to lose his balance. Dalbir's mouth was getting thinner with each new complication.

"But you remember who you are?" Sezal urged him. "*What* you are?"

Tav frowned a little at the wording. "Yes. I am the crown prince of Dharati, Advaith Thakar."

Vivaan and Sezal didn't seem reassured. The two rebels shared another of those silent conversations Kajal couldn't read. Vivaan's earlier awe had turned to something darker, harder, as he turned his gaze on Kajal and then Tav.

With a jolt, Kajal realized it was suspicion.

"We can't bring him to the Sodhis with his memories damaged," Sezal concluded at last. "Kajal, do you think you and Jassi can work with him on this while we retrieve your sister's body?"

It was a feat to keep her face impassive under the sheer force of her relief. "Yes," she said while Jassi nodded.

"I won't tell my parents," Dalbir vowed when the rebels glanced at them. "Honest. I only want to finish my coursework."

"Then I suppose it's settled," Sezal said. "Kajal, if you tell us exactly where Lasya is, we'll set out at dawn. By the time we get back, hopefully His Highness will remember more."

After all the panic and dread of the last couple days, Kajal's hope was bright enough to rival Tav's magic, preventing her from looking too closely at this fortunate turn.

Fortunate, that is, if she could last another few days with the bhuta haunting her every step, waiting for her to slip up again.

Chapter Seventeen

KAJAL HEADED STRAIGHT for Jassi's bedroom to avoid speaking to Tav and woke groggy and disoriented the next morning. Jassi had already left to prepare for classes; she must have let Kutaa out, since Kajal didn't see him. She rolled over and reached for her slippers, but they were gone too.

With a grumble, Kajal slid off the bed and peeked under.

Her slippers were there, sure enough, but guarded by tiny yakshas. They were no bigger than mice, puffy and white with shining black eyes that stared unblinkingly at her.

"Hi," she said. "Can I have my slippers?"

One of them made a high squeak, almost a question. Another nuzzled itself down into a slipper, as if attracted to the smell.

Kajal recalled Lasya dealing with these types of yakshas before. They had refused to give her boots back and hadn't relented until Lasya had given them an offering of rock sugar.

A brief search of Jassi's room revealed a tin of candied fennel seeds. She knelt again with a few on her palm. The yakshas inched forward with curious squeaks. Then tiny claws emerged from their fuzzy bodies to grab handfuls of colorful seeds before they retreated.

"Thanks," she muttered as she grabbed her slippers.

Out in the main room, Tav sat at the table with an empty cup before him. Kutaa had put his head on the prince's lap, and Tav idly stroked the dog's head while he stared out the window.

For a moment, she was struck by the sight of them, two bodies housing hearts that had stopped until she'd made them pump again. Limbs that had been stiff and cold now warm and shifting. Minds that had become empty filled once more with thought.

Tav sensed her stare and gave her a bemused look. "What?"

"Nothing," she said. "Just admiring my boys."

He glowered. "I'm not your *boy*."

"You're my creation, aren't you?"

"My *mother* created me." The beginnings of Kajal's smile fell away as he went on, "You didn't tell me about your sister. Or the student."

"I distinctly remember telling you I had a sister."

"But not that she's dead!"

"Only temporarily," Kajal countered. "Besides, it doesn't involve you."

He stood, gaining the unfortunate advantage of height. "It does if I'm lying to these people for *your* sake."

She flapped her arms in frustration. "All right, so maybe I omitted a detail. But I had to make sure they would get Lasya for me. And while they do that, I'll make good on my promise to help you find Advaith."

"That doesn't mean you should have— Oh, yes, sorry." Kutaa had nudged Tav's hand. Tav obediently continued to scratch behind the dog's ears. "You *manipulated* me."

Kajal sneered at her traitorous dog. "You grew up in a palace sucking on a gilded spoon, so I'm going to state this as simply as I can: When you see an opportunity that means survival, you take it."

He drew in a breath to speak, then let it out.

"You should have told me about your sister." His voice was quiet. "I woke up from being dead only to learn that everyone I love is also dead." He made to reach for his pendant before dropping his hand. "I would have understood."

"I'm being haunted by my own sister," she said flatly. "What do you understand of my situation?"

He looked away. Kutaa, sensing her distress, came and sat beside her instead.

She briefly revisited her fragmented memories of the days after she'd buried Lasya. The intervals of gnawing pain and numbness, the desire to simply build herself a pyre and be reborn as something better. Some*one* better.

She exhaled slowly. "Sorry." Kajal wasn't used to apologizing, and the words were stiff. "I shouldn't be comparing our grief."

He shook his head, whether to accept her apology or dismiss it, she wasn't sure. "Bhutas form when a body hasn't been burned," he said. "Which means your sister must have been buried."

"Yes. Same as you."

"Did I . . . Was I also a . . . bhuta?" The mere thought turned his skin ashen.

"Of course. A particularly rude one, at that. I risked my life to drag you out of there, and now I have to do it again with your brother. But make no mistake: Once my sister and Advaith are alive, I'm gone."

The rebels would bring the princes to the Sodhis and launch their coup, a campaign that would inspire civilians and soldiers alike to rise up against Bakshi. Kajal would be more than happy to leave them to it while she and Lasya picked up where they'd left off.

His gaze flickered to hers. "Then I owe you a debt. Not only for bringing me back, but also Advaith, when we find him. Based on what I've seen, I know your skill will be more than up for the task." He inclined his head deeply. "Thank you."

"You— That isn't—" She cleared her throat. "You can't *talk* like that. Warn me next time."

"Why?"

She turned away before he could catch the flush scalding her cheeks. "I'm helping you because my life and my sister's life are on the line."

"Is that really the only reason?"

She thought of the blighted crop she'd held in her hand. The diseased deer, and the pujari. The corpse of a woman swinging from a noose.

When she said nothing, he gave a weary sigh. "All right. No matter your motivation, our current goals are aligned."

There was movement in the corner of her eye. He'd extended a hand toward her. She took it and clasped hard, his tendons shifting within her grip.

Her finest creation. Her potential downfall.

"By the way," she said when she dropped his hand, "you're attracting yakshas. I had to haggle with some for my shoes."

"The juti cora? They're harmless."

"If you attract more, it could jeopardize your identity." Although what really worried her were the demon hunter and the Vadhia searching for the slightest trace of the supernatural on school grounds. "Also, now that the rebels are gone, we should prepare to leave too." As reluctant as she was to return to the Harama Plain, any distance she could put between her and the university right now was welcome.

"How do you propose we do that?"

"I'll talk to Jassi. I think I know how to convince her." She turned to the door and jerked her thumb over her shoulder. "In the meantime, get rid of those yakshas."

The students she passed were subdued. She walked through the archway of the Serpent Court, then stopped in her tracks. By the main gates of the university was a small congregation of people—a mix of staff, the Vadhia, and students. On a cart before them lay a plain wooden coffin.

A sobbing woman and man stood over the coffin with Siddhi beside them, dry-eyed and blank-faced, as if her emotions were too large to fit within her body. No doubt the family would be traveling home to their local cremation grounds, where they would then set fire to the coffin and release Riddhi's soul to travel to Patala, drink the tea of forgetting, and be reborn.

Vritika had an arm around Siddhi's shoulders. As if sensing Kajal's stare, she lifted her head. Next to her, Jagvir noticed the movement and caught sight of Kajal as well. His shoulders stiffened.

In her ear blew a breathy, rasping laugh.

Kajal forced herself to keep walking, eyes lowered. She didn't dare look up until she approached the laboratory. As she ascended the stairs, she recalled the state she'd left the room in and quickened her pace.

To her surprise, the door was already fixed. When she opened it, the interior beyond was clean. Had Jassi done this?

Kajal took out the pouch she'd been carrying since she and the rebels had been on the road. There were roughly thirty bitter almonds inside, their skins dry and wrinkled.

Just in case.

She ground them down, adding a bit of water until she ended up with a lethal, cloudy liquid. She strained it and poured the final result into a small blue bottle she found on the worktable, which she stoppered tightly.

The look Vivaan had given her in the rebels' hideout plagued her. And, as she'd told Tav: When you see an opportunity that means survival, you take it.

Familiar voices came from the hallway. Kajal slipped the bottle into her pocket before she crept to the door and pressed her ear against the wood.

"I'm so sorry." That was Jassi. "I know this must be difficult for you. I could put in a request for you to take a few days off from classes."

"That's all right, Professor." Vritika's voice sounded hoarse, like she'd been crying. "I don't want to fall behind."

"You lost a friend. You need time to grieve."

"With all due respect, Professor, I'd rather keep myself busy."

A soft sigh. "You still believe this was the work of a bhuta?"

Kajal held her breath.

"I do. The Vadhia wouldn't let me join their search, but I used turmeric incense to dowse for bodies. There were none." She grew winded with excitement. "My family's methods have been developed for this exact scenario. I want to find it and exorcise it."

Kajal twitched with indignation. *Like I'd let you.*

"You know more than anyone how dangerous bhutas are," Jassi said. "Your family—"

"Expects me to live up to my older siblings," Vritika cut in, irritation winning out over respect. "If I exorcise a bhuta terrorizing the university, the Meghani name will be even more revered." A pause. "Which means Bakshi won't target us."

Jassi's tone sharpened. "Has he been making trouble for your family?"

"No, no . . . At least not yet. My parents like him, like that they were able to keep their trade because of him, but I . . ."

"I understand. I'd like nothing more than to see you reach your full potential and do your family proud."

The conversation went on a little longer, but Kajal stepped away from the door as her chest filled with hot pressure. The feeling was foreign and uncomfortable, and for a moment she wondered if she had accidentally ingested some of the bitter almond extract.

But no—this was jealousy, plain and simple. Jealousy over someone like *Vritika*, because a professor saw greatness in her and wanted to shepherd her toward it.

No one had ever seen greatness in Kajal. Lasya had believed in her, but that was the biased loyalty of a sister. The rebels had sought her abilities, but that was exploitation. She had allowed herself to be used. Was still being used.

If she had been able to come to the university on her own, perhaps with Lasya at her side, would someone like Jassi have seen her potential and taken them under her care?

The door whisked open, and Kajal jumped, blinking the wetness from her eyes. Jassi was equally startled at the sight of her.

"Kajal," she said, closing the door. "I thought you'd be with the prince."

"I wanted to clean up." Kajal gestured at the already clean laboratory. "Seems I was beaten to it."

"I had the janitorial staff come by as soon as I could. Didn't want anyone else to see the broken door."

Kajal tried to reorient herself for the conversation she'd been planning to have, but she couldn't let one thing go. "You're not going to help Vritika, are you?"

"I'm not going to point her in the direction of your sister's bhuta, if that's what you mean."

Kajal forced herself to nod despite that hint of betrayal tasting like a rotten confection on her tongue. "I think I know how to restore the prince's memories."

Jassi's eyes widened behind her glasses. "How?"

"There's a place to the north where he used to go with his family. He can't remember the exact name or what they did there, but if we visit, it could help trigger his memories."

"Oh . . . Kajal, I don't know. We should probably wait for Vivaan and Sezal to return first."

"The rebels said that time isn't on our side. The blight is getting worse every day."

"That's true, but—"

"So we should do this while they're retrieving Lasya."

Jassi sighed. "Where is this place?"

"He said it's near a town called Pahari. Or maybe it's the town itself. It's hard for him to remember clearly."

Jassi chewed on her thumbnail. "I have classes, and the administrative staff has to approve all my extended leaves."

"There's no need for you to come. Advaith is a soldier, remember? And besides, I have my sister's bhuta. No one's going to attack us and walk away from it."

Jassi still seemed conflicted.

"It's imperative we restore his memories," Kajal said. "Not only for your plans, but for mine. If I can fix *his* memories, then that means I'll be able to help Lasya if hers are missing too. The sooner this gets done, the sooner I can put the bhuta to rest. I don't . . . I don't want another Riddhi."

Jassi winced. After a long, painful moment, her shoulders fell.

"All right," she whispered. "But please make it quick. And be careful. If anything happens to him, the blame will fall on me."

"Don't worry," Kajal said with a smile she didn't feel, remembering how the bhutas had grabbed and scratched at her. "I'm sure the danger will be minimal."

She was on her way to tell Tav when she ran into Vritika outside the building. The girl's eyes were bloodshot, her hair halfheartedly brushed yet maintaining its usual luster. Recalling what Vritika had said about exorcising Lasya, Kajal scowled.

Vritika mirrored the expression. "What?" she demanded.

"Nothing." Kajal turned toward the dormitories, but Vritika blocked her. "What do you want?"

"Jagvir told me you ran into Riddhi before she collapsed. What happened between you two?"

"I accidentally saw them in a compromising position," Kajal answered, trying to keep her voice level as she ignored the drum-quick rhythm of her pulse. "I left quickly."

"That's it?"

"Are you trying to insinuate something?"

Vritika pressed her lips into a thin line. Kajal knew better than to agitate her, but Vritika's conversation with Jassi kept itching in the back of her mind.

"They said she died of heart failure," Vritika said at last. "But she's too young for that, and she didn't have any illnesses."

"Maybe she thought she saw a rakshasa," Kajal said with a flip of her hand. "She seemed eager enough to find one."

Vritika curled her hands into fists. "They also suggested poison."

"What does that have to do with me? *I'm* not the one she was kissing. Maybe you should question Jagvir instead."

Vritika moved closer, and Kajal took an unconscious step back, all too aware of the freshly made almond extract in her pocket.

"I come from a family that studies rakshasas," Vritika said softly. "How they hunt. How they kill. Riddhi didn't die from a heart failure or poison. She died from a *bhuta*."

Kajal did her best to keep her expression impassive. "I don't know what that means." Thinking of Jassi in the laboratory, she slipped on a confused smile. "I'm just a girl from Malhir. I'm not that knowledgeable about rakshasas."

"Really," Vritika said flatly. "Because that's not the impression you give me."

The whine built so gradually she wasn't aware of it until it became a thin scream. Phantom fingers plucked Kajal's clothing as a low laugh cut through the whine.

Vritika took another step forward, determination and grief making a grim mask of her face. Over her shoulder, a pair of red eyes glowed.

Kill, came a whisper in her ear. *Kill?*

"No," Kajal breathed. "Don't."

Vritika paused. Then she hissed, raising her arm and staring at her sarbloh bangle. The bhuta formed fully behind her, white kameez fluttering, dark hair like tendrils of shadow. Lasya's normally placid expression was twisted into a sharp grin—eager, wanting.

Hungry.

Kajal bolted.

The dormitories weren't far, but they might as well have been across the country as she darted between startled students and staff. The dissonant notes of *Lotus Blossom* wove around her like a net ready to ensnare her.

She managed to stumble into the flat right as the hum reached its peak and cold fingers clamped around her throat.

Kajal fell to the floor with a choked gasp. Above her, Lasya stared down with burning eyes the crimson of fresh blood, that unnatural smile distorting her face into a stranger's, a monster's. Kajal kicked and fought, drumming her heels against the wooden floor and scrabbling at her neck, doing little more than scratching up her own skin as her fingers passed through the bhuta's.

But those spectral fingers were substantial enough to close up her arteries, to cut off the rush of oxygen to her brain. Her entire skull felt like it would shatter, the pressure growing intolerable, maddening, while her heart fell out of rhythm.

Part of her wondered if it would be better to let it happen. To give her sister the satisfaction of revenge: one life paid with another. They had once done everything together—why not die together too?

A bark pierced through the roaring of her ears. Lasya snarled as a dozen butterflies descended on her, forcing her to dissipate into clouds of purling white smoke.

Kajal struggled for breath. Someone gently rolled her onto her side.

"*Kajal!* Kajal, can you hear me?"

She couldn't speak, so she weakly lifted a shaking hand and patted the closest thing to her. By the feel of it, it was Tav's knee.

"Damn. All right. Hold on," he was mumbling above her. Something wet and cold touched her temple. "Kutaa, sit."

The dog sniffed at Kajal's face a second longer before obeying. *How does he do that so easily?* she thought in a bleary, out-of-focus way as fingertips came to rest lightly at her bruised throat.

"Focus on breathing," Tav said. Her vision was murky, but she turned to the sound of his voice like a flower to the sun. "You'll be all right."

Logically, she knew the words were an empty comfort. But her body reacted to them like they were steeped in truth, turned to gilded law.

Warmth, sweet and mellow, soaked into her skin. Kajal shuddered and relented to its slow devouring of her body, the way it traveled from the crown of her head to the bowl of her pelvis to the tips of her toes.

Her throat flared with pain, sharp and dull at once. Every breath was like swallowing fire. But as the warmth sank deeper, the pain lifted from heavy fog to light mist, leaving her a little less lost and a little more at ease.

There was music in her blood, familiar, as quiet and essential as her next breath. All the vulnerable, creature parts of her body relaxed and gave in to it, acknowledging that the danger of the storm had passed—that this, finally, was shelter.

For the first time in years, she fell asleep knowing she was safe.

She woke not in Jassi's bed, but her own. She blinked, disoriented, and turned her face into a mound of fur.

"Mmph," she grunted. Kutaa lifted his head. "You're too warm."

Her voice was hoarse, but the pain was only a fraction of what it had been before. She touched the base of her throat and pressed experimentally. No bruising.

"Kajal?"

Tav sat on the edge of the bed, haggard and troubled.

"You healed me," she said.

He reached out and then paused, waiting for her consent. She nodded. His calluses were rough against the soft skin of her throat.

"Hopefully I managed to undo most of the damage," he said. "How do you feel?"

She sat up and leaned against Kutaa. "Fine, actually." Being strangled was a traumatic experience for the body, but she was only tired and sore, as if she'd done a hard day's labor. "I guess being the deva has its perks."

His healing was nothing short of a miracle, which surpassed Ayurveda by leagues. The wheels in her mind immediately began to turn, wondering what would happen if she could channel that magic. Could she better detect illness and injury, or modify bodies? Could she resurrect multiple people at once?

She'd spent years learning the mechanics of the body and how it worked, how it could be healed, how it could be altered. Yet it had taken Tav moments to do what would have taken her hours, if not days. The itch of jealousy returned.

At least it seemed to have taken a lot out of him, which meant his powers had a limit.

"So that was the bhuta," he muttered. "Your sister."

"You could see her?"

"No." He lifted a hand in reply. His bangle shone silvery on his wrist. "But this grew ice-cold when I came near."

Sarbloh bangles were made of pure iron, and rakshasas—including bhutas, apparently—were known to detest the metal. Kajal thought back to Vritika's hiss; her bangle must have grown cold too.

Kajal paled. "Vritika, is she—?"

"No one's died," he assured her. "I think my yakshas have weakened the bhuta for the time being."

Kajal slung an arm around Kutaa's thick neck with a relieved sigh. "When I refuse the bhuta a kill, it attacks me instead. But last time, that didn't stop it from taking a life. That's why Riddhi . . ." She quietly cleared her throat. "I can't control it, at least not anymore. Maybe I never could."

His expression tightened. "Then I hope the rebels come back with your sister's body soon."

"They better."

She'd gotten lucky that Vritika hadn't also dropped dead. But Kajal knew how suspect she must look to the demon hunter in training. Her days at the university were numbered.

"We need to leave for the Harama Plain," she decided. "Now."

"But you were just—"

"We're going *now.*" She touched her neck again. Even the scratches she'd clawed into her own flesh were gone. "And if you think one bhuta is troublesome, then be prepared to have a really bad day tomorrow."

Chapter Eighteen

THEY NEEDED A horse.

"It doesn't feel right to steal an animal," Tav muttered as they crouched in the foliage outside the university walls. There was a separate gate for guards and soldiers that led into the Tortoise Court, where the barracks were. A few guards were riding up to it after what Kajal assumed was sentry duty.

"We're not stealing one," she whispered back. "We're borrowing one."

"That's not much better."

"Do you have money for a mount, O Hallowed Deva of One Hundred Morals?"

He sighed in resignation.

The guards dismounted. Kajal patted Kutaa's side, and the dog slipped through the underbrush, making enough racket to cause the horses to grow skittish. That, combined with Kutaa's smell, had them pulling at their reins.

"What's wrong with you?" one of the guards complained. "It's probably just a monkey."

Beside her, Tav's eyes glowed blue. The horses bolted. The guards gave chase and Tav held out his hand, making a beckoning gesture. One of the calmer horses stopped, tail swishing, before it turned and sedately walked toward them.

"How does that work, exactly?" Kajal asked as Tav took hold of the fallen reins. "This thing you have with animals."

He shrugged, the light leaving his eyes. "I'm not entirely sure. It's innate. I can't sense their thoughts, but I can feel their sattvic energy. It's sort of like a string between us."

"Like a puppet master and his puppet."

He narrowed his eyes. *"No."*

"Does the asura have a similar connection?"

"Mostly with rakshasas, but yes. Although he was always better with people than I was." His hands were suddenly on her waist. "We don't have long until they return."

"Hey!" She smacked at him, and he yanked his hands away.

"Do you want to get on the horse or not?" he demanded.

"I can get on myself." Although the only horse she'd mounted on her own had been an aga ghora, and it had gone to the trouble of kneeling to make it easier.

Tav passed her the reins. "Fine. Go ahead."

Kajal stood up straighter at the challenge. The horse was standing placidly beside her, a brown gelding that probably weighed the same as about a dozen of her. She shoved her right foot through the stirrup.

"Wrong foot," he said. "You'll end up sitting backward."

Before she could snap *I know that,* the guards' voices filtered through the trees as they returned with the runaway horse. The gelding, hearing them, began to walk forward.

"No no no *no.*" Kajal awkwardly hopped along beside it, frantically grabbing at the saddle. "Stop! *Stop!*"

She craned her neck to see Tav standing in the same spot, arms crossed and eyebrows raised. "Good job," he drawled. "Interesting technique."

"Shut up and *help me.*"

"I thought you didn't need help."

Kajal held in a strangled scream and launched herself at the saddle. There was only minimal flailing as she hauled herself over and landed on her stomach with an *oof*.

A choked-off noise came from where Tav was standing.

"You better not be laughing at me," she warned. "I can and *will* poison you when you least expect it."

"Noted." Tav took the reins and led them farther into the trees. "Are you done?"

"I got on, didn't I?" Never mind that she felt like a sack of rice thrown over the saddle.

Kutaa came out of the brush as she slid one leg over the beast to properly sit up. When Tav made to get up behind her, she shoved a hand in his face.

"Get your own horse," she demanded.

"The guards are almost here," he said, muffled by her palm. He pushed it away. "We can't risk taking another."

"Ride in front of me, then."

"Why?"

"Just do it."

Tav's brow furrowed, but she didn't relent. Muttering to himself, he shifted his stance and effortlessly swung up in front of her.

They were nestled far too close for her comfort. But at least this way she wouldn't be ensnared by his arms, made to feel small and trapped.

"Hold on to me," he said. He shifted his weight forward to get the horse moving, swaying with its momentum.

She wrapped one arm around his waist. She'd never been pressed up against a boy before. He carried the scent of grass and the cha he'd had this morning, a gentle blend of nature and spice. His back was a flat, warm expanse, unfamiliar and also oddly inviting, as if encouraging her to lay her cheek upon it.

Kajal shook the thought away. She was only marveling that her creation could exude such heat when she herself ran so cold.

They traveled for a few hours, avoiding the roads. When the sun sank, they were forced to stop for the night in a wooded area. Like during her travel with the rebels, Kajal's legs were sore when she slipped off the saddle, and she braced herself against Kutaa. She didn't have Sezal's pouch of chamomile, but she had something better.

"To what extent can you use your power?" she asked once Tav pulled the saddle off the horse. "What's an injury you couldn't heal?"

"You're still on about this?"

Earlier, Kajal had pressed her fingertips as softly as possible over the knob at the top of his spine, using the point to try and delve into his channels and suss out what fueled his power. He'd immediately told her to cut it out.

"It's not every day I get to study a deva," she argued. "If I learn more about your healing, it could help when I revive Advaith and Lasya."

Tav thought it over, then gave the horse a pat and approached her. "I don't know what my limits are. During Bakshi's campaign, I volunteered a lot in the triage tents, but I couldn't use the full extent of my power without being discovered. The soldiers whose wounds were fatal . . ." His eyes grew distant, rousing only when Kutaa butted his thigh. He reached down to scratch behind the dog's ears. "I don't know if I could have saved them."

Kajal pretended she hadn't seen his lapse. "What about sickness?"

"Same thing. Smaller issues—indigestion, headaches, sore throats—I could cure without a problem."

"And the terminal ones?"

Tav didn't answer, his hand stilling on Kutaa's head. Too late, Kajal recalled that his mother had died of fever.

Of course he would have tried to save her, even as a young boy who probably hadn't gained control of his abilities.

"Sorry," she whispered.

He shook his head and knelt before her. Kajal tensed, her stomach turning fluttery and strange as he pressed his fingertips to just above her knees. Blue ringed his brown irises, and though the process was too gradual to discern any sudden change, her soreness was gone by the time he leaned away.

"Amazing." She bent one of her legs; there was no twinge, no ache. "When we get back to the university, I'm going to need you to do this again so I can better focus on how this works."

"You'd have to be injured for that."

"Then I'll injure myself."

He made a sound like a dying eagle in free fall. "Don't do that! What's wrong with you?"

"You want the long list, or the short one?" She nodded toward the lake. "Let's refill our waterskins."

The field around them was shadowed, the moon a smiling crescent. The lake looked touched by silver, broken only by the rushes and milk-weed growing along its perimeter. Kajal debated plucking some of the milkweed to squeeze its poisonous sap into her almond extract.

Then she noticed that the center of the lake was dark. Something floated on its surface.

Something dead.

She flung her arm in front of Tav, who was leading the horse toward the lake.

"What is it?" he asked.

"I don't know. Stay here."

Of course he didn't listen to her. As she crept forward, his footfalls and the horse's hooves were heavy in the grass behind her. The night was eerily quiet otherwise, not even the hoot of an owl or the sigh of wind to disturb it.

Once she reached the rushes, she could better make out the shape. It was a large fish, its scales iridescent in the moonlight.

"A pani sudhata?" Tav took a few steps forward, water lapping at his boots. "How—"

"Stop!" Kajal pulled him back. "Look closer."

Between its rainbow scales were twisting veins of black. Even from where she stood, Kajal smelled a hint of putrid smoke.

"It's blighted," she whispered.

Tav's eyes were round as he stared at the dead yaksha. "*This* is the blight you spoke of? I thought it was only affecting the land."

"And what's tied to the land?" She gestured at the nature yaksha. The pani sudhata were meant to keep bodies of water purified. She couldn't imagine a more ironic death. "I've seen blighted crops, a deer, and even a pujari, but this is the first blighted yaksha that I know of."

This new development set off an internal alarm bell. If even the yakshas were dying, had the corrupted soil already distorted her sister beyond recognition, like it had the pujari? Would she even be able to revive Lasya if her body was afflicted?

Ride fast, she urged Vivaan and Sezal. No matter the reckoning she'd meet with when she and Tav revealed the truth, so long as she had Lasya, she could weather it.

The horse, catching the scent of blight, nervously backed away with flicking ears. When Tav pulled on its reins to keep it close, it spooked and shook its head with a shrill sound, yanking out of Tav's hold and bolting. Tav cursed and chased after.

Kajal's heart was in her throat, goosebumps running up and down her arms with the horse's cry. She knew exactly how it felt.

Facing the dead yaksha, she took a deep breath. Then, slowly, she waded into the lake.

It was perhaps not the smartest thing to do. If the pani sudhata was corrupted, there was a chance the water was too. But she felt compelled to understand what had caused it to suffer the same fate as the pujari.

The rippling water and her breaths were the night's only sounds. The fish bobbed gently under the current she made with her steps. Was it truly dead, or only pretending? Did it want her to come near enough to infect her? Kajal tried not to choke on the burning smell as she reached for the yaksha's glimmering scales.

Something yanked the body under the water's surface.

Kajal lurched backward, nearly tripping over the lake bed as she rushed to the shore. She crawled onto the grass, breaths wheezing out of a tight chest.

A soft laugh sounded behind her. She turned around.

In the place where the yaksha had been floating was a head. A familiar one.

"Bad idea, little girl," the nagi crooned, the same one who'd accosted her under the hawthorn tree. "Were you not warned to beware dark things?"

Kajal swallowed hard. "Did . . . Did you do this?"

The nagi's smile twisted into a frown as she rose higher from the water. She tossed the yaksha onto the grass, and Kajal scrambled away from it.

"We do not control the halahala," the nagi whispered. "It spreads in a tide no living thing can outrun."

Kajal wrenched her gaze from the yaksha. "'Halahala'? What is that?"

The nagi swam closer. "Poison. Scourge. *Death.*"

Kajal scanned the field for Tav, silently begging him to return. But questions rattled behind her teeth.

"What else do you know about it?" Kajal asked. "The blight. What you call halahala."

The nagi preened, as if satisfied to hold knowledge over Kajal's head. "That it is ancient. That it is vile. That it is a thing born of hatred and violence."

The Harama Plain. "Would a battle resulting in thousands of deaths be enough to cause it?"

"No."

Kajal was taken aback, though she tried not to show it lest it excite the nagi more. "Then how?"

The nagi swam in a lazy circle, her tail rising above the surface like the hump of a whale. "It must be a clash of power." She revealed her sharp teeth in a grin. "Of opposites."

Although the night was humid against Kajal's skin, her soaked trousers made her shudder.

The nagi laughed with a sound like rattling pebbles and flicked the end of her tail out of the water. She began to recite:

"Side by side they make their stand,
Together fighting hand in hand.
The earth blooms green, the nectar sweet.

Churning waters and blood-soaked ground,
Metal strikes with fearsome sound.
The venom swells below their feet."

Kajal had never heard the rhyme before, but it was familiar regardless. "I don't understand," she admitted at last. "Say it plainly."

"It is all I know," the nagi said, solemn. "The nagas were there at the beginning, and we will be there for the end. That end is not for us to determine."

She glided back to the middle of the lake. Kajal gained her feet.

"The water," Kajal blurted. "Won't it hurt you if it's poisoned?"

The nagi turned, black hair fanning out around her.

"The nagas commune with death, but it's a realm that is beyond us," she said. "As you should know."

The nagi silently slipped under the water.

By the time Tav returned with the horse, Kajal was sitting by the yaksha's body, staring unseeing at the black threaded through its scales. Tav fell to his knees before it.

Kajal lunged toward him. "Wait—!"

But he was already pressing his fingers to the unblighted scales and delving into his power, eyes glowing like ghost lights against the dark. The rest of him pulsed a steady blue, which crept over the yaksha's still body.

"Tav," she whispered.

He didn't relent. He pressed his lips into a thin line, arms shaking at the strain. Minutes passed, but the black threads remained. Blood trickled from his nose.

Kajal grabbed him by the shoulders. *"Tav."*

He finally let go with a gasp. He fell back, shoulders trembling under her hands.

"Damn it," he growled, punching the ground hard enough to leave an indentation. *"Damn it."*

She had asked him what the extent of his power was, if there was an injury he couldn't heal. Now she had her answer.

Chapter Nineteen

KAJAL DECIDED TELLING Tav about the nagi could wait. He'd become withdrawn after failing to heal the yaksha, and Kutaa slept beside him through the night. He barely spoke, even when they resaddled the horse the next day and took off in the dreary, gray dawn.

She handed him some nuts she'd packed away, but he only murmured a faint thank-you. They lay forgotten in his palm while he fiddled with his amber pendant. She couldn't see his expression from this angle, but she didn't need to; his grief lay like a thick cloud over them.

She didn't know how to comfort others. That was Lasya's strength. Instead, she ran the nagi's words through her head over and over, trying to make sense of them.

The nagas commune with death, but it's a realm that is beyond us. As you should know.

Kajal's hand flexed, remembering the way her coffin lid had scraped her knuckles.

In the end, she couldn't stay silent. "Your memories," she began, keeping her voice quiet yet feeling Tav flinch against her anyway. "How much do you remember?"

"About the battle?"

"All of it."

"I remember most of my life, if that's what you're asking. My family. My responsibilities. Journeying to Patala and Svarga with Advaith. Di—" He cut off sharply, and his shoulders curled inward. Kajal was glad she couldn't see his face.

"I remember Bakshi's campaign," he whispered once he'd regained his composure. "With growing prejudice against the rakshasa races, demon hunters became popular. Advaith and our father worked to dismantle them, to lay down protections for the rakshasas, but Bakshi twisted it by saying the king cared more for the safety of demons than for his own people. He used the resulting outcry to point out every minor mistake my parents had made: broken trade agreements, how much money was spent on military instead of infrastructure, the supposed increase of witchcraft . . ."

Kajal grunted at that last part.

"Bakshi's influence was strong enough for him to build a small yet dedicated army. My father wasn't a perfect king, but a perfect king does not exist. Bakshi killed him for it anyway. I remember riding toward the Harama Plain with my troops after I learned he was dead, thinking Advaith was safe at the fort." A bitter laugh fell from his mouth. "And that's it."

"Your memories stop at the Harama Plain?"

"The battle is just images, sounds, feelings." He hesitated. "Although I remember my life, there are holes. Missing faces, names, places. I feel as if I *should* know them, but they're . . . gone."

Kajal hummed and wondered how to remedy that. To ensure that when she resurrected Lasya, she would come back as perfect and whole as she'd been in life, with not a memory out of place.

And beyond that, because it was the least she could do for Tav.

"Tell me about Advaith," she said. It was partly a bid to drag him out of his gloomy demeanor, partly because she wanted to know more about the crown prince. "About how you grew up together."

"Well . . . when we were fifteen, there was a military parade in Malhir. Baa-Ji wanted Advaith to do a demonstration—with a sword, not his trishul, of course—and Advaith, loving attention, was more than happy to oblige him."

Tav rubbed a thumb against the rein's stitching. "He could tell I was jealous, though. Growing up, Adi had always been more of a scholar, while I spent most of my time training and learning how to wield different weapons. So he came to my room that night with some spicy chakli to bribe me into switching places with him for the demonstration."

"Spicy chakli?"

"Mm. It was—is—my favorite snack. I tried to warn him that Baa-Ji would know, but Advaith didn't care about those sorts of things." She could hear the eye roll in his words. "He *never* got in trouble," he mumbled with no small amount of annoyance. "He could charm even the surliest rakshasa. He could probably charm a rock."

Kajal's lips turned up at the image of Advaith's beaming smile next to Tav's scowl. "Did you switch places?"

"Yes. And I *loved* it. The crowd cheered as I went through my sword forms and sparred against one of the generals. Who did *not* let me win, by the way," he said quickly, like it was an old argument. "But, as I had warned Adi, Baa-Ji was furious at us for making the switch. I didn't regret it, though. And after, Advaith brought more spicy chakli to my room to go over the fight beat by beat."

There was pride in his voice, and the same fondness Kajal felt for Lasya, an exasperated affection that laid the foundation for their relationship. But now that his story was done, Tav began to slump again, remembering exactly what he had lost.

His grief seemed impenetrable. Kajal understood that, respected it, but wondered if she should acknowledge it. Tav might harbor the same inner desires Kajal had once had, the desperate plea to not be alone.

Carefully, she rested a hand against his back, rubbing a small circle the way Lasya would have. Tav tensed for a second before his muscles loosened under her touch, and a long, weary sigh left him. Kajal kept her hand there a moment longer before letting it drop, the two of them riding on in somewhat lighter silence.

An hour later, Tav reined in the horse. Beyond them stretched the field Kajal had never wanted to lay eyes on again, its barrows bleak and eerie under a stormy sky.

But there was one difference. Black streaks had snaked through the dirt and veined over the mounds, pulsing and putrid. The horse danced sideways with a snort and Kutaa raised his hackles.

"This is . . ." Tav's voice cracked. "This is where we . . ."

He dismounted and made to run straight into the field. Just as she'd prevented him from careening into the lake last night, Kajal grabbed his collar.

"Bhutas," she hissed. "They're attracted to loud noises and big emotions. Calm down first."

Uttering a sound of frustration, he folded his legs to sit on the ground in a meditative pose with his hands in the dhyana mudra, one hand on top of the other, with thumbs touching. Kutaa sat beside him, ears forward, on alert.

Kajal slid off the horse and tied its reins to a tree. Then she approached the nearest black vein and squatted to inspect it. The smell was the same as the blighted yaksha's—smoky and rotten. *Wrong*. It wasn't liquid or solid but something in between, tar-like yet alive. She imagined if she touched it, it would rise up and devour her whole.

Halahala. Poison. Made from violence—but how?

When she returned to Tav, his shoulders were crowded with white butterflies. Though he remained in his meditative pose, his eyes were open, staring at the Harama Plain.

Kajal had no intention of returning to Siphar, to the place where she had almost died. Where Lasya *had* died. If she did, she'd probably look something like this, a cacophony of fury and anguish. It was strange—almost absurd—how one physical spot could hold so much misery.

"You know," she said, breaking him out of his thoughts, "you very nearly stopped me from taking your body."

"I did?" The way his face fell into concerned dismay made her want to smile, though she had no idea why. "I . . . The bhuta didn't hurt you, did it?"

"No, just gave me a scare. Lasya fought you off."

Tav dropped his hands out of the mudra and settled them on his knees. "I don't remember any of it. Just pain, and . . ." He swallowed hard, his throat bobbing.

Kajal recalled the two identical wounds on his abdomen and wondered yet again what had caused them. One of the butterflies landed on her sleeve. "They helped me. Before."

"Really? How?"

"When we were trying to find Advaith, one of them appeared and led me straight to your body."

Hope lightened his expression. "Maybe they can help us find my brother."

He stood and lifted his arms in a silent order. The butterflies took off, heading into the field as if they had nothing to fear. But Kajal could already feel the chill of the bhutas, the faint whispering menace calling to her. There had to be a faster way.

When she had chased Tav through the university, Kutaa had followed his scent. She didn't know if twins shared a smell, but it was worth a shot. Besides, dogs were supposed to be good at scavenging in places like this.

She grabbed Tav's arm and shoved his hand in front of Kutaa's nose. "Can you find a scent like this one?" she asked.

Kutaa sniffed Tav's hand, pressing his nose into his palm. He sneezed slightly and stalked forward.

"Will that work?" Tav asked.

Kajal steeled herself to follow after Kutaa. "It better."

It was like walking through a veil of icy water, stepping from spring to winter. Tav shivered as his eyes darted from mound to mound. The air was dense here, leaving an ashen taste in Kajal's mouth. She sensed them being watched. Followed.

"Steady," she whispered as Kutaa searched, head down and ears flat. The butterflies kept landing on the mounds and fluttering away quickly, repelled by the blight crawling over them. "Keep calm."

She knew it was a useless thing to say. Tav's soldiers had fallen here, and now he was wending through their graves, the set of his mouth grim and his eyes overly bright.

Something plucked the sleeve of her kurti, tugged the end of her braid. She kept moving forward, trying to ignore the pounding of her heart. The distant cries of battle rose and waned with the wind.

A low hum on her right snagged her attention. There was nothing there—only diseased, forsaken ground. But when she looked away, the hum grew persistent, eventually forcing her gaze back to the same spot.

Where there was emptiness before now stood a soldier. Not the wraith-like form of a bhuta, but a tangible, walking corpse.

Kajal collided into Tav. He grabbed her arms and whispered, "What—?" before he saw the same thing.

The soldier was filthy, the green fabric and brass nails of his chilta hazar masha covered in dirt and dried, browned blood. His helmet was gone, revealing a head that had been brutally caved in on one side by some large, blunt weapon. Bits of stark white bone peeked through, one of his eyeballs dangling from its socket.

"What's happening?" Tav's fingers dug into Kajal's arms. "I thought there were only bhutas here?"

Kajal couldn't take her eyes off the soldier. He stood listing to one side, mouth slack, arms hanging loose. There was no sign of decay on him, but through the blood and dirt she detected thin ribbons of black creeping down his hands and up his neck, toward his face.

The blight had taken over the barrows, infecting the bodies. Had their bhutas been forced back inside their ruined flesh, allowing them to break free of their graves?

Whispers rushed by on the wind as her heart pounded, and the soldier took an ungainly step forward. Tav pulled her behind him.

"What do we do?" he whispered.

It took her a couple attempts to speak. "D-Don't react. Keep going."

"Don't react?"

"It's what they want." The bhutas may have repossessed their bodies, but they likely hunted the same way. Kajal twisted out of his grip and gestured for Kutaa to go on ahead. "If we leave them alone, maybe they'll leave *us* alone."

Tav's mouth worked soundlessly. Even Kutaa looked between her and the shuffling soldier as if trying to decide whether to heed her order or attack. At her insistent nod, he continued to sniff his way through the barrows.

Despite the cold, the dogged pursuit of the soldier behind them sent hot sparks of panic through her. For the first time, she realized they should have procured some sort of weapon for Tav. She had a scalpel, but what good would that do against the undead?

A fist punched through the nearest mound, and Kajal slapped a hand over her mouth. The soldier that broke free stared at them with blank eyes, blood splashed across her face. She pitifully crawled after them, gray hands clawing through the dirt, the ropy intestines that spilled from her stomach dragging behind her.

"Geetha," Tav breathed. Kajal read horror in the rounding of his eyes and the trembling of his mouth.

"Don't look at them," Kajal warned. "Stop feeding your emotions."

Tav labored for breath. He shut his eyes and assumed the mudra again, whispering mantras under his breath. The corpse slowed down, but barely.

All around them, the barrows shook and cracked. Kutaa growled as bodies rose, more and more of Tav's soldiers coming to welcome their leader back.

Kajal pushed Tav between the shoulder blades. "Kutaa, hurry!"

The dog started trotting. The butterflies abandoned their search, fluttering above crumbling earth and flailing limbs. Tav continued to whisper mantras, which kept the soldiers sitting in their graves or swaying where they stood.

The harder Kajal's heart beat, the louder she heard the tune of *Lotus Blossom*. If Lasya showed up, would she attack the bhutas, or return to strangling Kajal?

She didn't want to find out.

Finally, Kutaa stopped beside a mound slightly smaller than the others. It was intact, and far enough away from the edges of the field to not yet be touched by blight. Only a few feet away lay the remains of Tav's own grave, his abandoned armor gleaming dully in the gray light.

Kajal didn't know whether to laugh or swear. Advaith had been *this* close?

"Is this . . . ?" Tav knelt beside Kutaa, hands hovering over the mound. In the distance, the undead soldiers watched on—unmoving, silent.

He glanced at the armor they'd abandoned last time. "Is that where you found me?"

Kajal nodded.

"This doesn't make sense. How could he have been here, next to me?"

Kajal wetted her chapped lips as the whine blew through her ears. "Maybe it has something to do with the holes in your memory."

Tav's butterflies flapped in agitation above him. The soldiers twitched and moved forward.

"Emotions," Kajal reminded him.

Tav took a deep breath. Another. The soldiers paused again. Kajal came around the other side, facing him, and their eyes met with determination.

Quickly, they dug through the mound with their hands. Dirt collected under Kajal's nails, carrying the iron-rich smell of blood. For a moment, she was outside of Siphar, carving out a grave in damp earth. The whine flared.

The soil gave way and revealed an arm, then part of a chest. Tav exhaled as if someone had kicked him, and dug faster. Even Kutaa helped by pawing at the base of the mound. The body was dressed not in the chilta hazar masha of the soldiers, but in a simple red padded tunic, which was stiff with old blood. Kajal uncovered a hand, a gold-and-ruby ring shining on its fourth finger.

Tav pushed away more dirt in an effort to uncover his brother's face. "It's him. He's—" Tav froze.

When Kajal realized why, a javelin of ice shot down her spine.

Advaith's head was missing.

Tav stared, uncomprehending, at the sharp line of his brother's neck. Kutaa whined, and Kajal tore her gaze away to see what the dog had found—or rather, not found.

The prince's bottom half was also missing. Everything below the waist was gone, his body ending in a stump of exposed meat and bone.

Kajal didn't know when her hands began to shake. Didn't know when the whine began to climb higher. Didn't know when the soldiers began not to shamble but to run.

Kutaa barked, jolting her into action. She leapt over Advaith's torso and grabbed Tav.

"Stop!" she yelled. "The soldiers—"

"Why?" The single word was strangled. *"Why is he like this?"*

"I don't know, but—"

"Where's his head?" Tav scrambled around in the dirt as if the crown prince's head was merely buried under its own tiny mound. "Where are his *legs*?"

"Tav!"

He noticed the advancing soldiers. He stood and held out his hands, squeezing his eyes shut as he chanted in a low voice.

"Sudarshana chakra, enlighten me with the gods' will." Sweat ran in rivulets down his temples. "Sudarshana chakra, grant me the power to defend."

He repeated the mantra once more, but the weapon refused to materialize in his waiting hands. The corpses were closing in. With a curse, Tav dove for the remains of his barrow, grabbing the rusted talwar Kajal and the rebels had left behind. Kajal took out her scalpel.

Tav pointed the talwar's tip at the soldiers. "I don't want to hurt you." One of them stepped out ahead, a large man with a mustache plastered in blood. "Jaideep, please—"

But whoever Jaideep was or had once been, he didn't recognize the prince now. The corpse lunged forward, ready to grab and rend.

Tav moved. It was swift and elegant, hardly more than a flash of steel and light, the deva's energy coating the blade like blue fire. Jaideep staggered, arms severed at the elbows.

As Tav fended off the soldiers, Kajal grabbed Advaith's arms to pull him away. He wasn't that heavy—missing half a body helped—and Kajal managed to wrap an arm around his chest.

"Damn it," she panted. Kutaa stood before her, snapping his jaws at the soldiers. "Why did you have to be—"

Her words fled. There, under the spot where her hand pressed against Advaith's chest, came a faint flutter.

It was weak and abnormally slow, but there was no mistaking it. Advaith's heart was beating.

Nausea roiled through her. She nearly hurled the torso away from her, but she was too stricken to do more than stare at the exposed stump of the prince's neck.

Kutaa barked, startling her into looking up. No matter how fast and skilled Tav was, there were too many blighted bodies around them, black veins pulsing along their skin. One woman staggered forward as black bile poured from her mouth and down her chin.

"Don't touch the blight!" Kajal called. "It's poison!"

Tav kicked the woman away and backed up. The tide of dead continued to press in. Tav couldn't cut down every soldier on his own. Kajal had to do something.

She had to make a path for them to escape.

Kajal ducked her head. Though she had ignored and resisted the whine before, she now focused on its thin, high note of warning. The melody of *Lotus Blossom* threaded through the sound, soft and discordant, and she joined in with her own harmony.

She had never called upon the bhuta before. It had always been Lasya's decision, Lasya's intention, to appear when she wanted. But if Kajal granted her permission to wreak destruction after having denied her . . .

"Lasya," she whispered under the din. "Lasya, I need help."

The whine faded and the melody cut off. Kajal opened her eyes. Before her floated her sister's specter, eyes burning crimson in the gloom. It was as if she was silently passing judgment—determining whether or not they should pick up where they'd left off. Lasya's face was inscrutable, terrible and cold, the darkened side of a globe when turned away from the light.

But there had to be light in there somewhere. Kajal couldn't risk believing otherwise.

At last, Lasya turned and moved toward Tav. As he lifted his weapon to block an advancing soldier, Lasya raised her hand and blasted Tav backward.

He tumbled through the dirt and stopped near where Kajal crouched with Advaith's body.

Coughing, Tav got to his knees. "What—?" He couldn't see Lasya, but he noticed Kajal's expression. "Is . . . Is that her?"

Kajal, throat too tight to speak, could only nod.

She wasn't controlling Lasya. She had only pleaded for protection and laid herself at her sister's mercy. It seemed Lasya had decided to be generous today.

Lasya faced the blighted bodies and spread her hands out before her. The whine kicked up again, shrill enough to make Kajal cringe. A vaporous light surrounded the bhuta, shooting out from the tips of her fingers as if they were arrows.

They pierced the soldiers through the chest. The bodies convulsed, staggering and shivering and letting out ghastly keens. Tav gripped his sword tight, the radiance along the blade sputtering.

Then, one by one, the soldiers turned and walked or crawled back to their barrows. Kajal's hold on Advaith loosened as they lay down and let the diseased earth creep over their bodies, shrouding them from further decay.

Lasya lowered her arms and looked over her shoulder at Kajal. Their eyes met, one pair dark and the other red.

"Burn me," Lasya said, her voice no longer a ghostly whisper, but flat and clear. "Kill me."

Then she was gone.

Kajal slumped over and caught her breath. Her vision spun as she dug her fingertips into the dirt, pulse pounding like a war drum.

Lasya had saved her before at the Harama Plain, but that had been a whirlwind of furious rage and strength, a stalling tactic. This time, her power had been controlled, deliberate, and strong enough to overcome the other bhutas' wills.

Her sister was becoming far too powerful. Then again, without her, Kajal and Tav would have been torn limb from limb. Was this something Kajal could replicate? Could Lasya be not just a vengeful spirit, but a weapon?

Kajal was immediately flooded with shame. Lasya was not something to be *used*. Her gentle sister would never have wanted to be a weapon—would never have wanted to become one of Kajal's experiments. Would never have wanted to be a bhuta.

"Kajal?" Tav put a hand on her shoulder. "Did she hurt you again?"

"No. No, I'm fine." She shifted and realized she was still holding Advaith. "I . . . His heart . . ."

Tav's hand dropped to his brother's chest, and he felt the unnatural pulse for himself. He turned nearly as gray as the corpses. "How is this possible? He's— He's *dead*, he—" His voice was thick with anguish. "No one can suffer these injuries and still be alive!"

"I have no idea. Do you smell any of his missing limbs around?" she asked Kutaa, who gave a soft huff, which she took to mean no.

Tav stared down at his dismembered brother, tears leaving clear paths on his dirty cheeks.

"How are we supposed to resurrect him if he's not whole?" Tav whispered.

Kajal didn't know. She had performed wonders with Kutaa and Tav, but to bring the crown prince back now would be a true marvel.

Chapter Twenty

THEY RODE BACK to Suraj in silence. Kajal had brought the same bag Tav's corpse had been stored in, packed now with unblighted dirt and what was left of Advaith's body. It lay behind her like saddlebags.

She couldn't stop dwelling on its faint heartbeat, or what it could possibly mean. She rubbed her hand against her thigh as if to dislodge the sensation. Still, the larger part of her longed to study the torso, wondering about its circulation—there was no *blood*—or whether this indicated Advaith wasn't truly dead.

She doubted Tav would appreciate the scrutiny, though.

Tav didn't want to exhaust their horse, so they took a couple breaks to sit in the grass and nibble on venison jerky and nuts. Whenever Kajal glanced at him, he was either staring off at nothing or at the canvas bag.

Kajal thought of the cracks in the walls of the royal quarters. The way they'd spread and fractured with time, growing more perilous with neglect.

She scratched behind Kutaa's ears and cleared her throat. "Once, I stole a sarbloh bangle for Lasya. She had been upset because we didn't have any, and I hated her being upset. When I found a vendor in a city we were passing through, I took one."

Tav's hand drifted to his own bangle, hidden under his sleeve—the reminder of the cosmic significance one person could have upon the world.

"I thought she'd be happy." Kajal scoffed, the noise making Kutaa's ears twitch. "I should have known better. The fact that I took something we didn't need to survive made her angry. Well, mostly sad. She hardly ever got angry. Truly angry, I mean."

"Did she make you return it?"

"Absolutely. But she was smart enough to know that if I apologized to the vendor, I'd get beaten for stealing it in the first place. So instead, she caused a distraction. She pretended to run into someone in front of the vendor's cart and break her nose. She even had a vial of pomegranate juice to use as blood. There was a whole commotion, and the vendor got involved, which allowed me to slip the bangle back without being seen."

The corner of Tav's mouth quirked. "I take it you didn't steal again after that?"

"Oh, I did." She held in a laugh at Tav's withering expression. "But I made a point to never let Lasya see." Though Kajal was fairly sure her sister had known and had chosen not to say anything. "Sometime later, we were searching through piles of trash for anything useful—things we could sell, eat, repurpose—and I found a copper ring. I cleaned it up and gave it to her as an apology. It was too small to fit on any finger except her pinkie, and it stained her skin green, but she loved it."

Tav's gaze had softened. On his chest, the amber pendant gleamed, the lotus petal inside trapped in time like all of Kajal's memories. Seeing his own memories stir behind his eyes, Kajal gently nudged Kutaa, who went to settle beside Tav instead. Tav wrapped his arms around the dog and leaned his weight against him.

"It must have been a difficult life," Tav said at last.

"That coming from someone who grew up in a literal palace." He side-eyed her, and she grinned. "We had each other. That's all we really needed."

He nodded, and his gaze strayed toward the canvas bag again.

"We'll find the rest of him," Kajal assured him.

Kajal wanted Lasya back, *needed* her back, and Tav deserved the same reunion with his brother. The world needed the asura and deva.

Tav hid part of his face in Kutaa's fur. Either he didn't believe her, or his hope was so riotous he was trying to keep it at bay.

Kajal understood the feeling.

By the time they reached the university, night had fallen. The sandstone fortress was dark atop its hill, its windows like eyes watching the field for their return.

Dread had been solidifying inside Kajal since leaving the Harama Plain. It had built up deposits in her veins, in the base of her lungs, pieces breaking off and dissolving in her bloodstream.

"What's wrong?" Tav's voice was quiet over the night's unobtrusive sounds, from the susurrous grass to the horse's plodding steps.

Kajal exhaled a mirthless laugh and rested her head between his shoulders. "Everything." Soon she would reunite with her sister's body and make good on her promise. She would also have to admit the truth to the rebels, and she had a suspicion they wouldn't be happy to find out their precious prince's body was in pieces.

He started at her touch but didn't move away. "Seems like an understatement."

"Is it ever."

They dismounted at the base of the promontory. After pulling Advaith down, Tav took the horse's head between his hands and pressed his forehead to the animal's, blue light flickering between them. The horse's tail swished once before it turned and made its way sedately up the hill.

Tav and Kajal went in the opposite direction, toward the royal quarters. They'd agreed it was the best place to store the body for now. Bringing it to the laboratory would be too risky.

"I don't even know where to begin with finding the rest of him," Tav said after he helped Kajal get the bag over the wall. She'd told Kutaa to go around and slip through the front gates. It was a new moon, and the overgrown gardens were thrown into deep shadow.

"Do you think Bakshi did this?" Kajal asked. "Would he have, I don't know, kept Advaith's head as a trophy or something?"

Tav hefted the bag into his arms. "That seems too crass for Bakshi. He always presented himself as someone of sophistication. But I guess it can't be ruled out."

They followed the same path they'd taken before to get to Advaith's room. The walls bore down on them from either side, their footsteps far too loud. Kajal felt as if the place were coming alive, recognizing the return of both its princes.

"When the rebels get back, I'm resurrecting Lasya first," Kajal said as they reached Advaith's door. "She's my priority. Then we can tell them about Advaith."

He met her eyes. "I know. If you need my help in any way, I'll do what I can."

Kajal was still unused to receiving things. It sent an uncomfortable itch between her shoulder blades. "And you're . . . all right with that?"

"Yes. We're in this together, remember?"

Together. It was a word she never thought she'd apply to anyone but Lasya. Strangely, it didn't leave her mouth coated in ash; every bone in her body wanted to embrace it, to revel in the simple statement of *I am not alone*.

Kajal didn't know how to respond, didn't want Tav to see her flush, so she opened the door and entered Advaith's room.

Too late, she realized there was a lantern lit on top of the desk, throwing three waiting figures into silhouette.

Kajal whipped out her scalpel, and Tav grabbed the rusty talwar he'd brought with him from the Harama Plain. One of the figures turned, and the planes of Jassi's face were highlighted in the lantern's glow. The other two followed, revealing Vivaan and Sezal.

"Kajal," Jassi whispered. "I'm sorry. I tried to explain—"

Vivaan raised a hand to cut her off and stalked forward, emanating the staticky tension of a thunderhead. Tav set the bag against the wall and stepped in front of Kajal.

"It was my idea," Tav said firmly. "We felt that there was no time to waste. We couldn't wait for your return."

Vivaan stared hard at the prince. Then his lips parted in an unfeeling grin.

"You really think that's what this is about?" Vivaan's gaze flitted over Tav's face, something vast and dark stirring behind his eyes. "Stop pretending."

Kajal played dumb. "Pretending what?"

"That this is Advaith Thakar."

The room fell so deathly silent that Kajal could hear the rustle of the lantern's flame. The pulse at her neck jumped, reminding her how much blood the rebels could spill on this dusty floor.

"What are you talking about?" Tav demanded, but the slight waver in his voice gave him away.

Vivaan's not-smile twisted. "I know Advaith. I *knew* Advaith. And you are not him, Tavinder."

Tav rocked backward. Kajal's gorge rose, her face flaring hot as she recalled the look Vivaan had given her that day in the rebels' hideout.

Suspicion. *Realization.*

They'd known this whole time.

"Why did you lie to us?" Sezal asked Kajal. Her voice was plaintive, sorrowful. "Was it just to be reunited with your sister sooner? If you'd told us the truth from the start—"

"They didn't want us knowing this is the deva," Vivaan said. "What was your plan?" he drawled at Kajal. "To use the asura and deva for your own purposes? Were you going to sell them to Bakshi for a place at one of his universities?" He sneered at Tav. "Or maybe you finally found an opportunity to step out of the shadows and take the throne for yourself."

Tav was too stunned to deny it, so Kajal spoke for him. "Have you lost your mind? How did you . . . How do you know what they are?"

Before Vivaan could answer, his gaze swept past Tav, to the canvas bag slumped at the base of the wall. Eyes widening, he hurried toward it.

"Don't," Kajal warned.

Vivaan tore open the bag and pushed away the dirt, stopping at the sight of Advaith's neck.

Sezal gasped and clutched at her throat. Jassi looked between Tav and the new body, brow furrowed in confusion.

"How," came a low growl from Vivaan's throat. *"What did you do to him?"*

"W-We found him like that," Kajal stammered. "We think Bakshi—"

Vivaan roared and punched the wall. His fist blew a hole through the wood, splintering the plaster all the way up to the ceiling. Jassi stumbled into the desk and the lantern wobbled, light tilting dizzyingly through the room.

"Vaan," Sezal called. "This obviously wasn't them."

Vivaan clutched his hair, bent over Advaith. When Sezal made a move toward them, Tav and Kajal retreated farther. Sezal paused.

"If you knew I was lying, then why did you leave?" Kajal asked her. "Did you even find Lasya's body?"

Sezal sighed; Kajal missed the girl's usual cheerfulness. Vivaan slowly rolled up to his full height.

"We left because bringing your notebook to the Vadhia was clearly not enough of a threat," he said lowly. "So we decided on another way to keep you in line."

When he turned, his face was like granite. He reached into his pocket and threw something onto the floor between them.

Kajal stared, uncomprehending. Even when Tav swore, her mind was simply unable to process what she was looking at. It started with the pounding of her heart, the rush of blood in her ears, and the furious heat building in her chest.

A severed pinkie finger. Small, brown, and stained green from where it had once worn a copper ring.

The world shrank to a pinpoint. Inside Kajal a wave was building, longing for nothing so much as to crash into everything in its path. She knew anger like she knew the shape of her hands—the creases and valleys, the low points and the high. Knew when to keep them at her sides for fear of a bigger wave knocking her down, crushing her into pieces.

But this was more than anger. It was fury and fire and the need to pick up her bones and march to battle. It was an unleashed scream that had been building behind her teeth since the day she took her first step into the world and realized she cared more for it than it did for her.

So she'd learned not to care. To trust in only one person, love one person, who'd stubbornly refused to accept that goodness did not exist.

And this boy—this unworthy being—had laid his hands upon her.

The noise that tore from Kajal's throat was barely human. The room shook as she called for the bhuta like she had on the Harama Plain, seeking not protection but destruction. To allow it all the pain and death it craved.

All around them rose a high whine. Lasya formed before her, white funeral dress whipping in a sharp wind that pushed Advaith's belongings off his shelves and made Jassi and Sezal shield their eyes. Though the bhuta was invisible to him, Vivaan stood unflinching, jaw clenched.

Kill him, Kajal seethed. *Make him pay for what he did.*

Lasya didn't move at first. Her eyes penetrated the shadows, hair flowing around her ashen face as if she were underwater. For a moment, Kajal thought she might turn and strike Kajal instead, the creator of her suffering, the reason they had found her body in the first place.

Then Lasya dove straight at Vivaan. Kajal longed for her sister's achingly cold fingers to wrap around his throat and drain the life out of him, making him feel the same helpless fear Kajal had felt in Jassi's flat. Satisfaction was already unfurling like a flower at her core, feeding off the violent offering of her imagination.

Vivaan pulled down his collar, revealing the mandala-like tattoo spiraled across his skin. He pressed his fingers against it and the black ink lit up red, the glow enveloping his body in a flash just as the bhuta reached him.

Kajal squeezed her eyes shut at the burst of light. Tav steadied her with an arm around her shoulders. The whine had fallen into a minor note, as if the bhuta were distressed.

Blinking against watering eyes, Kajal squinted into the crimson glow and found Lasya going in for another attack, only to be pushed away by some invisible force. As the light finally diminished, she got a better look at Vivaan.

Or, rather, the rakshasa now standing in his place.

He was of a similar size—humanoid and tall, with broad shoulders. But his skin was dark gray, like a rhino's hide, and the ears that parted his fall of black hair had elongated into points. On the middle of his forehead below his horns sat a mark like a bindi, a half-moon on its side with three dilating dots rising from its center. His eyes were red, the pupils vertically slitted, and burned furiously as they landed on Kajal. When he bared his teeth, the canines were fanged.

"You . . ." Kajal would have sunk to the floor if Tav hadn't been holding her up. "All this time . . . ?"

All this time, he had hidden his true form under a glamour. All this time, he had been a danava, a demon skilled in illusions.

Vivaan glanced meaningfully at Sezal just before the bhuta turned to her, longing to enact its vengeance on someone. Sezal ripped her sleeve and activated her own glamour tattoo in another flash of red. Like Vivaan, her skin grayed, and black horns sprouted from her skull, though the mark on her forehead bore diamonds instead of dots.

Jassi scurried away from Sezal and pressed her back against the wall. "No," she whimpered. "No, no, no!"

The bhuta, growing more enraged, kept striking at Sezal. But the rebel—the *demon*—blocked her attacks with a shield of crimson light that activated whenever Lasya got too close.

"Stop!" Kajal cried. Any control she'd had over her sister snapped as Lasya, determined to find a victim, turned with a silent snarl on Jassi.

The professor's glasses hit the floor before she did. Jassi choked and fought against an enemy she couldn't see, tears escaping the corners of her bulging eyes.

"Lasya, stop!" Kajal screamed. She tore out of Tav's hold. "Don't hurt her!"

White butterflies swarmed ahead of her. They descended on Lasya like they had in Jassi's flat, making the bhuta writhe until it dissipated into wisps of smoke.

Jassi cried weakly as Kajal moved her onto her side. Tav crashed to his knees and pressed shaking fingers to Jassi's throat, their blue light like sapphires around her neck.

"Why didn't you do anything?" Kajal shouted at the danavas. Vivaan was holding Sezal back by her arm, his expression stony and hers regretful.

"Because you needed to see that your actions have consequences," Vivaan said. "Attacking us is futile. Rakshasas are immune to a bhuta's powers."

"But you . . . on the Harama Plain . . ." Though they'd been scratched up in their human guises, it had been nothing but a clever act. They hadn't been in danger at all.

She was the one in danger, and always had been.

Kajal's gaze drifted to Sezal. The rebel seemed like she wanted to say something, to apologize, to explain, but she only turned her face away.

Blue ringed Tav's irises as he glared at Vivaan. "I didn't lie when I said my memories are affected. I didn't recognize you in your human forms, but I know you now. Vaan. Sezal. My brother's aides."

Sezal looked like she wanted to cry. Even Vivaan's icy demeanor melted somewhat when he glanced at Advaith's body. He let go of Sezal and returned to the crown prince's torso, gently scooping the dirt back inside the bag before retying it.

"The world needs him," Vivaan whispered. "*We* need him."

"You think I don't know that?" Tav snapped. "Of course we need him. We have the same goal, but you're treating me like the enemy. I'm not out to take my brother's throne."

Vivaan's laugh was soft and mocking. "I'm not so sure. I remember how you two fought, toward the end. And more than that . . ." He peered over his shoulder. "I'm worried about what *she* is hiding from us."

Kajal stiffened. She didn't like the way he and Sezal were assessing her. "I'm not hiding anything. You know about the bhuta, my experiments. There's nothing else."

"Do you know what they told us, when we went to Siphar?" Vivaan asked. "They said the day of the accident, the ground shook like an earthquake, and veins of black energy streaked the sky. Like a sudden surge of blight. Of *tamas*." His eyes flashed.

She pressed her lips together to stop their trembling. Vivaan stood and picked up Lasya's finger. He shoved it at Kajal, and she cradled it against her chest.

"The Sodhis are now in possession of your sister's body," Vivaan said. "You will help us find the rest of Advaith and resurrect him. If we find out you've tampered with either prince's body, your sister will burn. Lie to us again, she will burn. Attack us again, *she will burn*. Do you understand?"

Kajal hunched over Lasya's severed finger, under the weight of Tav's troubled gaze. She was a child again—powerless, furious, trying desperately to survive. Choosing any option that would ensure she could make it at least one more day.

"Yes," she whispered. "I understand."

How ridiculous she'd been to let her guard down for even a second. She should have known better—known there was only one person who had ever been worthy of her trust.

She wouldn't make that mistake again.

Chapter Twenty-One

WHEN KAJAL WAS younger, she had a recurring nightmare of a volcano.

She had never seen one in real life, but she had read about how magma built under heat and pressure until it finally exploded in a geyser of destruction. In her nightmares, she stood at the volcano's rim and watched, mesmerized, as lava bubbled and surged. Sometimes it came right up to the rim, burning away her feet. Sometimes it lurked far below.

Kajal felt as if the lava had spilled from the volcano's lip and down its sides, a hissing, scorching warning.

Last night, Jassi had explained the situation to Dalbir in her flat. As the Sodhis' representative, the rebels had conceded that Dalbir needed to be involved.

"Hold . . . Hold on," Dalbir had said, more than a little perturbed as they stared at Tav. "So this one *is* a prince, but not the *crown* prince, who's been carved up like a prize lamb." Jassi and Kajal had nodded while Tav glowered. "Advaith Thakar is actually his twin and also happens to be the *asura*?" Another nod. "And this one here, he's . . . he's the—?"

"The deva," Kajal had said. "Yes. Glad you understand."

"I *don't* understand!" Dalbir had given a near-hysterical laugh, grabbing their hair with both hands. "This must be a prank. No—it's a myth. We're living through an actual myth right now."

"That *is* your strong suit," Jassi had said with a weak smile. "Maybe your knowledge of asura and deva lore will come in handy."

Dalbir's eyes had gone round. "Oh. This is real." They'd approached Tav, but one sharp look and Dalbir had immediately retreated. "I— I can't pass up this chance to see him in action. I *have* to come along." Their face dropped a little. "But my classes . . . No, no, this is far more important. I'm going to get *such* good material."

"Why are you still going through with this?" Kajal had demanded once Dalbir had left to pack their things. "The rebels are *demons*."

Jassi's fingers had reached for her throat. Tav's healing had reversed the effects of the strangling, but not the dread that had settled in her eyes. "They told me I could learn how to resurrect the dead."

"Who did you lose?"

Jassi had looked away, whether out of shame or a desire to not bare the raw nerve of her grief. "I haven't lost him yet, but my father has been sick for a long time. And if he goes, what'll happen to my sister? Professors are only allowed to bring spouses and children to live with them at the university. I can't afford a place in the city. So what am I supposed to do?" She'd furiously wiped at a fallen tear. "Now that I've come this far in their plot, how can I walk away without them killing me? I know too much."

Kajal didn't have an answer. Like Jassi, she'd been backed into a corner.

It had been a mistake to agree to the rebels' terms when she was in that cell awaiting an ordeal of poison. It had been a mistake to ever leave Lasya's body. It had been a mistake to—

"What you're doing isn't natural."

Cracks in the earth, the frantic pounding of her heart.

"Kajal!"

"Kajal?"

A touch jolted her back to the present. Tav's hand was on her arm, warm yet tense. She shrugged it off.

Outside the university, in the blush of dawn, they'd each found a horse waiting for them. Vivaan and Sezal had reverted to their human guises, the latter speaking to Dalbir.

"You're studying to be a lorist," Sezal was saying. "And we know Bakshi is well versed in mythology. Are there any places in particular you think he would have hidden parts of an asura's body?"

"Unless you can think of any, Tavinder?" Vivaan asked coolly. "Ah, but that's right—you often skipped such lessons to go play by the river."

Tav bristled.

"Are you sure Bakshi would have known Advaith Thakar was the asura?" Jassi asked.

"Yes," Vivaan said without further explanation.

Dalbir chewed on their lower lip. Despite their excitement last night, they were more subdued in front of the rebels, their gaze often straying toward the canvas bag slung over Vivaan's horse.

"There are several places tied to the asura," they ventured at last. "But when it comes to the best places to hide a body . . . uh, parts of a body . . . there's the Varajita Flat, in the north, which is where the asura met a seer who told them to never fire an arrow. But the asura was curious and proud, so they challenged the deva to an archery contest, which they lost. The asura's anger was so potent it made the rivers dry up, causing a drought. To make up for it, the asura stole a flock of chatakas and had them plead to the clouds for rain. But the monsoon they brought flooded the plains."

Dalbir spoke faster, losing themself in the stories. "A lot of myths mention Lake Hira, in the south, which some think is where their holy weapons first appeared. It's also near the Chaandanee Woods, where the asura and deva discovered chakoras. They were amazed to discover the birds only sustained themselves with moonlight. The asura was so enthralled, they took a chakora for their own. Obviously, the chakora didn't like that too much, and the deva convinced the asura to free it, but the chakora would return once in a while—"

"All right," Vivaan cut in. "We'll start there."

Why is it only the asura who makes mistakes in these myths? Kajal thought. She glanced at Tav, who was also frowning. Then again, frowning was his default expression.

"We'll need to split into two parties, though," Sezal said. "There have been more rakshasa sightings in the south, so Vaan and I will go there while the rest of you go north."

Kajal was surprised to hear it, but also thankful. The last thing she wanted was to be subject to Vivaan's dark, knowing stares for days.

Vivaan nodded to Tav. "Don't get any ideas. Remember: The fate of your brother and your country rides on this." Tav only clenched his jaw.

"Wait." Kajal nudged Kutaa to go up and sniff the bag with Advaith's torso. Once he'd gotten its scent, he sneezed.

The two groups parted ways. Tav went to help Kajal into the saddle, but she elbowed him away and did it herself, remembering to put her left foot in the stirrup first this time. It still amounted to little more than an awkward flapping of limbs, but neither she nor the mare cared.

A shiver rolled down her spine. She looked over her shoulder, but the rebels were already heading south. There was only the university on the promontory, its sandstone walls glimmering with the rising sun, with no one else in sight.

"Well, this is nice," Dalbir said with false cheer. "Getting out to explore the world instead of only reading about it. Don't get me wrong, I'll miss my bed and my books, but this is a refreshing change of pace."

As Kutaa led the way north, Tav came up beside Kajal on his black gelding. "I give them two hours until they start complaining."

When she didn't respond, Tav lowered his voice. "What's wrong? You're not acting like yourself."

Kajal's scoff was subdued. "What's *wrong*? Look around, Your Highness."

He winced at the title. "And how do you know what I'm like? You barely know me."

"I . . ." He seemed ready to say more, but seeing her shoulders stiffen, he tactfully fell back to ride behind her.

Kajal was both resentful and glad for the space. Loneliness was her only companion and her constant enemy; she didn't know how to exist without it. Didn't know how to exist in a world where Lasya couldn't be her counterweight.

She had once thought if she could resurrect her sister, everything could return to how it had been, but she realized now that wasn't true. She had used Lasya as a weapon—her gentle and courageous sister, who would be ashamed of how Kajal had disregarded the collapse of their world to pursue her own selfish desires.

Like the asura in Dalbir's stories, Kajal was a proud and curious thing. Wherever she went, people made up their minds about her with a glimpse: That she was feral, repellant, bothersome, strange. That just because she spoke her mind and displayed her intellect, she was a witch and a servant of evil.

Lasya had always told her those people were wrong. But with the pressure and heat building inside her, ready to make her shatter and burn anything that got close, Kajal worried they'd been right.

Kajal quickly learned her tolerance for travel companions was nonexistent.

Jassi kept shooting her sad, apologetic looks, which Kajal tried to ignore. And Dalbir, who had indeed started complaining a couple hours in—the air smelled weird, it was too windy, the sun was too bright, would there be rakshasas lying in wait?—took turns gazing around the landscape and gazing quizzically at Tav. They had a journal propped open on their saddle horn, where they occasionally scribbled down observations. It made Kajal yearn for her notebook; even the notes she'd left in the laboratory had been confiscated by the rebels.

"My parents would *never* let me do this," Dalbir said. "The farthest I ever got as a child was a mile from the estate. One time, I thought I saw a rakshasa, but it turned out to be a water buffalo. Very disappointing."

"Yes, too bad it wasn't a rakshasa that would have torn you limb from limb," Kajal muttered. "This isn't an adventure from your books. You know that, right? It's important to me that you know that."

Dalbir made a lazy gesture with their hand. "As long as I get enough material to write a book of my own, it'll be more than worth it. I'm going to be *famous*."

Tav, likely not fond of the idea of Dalbir getting famous from *his* story, offered a low grunt.

"Besides," Dalbir said, "you know there are plenty of rakshasas who wouldn't tear me limb from limb. It's only recently that some have become more, ah . . . violent. Would you know more about that?" they asked Tav. "I guess that's a better question for your brother, though."

Tav didn't answer, his focus trained on Kutaa. He hadn't said a word since Kajal snapped at him earlier. She'd felt his eyes graze her from time to time, as if gauging whether it was safe to approach again.

In the silence that followed, Kajal urged her horse closer to Dalbir's. "Have you ever heard of 'halahala'?" She'd been mulling over the nagi's poem for days without any breakthroughs.

Dalbir closed their journal. "I believe that's the name of the demon lord."

"I thought his name was Dukha?"

"It is. This was at the beginning of everything, before the creation of Patala." Dalbir rubbed their chin, studying the scenery. The others were doing a poor job of pretending not to eavesdrop. "When the Brahimada was formed, the order was Martya, Svarga, then Patala. Patala was last because for a long time the demon lord was alone, without a means by which to create his realm. In that state, he became Halahala, a sort of cosmic toxin."

"Cosmic toxin?" Jassi repeated.

"I'm not entirely sure what it means." Dalbir shrugged. "What few translations we have of ancient myths are vague. It's more of an abstract idea than a physical thing. Some think halahala is something that resides within Naraka, where the most wicked souls go, but it's more commonly associated with tamas."

"Why's that?" Kajal asked.

"You remember Professor Manraj's lecture, right? Svarga, Martya, and Patala all share three interwoven energies: sattva, rajas, and tamas. Sattva is pure and clean—a baby's first breath, new growth in soil, a healthy body—and is usually associated with the yakshas. Rajas is the passion and exertion of living things, and most commonly associated with us humans. The sweat on our brow, a loud belly laugh, lust. Tamas, then, is the chaos of the rakshasas: turmoil, instability, and death." They shrugged. "That certainly sounds like something toxic."

Thinking of the tar-like veins on the Harama Plain, Kajal swallowed.

The nagi had said the blight was halahala, and Vivaan had inferred the blight was tamas. Just as those who studied Ayurveda were able to manipulate sattva and rajas, could there be a way to manipulate tamas?

The land faded from lush green fields to yellow scrub over gently rolling hills. They took a break to stretch and eat, but Kutaa seemed anxious to continue on. Kajal felt it too; there was a strangeness in the air. They weren't near the Harama Plain, but Kajal thought she could sense its threatening call, the pulse of diseased veins under her feet.

As the sky tinged pink and purple with dusk, Kajal remained on edge. She kept scanning the hilly terrain, expecting to see someone or something staring back at her. They passed a murky pond, and she swallowed at the reminder of the dead pani sudhata.

Tav risked riding beside her again. Although he didn't speak, it took her a while to notice he was humming. His voice was smooth and soft, and she found herself relaxing as if he were casting a spell over her, like this was merely another form of healing. Then she recognized the song.

She whirled toward him. "What are you doing?"

Tav was startled into a cough. "I'm . . . humming? I can stop."

"No, I mean that song. How do you know it?"

"I made it up."

Kajal stared at him. She wondered if he was joking—was Tav even capable of joking?—or else trying to get some sort of rise out of her. But he only showed genuine bewilderment at her reaction.

"That's not funny," she said at last.

"Why would it be funny?"

"Because *I* made up that song," she insisted. "For Lasya. So how do *you* know it?"

Tav's brow furrowed. "I know it because *I* made it up for—" His voice caught, and he turned away. "You must be mistaken."

She pulled her horse closer to his. "What do you call it, then?"

"*Lotus Blossom*," he and Kajal said at the same time.

Dizziness hit her like a blacksmith's hammer. Had Tav heard her humming the song? Or had he heard the lullaby within the whine of Lasya's bhuta, like Kajal did? He still had holes in his memory—maybe he'd filled one with something that wasn't his.

Tav's hand drifted to the amber pendant hiding under his shirt. His frown softened, more confused than upset. Her skin heated at the scrutiny.

Kutaa's bark snatched her attention. Ahead, the others had reined in their horses. Their way was blocked by four riders, the gloaming casting dull light across their naked weapons and the coiled whip one wore at his belt.

Across their uniforms of blue and marigold.

The mare Kajal was riding danced back as anxiety spiked through the roof of her mouth. The hills must have shielded the Vadhia from sight, allowing the soldiers to cut them off.

Jassi gestured for the students to stay put. "Jagvir? What are you doing here?"

"We have reason to believe you travel with a witch," Jagvir said, cold and commanding. "One who is responsible for leaving death and chaos in her wake. She has not only killed an innocent girl"—at this, his voice went thin—"but left multiple victims in Siphar and Kinara. She will no doubt kill again."

We're not the only ones who heard about the mishap in Siphar.

He was on some mission that didn't go well.

Jagvir and the other Vadhia made the sign against the evil eye, touching their foreheads and flicking their fingers at Kajal. Before, she could have easily brushed it off as superstitious nonsense, rolling her eyes at how easily people demonized that which they didn't understand.

But now she was roiling magma and exposed nerves. The parts of her she'd kept soft for Lasya were sharpening again.

Kajal clumsily dismounted. As she walked toward the Vadhia, Dalbir hissed, "What are you doing?"

Jassi tried to put her horse between them, but Kajal stepped around and faced the four soldiers, gazing up at the young man who regarded her with so much disgust.

"You killed her, didn't you?" he snarled. "She enraged you. I could *see* it. And then you—"

"Jagvir, stop!"

A rider was approaching from the south. *Vritika*. Both she and her horse were gleaming with sweat; it was the most disheveled Kajal had ever seen her. As Vritika galloped closer, Kajal noted the crossbow slung across her back and the quiver of iron bolts at her hip—the tools of a demon hunter.

"Why are you here?" Jassi demanded in alarm.

Vritika ignored her and slid off her horse. "Jagvir, please," she panted. "What happened to Riddhi is terrible, but this isn't the work of a dakini. *She* isn't a dakini. I told you, Riddhi died of a bhuta attack."

Vritika's dark eyes landed on Kajal. Though she'd claimed Kajal wasn't a witch, her glare harbored bitter accusation, a hatred that would have unsettled Kajal more had the pressure within her not been climbing steadily higher.

"There were no bodies to suggest it was a bhuta," Jagvir argued. "Riddhi was struck by the evil eye!" He pointed his talwar at Kajal. "*You* are to blame for this disease on our land. And it can only be cleansed with your death."

Vritika's cheek twitched in annoyance, and Kajal nearly uttered a dark laugh. Of course someone like Jagvir thought he knew more about rakshasas than the daughter of demon hunters.

"It isn't a typical bhuta," Vritika insisted. Some of her curly hair had escaped her braid, sticking to her sweat-slick face. "Somehow, it's attached itself to *her*. And I'm here to exorcise it."

The pressure rose, threatening to crack Kajal's ribs, her teeth.

Jagvir let out a broken sound and grabbed his whip. He unfurled it with a loud snap. "She's already cast you under her spell! She's not *normal*. She—"

He didn't have time to finish. A thick black vine punched up out of the earth and stabbed him through the chest.

Jassi's scream and Dalbir's curse were lost under the roaring in Kajal's ears. Kutaa barked again and made to pounce, but Tav unsheathed his rusty talwar and ordered him and the others to stay put.

Kajal stared at the gaping hole where the tendril of blight had penetrated Jagvir's chest, seeping blood and gore, until the Vadhia slid off his horse and fell into the grass. The horse whinnied and took off as the other soldiers cried out and raised their weapons.

Another vine burst out of the ground and wrapped around Jagvir's neck.

It hauled him up and strangled him like a noose, digging into his flesh while his face purpled.

Kajal could *feel* the vines, could sense them with something beyond sight and sound and smell. Like she was the rot that fed them, driving one to pierce the throat of the second soldier, another to flay the back of the third.

Tamas. Blight. Halahala.

Tav clutched her arm, and he was yelling something in her ear. But her voice had fled, her body frozen in place as the yellowed grass was sprayed scarlet.

The crack of Jagvir's neck breaking resounded louder than the unfurling of his whip. His body crumpled to the ground, but only a moment later it twitched and rose. Its movements were clumsy yet determined, like the soldiers' on the Harama Plain. Black veins spread across his skin, and his eyes had paled to milky white. He picked up his fallen talwar and staggered toward them.

"What's happening?" Vritika shouted. She grabbed one of her crossbow bolts. "Jagvir, stop!"

Tav's talwar lit up blue, and he ran forward to swipe at Jagvir's lolling head. The deva's energy crackled as his sword bit through diseased flesh, severing the Vadhia's head from his shoulders.

But that didn't stop his body from moving forward, swinging his sword in broad, wild strokes, which Tav blocked. Vritika fired her crossbow, and though it landed in Jagvir's shoulder, he didn't let up in the slightest. The other three soldiers also gained their feet and stumbled forward, eyes white and unseeing.

Kajal couldn't move. Couldn't feel anything beyond the blight, the wretched core of it like the shush of blood through her body. It was only when the vines slithered under the ground like a snake hiding from a mongoose that she could finally draw in a gasp and crash to her knees.

"Kajal!" Jassi grabbed her shoulders. "We need to run!"

Tav was trying to fend off all four soldiers. Even with his inhuman strength, he was having trouble keeping track of them all, and one of the corpses slashed a line across his back.

Lasya, she thought, reaching a shaking hand toward him. *Lasya—*

She didn't want to keep using her sister like this, but what else could she do? How else could they escape this?

The whine rose like the swelling of a gale. Vritika glanced at her iron bangle and then at Kajal.

"It's here." Vritika yanked a hanging incense burner from her belt. Kajal knew it held turmeric, the burning of which was an essential component to purifying a bhuta's energy.

Before Vritika could light it, Jagvir's headless body was suddenly bound in what Kajal first thought was writhing rope, but was actually a long, thick snake. It coiled around his torso, pressing his arms to his sides and binding his legs together.

Beyond the Vadhia were two nagas with astras, the bows creaking before they let their arrows fly. Midway through their arcs, the arrows turned to snakes, wrapping around the other undead soldiers and sending them to the ground. Their fangs punctured the Vadhias' black-veined necks until their bodies lay unmoving.

Vritika trained her crossbow on the nagas with one hand, incense burner dangling from the other. Kajal recognized one as the nagi who had appeared under the hawthorn tree and at the lake. There was a piece of algae on her bodice; the nagas must have come from the pond. The other was male, with a bare chest and long hair threaded with silver rings, which chimed when he moved toward them.

"Yakshas preserve us, we're going to die," Dalbir croaked even as they fumbled to get out their journal. They and Jassi had followed Tav's order to stay back, but Jassi dismounted now with a dagger in one trembling hand.

Tav kept his talwar at his side, watching the nagas draw closer. They eyed him just as warily, the moment stretching uncomfortably until they let their astras disappear. Both of them pressed their hands together at their chests and bowed.

"Greetings, Holy Deva," they intoned as one.

The barrel of Vritika's crossbow lowered in shock. "Deva?" she repeated.

Tav's face went utterly blank. Kajal wondered when he'd last been addressed like this. Eventually, he sheathed his sword and gently touched their heads, a silent order to rise. Kajal was certain they were both taller than Tav, but they sat lower on their tails in deference. Jassi nodded to Vritika, who lowered her crossbow all the way but kept a finger on the trigger.

"Thank you for your help," Tav said. "I'm . . . not sure what happened."

"Halahala spreads quickly when it is fed," said the nagi in her sibilant voice. She glanced at Kajal, eyes gleaming.

"Halahala?" Tav repeated.

The naga inclined his head. "An ancient poison of the earth. The result of two opposing forces that meet in hatred."

Metal strikes with fearsome sound. The venom swells below their feet, the nagi had recited at the lake.

"How can we stop it?" Tav asked.

The naga shook his head. "Such a task can only be accomplished by the asura and deva. As for how, we cannot say."

Jassi took a few steps forward, faltering slightly when the naga turned to appraise her. "W-We are looking for the remains of the asura. To— To bring him back."

"There is somewhere nearby where you may find answers," the nagi said.

"Where?" Tav asked.

"A forest to the northeast. You will know it by its gnarled trees. Stop at the border, for those who dwell within will not let you pass without consent."

"Who dwells there?"

The nagi glanced again at Kajal. "The dakinis."

Chapter Twenty-Two

KAJAL THREW UP once the nagas left. Jassi fretted over her while Tav rubbed her back, but Kajal swiped angrily at them, allowing only Kutaa near. She expected some sort of venomous remark from Vritika, but the girl had been shocked into silence.

That is, until Jassi rounded on her. "You shouldn't be here."

Vritika straightened. "I'm perfectly capable of taking care of myself. More so than *Dalbir*."

"Hey." Dalbir rubbed their nose. "I mean, you're right, but *hey*."

"I know you are, but this . . ." Jassi sighed helplessly. "This is something big, Vritika. I don't want you caught up in it."

"I already am." The girl glared at Kajal, finger lovingly curled around the crossbow's trigger.

"Let me guess," Kajal rasped, wiping her mouth with the back of her wrist. "You want to avenge Riddhi and prove your worth to your family. Well, no need. I'm going to get rid of the bhuta myself."

"How can you possibly—?"

"Can we maybe not do this next to a bunch of corpses?" Dalbir said. "Vritika, if you promise to not stick Kajal full of bolts, you can at least ride with us to this forest. Uh, if that's all right with you, Professor."

Jassi wavered, but at the stark pleading on Vritika's face, she finally caved. "I don't want you traveling alone. It's best if you come with us for now."

If Kajal had been miserable before, she was downright wretched as they continued north. A long argument ensued between Jassi and Vritika, the latter trying to piece together what their mission was and the former unwilling to divulge it.

"I've already guessed you're dissenters," Vritika said. "You wouldn't be traveling with a Sodhi otherwise. I won't relate any of this to my family, if that's what you're worried about."

"Are you sure you want to be involved?" Dalbir asked. "I mean, we saw nagas. And that—that *thing*, the blight. It's like a creature all its own." Yet Dalbir was smiling, holding their journal to their chest. "And now we're heading into a commune of *dakinis*."

"You should be more concerned about *her*." Vritika nodded toward Kajal. "Get on her bad side like Riddhi did, and she won't spare you. I'm surprised she hasn't unleashed the bhuta yet."

"I don't need the bhuta for *you*." Kajal knew a taunt when she heard one, but she couldn't help herself; the magma was rising, dribbling over the volcano's rim. "Because I'll leave your viscera to stink in the sun if you say another word."

Tav inhaled sharply while Dalbir muttered a quiet "Damn." Vritika drew herself up and reached for her incense burner, but Jassi nudged her horse between them, shaking her head in warning at Kajal.

Just get through this, Kajal thought, the forest looming in the distance. It was as if her own veins had turned black, filled with whatever decaying sludge made up halahala.

She held the pouch containing Lasya's pinkie finger tight in one hand. Kajal's heartbeat was irregular, and every so often she heard whispers in her ear, weeping and pleading. In her mind, she replayed the instant the blight had stabbed Jagvir through the chest, through the hard pillar of his sternum and cartilage and into the membranous mediastinum, punching through vertebrae on the way out.

She's not normal.

Something entered her line of sight. Slowly, her eyes focused on a waterskin.

"Drink," Tav said.

She didn't move for a long time. He continued to hold it out for her, waiting patiently. It made her want to scream and knock it out of his hand.

Instead, she accepted the waterskin and took two large gulps. It marginally helped.

"How do you feel?" Tav asked softly.

Kajal didn't bother wiping her chin before shoving the waterskin back at him. "You're the one who got hurt."

After a moment's confusion, he tried to peer over his shoulder at the shallow gash one of the undead Vadhia had made. "That? It's already mostly healed."

Of course it is. How nice to harbor such a benevolent power. How nice to not have anyone question his goodness.

"Oh, this is appropriately spooky," Dalbir murmured as they approached the forest's edge. It was made up of tall, thick pines, the canopy so heavy it blocked out most light. Between the trunks wove a thin, low mist. "The trees look odd. Don't they look odd?"

Kajal silently agreed. Pines usually grew straight, but these were leaning and bent in different directions. Some of the trunks held strange bulges like tumors, and their roots had burst out of the ground to form a weaving, tangled web across the forest floor. She wondered if the blight had reached here as well, but no matter how hard she concentrated, she couldn't detect any black veins. There was also no rotten, smoky smell—just the fresh, clean scent of pine needles and fertile soil.

Tav chewed his lower lip while his gelding danced to the side at either his nervousness or the general wrongness of the place. He was about to say something when he abruptly looked to the left.

Two tall figures emerged from the mist and shadows. They wore simple, threadbare clothes, and bows dangled from their hands. Kajal's first thought was that the nagas had found them again, but as they came closer, Kajal saw they were women with lustrous brown skin. Each of them had braided their long, thick black hair into plaits that rested over their shoulders.

They could have almost passed for human were it not for their sharp black nails and the vertical blue eye that sat upon each of their brows.

Dalbir gasped as they and Vritika automatically warded against the evil eye. Jassi stayed very still, though her hand twitched to do the same. The two dakinis cast their gazes over all of them before settling on Tav.

They didn't bow like the nagas had, but they did incline their heads. "Greetings, Holy Deva." Their voices were deep and musical. One continued, "It has been some time since you walked this plane."

Tav dismounted and approached them, returning the greeting. "We're sorry to intrude on your sacred land. But we wouldn't be here without reason."

"We know why you are here," the other said before they turned to the tree line. "We have been waiting. Come."

Everyone exchanged wary glances. But as Jassi rode forward, one of the dakinis raised a hand to stop her.

"Only the deva may cross our border," she said.

Jassi touched her throat, likely thinking about the rebels and how mad they would be if she ended up losing Tav.

"I'll return," he said solemnly. "No matter the weapon held at my neck, we both want my brother back."

Jassi nodded. Vritika scowled, though she stayed a healthy distance away. One of the dakinis, no doubt sensing the blessed bolts Vritika carried, gave her a cool, assessing once-over.

The other dakini studied Kajal. They locked eyes for a lingering moment, Kajal's skin clammy and tight, until the dakini tilted her head toward the forest.

"You as well," she ordered.

Vritika made a choking noise. Dalbir grumbled, "How come *she* gets to go? This is a prime opportunity for research!"

Even Tav seemed uncertain why Kajal had been chosen to come along. Kajal flushed, not with embarrassment but with shock. She fumbled her dismount and staggered, but Kutaa was there to steady her.

"Stay with the others," she whispered while petting him. "Hopefully we won't be gone long." Kutaa sighed but stayed put.

The low-hanging mist curled around their ankles and calves as they entered the dark forest. It was far colder in the shade, making her shiver. Some of Tav's butterflies appeared out of nowhere to cast their moonbeam light.

There was a hint of something metallic in the air. It grew stronger the farther they walked, following the dakinis toward the heart of the forest. The roots were gnarled and twisting, rising from the base of the trees like the dead crawling from their graves.

Her foot snagged on one, and she lurched forward. Tav caught her as she grabbed hold of another root for balance.

It was in the shape of a hand, holding hers.

She scrambled away until she bumped against Tav's chest. The dakinis turned, and when one of them noticed the root, she smiled grimly.

"They won't hurt you," she said. "They're long dead."

Tav cleared his throat, his hands on Kajal's shoulders. "Who is?"

"Those we feed to the forest." The other dakini gestured broadly to the thick, contorted trunks surrounding them. "Murderers. Rapists. Abusers." Her eyes darkened. "So-called witch hunters."

Kajal saw them clearer now. The shape of a leg. Clawing fingers. An eroded, screaming face in the bark.

"We hunt those who have committed grievous assault," the dakini went on. "Once they've been mostly drained of blood to feed the village, we feed the trees. The roots absorb the nutrients of their flesh. It is the only use for them in this world."

A thin trickle of sap seeped from a nearby tree. No—blood. The source of the metallic smell in the air. The other dakini scooped it up with her finger and licked it clean. Meeting Kajal's stare, she smirked as the eye upon her forehead narrowed.

"Nothing goes to waste," the dakini said.

Kajal and Tav silently followed them onward. The yaksha butterflies trailed behind, either warded from going any farther or affected by the heavy energy of the forest. Now that she knew the bodies were there, Kajal sensed a restless stirring beneath her feet. The trees creaked and groaned every so often, their bark sheltering bones that cried for the relief of fire. So long as their bodies remained unburned, their souls would never journey to Patala to begin the process of rebirth. They were stuck here in endless torment.

Whispers kissed her ears, begging for justice, for pain, for revenge.

This is *justice,* she thought viciously.

They quieted at once.

"Haven't they formed bhutas?" she asked.

The dakinis shook their heads. "Their bodies are absorbed by the trees, so anything that remains of their spirit gets absorbed as well. It's why the forest is so well protected. If anyone tries to enter without our permission, they're swiftly stopped."

Curious, Kajal prodded her enigmatic connection with Lasya, wondering if her bhuta would form despite the dampening effect of the forest. She couldn't tell if she was relieved or dismayed when nothing happened.

Eventually, they emerged into a spacious clearing surrounded by small white buildings with domed, thatched roofs. It left the center free for a wide communal well and mud chulhas, where pots bubbled and simmered, their steam smelling of meat and herbs. Women squatted before flat iron pans, flipping rotis with their bare fingers. Laundry hung up to dry on long stretches of rope, and a couple of children were using the long kurtas and uttariyas to hide from one another as they played.

Kajal couldn't help but gawk. Roughly half of the population were dakinis, but the other half were humans of all ages. The majority seemed to be women, from an old auntie clucking her tongue and swatting her hand at the rowdy children to a young woman—hardly older than Kajal—who sat sewing on a stump.

It was that young woman who looked up with haunted eyes and froze at the sight of Tav. The others gradually became aware of him as well, and though the dakinis didn't seem particularly fazed, the humans either tensed or hurried back inside.

The two dakinis who had led them through the forest said something in a dialect Kajal wasn't familiar with. The humans' reactions ranged from shock to doubt to intrigue. Many remained fearful and stayed close to whichever dakinis were nearby.

Tav scanned the village as if looking for something, then lowered his gaze in an effort to alleviate their discomfort. "I'm sorry. I can leave, if that would be easier."

"So long as you don't stray deeper into the village, it's fine," said one of their guides. "We've told them you are the deva. We've allowed you to cross our border for this reason and this reason alone."

"Most of them haven't laid eyes on men in years," added the second.

"I understand." Tav kept his gaze averted. "I apologize for disturbing the peace."

The other dakini smirked. "You'll know if you've disturbed the peace." Her hand tightened on her bow. "Come."

Kajal and Tav followed their guides around the outskirts of the village. Kajal wondered where all these people had come from, how they had found this place, or if the dakinis had rescued them. The woman sewing on the stump shut her eyes tight as they walked by, and Kajal noticed a long, jagged scar near her temple.

She remembered the day villagers had thrown rocks at her and Lasya. How one had struck her sister, making her bleed.

A sound left her throat, and Tav turned. Whatever showed on her face made his own tighten in . . . what, concern? He had no reason to be concerned about her. She'd done nothing to deserve it.

She shouldered past him and hurried behind the dakinis until they reached a spot outside the village where a handful of elders were sorting through plants, either putting them into clay pots or grinding them into pastes or pressing them to dry. Their braids were threaded with silver, and some were using those long, thick plaits as an additional limb to grab shears or jars when their hands were full.

When they spotted Tav, they stopped working and got to their feet.

"Please don't stop on my account," Tav said.

One of the older dakinis stepped forward with a hoarse laugh. "It is not every day the deva comes calling." She reached up to pinch Tav's cheek, and he let her. "Especially when that deva is supposed to be dead."

"I . . ." Tav glanced at Kajal, then away. "I'm not dead. Anymore." The other dakinis laughed. "But the asura is."

They sobered at this. Dakinis were considered rakshasas and were therefore under the care of the asura. Without that pivotal tie between Martya and Patala, between the humans and the other rakshasas, they had considerably less protection against any who decided to do them harm. Humans, mostly; the Vadhia, specifically.

Kajal stared at their third eyes, thinking of all the times people had flicked their fingers at her.

"The usurper called Anu Bakshi killed my brother and scattered pieces of his body." Tav swallowed hard. "We were told there would be more information here."

The dakini elder brushed her hands off on her uttariya and nodded to the others to resume their work. They did so with reluctance, obviously piqued by the drama.

"You may call me Ruhi," she told Tav. "Follow me."

They walked farther into the forest, along with their two original guides, who seemed to act as bodyguards; whether for the elder or for Tav and Kajal was uncertain.

"For some years now, we have not been alone in this forest," Ruhi said. "To the east prowls a being of immense strength and power. He does nothing but pace the same spot over and over. He is guarding something, though none of us have been able to get close enough to figure out what, and the forest's protections have done nothing against him. We do not let the humans near, for fear that he will perceive them as a threat."

Out here, the pines weren't as gnarled, and there was more foliage. Apparently, the dakinis kept this part of the forest unfed. They passed under a tree where a dakini sat among the branches, bow balanced on her knees. She nodded at them.

"Nothing unusual today," she called.

"We keep him watched," the dakini elder explained. "Though for nearly two decades he has never strayed from this spot."

Nearly two decades. The amount of time Tav and Advaith had been dead.

Their guides silently gestured for them to crouch. Peering through the trees and underbrush, Kajal could see a clearing lush with grass except for a ring of hardened dirt around its boundary.

Kajal heard heavy, stomping footsteps. She tensed as they grew closer, expecting to find a rakshasa of some sort—a daitya, perhaps, with tusks and a thick, impenetrable hide.

But the figure that came into view was that of a man. A *large* man, easily close to seven feet tall, with broad shoulders and densely packed muscles along his chest and arms. His dark hair hung loose and unwashed, his clothes thin and disintegrating under stained armor. In one meaty hand, he gripped a heavy gada, the spherical head of the gilded mace crowned with a deadly spike.

The sight of him dried Kajal's mouth. How were they supposed to get past him and see if he guarded a piece of Advaith's body?

As he approached their hiding spot, Kajal noticed that his eyes were blank and filmy. Not the disturbing white of the blighted soldiers but instead unfocused, as if he were trapped within his own mind. Even more disturbing was the spot in the middle of his forehead where a small wound rested like a horrific imitation of a third eye, continuously weeping blood. Trickles of it ran down his nose and dripped off his chin.

Tav's gaze was fixated on the warrior. Not in fear, but in recognition.

"Ranbir," he breathed. "He was Advaith's personal guard." His fingertips paled against the bark of the tree. "My brother is here."

Chapter Twenty-Three

KAJAL RECALLED TAV mentioning Ranbir in Advaith's quarters, when they'd searched for where he'd gone. He explained again for the dakini.

"My father chose his best warrior to be my brother's guard," Tav whispered once Ranbir had walked past. "But he was still only human, and Advaith worried he'd get hurt during his asura missions. So he put some of his own power into a ruby that he fused to Ranbir's forehead to grant him extra protection." He touched the spot between his brows where Ranbir was bleeding. "Someone must have forcefully removed it, and the loss affected his mind."

Ruhi gave a thoughtful hum. "Our most skilled have tried to confront him, but they returned heavily injured. One did not survive. But you are the deva."

The way she said it wasn't an admission that his power was greater; it was merely an acknowledgment that his power was *different*, and therefore might have a better chance than they did. Tav took a deep breath and settled a hand on his rusty talwar.

Kajal's chest ached with foreboding. If they were going to get past Ranbir, that meant *fighting* Ranbir, and she very much did not like the sound of that. When she took out her scalpel, the dakini nearest her scoffed.

"What are you going to do with that? Prick a couple holes in his boots?" The dakini tugged a sheathed dagger from her belt and handed it to Kajal. "Here."

The sheath was plain leather, and the blade she drew was gently curved, like a tusk. Its hilt was narrow at the grip and wide at the pommel, and it was unadorned save for a subtle swirling design.

"You know how to use it?" the dakini asked.

"Point the sharp part away from me and hope for the best?"

The dakini's three eyes narrowed. "Good enough."

Lasya's bhuta had materialized in situations of extreme duress. Would it do so again, Kajal wondered, when she faced a huge, mindless warrior who could cave her skull in? But there was that strange, stagnant atmosphere in the forest, the sheer number of dead muting her connection with her sister. Every so often, the breeze carried a whisper in a voice that was not Lasya's. No one else seemed to hear it.

"There's a spot in the middle of the clearing where nothing grows," Ruhi told Tav. "Whatever he guards is buried there."

Tav quietly unsheathed his talwar. He gave Kajal a look that conveyed she didn't have to go. She shook her head, and he made a face at her stubbornness before he crept into the clearing. She followed after.

The dakinis stayed behind, their bows primed in case Ranbir decided to break out of the clearing. They had to think of the village's safety first and foremost, but Kajal wished at least one of them would have come along. As far as backup went, Kajal was the pesky flea to Tav's hunting dog.

The clearing was large enough that Ranbir didn't notice them at first. He kept his steady, slow pace, circling the mound in the center. But when Tav took a step toward it, Ranbir's head snapped up, vacant eyes pinning him in place.

"Ranbir," Tav whispered, then raised his voice. "Ranbir! Do you recognize me? I am Tavinder Thakar, Advaith's brother. He—"

Ranbir had no patience for the prince's speech, raising his gada with a roar before he charged.

Kajal yelped and dove to one side. Tav dodged and held out his hand.

"Sudarshana chakra, enlighten me with the gods' will," he said quickly as Ranbir turned. "Sudarshana chakra, grant me the power to defend!"

But like before, the weapon refused to appear.

"Damn it."

Instead, he covered his talwar in crackling blue energy and rushed at Ranbir. The warrior thumped his mace so hard against the ground that it trembled underneath Kajal's feet.

While Ranbir was distracted, Kajal scrambled toward the mound and started to dig, uneasily reminded of the Harama Plain as she used the dagger to loosen the soil.

She heard Tav's yelp of pain before something grabbed her and flung her away. She didn't have the breath to scream as her elbows and knees banged against the ground until she rolled to a stop at the base of a tree.

Tav attacked Ranbir from behind, grabbing his attention once more. "Stay away from him! Let me tire him out first!"

Kajal struggled to push herself up. "I don't think he *can* get tired!"

Ranbir was about to slam the gada into Tav's chest when an arrow whizzed by and struck the warrior in the neck. Ranbir barely staggered, but he did stop to wrench the arrow out with a spray of blood. In response, the hole in his forehead bled harder.

The dakini's arrow only made him angrier. He roared again and swung his gada at Tav, who blocked it, impossibly, with his reinforced talwar, his arm pressed against the blade's blunt side. Tav's feet made trenches in the earth as he was pushed back, teeth gritted and the tendons of his neck protruding.

Kajal lunged for the mound to start digging again.

"No!"

She stopped at Tav's cry. Ranbir towered over her, gilded mace hurtling straight for her head. She unthinkingly called for Lasya, but the forest's protective spells were too thick, filled with the wailing whispers of the dead seeking vengeance.

Tav dove into the gada's path, stopping it with his body. He grunted as he caught it in his arms.

"Tav!" she yelled.

"I'm all right," he ground out, his inhuman strength the only thing between him and a broken rib cage. "Hurry!"

But even if she did dig up what they assumed to be part of Advaith, she was sure Ranbir would chase after it. Kajal glanced at her fallen dagger, mind racing while the clearing filled with vehement whispers. Among them came the memory of Dalbir's voice.

Tamas, then, is the chaos of the rakshasas: turmoil, instability, and death.

She grabbed the dagger and stood, backing away from Ranbir and Tav's ongoing struggle. Tav was flagging, being pushed down by the warrior's undaunted force.

There was no halahala here—at least not yet. But there was something else just as restless. And if she could wake the dormant energies within a body, perhaps there were other things she could awaken.

Kajal made a jagged gash in her palm, her blood dribbling into the grass.

"Spirits, awake and come to me." She invented her own mantra on the spot as she pressed her wound to the bark of the nearest tree. "Spirits, awake and do my bidding."

All around her, the forest groaned and screeched. The earth trembled harder than it had when Ranbir pounded his mace, and the bark under her hand burned so cold she nearly yanked her arm back.

The whispers grew into a raging crescendo. Kajal gritted her teeth and focused on the lure of her blood. Fissures split the ground, and Tav lost his footing; Ranbir bore down on him with the mace's spike aimed at Tav's eye.

But before Tav could be skewered, roots in the shape of human arms emerged from the fissures and grabbed Ranbir.

The warrior swung his gada fruitlessly as the root arms took hold of his shoulders, his wrists, his thighs. They kept piling on, wooden fingers digging into Ranbir's flesh, until the warrior fell and was pinned to the grass.

Ranbir fought even while the roots snaked over his prone body. Tav dropped to his knees above Ranbir's head and pressed his fingers to the warrior's bloodied temples, his thumbs covering the open wound in Ranbir's forehead.

Tav closed his eyes and lit up with his power. It washed the clearing in an aquamarine radiance, giving Kajal a feeling of unreality. Like she was drifting somewhere at the bottom of a lake, looking up at a sun-dappled surface she could never reach.

"Ranbir," Tav called, his voice echoing. "Return, Ranbir."

The warrior struggled against the root limbs, baring bloodstained teeth. But eventually, he calmed down, his breaths coming in great, heaving gasps. He blinked until the filminess left his eyes.

Tav opened his own eyes. The light around him shrank and faded. Kajal pushed her palm harder against the bark.

Go back, she thought. *Go and fulfill your punishment.*

The whispers snarled and hissed in her ears, raising the hairs on her arms. But the roots let go and retreated into the ground like the vines of blight that had killed the Vadhia. Kajal's legs gave out, and she sank to the grass.

Ranbir lay dazed and wounded in Tav's hold. He was staring up at the prince as if it were the first time he'd ever seen the sun.

"A . . . Advaith," the warrior croaked, his deep voice so broken Kajal wondered how it worked at all.

Tav's expression of relief fell into despair. He opened his mouth, then decided against whatever he was going to say. Instead, he nodded. "Yes. You're safe now, Ranbir."

But even Kajal could see that wasn't true. The years of mindlessly guarding this clearing had taken a toll on the warrior's body that he had been unable to succumb to until now. The spot on his forehead where the ruby had once been fused had stopped bleeding, but his other wounds hadn't.

"I'm . . . sorry, Your Highness," Ranbir rumbled. He tried to raise his arm, but he was too weak even for that. "For whatever . . . I did wrong."

Tav took his hand. "You did nothing wrong."

Ranbir's eyelids fluttered closed. "I must . . . have done something. For you to . . . revoke your protection."

Tav glanced at Ranbir's forehead. "What? Why would he— Why would I do that?"

"So sorry, Your Highness," Ranbir was whispering, his voice fading. "You have . . . my devotion, even unto the next life . . ."

"Ranbir? *Ranbir!*"

Kajal saw the moment Ranbir's life severed from this world, between one heartbeat and eternal silence. Tav's power flowed through his hands again.

"Tav," Kajal called. "He's gone."

Unlike when he'd tried to heal the dead yaksha, this time he didn't need telling twice. The blue light faded, and Tav hung his head, whispering a prayer over Ranbir's body.

The dakinis cautiously entered the clearing. Ruhi went to kneel beside Tav and offer condolences while the other two gave Kajal strange looks.

Kajal wiped her bloody hand on her kurti before handing the dagger back. The dakini who'd offered it to her shook her head.

"Keep it." She glanced at the fissures within the clearing, then at the tree where Kajal had pressed her wounded palm. The blood was gone, absorbed by the wood. "You . . ."

The other dakini gripped her partner's wrist. Kajal flushed at the thought that *they* could be scared of *her*. That someone who had always been called a witch could unnerve an actual dakini.

She stared at her cut palm until a shadow fell over her and two gentle, shaking hands cupped hers.

Tav quietly focused on her wound. The magic flowing into her was warm and sweet: the smell of sunshine on a late spring day, the swirl of pollen in a field of marigolds, the soothing light on a lazy river. Her eyes stung, and she had to squeeze them shut.

"I'm sorry," she whispered. "About Ranbir."

She felt more than saw him shake his head. "He was suffering. Ruhi says they'll burn his body, so at least he can move on." He pulled in a shuddering breath. "What you did . . ."

Kajal stilled, but he didn't stop feeding power into her, her palm itching and tingling where the flesh knit back together.

"I didn't know something like that was possible," he said at last.

She opened her eyes. Her wound had healed into a tender brown line, but he didn't let go yet. "It's the forest. It's sort of like the Harama Plain, but . . . different. *Those* bodies were being controlled by blight."

"And these bodies exude tamas," Tav guessed.

Her mouth twitched at how fast he'd caught on. "Yes. I thought if I could tap into the body's sattva for healing, then maybe I could also tap into tamas."

For a moment, her head rang with the reverberation of Lasya's scream. Kajal swayed, but Tav kept hold of her. They remained like that as the dakinis stripped the armor off Ranbir's body.

"He said something about Advaith revoking his protection," Kajal said. "Does that mean Advaith was the one to remove his gem?"

"I don't know. He wouldn't have done something like that. Not without good reason. I don't . . . I don't understand any of this."

He didn't seem to notice the tear that escaped the corner of his eye. Before she realized what she was doing, she lifted her other hand to catch it on her thumb.

"Nothing eludes us forever," she said. "Not even death."

He stared at her. His tear clung wetly to the pad of her thumb.

What am I doing?

She lurched to her feet and nearly fell against the tree behind her. But when she turned to the half-dug mound, Tav stopped her.

"I'll do it," he murmured.

Tav gradually unearthed a small wooden trunk. He hesitated before undoing the latch and opening the lid. The inside was packed with dirt, and when he brushed it away, he recoiled.

Within the dirt was a head with the same thick black hair and long lashes as Tav. Advaith's eyes were closed, and unlike the expression of serenity that had been on Tav's face, his brother bore a small furrow between his brows.

The dakinis fell to their knees and prostrated themselves to the asura's head. Kajal was the only one who remained standing, the only one who kept her gaze on Tav's bowed shoulders as she traced the slant of her new scar.

They now had two-thirds of Advaith's body. They were a step closer to the possibility of the asura and deva walking the mortal plane together once more.

They set up a pyre for Ranbir in the clearing. Kajal helped them make a firebreak, remembering how the rebels had burned the body of the blighted deer in Kinara's forest. It felt like centuries ago.

As she brushed the dirt off her hands, Ruhi approached her. "Let us give the deva privacy to mourn." She nodded at Tav. Holding the box in his arms while fire licked up Ranbir's body, he looked the embodiment of exhaustion.

"Thank you for your help," Kajal said hoarsely as the dakini elder led her toward the village. She continued to run her thumb over the scar on her palm, wondering if Ruhi would ask about what she'd done.

"It is our duty to assist the asura and deva." Ruhi seemed to want to say something else, but she remained silent until they reached the edge of the village.

The elder stopped. The two of them studied each other, Kajal appraising the blue eye upon the dakini's forehead until Ruhi stepped forward and pressed a cool thumb to the center of Kajal's brow.

Kajal gasped when a cool sensation traveled through her body while the spot upon her forehead burned. Her eyes prickled as Ruhi stared into them—into *her*—through bone and tissue and muscle, into whatever fragile, pathetic thing made up Kajal.

The dakini stepped back with a sigh. "You have killed. Your actions took the lives of innocents, and even that of your sister."

Kajal couldn't move. Couldn't speak. The cold sat inside her, churning and aching, a storm of her own making. Everything that was the inverse of Tav's warm light.

"You believe it is your fault," Ruhi went on. "It's true that our mistakes often harm others. Sometimes they cause a grief too great to bear. But there are moments when we must take action despite this. There is a difference between making the right choice and having a choice at all."

The pressure building in Kajal's throat released in a sob. There was a dark, twisted root inside her like the roots of the forest, made of death and blood and horror. She couldn't pry it out—had to instead grow around it, forever gnarled and bent.

The dakini held her shoulders and pressed the top of her forehead to Kajal's. They stood there for a while, saying nothing and saying everything. The tears on Kajal's face were warm.

"Remember that darkness takes many forms and comes in many shades."

Kajal sniffed and nodded as Ruhi leaned back.

"Come, you need cha."

When Tav returned, Kajal was more or less put together, sitting with Ruhi and a couple of curious women—both widows, and both by choice—as she finished her cha. He took one look at her and rushed over, kneeling by the stump she was perched on.

"What happened?" he asked. "Are you all right?"

She was momentarily rendered speechless. Why was he still so concerned over her when he held his brother's head in his arms? But his attention was on her, not the box, and it gave her newfound satisfaction.

She handed him her cup, which contained the last couple sips. He took it, confused, but under her watchful gaze he obediently drank it down. His lips touched the place where hers had been.

Eventually, she whispered, "I'll be fine."

Maybe it was true. Maybe it wasn't. Like with so many things, it was something she would have to find out in time—time that was slipping faster and faster between her fingers, like grave soil.

Chapter Twenty-Four

THE BOX PUT everyone on edge. Tav insisted on riding with it, his hand a protective weight on its lid. Vritika kept casting it wary glances; Dalbir must have filled her in on the purpose of their journey. A potentially dangerous decision, Kajal thought, but considering it was Dalbir's family at the heart of this, the choice was theirs to make.

Tav had been silent when he and Kajal returned from the forest, leaving Kajal to answer Jassi's questions: if they were all right, what had happened, if they needed anything. Not to mention Dalbir had pressed her for descriptions and "sensory details." Kajal's answers had been short and flat; she didn't want to relive it so soon.

"We have what we need," Kajal had said. "That's all that matters."

The ride to the Sodhi estate, where the rebels had told them to meet, took two days. When they stopped the first night, Kajal watched firelight play across the dark grass while idly rubbing her forehead. Tav sat by himself, and Jassi and Dalbir were quietly arguing about some Ayurvedic theory. Vritika stood apart from them, staring up at the stars. Her posture was more slouched than the confident way she typically held herself.

It's true that our mistakes often harm others, Ruhi had told Kajal. *Sometimes they cause a grief too great to bear.*

Kajal's mistakes had cost not only her, but those around her. Because of her—because of the bhuta—a mother, a son, and a friend were gone. A daughter. A sister.

Kutaa lifted his head when she stood, but she told him to stay put and approached Vritika. Perhaps thinking Kajal was Jassi, Vritika turned her head with a surprisingly open expression. It hardened at the sight of her.

"What do you want?" the girl bit out.

A good start. Kajal stood beside her, mostly so that she didn't have to look at Vritika's face while she did this.

"I wanted to apologize," Kajal said. "For Riddhi."

She sensed the tension in Vritika like a taut bowstring, ready to launch its accusing arrow. Before she could, Kajal lifted her hand. "Hear me out before you throw incense in my face."

When Vritika remained silent, Kajal said, "The bhuta is my sister."

Vritika's eyes widened. "I was wondering why it was able to cling to you." She frowned with a scholar's bemusement, like she was the kind who savored the contemplation as much as the breakthrough. "Is it because you're related, then? But no, there have been plenty of bhutas who couldn't travel with their loved ones . . ."

"I'm not entirely certain. She . . ." Kajal waited to ensure that her voice wouldn't break. "Her name is Lasya."

Crickets sang in the long grass, and for a few moments all Kajal heard was their chorus amid the rustle of the breeze and the murmurs of Jassi and Dalbir.

"She died," Kajal whispered. "And it was my fault. I wanted—I *want*—to bring her back like I brought back Tav. But until the rebels allow me to resurrect her, her bhuta haunts me. It feeds on my anger, my fear. Riddhi—"

"I can guess." Vritika came to stand before Kajal, forcing her to meet her venomous gaze. "Riddhi kept riling you up, so you unleashed your bhuta on her."

"It was an *accident*," Kajal stressed. "I tried to stop Lasya, but she's far more powerful than I am. And when I deny her a kill, she turns on me instead."

"You considered your life more important than Riddhi's, then."

Kajal supposed that was true. But she couldn't properly explain that a body would give in to any demand if only to lessen its agony.

"If that's how you see it, fine," Kajal said. "But I tried to save Riddhi. Whether you believe it or not, I wanted you to know. And to apologize on behalf of me and Lasya. It isn't enough, but it's all I can offer." Kajal had little practice in apologies and wasn't fond of how squirmy it made her feel, but she bowed her head anyway, hoping it conveyed her sincerity.

Vritika didn't say anything at first, glaring at the grass between their feet. Then she aggressively wiped her eyes.

"Get out of my sight," Vritika muttered.

Kajal was more than happy to oblige. She returned to where Kutaa waited, ears pricked as if he'd been listening in on the conversation.

He wasn't the only one. Kajal froze under the mantle of Tav's gaze, unable to decipher the peculiar look on his face until he nodded at her.

Sadness. Empathy. Respect.

Already jittery from the conversation, Kajal settled down with Kutaa, filled with an uncomfortable chagrin. Her sleep was broken and uneasy, but she managed a few hours of dozing, on the edge of true dreaming.

When she opened her eyes to the spreading dawn, she found something wooden in the grass beside her. Kajal lifted it to better see. It was a small figurine, somewhat crudely whittled but unmistakably in the shape of Kutaa.

Kajal turned. Tav sat cross-legged facing her, as if he'd been awake awhile. As soon as their eyes met, he scrambled to his feet and busied himself with saddling the horses.

Fighting back a smile, she held the figurine out to Kutaa for his appraisal, and he gave it a cursory sniff. Then she slipped it into her pocket and got ready for what was sure to be a challenging day.

Kajal mused over Ranbir's last words while Kutaa trotted beside her horse. On her opposite side, Tav was tight-lipped and wan. The other three were in the lead.

"Maybe Advaith removed Ranbir's jewel so that he could get past him," Kajal said, her voice creaking with disuse. Other than her apology to Vritika, she'd hardly spoken since leaving the forest. "To join you in battle."

Tav stirred. "I thought of that. But if so, why remove his jewel instead of bringing Ranbir with him to fight Bakshi?" He shook his head. "It doesn't make sense."

Kajal had to agree. There were still so many pieces missing, like the burned-out holes in Tav's memories.

"He thought you were Advaith," Kajal said after a long pause.

"Most people do." His voice was flat.

She fidgeted with the reins. "Lasya and I once stayed in a town where there was a girl named Hafa. When we found work dyeing fabrics at the river, she taught us the basics. She was pretty and had a contagious laugh."

Tav silently yet bewilderedly allowed her to go on.

"But Lasya was better at flirting than I was. I always ended up being mean. I accidentally pushed Hafa into the river, and Lasya was the one who pulled her out." Kajal was torn between laughing and cringing at the memory. "Naturally, Hafa liked Lasya more. I found them kissing behind a shed."

"I'm . . . sorry?"

"Don't be. It was silly, and pointless. We ended up leaving town a couple days later." She swallowed, thinking about the rock that had struck

Lasya's temple. "What I'm trying to say is, I understand what it's like to be the lesser-known sibling, the less favored. I didn't mind being in Lasya's shadow—she was the better of us, it made sense—but once in a while, I could see just how far apart we were."

Tav processed her words while she stared straight ahead and pretended she hadn't just yanked a rotting tooth from her mouth.

"I also didn't mind being in Advaith's shadow," he said at last. "Most of the time. But there were moments I didn't feel like my own person. Even now, I don't." The hand resting on the box curled inward. "My whole life was dedicated to him. I guess I'm learning who I am without him. I don't know who that is, really."

She recalled that first horrible month after Lasya's death, the numbing, endless abyss of it. Like crawling without a destination, a hopeless, half-hearted shuffle to move forward without knowing why you needed to move at all or what waited for you ahead.

Kajal gripped the saddle horn tight. Who she was without Lasya was only a worse version of who she'd been before: a girl who didn't care about consequences so long as she got what she wanted. Selfish and uncaring and dishonest.

"I killed her," she whispered. She thought of the dakini's forehead against hers, the affirmation she'd longed to hear but didn't deserve.

Tav's gaze was heavy. "How?"

"Does it matter? She's gone because of me. The best one died, leaving the other to cause problems." She stole a glimpse at Vritika and found the girl's head turned toward them. Realizing she'd been caught, Vritika nudged her horse faster.

"That's not true." Strength had returned to Tav's voice, and he shifted his horse closer to hers. "Your help has been invaluable. Without you, I . . ." He gave a feeble huff. "Without you, I'd still be dead."

Any appreciation Kajal would have felt at the words was lost in the maelstrom of doubt her thoughts had become since her time in the dakinis' forest. Since Vivaan and Sezal had revealed themselves and given her their ultimatum. Since that vine of blight had broken free of the earth.

"Kajal?"

She looked up. Tav was toying with his amber pendant, the hope in his eyes so delicate it made her throat constrict. He opened his mouth, but suddenly she couldn't bear to hear whatever he was about to say.

That's when Jassi's voice called out, "We're here."

In the distance rose the spine of the eastern mountains, the ridges dark purple against the oncoming sunset. Less than fifty miles north lay the village of Siphar, where all this had started. Where Kajal had buried Lasya with the promise to return and revive her.

Kajal's vision darkened under the force of her heartbeat, and she reached for the pouch containing her sister's finger. The rebels would pay for what they'd done, but first and foremost she had to make sure they had no reason to set fire to Lasya's body.

"Ride for the nearest city and get someone to escort you back to the university," Jassi told Vritika. "I know the Meghanis favor Bakshi and wouldn't want you caught up in this."

"But I—"

"Unlike us, you actually have a choice," Dalbir said. The closer they'd gotten to the estate, the more reticent they'd become, and they'd even tucked their journal away. "Take advantage of that, and leave while you can."

Vritika clearly wanted to argue, but Jassi's plaintive expression made her shoulders fall. "I won't go far," she warned. "Not until I learn the bhuta's been taken care of." She spared Kajal a glare before turning her horse north.

The rest of them continued south, to the estate. It was ringed by a stone wall, its gates armed with guards in dark uniforms. At Dalbir's order, the gates opened, and they were admitted into the courtyard.

"Well, this is it," Dalbir said gloomily. "Welcome to my family's seat."

It was the biggest home Kajal had ever seen. The exterior was made of white brick and stone, with long columns and square balconies, framed by scalloped archways. A rectangular pool in the courtyard was surrounded by palms and geometric hedges. Kajal would have appreciated it a lot more if every inch of her hadn't been screaming to run inside and demand they tell her where they had put Lasya.

A small welcoming party appeared at the front entrance. Kajal's upper lip curled when she spotted Vivaan and Sezal in their human guises. Beside them stood a woman and a turbaned man in their midyears, their clothes colorful and immaculate next to the rebels' travel-worn garb.

They all dismounted, and Dalbir touched their parents' feet in respect. Their mother reached down to cradle the back of their head.

"We missed you, beta," Shrimati Sodhi said. "Has there been any trouble?"

Dalbir looked over their shoulder, as if debating whether or not to mention the blight, the Vadhia, the dakinis' forest. At Kajal's small headshake, they smiled at their mother.

"No trouble," they lied.

Vivaan's gaze fell upon the box Tav held. "Is that . . . ?"

Tav held the box closer, regarding him frostily. "Did you find the rest of him?"

Vivaan visibly had to restrain himself, hands fisted at his sides.

Sezal spoke for him. "We did. All that's missing is his head."

The Sodhis stared at Tav. Kajal wondered if they were now fretting over a succession crisis, like Tav's father had.

"Astounding," Shrimati Sodhi murmured. She turned to Vivaan and Sezal. "I was skeptical when you first said there could be a way to revive the prince. But you truly came through. Well done."

It was because of me, Kajal thought, indignant at having her praise stolen.

When Tav caught the husband's eye, the man brushed down his mustache before bowing. "We welcome you into our home, Your Highness. We must admit it is a surprise to know of your existence, but by no means a bad one. To think the crown prince had a brother, and that you were the asura and deva . . ."

His wife laid a hand upon his shoulder as Tav's expression grew chillier. "We will discuss this inside. Please, follow us."

Kajal stepped forward. "Where is my sister?"

The Sodhis looked puzzled. Did they not even know they had the corpse of a dead girl in their lavish estate?

"You'll see her once the crown prince is resurrected," Vivaan said. "And only then."

Kajal would have pressed, but Shrimati Sodhi had cocked her head to one side, her large golden earrings swaying. "You must be the girl they mentioned."

Kajal's skin prickled under the woman's assessment. Unimpressed with what she saw, Shrimati Sodhi turned without further comment.

Reluctantly, Kajal passed the threshold. The interior boasted white walls with hanging tapestries and silver-framed mirrors, wooden floors that shone like glass, and a wide, curving staircase that led to an upper floor. She had peeked into fancy homes before, had even been inside a couple when she and Lasya had been hired for the odd job here and there, and every time she was rocked by the realization that there were people in this world who could throw away their money on things they had no use for. The hanging jeweled incense holders, for example, or the decorative glazed vases that had no purpose other than to sit there collecting dust.

She was a second away from sprinting off in search of Lasya. Kajal thought she could sense the bhuta at the edge of her consciousness, ready to be called on. She was closer than she'd been in months and still so far away.

Dalbir seemed embarrassed at Kajal's assessment, but they relaxed when two brown dogs ran up to them. Unlike rural mutts that people considered little better than scavengers, these hounds were sleek and powerful, clearly bred for guarding the estate. Dalbir greeted them with enthusiastic pets until the hounds turned to Kutaa, who only stared at them until they flattened their ears with soft whines.

Seeing that Kutaa had followed Kajal, Shri Sodhi wrinkled his nose. "The dog stays outside."

Kajal scowled and knelt to whisper to Kutaa, "Keep an eye on the surroundings." He pressed his cold nose to her cheek before trotting back outside.

"We were worried the process would take much longer," Shrimati Sodhi said as she led them through wide double doors into another open courtyard cut into the middle of the estate. "The Vadhia are passing through this area more and more of late, as if Bakshi wants us to know that he is keeping an eye on us. Not to mention all the trouble they're stirring in the countryside."

Trouble. As if such a mild word could encompass the torture, interrogation, and death brought about by their hands.

"We've received multiple reports of hangings," her husband added. "Dharati is being decimated with blight more and more each day. The farms around here are failing. The people want an easy way out, and the Vadhia are preying on their fear."

Vivaan and Sezal both glanced at Kajal. She flexed her fingers, remembering how it had felt to hold a jar of poison to her lips.

They were led into a wide parlor at the rear of the estate. There were no guards or servants here, and the whole wing had an empty, unlived-in atmosphere. The room featured dark wooden floorboards and furniture in red upholstery, with ceramics and decorative weapons lining the walls. Incense burned in every corner, and Kajal immediately recognized the five elements used in Ayurveda, tangled in a cloying braid of scents: cassia for water, anise for ether, valerian for earth, vetiver for air, and clove for fire.

The last one burned at the head of a shrouded body that lay in the middle of the room. Or, rather, the incense burned where the head *should* have been.

Tav released an unsteady breath. The rebels must have removed Advaith's body from the soil as soon as they'd seen their horses on the horizon. They wanted this done immediately.

"We gathered the materials you requested," Shrimati Sodhi said with dip of her chin at Vivaan and Sezal. "Thank you for providing us with instructions."

They had used her notebook. Kajal fought against nausea at the idea of these people looking through her notes—her simple, hard-to-read handwriting and nonsensical doodles—and focused on the tall slab of limestone the body was lying on.

"Well?" Vivaan directed at Kajal.

Everyone looked to her. This would not be like working in the laboratory, where she'd had blessed privacy; this was a stage, an ordeal, and if she didn't perform to their liking, there would be a price to pay.

She will burn.

Heart racing, Kajal gestured to Tav. He knelt beside the shroud and unlatched the box. Vivaan crouched beside him as Tav lovingly lifted out Advaith's head, brushing dirt from his brother's face and hair. Vivaan made a soft, punched-out sound, and Sezal squeezed his shoulder. The Sodhis looked eagerly on, as if this really were some morbid play.

"The body's already been washed," Sezal told Kajal. She indicated a wooden basin with water nearby, next to a bowl of thick, granular pink salt. "We noticed he—"

"Has a heartbeat," Kajal finished. Sezal nodded, discomfited.

"Wait," Dalbir blurted, "are you telling me he's actually *alive*?"

"Yes and no." Kajal pressed her fingertips to Advaith's shrouded chest. "He does have a faint pulse, but it's not providing any circulation or keeping his organs active. I don't know what's causing it."

"Will it make reviving him easier?" Sezal asked.

"I suppose we'll see." Kajal lightly touched Tav's forearm. "Tav?"

Hearing the question in her tone, he picked up the cloth draped over the water basin. Carefully, he washed Advaith's face, threading water through his hair and detangling it with his fingers. Kajal couldn't watch, so she turned to the Sodhis.

"We'll need thread," she said. "Thick and durable, as well as suturing needles."

Once Advaith was fully clean, Kajal knelt at his head where the incense had been burning, the lingering smell of clove in her nose.

Advaith was in three pieces. Even if it were possible to bring him back on her own, the body had suffered more trauma than Tav's. It would be a challenge even with the aid of his weak heartbeat. As much as she didn't want to ask for help, she needed Jassi's assistance.

First, they'd have to sew him up. The shroud was lifted away, and Tav hissed at the sight of the long, nasty stab wound above Advaith's heart. The skin there was dark red and puckered, like it had attempted to heal. Even Kajal was unsettled by it.

"Bakshi," Tav growled. "I'm going to repay him twice over for everything he's done to us."

"One step at a time," Kajal murmured.

Tav's face was grave as he held his brother's legs in place. Kajal and Jassi reattached Advaith's middle, a process that left them with cramped hands and faces damp with sweat. The head was difficult to keep in place, and the sensation of the thick, curved needle sliding through dead flesh left Kajal queasy.

When they were done, a line of black *x*'s surrounded Advaith's neck like a torc and riddled his midsection like a belt. Tav scrubbed him down with salt—he'd insisted on doing it alone, and no one opposed him—while Kajal instructed Jassi on what to do next.

She had a sense of déjà vu while she worked, remembering doing this to the boy currently kneeling at her side. Jassi applied adder's-tongue oil to Advaith's doshas while Kajal carefully pried the prince's mouth open to pour a mixture of haw and zinc down his throat. She trembled as she sprinkled the gotu kola and the goldenrod. Tav covered her hand with his.

"It's all right." His voice was as strangled as her chest felt. "No matter what happens. It's all right."

Kajal bit her lower lip nearly hard enough to draw blood. She didn't deserve this gentleness, this preemptive forgiveness. None of it.

The Sodhis sat on one of the couches, Dalbir watching the proceedings intently. The rebels stood motionless and grim, ready to put a halt to everything should Kajal try to pull something. When the preparations were done, Kajal stared at the face between her hands, a mirror of Tav's.

The crown prince of Dharati. The asura of Patala. The other half of Tav's soul.

It was absurd, how so much depended on one person.

Tav's shoulder pressed into hers. "I believe in you," he whispered.

They were the same words Lasya had once spoken, so sure that Kajal could fix anything she set her mind to.

What if I can't fix this? she thought. *What if I'm only destined to break?*

She focused on the warmth of Tav's shoulder until she got herself under control. Pressing her palm to the top of Advaith's head, she whispered, "Sahasrara, open." An ember of the silent chakra flared to life, far faster than Tav's had. As if it had been waiting, dormant and patient, for this very moment. She moved her thumb to the center of his forehead. "Ajna, open."

She traveled down Advaith's body, following the trickle of energy that began to circle through him. Jassi kept her hands on the prince's chest, ready to keep the energy flowing once the chakras in those sections were woken.

"This should be impossible," Jassi murmured. "It shouldn't be this *easy*. If this were public knowledge, any physician could revive a dead body."

"It doesn't matter," Vivaan cut in. "We only need *him* revived, and then the knowledge can die out."

Kajal's fingers twitched. *Die out*. Did the rebels mean to kill them once this was done? Throw her notebook onto the pyre that held their bodies? She could sense Jassi's apprehension growing too, and Kajal wondered if she was thinking about her younger sister being left to fend for herself.

By the time she reached Advaith's chest, Kajal was drenched in sweat and shivering with nerves. Tav kept her upright as she pressed her fingers above the prince's miraculously beating heart. She traced the groove of the lethal wound, the spot that had proven the asura's mortality against a single blade.

"Anahata, open."

The chakra unfurled and flared so fast that Kajal would have been knocked over if it hadn't been for Tav. She sensed his power shooting through her, past her fingertips and into his brother's heart. She groaned through her teeth at the charged current of it.

Advaith's body jerked and arched. The limestone underneath him cracked and crumbled. Behind them, the Sodhis had begun to pray.

A painful second later, Advaith's feeble heartbeat gave a thunderous jolt, and his eyes flew open.

Everyone flew back by some invisible force. Kajal landed in a tangle with Tav on the rug. Jassi hit the wall, and some of the Sodhis' delicate ceramics fell, crashing around her. Shri Sodhi covered his and his wife's heads with his arms while Dalbir ducked behind the couch.

The crown prince sat up with a gasp amid the broken chunks of limestone. His hair fell in lank strands, hiding his face as he frantically felt the sutures at his throat. Blood trickled from his chest wound.

Tav pushed to his knees. "Adi!"

Advaith whirled around and froze. The twins stared at each other: inverted images, identical yet not.

Tav stretched out a shaking hand. He touched Advaith's cheek, and his brother's eyelids fluttered.

"Tav," Advaith whispered. His voice was wrecked, hoarse, like gravel siding down a ravine.

Tav's chest hitched, and he settled his hand on Advaith's shoulder. "It's me. You're here. We're . . . We're all right. We're *alive*."

Advaith licked his chapped lips, removing the granules of salt that clung in the corners. "Alive." He took in the room. His eyes were half a shade of brown darker than Tav's, and they slid impassively over Kajal until they lit in recognition at Vivaan and Sezal.

They fell to their knees and prostrated themselves, just as they had when they'd thought Tav was Advaith. "Your Majesty," Vivaan whispered, the words laid bare like a heart cradled within careful hands. "Blessed Asura, welcome back."

Advaith took an uneven breath, his eyes bright.

Tav scooted closer to him, his hand burning blue as he pressed it to Advaith's stab wound. "Do you remember what happened?" Tav asked.

"I . . . I think so. Why am I here?"

Kajal could only sit in stunned exhaustion while Tav quickly told him about the Harama Plain, the note they'd found in his room, how the Sodhis wanted to restore his rightful title as heir to Dharati. The Sodhis themselves had fallen into postures of deference, except for Dalbir, who stared at Advaith from behind the couch and mumbled soundlessly to themselves; likely what they were planning to jot down in their journal later.

Advaith looked to Vivaan. Something passed between them, something that made Kajal's gut twist. Advaith's confusion had mellowed into an unusual calmness.

"I see." Advaith smiled up at Tav, but the smile was small and sad and didn't reach his eyes. "And here we are, together again."

"Advaith . . . why did you follow me to the Harama Plain? You were supposed to stay protected at the fort. Ranbir was . . . Did you . . . ?"

Advaith tucked some of Tav's hair behind his ear. Kajal noticed that the ruby in the ring he wore had a shape similar to the hole in Ranbir's forehead. "So there are things you don't remember. Maybe that's for the best."

"What? Why?"

"It wasn't meant to turn out this way. He promised so many things, and I believed all of them." Advaith gave a rueful laugh. "I suppose that's my fault, isn't it?"

The knot in Kajal's stomach tightened as Tav leaned away from him. The wound he'd been healing was now covered in a thin layer of fragile skin.

"What are you saying?" Tav whispered.

Advaith's smile twisted, and he dropped his hand to the place on Tav's torso where Kajal knew his own fatal wounds lay.

"Did it hurt," Advaith asked, "when my blade found you here?"

Chapter Twenty-Five

NOBODY IN THE room moved. They may as well not have existed save for the two brothers locked in their half embrace, one stricken and the other wearing a pained, crooked smile.

"Ah, Tav," Advaith whispered. "Are you remembering now?"

Tav's breaths shortened. Kajal wanted to drag him away, but there were red tendrils emanating from Advaith's bare shoulders, and the rings of his irises were glowing scarlet—an unspoken warning to anyone who dared interrupt them.

"You . . ." Tav put his hand over Advaith's, over the closed wounds. "You were with him. Bakshi."

The scarlet in Advaith's eyes flickered. "That fool. He told me—" He cut himself off with a shake of his head. The ends of his hair brushed his shoulders. "No. I'll deal with it later." He turned to Vivaan and Sezal. "I believe you're to thank for this?"

Vivaan, still kneeling in genuflection, seemed torn over whether to admit or deny it. "You didn't tell us you were leaving the fort," he said instead. The accusation was quiet but all the more palpable for it.

"Or what you planned to do." Sezal glanced at Tav, clearly wanting to ask if it was true—if the asura had really killed his own brother. "Since that battle, we've been stuck in Martya. Our only source of news from Patala has been from the nagas."

There was a flash of . . . regret? hurt? . . . on Advaith's face, too quick for Kajal to process. "I'm sorry. It all happened so fast." Lowering his voice, he asked, "Did it work? The halahala?"

Sezal frowned. "You mean the blight?"

"Blight? No, that's not . . ." Advaith's fingers tightened against Tav's wound until his brother grunted. "Something must have gone wrong. Which means there's still work to do."

Advaith looked back up at Tav, his next smile showing teeth. "And now we can do it together, bhara."

The Sodhis offered Advaith a change of clothes, a rosewater bath, almond oil for his skin, and someone to treat his hair. He donned a black-and-silver dhoti sherwani but waved the rest away; his thick hair, which fell in waves of black, was tamed only by his fingers.

The rebels explained the situation to him while he dressed. Jassi sat, reticent, on the couch and stared at the line of sutures around Advaith's throat. Dalbir stood near their parents with arms crossed, their earlier excitement long since faded to disquiet.

Tav sat on his heels beside Kajal with his hands held open in his lap, as if asking for an explanation to fall into them. His expression was bemused, the face of someone forced to accept something they could not.

Did it hurt when my blade found you here?

Everyone thought Bakshi had killed Tav on the Harama Plain. Yet somehow, inexplicably, the one who had spilled his lifeblood was his own brother.

Why? Kajal thought as a shudder racked through her, remembering the pain in Lasya's cry. *Why?*

She reached for Tav, but he flinched when her fingers brushed his thigh. She snatched her hand back and continued to shiver on her own.

"I remember you," Advaith said. "If I recall correctly, you come from a line of cousins."

Dalbir raised an eyebrow. "We're related?"

"Distantly." Advaith smiled with disarming cheer. "I believe my father often invited your parents to the palace," he said to Shrimati Sodhi.

"Yes," she agreed. "I would sometimes accompany them."

Advaith snapped his fingers. "That's right! You and I played pachisi. You were quite good."

She flushed and ducked her head while her husband looked on with discomfort. "We knew that what Anu Bakshi did was unjust," she said. "So we moved out of the capital and kept our relationship to the royal family quiet. I vowed to find some way to undo the damage he's caused in your absence."

"So *you* are the ones responsible for reviving not only me, but my brother."

She reluctantly shook her head. "I did not revive you. I merely supplied the necessary Ayurvedic resources."

"Then who did?"

Vivaan stepped forward and jerked his chin at Kajal. "That one."

The crown prince turned, and his eyes met Kajal's for the first time. His maintained a tinge of red while they studied her with focused intensity, like a scavenger looking for the best pieces of meat to strip from the bone.

Then those eyes narrowed. "Such a miracle can be performed with Ayurveda?"

When Kajal remained silent, Vivaan snapped, "Answer your king."

She couldn't help the wry twitch of her mouth. "Who's a king? Pretty sure someone else's ass warms the throne. Goes by the name Bakshi. Maybe you've heard of him. Felt his sword go through your gut, even."

Before Vivaan could retort, Advaith threw his head back and laughed. The prince's laughter shocked Vivaan into silence, but his shock quickly gave way to soft wonder. Beside him, Sezal looked similarly torn between concern and fondness.

"You're not wrong!" Advaith agreed. "But we'll change that soon enough."

He strode over and grasped her chin, forcing her gaze higher. All traces of humor fled, leaving him solemn and searching. She held her breath and focused on the ring of scarlet around his irises. She might as well have been a bird pinned under the curious, cruel hands of a boy yearning to understand how she worked.

A cold, familiar wisp curled around her. The faintest hint of a whine. The barest caress of a whisper. Advaith's grip tightened on her chin, squeezing painfully as two of his fingers pressed into her pulsing carotid artery.

"Ayurveda," he repeated slowly, and if she didn't know any better, she'd say he was amused.

In a flash, Tav was on his feet. He grabbed his brother's wrist to wrench Advaith's hand away, glaring at him with eyes burning blue. In that moment he was beyond boy or animal, a creature of both divine and feral construct.

Advaith inhaled sharply, then let it out as a breathy laugh. "Bhara, why so grim? I won't hurt her. I'm merely interested in how she came to learn such an unorthodox procedure."

"We aren't answering questions now," Tav said in a low voice, and Kajal's mind snagged on the word *We*. "Not until you answer mine. Why did you work with Bakshi?"

Advaith tried to tug his wrist away, but Tav squeezed until he made a pained sound. Only then did Tav let go, and Advaith took a couple steps back. Vivaan put a warning hand on his sword's hilt with a glower at Tav.

"Working with Bakshi," Advaith muttered. He touched the sutures lining his neck, fingertips bumping along their black ridges. "I was *betrayed* by Bakshi."

"What are you talking about?" Tav demanded. "Speak clearly, Adi."

Advaith stilled at the nickname. A mask slipped over his face, shuttering the flashes of bright life that had been returned to him. Like he'd brushed up against something that burned and immediately retreated, a hand feeling the kiss of a hot stove.

"You wouldn't understand," he whispered at last.

"How do you expect me to understand unless you explain?" The glow of Tav's eyes had dimmed, but at this they blazed again. "Explain why it was *your* weapon that gave me these wounds. Explain why you're the one who killed me!"

His voice rose with the same ferocious grief that howled in Kajal's chest. The whine in the back of her skull rose higher.

Advaith shut his eyes. "I didn't . . . Tav, I didn't mean for it to happen. He told me all we had to do was fight."

"Who told you? Bakshi?"

"No. Lord Dukha."

The Sodhis touched their foreheads to the floor with fervid, whispered prayers against the name of the demon lord invoked in their household. Shri Sodhi drew out a small marble icon of the Elephant. Advaith, seeing this, snatched it out of his hand.

"Does a mere name scare you into theatrics?" Advaith demanded. "Has the demon lord been reduced to nothing but a tale to induce nightmares?" He closed his hand around the Elephant icon, and it crumbled to white dust between his fingers. The Sodhis gasped.

"There would be no balance in this world without his existence, without the rakshasas! And yet," Advaith went on with a bitter laugh, sweeping his arm around the room, "everyone believes it's solely the yakshas that keep this plane stable. They are taught that yakshas are *good*, that they are *necessary*, but the rakshasas . . . We become cautionary tales, things to be feared in the dark. The yakshas become saviors, and we become *monsters*."

He threw the white dust at Tav's feet. Tav stared at him with hands clenched at his sides, imploring, as if they'd had this argument before.

"No one thinks you're a monster, Adi," he said carefully.

Advaith's smile was pitying. "Of course people think the asura is a monster. The asura always works for the demon lord. They're associated with rakshasas. They could raise an army of demons, if they so wished."

Kajal thought back to the vendor Tav had been aggravated by in Suraj. The drawings that had rendered the asura with hideous features.

"For too long, Martya has been crying about the horrors of demons," Advaith continued. "Never mind that the majority keep to themselves and don't interfere in humans' lives. Never mind that yakshas are not always benevolent—that they are capable of greed, anger, and capriciousness. From the hungry ghosts who waylay travelers to those who drag unsuspecting creatures into their dens."

Realizing white powder still clung to his hand, Advaith brushed it carelessly on his new clothes. "But humans seem to have forgotten this. Just as they forget that every living thing within the Brahimada carries the same three energies. Although the yakshas are high in sattva and the rakshasas high in tamas, they're *both* necessary in balancing out Martya's rajasic energy. But when the hunting of demons became commonplace, tamas receded, and the yakshas' energy surged. The natural balance of Martya was thrown off, and rakshasas suffered as a result."

His gaze grew distant. "There was a field full of oleander shrubs. A herd of aga ghora liked to graze on them. Do you remember, Tav, how we used to race the horses across the plains? They were so *fast*, and so beautiful. We'd sit and watch them for hours."

He flexed his hand, red light flickering at his fingertips. "When the herd grew, do you know what the yakshas did? They poisoned the flowers. Do you have any idea what it was like, seeing the field strewn with their bodies?"

His voice broke. Tav made an aborted move toward him.

"Lord Dukha revealed to me that the yaksha deities do not care for us," Advaith went on softly. "He himself suffered great hardship due to their neglect, and knew they favored humans over rakshasas. So we planned to create an abundance of tamas, to balance out the overflowing sattva."

"How?" Tav asked.

"Conflict. Lord Dukha helped Bakshi gather power, with the intention of killing him once he'd served his purpose. Then Lord Dukha told me we had to set the stage for a battle."

"*What?* Why would Lord Dukha bring such chaos to Dharati?" Tav demanded. "And why didn't you tell me any of this?"

"Because I knew you would try to stop me." Advaith stubbornly lifted his chin. It reminded Kajal of the moments she had tried to pester Lasya into doing something she wasn't comfortable with. "Because this was our attack on the gods."

Tav reeled back, and even Kajal was stunned by his audaciousness. *Attack on the gods?*

"We would find a way to make them retreat, to let the rakshasas grow in number until proper balance was attained," Advaith explained. "We would show the world that we are not things to be hunted or killed. That we are not *evil.*"

"And starting a war would accomplish that?" Tav retorted.

"It wasn't only about starting a war." Advaith kept running his fingers over his sutures, tracing each black *x* sewn into his skin. "As Lord Dukha explained it, the battlefield was to be our stage. One where you and I had to face each other as opponents."

There was a flicker in Tav's eyes, like a memory was trying to break free. "Opponents . . . ?"

"It was the only way to produce the kind of tamas that would make the yaksha deities go into hiding." Advaith turned to him. "A clash of opposites. Of the asura and deva."

Kajal's mind spun back to a night by a diseased lake, the nagi's sibilant voice traveling through the dark:

"Churning waters and blood-soaked ground,
Metal strikes with fearsome sound.
The venom swells below their feet."

"Halahala," Dalbir said, coming to the same conclusion. "The cosmic toxin."

"So what the nagas said was true." Kajal started at Jassi's voice, having forgotten she was there. The young woman's face was slack with shock. "Halahala *is* the blight. That's what has been slowly killing Dharati."

And it had been created when the asura and deva had turned against each other.

Advaith frowned at Jassi, then looked at Vivaan for confirmation. Vivaan hesitated before inclining his head.

"The bl— The halahala has spread wide these last two decades," Vivaan explained.

"It started after the battle on the Harama Plain," Sezal added delicately. "And lately, it's growing worse. It's finding its way into farms and fields. Animals. Even people."

The living warmth that had returned to Advaith's face leached away. "It . . . ? No. No, it was never supposed to spread that far. Lord Dukha would have stopped it."

Vivaan and Sezal had one of their silent conversations until Sezal said, "We haven't seen Lord Dukha in many years. According to the nagas, no one in Patala has."

Kajal's head flared with pain. The whine was almost loud enough to drown out the others' voices.

"I don't understand." Advaith pressed the heel of his hand against his forehead like he was also in pain. "The whole point was to make for a more equal world, to balance Martya. Why wouldn't he stop halahala from destroying everything? Why did—?" His breaths stuttered, the red in his eyes growing brighter. "Why did he allow Bakshi to kill me? I was supposed to rule. He— *Why is he on my throne?*"

The ache in Kajal's head made her want to scream. She doubled over with the sound caught between her teeth, fingers digging in her hair. Tav grasped her shoulders, but she couldn't hear him over the droning whine, the buzzing hum of *Lotus Blossom*.

Kajal forced her head up. Lasya's bhuta floated in the middle of the room, wind whipping so violently around her that pieces of broken limestone rose and crashed into the walls, the ceramics and decorative weapons falling from their hooks.

Vivaan and Sezal instantly dropped their glamours and flanked Advaith. At the sight of the two demons, the Sodhis screamed and dragged Dalbir with them against the wall.

Kajal expected Lasya to be invisible to Advaith. Instead, his eyes widened, and he quickly muttered something under his breath that sounded like a mantra; Kajal heard the word *trishul*. But just as the sudarshana chakra had refused to materialize for Tav, the asura's weapon didn't come to its master.

Lasya rushed at him. The bhuta rammed into the demons' shields, hissing and making terrible, high-pitched keens.

"Don't," Kajal gasped around the agony in her skull. "Stop her!"

Tav flung his arms out, and blue light engulfed his hands. The walls around them groaned until cracks splintered from the ceiling. Through the cracks floated white yaksha butterflies, descending on the bhuta with single-minded purpose. Lasya twisted away from them, their light paling her contorted features, until she shrieked once more and disappeared.

Kajal collapsed. Her head rang in the aftermath, the corner of her mouth wet with either spit or blood. Tav turned her over, saying something she couldn't register.

Advaith appeared upside down above her, lips parted and eyebrows furrowed in thought.

"So you can bite with more than words," the crown prince murmured. "You grow more interesting by the minute." He turned to his aides. "Find a place to keep her locked up for now, until we can figure out our next moves."

"N-Next moves?" stammered one of the Sodhis, still staring in horror at the danavas.

"I'm getting rid of Anu Bakshi. I will need you to tell me every piece of information you have on him." Advaith looked back down at Kajal, and she had the disorienting view of his face above Tav's, so similar and so different. "Then I will open the gates to Patala and demand answers from Lord Dukha."

Chapter Twenty-Six

VIVAAN SHOVED KAJAL and Tav into a dark cellar below the estate, filled with dusty jars of wine and sura. Kajal charged at the demons but only ended up running into the heavy door as they slammed it shut and turned the lock.

"Take me to my sister!" she screamed. "At least bring her body to me!"

"Wait here until His Majesty decides what to do with you," came Vivaan's uncaring voice from the other side.

A murmur from Sezal was followed by a scoff, and then they were gone.

Kajal's vision spun, her heart beating too fast. It was like being holed up in that cell in Kinara, Kutaa howling outside while she waited for dawn and the promise of poison.

Her hand slipped into her pocket. The demons had taken her dagger, but she still had the pouch containing Lasya's finger and the vial of bitter almond extract. *What a pointless thing to make,* she thought. It wasn't as if she could grab the demons and shove the extract down their throats. Would such a base poison even work on them?

Her fingers brushed the edge of something wooden. She pulled it out and stared at the little Kutaa figurine Tav had carved for her.

A touch on her shoulder. "Kajal."

She jerked away. "What are you even doing here?"

Advaith had been baffled when Tav had insisted on being locked up with her. "Bhara, come and help me," Advaith had wheedled. "We need that tactical mind of yours."

"Help you with what?" Tav had spat. "Killing yakshas? Making demons the superior power in Martya?"

Advaith had blinked. "It's not about killing yakshas, Tav. It's about balance."

"The halahala has thrown *everything* off-balance!"

"Which is why we need to work together to end it. We'll stop Bakshi *and* the blight." He'd taken Tav's hands in his. "Let me make it up to you. The things that went wrong, I . . . I can make up for them. Trust me."

Advaith had even allowed Jassi to sit in on his counsel with the Sodhis, after being told she'd helped resurrect him and that she had considerable knowledge of Ayurveda.

Kajal hadn't missed the hurt on Advaith's face at Tav's stubborn refusal.

"I don't need your . . . your protection, or whatever this is," Kajal said now. She threw the carving at Tav, and he caught it.

"I'm not doing anything with Advaith until I know more about the deal he made with Lord Dukha." Tav's hand strayed to his mostly healed wounds. "And what about it went wrong."

"You're more useful with him than rotting in some cellar, then."

"*You're* here," he said softly. As if that were any rational justification.

A feverish heat swept through her—fury and desperation, and something so small and weak it couldn't possibly survive if she acknowledged it. She held her head in her hands even though the pain had long faded, still caught in its spindrift.

"Kajal—"

"Don't." Somewhere in this estate lay her sister's body, and in a twisted sense of fate, it was now Kajal beneath the earth. A broken laugh tumbled from her lips, and once she started, she couldn't stop.

She'd thought all her problems would fall away once the prince was resurrected, once the rebels had their ticket to the throne, once she reunited with Lasya. But the situation was so much more hopelessly knotted than that. She was a gnat stuck in the web that Advaith and Bakshi and the demon lord had spun years and years ago. A web that not even Advaith fully understood.

A web she had tried to untangle, with fatal consequences.

"I couldn't do it." She sobbed, or maybe she was still laughing. "We tried, but nothing worked. And I thought . . . When you said you were the deva, I thought . . ."

Thought that everything would be fixed. That she would be absolved. Forgotten. Left to do as she pleased.

She should have known that fate had other plans for her.

"What are you talking about?" Tav asked.

She didn't answer.

Several minutes passed until the tide of mania washed away, leaving her exhausted. Not two hours ago, she had brought a boy back to life. She swayed, and Tav propped her up against him.

"You should lie down," he said.

But her thoughts were racing. "He never said anything to you about his plan?" she mumbled into his chest.

She heard the click of his throat as he swallowed. "I always agreed with him that Martya's view of the rakshasas was unfair, that we should look for ways to unify them." He took a deep breath, which expanded his chest beneath Kajal's cheek. "I didn't think Advaith would resort to something this extreme. That he'd work with Anu Bakshi, or that Bakshi was under the patronage of Lord Dukha."

I remember how you two fought, toward the end, Vivaan had said. "He didn't act differently before the Harama Plain?" Kajal asked.

He thought about it. "It's difficult to say. When Bakshi began to rise to power, everything was chaotic. Advaith frequently went to Patala. I thought he was asking for Lord Dukha's assistance, since the demon lord doesn't normally interfere in Martya's affairs." A wry laugh. "Apparently, it was the other way around."

Kajal's mouth was so dry. She pushed away from Tav and found the nearest jar, shoving off the lid before tipping the rim toward her mouth. Distilled liquor the color of honey dribbled down her chin. She'd only tasted sura on a couple of occasions, both times finding it less than ideal, but now the astringence was a welcome reprieve.

"Kajal," Tav whispered, half admonishing.

She ignored him and took another large gulp that burned on the way down. It immediately kindled a warmth in her stomach to combat the chill of the cellar. "All I wanted was my sister. That's all I wanted."

"I know."

"I didn't want all of this asura-and-deva nonsense. I didn't want to be involved in bids for a throne."

"I know."

If he noticed the tears making tracks on her face, he wisely kept it to himself. Instead, he sat near her—with enough space between them so she wouldn't feel crowded—and held the amber pendant in one hand, the figurine in the other.

A low sound filled the cellar, and it took her a moment to realize it was coming from him.

Lotus Blossom. The song she'd sung to Lasya on lonely, desolate nights. The song Kajal had woven into the muscle and tissue of who she was until it had gotten warped through the bhuta's perversion.

Kajal squeezed her eyes shut to stop the tears, but they only came on faster, the sobs trapped in her throat hardening into walnut-shaped knots that refused to crack open. Unthinking, she reached for her sister's bhuta, frantic for any trace of her. But either the sura was dampening her connection or

Lasya had tired herself out on the demons' shields, because the only hum she heard was Tav's.

We're in this together, he'd told her in the old palace, and here he was proving they hadn't been empty words. That no matter how much Kajal bit and pushed, revealing the feral thing she was underneath the skin's surface, he stood resolutely at her side.

She wanted to be angry, wanted to fight and claw until he finally saw what she truly was and abandoned her. But for the first time in a long while, she was not alone. As selfish as she was, she would not give that up.

The night crawled on until the cellar door was unlocked with a loud scrape. Kajal was sufficiently numbed by this point, and needed Tav's help to stand as the door swung open. Sezal stepped in, carrying a tray.

"Lasya," Kajal began, but Sezal held up her hand. The young woman remained in her demon form; clearly, there was no more need to hide.

"His Majesty is speaking with the Sodhis. While that happens, you should eat." Sezal set the tray on the floor, but Kajal barely looked at it. "He also asks if you've changed your mind."

She'd directed this at Tav, who said nothing. Sezal sighed and turned to leave.

"Sezal," Tav blurted. "Did you really not know what Advaith was planning with Lord Dukha? You and Vaan were always with him."

Sezal hesitated. Some of her hair slipped over one of her horns. "I knew he was speaking with Lord Dukha about Bakshi, though not about their plan to create halahala." Kajal wondered if she was imagining the resentment in her voice. "Regardless, we all want to see it come to an end."

"I want my *sister's body,*" Kajal pressed.

Tav put a steadying hand on Kajal's arm. "I'll help put an end to halahala, but he'll need to tell me everything first. Everything he can remember. And Kajal gets to bring her sister back. Now."

Sezal nodded and left. Kajal sank to the floor and cradled her emotional-support jar of sura, staring into the shadows while Tav restlessly paced.

The lock scraped open again much sooner than either of them anticipated. But it wasn't the demons or Advaith who stood in the doorway.

"I just want to say," Dalbir panted, "that adventures are overrated."

Kajal knocked the jar over in her attempt to get back up. "Dalbir? What—?"

"Shh, I'm trying to do a heroic rescue here." They gestured for Tav and Kajal to hurry. "Come on, before my parents notice how long I've been gone."

The sura's effects became far more obvious once Kajal tried to walk. Tav clicked his tongue when she stumbled, and held on to her elbow as they followed Dalbir into the dark hallway.

"What's happened so far?" Tav asked.

Dalbir led them to the set of curving stone stairs they'd descended hours earlier, which immediately became Kajal's worst enemy. "My parents have been filling the prince in on current affairs, like how the Vadhia are roaming Dharati unchecked and targeting citizens. There's even a group of Vadhia who passed by not too long ago on their way to the border. What is wrong with you?" they snapped at Kajal when she tripped again.

"What's Bakshi doing at the border?" Kajal mumbled. Her hazy mind was floating several steps beyond the conversation, and she had the feeling she wasn't nearly as worried as she should have been. "Weeding out more *witches*?"

Dalbir sighed as they emerged into a dim hallway and rounded an increasingly dizzying number of corners. "Possibly. My parents aren't too happy about that—or about any of this. At first, their idea was to just assassinate Bakshi, but when those demons got wind of you, their plans changed. They wanted to restore Advaith to the throne and be rewarded handsomely for it with titles and land. They didn't expect to deal with the long-lost asura and deva."

Kajal snorted loudly, and Tav squeezed her elbow in warning. "Know the feeling."

"The prince said something about opening the gates to Patala, but his trishul isn't materializing. The gates can't open without it."

"My sudarshana chakra isn't appearing either," Tav said.

"Huh." Dalbir glanced at Kajal. "He, uh . . . also asked for more information about you. I had to tell him what happened these last few days. For some reason, it seemed to raise his spirits."

A spike of nausea hit her. She slid between present and past, standing within an extravagant estate one second, and the next kneeling before a twisted vine of blight punching a hole through a soldier's chest.

She fell upon the nearest vase and emptied the sour, acidic contents of her stomach. Tav held her braid out of the way, and Dalbir made a strangled sound.

"That vase was from my grandmother," they complained.

Kajal coughed and wiped her mouth. "We need to get out of here."

"*Yes*, that's what we've been trying to do, thanks for paying attention!"

"I can help with that."

Vritika stood breathless in the hallway. Her crossbow was slung over her shoulder, and her eyes were spooked.

"Oh, why am I not surprised," Dalbir drawled. "Of course you didn't do as Professor Jassi told you."

"I had a bad feeling," Vritika said. "And I was right. There are *rakshasas* here. I saw two danavas through the window."

"Those would be the rebels," Kajal said.

"How are—? No, you can explain later." She unslung her crossbow, carrying it like she'd been born with one in her hands. "We need to get going."

"I have to get my sister first," Kajal protested.

Vritika huffed. "Exorcising her would be a great deal easier."

"Over my cold corpse."

"Are you volunteering?"

"All right, all right," Dalbir hissed, getting between them. "Vritika, so long as you're quiet you can lead these two out while I go find this fabled sister."

Vritika frowned. "Aren't you coming with us?"

Dalbir shook their head. "I don't want to leave my parents alone with the demons. But it seemed like the prince was getting ready to ride out soon, and he wanted to talk to his brother and Kajal before then. We don't have much time."

"You don't have *any* time, unfortunately."

That hoarse, cheerful voice made everyone freeze—except for Vritika, who turned and fired off a bolt with lightning reflexes.

A flash of red, and the bolt broke apart midair. Advaith stepped over the splinters with hands tucked behind his back, flanked by Vivaan and Sezal. He wore an apologetic smile.

"Didn't mean to break up the escape attempt," he said. "I was curious to see how far you'd get." He studied Vritika with disdain. "I take it this one is a demon hunter?"

Tav approached his brother. "Adi, let Kajal and the others go. I'll stay."

Before Kajal could argue, her tongue clumsy under the effect of the sura, Advaith spoke first.

"I can't do that."

"Why? You don't need them."

"I do, actually." Advaith's gaze met Kajal's, and something zapped through her at the contact. "The hallway's too crowded for this. Come."

Vivaan confiscated Vritika's crossbow and quiver before corralling them to follow Advaith back to the parlor. The broken limestone and pottery had been cleaned up, and the Sodhis sat grim-mouthed and silent on the couch. Jassi was nowhere in sight.

"Sit," Advaith said pleasantly, gesturing at the couches. "Make yourselves comfortable. No need to stand around awkwardly on my account."

Tav sighed. "Adi."

"What? Oh," he said with a small bow toward the Sodhis. "Apologies. This is your household, after all."

But the two merely shook their heads, tight-lipped. Dalbir went to sit with them. Their mother gripped their hand.

"What are you planning?" Tav asked, clearly tired of the theatrics.

"Tav, *please* sit down. All of you, just . . . sit."

Vivaan looked like he would force them one by one onto the couches. Since Kajal felt like she was ready to keel over anyway, she didn't sit so much as collapse onto the couch opposite the Sodhis. After an impressive face journey ranging from uncertainty to annoyance, Vritika joined them.

"Better." Advaith gave them a sunny smile.

Kajal couldn't help but stare; seeing Tav's face with such a broad grin was bizarre.

Shrimati Sodhi noticed Vritika. "Who is this?"

"She's a Meghani," Dalbir mumbled. At the name, their parents' eyes flashed with hope. "She—"

"Is of no consequence," Advaith finished, earning a sharp glare from Vritika. "All right. So. There is an issue."

He waited until he had everyone's attention before holding his hands out before him. "The trishul is the asura's weapon. It is ancient and unbreakable, and appears whenever the asura calls for it. It is not only a weapon, but a tool. A key. A way for humans to enter Patala from Martya."

His fingers curled into his empty palms like flowers at night. "But no matter how often I try, the trishul does not come."

He turned toward his brother. Tav nodded silently, confirming his suspicion.

"It should be impossible to hide the asura and deva's weapons," Advaith went on, "but somehow, I believe Bakshi is the one behind this. Or perhaps Lord Dukha. I don't know. I don't . . ." He faltered, and Vivaan took a half step toward him. "Either way, I need a new method to return to Patala and find the demon lord. To ask him how to reverse halahala."

Dalbir breathed in suddenly. That got Advaith's attention, and he made a motion for Dalbir to stand. Dalbir did so with some reluctance, their mother refusing to let go of their hand.

"I was told your knowledge of the asura and deva was useful in finding me," Advaith said with a smile. "Thank you."

Dalbir was stricken by that smile—or perhaps at being thanked for a passion their parents hadn't wanted them to pursue.

"Does this mean you are also knowledgeable about our holy weapons?" Advaith went on.

Dalbir swallowed. "Y-Yes? Um. As you probably know, these ancient weapons were forged out of the cosmic matter between the planes. The trishul appeared on Lake Hira, and the sudarshana chakra appeared at the top of Taara Peak. The yaksha deities held on to the latter, and the nagas possessed the trishul—until the asura and deva came along. These weapons became conductors for their unique energies."

Dalbir had gotten lost in the explanation, shaking off their mother's hand to gesticulate while talking. "The deva's power is related to sattva, or 'pure' energy, which connects to Svarga. The asura's power comes from tamas, 'unruly' energy, which connects to Patala. Since the weapons are conductors, that allows them to be used as keys, like you said. But even without the weapons, the asura and deva are still wielders of their respective energies, which means they each should have the ability to forge something else into a conductor."

Advaith had tilted his head to one side, listening with the raptness of a scholar. "Go on."

"The story of halahala claims it first originated with the demon lord while he was trapped within the ocean, and the demon lord is supposedly the source of tamas. Which means that the asura, who wields tamas with or without their trishul, is also tied to halahala."

Advaith silently began to pace the length of the room. Everyone else was thrown into strained silence, and Dalbir took this as their invitation to sit back down. Sweat dotted their forehead, and their breathing was somewhat erratic.

"I've learned that some of Bakshi's soldiers have traveled through here recently," Advaith said eventually, eyeing his ruby ring. "This is good timing."

Tav stiffened. "What do you mean?"

Advaith turned to Kajal. "Would you like to explain it?"

All eyes turned to her. Blood stung her face, even as the rest of her grew cold. Vritika edged away from her, as if Advaith's attention were contagious. Or maybe she smelled like sura and bile.

"The elements of Martya are composed of both life and death," Advaith said, undeterred by her silence. "An overabundance of sattva, and the world blooms too wildly to maintain. An overabundance of tamas, and the world withers." He held out his hands in imitation of scales, tipping steeply in one direction. "Just as Martya was once ruled by an excess of sattva, it is now becoming ruled by tamas."

Everyone hung on to his words. Even Tav watched his brother with unblinking concentration.

"But if the blight or halahala *is* tamas, or at least has a connection to it . . ." Advaith's eyes flitted toward Dalbir.

"Then the asura can control halahala, to some extent," Dalbir finished quietly.

"You're going to attack the Vadhia with *blight*?" Tav demanded.

"You were always sharper than you let on, bhara."

"What will that accomplish, other than taking out a small fraction of Bakshi's forces?"

"As the young shri just said, we need a conductor." Advaith inclined his head to Kajal. If she didn't know any better, she'd say it was deferential. "It was the manipulation of tamas that killed those soldiers you encountered on the road, wasn't it?"

Kajal pressed her trembling lips together. Tav studied her, no doubt recalling what she had done in the dakinis' forest.

"And the fact that they were *controlled* by the blight afterward . . ." Advaith grinned. "Their bodies became conduits for tamas, amplifying it to new levels. That is exactly the sort of energy that can force the gates of Patala open."

Kajal was caught in a spasm of vertigo, tremors spreading through her body like she was standing at the epicenter of an earthquake. Someone called her name as the echo of breaking stone jarred her bones and rattled her teeth.

"What's wrong with her?" Vritika asked.

"Kajal," Tav whispered, and his voice reverberated through her. "Breathe."

She tried to. Her vision had gone dark, but with each inhalation the shadows eased, until she could make out her hands curled in her lap. Floating above them were two small yaksha butterflies. They landed on her fingers and flapped their wings slowly, in time to her breaths.

"Kajal." The voice was similar to Tav's, but hoarser, the inflections slightly off. She glared up at Advaith, who had come to kneel before her. "This is a lot to take in, I know. But I'll need your help."

She exhaled through her teeth. "No."

Advaith wasn't deterred. "Please?"

"Piss off."

He didn't bother to mask his disappointment. He stood and made his way toward the door. "Then perhaps this will convince you."

He opened the door and peered into the hallway. When he returned, Jassi tagged along behind him, her face pinched with fatigue and guilt. She quickly glanced at Kajal, then away.

But it wasn't Jassi who Kajal was focused on. It was the person who entered the room after, her white funeral dress exchanged for a plain blue salwar kameez, the dirt washed from her face, her right hand missing its pinkie finger.

Kajal rose to her feet like a dreamer, without conscious will. She occupied the moment between a cut and the first seep of blood, before nerves recognized pain.

Lasya's eyes watered. Not red like cinnabar but rich brown. "Kajal," she whispered, the same voice that had been whispering to her for months, begging Kajal to kill her for good. But here she was, flesh and bone and muscle, miracle and impossibility and memory.

Tav looked between them with growing bewilderment. Vritika's eyes widened, and Dalbir's mouth fell open.

It was no mystery why. In all the time the bhuta had haunted her, they hadn't been able to see Lasya, not the way Kajal had. None of them had known what to expect of her sister.

She was certain they hadn't expected the face staring back at Kajal to be a mirror image of her own.

Chapter Twenty-Seven

THE ROOM FELL away. If anyone spoke, it didn't register; nothing mattered more than the rise and fall of Lasya's chest, the wetness of her eyes, the small yet undeniable proofs that she was *alive*.

Alive by someone else's hand.

Fury unlike any Kajal had felt before eddied through her. She was a summer storm, all crackling pressure and heat, as she forced herself to turn toward Advaith. He watched her placidly, though the curl of his mouth hinted at triumph.

"What a scary face," he muttered with a mock shudder. "I figured out your little trick, thanks to Professor Jasmeet." Jassi's gaze stayed rooted to the floor. "I'd say something like this would be cause for thanks. You brought back my brother, so I brought back your sister."

Kajal's fury ratcheted up, banging against her rib cage, her chest, baying to be let out. How dare this boy lay his hands on Lasya. How dare he revive her without Kajal's consent, without her present to ensure that he had done it right, if her chakras had been opened correctly, if—

"Hold on," came Dalbir's voice. "You're twins too? What's the statistical likelihood of this? It's weird, right?"

"Dalbir," Vritika snapped.

"I think," Advaith said, "this should be enough to convince you to help me. More than anyone here, you understand the intricacies of how energies interact." His smile was as knowing as Vivaan's glare had been, and Kajal's heart sank. "I'll need you if we're to open the gates to Patala."

Kajal yearned to check Lasya's pulse, her channels, her lungs, and her heartbeat, but she couldn't force herself away from Advaith's smugness. She *burned*, and she longed to burn *him*, this terrible creation that had been sewn together and breathed to life under her hands.

She moved forward, and Advaith's smile faltered. She felt bigger than herself, outside her own body, propelled by little more than a wild urge to bite through his sutured throat.

"Kajal."

Her whole body flinched. Lasya faced her with that same grim, sorrowful expression, one hand curled loosely at her chest. Her dark hair fell around her shoulders, hair that had whipped in the eerie silence of the bhuta's wind.

"Don't," her sister whispered. A warning. An order.

Kajal's lungs heaved for breath; she was starved of air, couldn't inhale enough of it. "He—"

"Don't put up a fight."

She wondered how Lasya could be this calm, this composed, in the face of everything.

And then she looked closer and saw the hairline fractures in Lasya's expression, the desperate way she was holding herself together for Kajal's sake. Something dark stirred behind her eyes, a flash of unnerving shadow under the water's surface.

The fury within Kajal guttered, a crimson flame doused with snow. Tears welled and spilled down her face.

"I'm sorry," Kajal whimpered, and it split apart on a sob, all her own hairline fractures threatening to shatter her into pieces. "Lasya . . ."

Her sister's face crumpled. Though Kajal didn't deserve comfort in any form, Lasya enveloped her in her arms.

"I'm sorry." Kajal hid her face in Lasya's shoulder as she wept. Her fingers dug into Lasya's back, hard enough to hurt, to make sure she was solid and warm and living. "I'm sorry."

Lasya petted a hand down her hair. Kajal might never earn Lasya's forgiveness, but at least she had this: a familiar touch, however brief.

"We'll have to do as he says for now," Lasya whispered, so soft Kajal could barely hear it. "Don't give in yet."

Kajal wasn't sure what she had expected—a fight, an argument, another escape attempt. Not complete surrender.

She pulled away. Lasya's face was just as wrecked as hers. Her sister sniffed, then brushed the wetness from Kajal's face.

"Later," Lasya promised. Helplessly, Kajal nodded.

Advaith exhaled as if he'd been holding his breath. "Well, that was touching. Did you expect more tears from me, Tav? I'm sorry I underperformed."

Everyone had been watching with fascination or bafflement, but Tav's expression was unreadable. At Advaith's words, he roused himself. "Drop the tone, Adi. Tell me what you plan to do with Kajal."

"About that." The crown prince turned to the Sodhis. "We'll need supplies for a short journey." His hand drifted to his unadorned hip. "And I'll need a weapon."

The Sodhis were reluctant to let Advaith go anywhere.

"I will return," Advaith promised, inexplicably beguiling, taking Shrimati Sodhi's hand in his. "Before I can reclaim the throne, I must first fix our land. I'm sure you'd agree." In the end, they did.

Although the Sodhis had enough horses for everyone, Advaith insisted that Lasya ride with him. With nothing more than a stern look, Lasya prevented Kajal from arguing.

It was a look Kajal was exceedingly familiar with. As they'd traveled, as they'd worked, as they'd encountered people of all creeds, Kajal had been the one to cause trouble when there was none, to turn a small inconvenience major with little more than an off-putting word or gesture. It had been up to Lasya to be the mediator, to hold the end of Kajal's leash.

Truthfully, Vivaan seemed more displeased with Advaith's request than Lasya did. Her sister was all grace and quiet dignity when Advaith assisted her into the saddle, staring straight ahead as he climbed up behind her.

"Nothing untoward will happen, I assure you," the crown prince told Kajal. "It's only for safety purposes."

Bullshit.

Kajal forced herself to turn and walk to Tav's horse, where Kutaa was watching the proceedings. Tav paused with his foot in the stirrup.

"You . . . want to ride with me?" he asked.

It was only then she remembered she'd been given her own horse. Painful heat flooded her face.

Tav set his foot down and held out his hand. "Come here."

She studied the somber lines of his face, the calluses on his palm, the wave of his dark hair. He and Advaith were identical, but it was hard to believe when the ticking mechanics within them were so dissimilar.

Slowly, she put her hand in his. He helped her up and settled behind her, keeping an inch of space between them. Then he tensed.

"Sorry," he said. "I can sit in front."

He recalled how she'd insisted on it during their trip to the Harama Plain. Her throat was tight as she shook her head. "It doesn't matter."

He relaxed and reached for the reins. She held on loosely to the saddle's pommel and tried not to dwell on the way his arms bracketed her, or how his chest radiated warmth against her back.

It was late afternoon when they rode from the estate, heading south toward the border with their neighboring country, Navarata. According to the Sodhis' informants in Malhir, Bakshi had been stirring up nationalist sentiment in the capital. One of his latest ideas was to cut off the flow of travelers, believing part of Dharati's decline was due to foreign contamination. Since Navarata was where the contingent of Vadhia who'd passed through recently were heading, it was also Advaith's destination.

Kajal thought Advaith would oppose Kutaa coming along, but instead he'd shown great interest in the undead dog, even going so far as to rub his fuzzy ears in delight. Kajal mentally urged Kutaa to nip or growl, but instead her duplicitous dog had allowed the prince to do as he pleased with a patience Kajal wished she possessed.

Vritika and Dalbir had been told to stay behind. Dalbir had seemed torn between relief and disappointment while Vritika fumed, but of course Advaith didn't want a demon hunter in their midst.

Jassi, however, had been invited. Advaith chatted amiably with her about Ayurveda while Vivaan and Sezal, wearing their human guises, each rode ahead and behind the traveling party, respectively.

The sky was heavy with cloud cover that rolled in from the mountains, a sheet of steely moisture that threatened to turn to rain. It made Kajal's whip scars ache. She glanced at Lasya and found her sister gazing back, as if knowing they pained her; Lasya used to rub gotu kola salve on the scars when the weather turned.

From within Advaith's arms, Lasya gave her a single nod. *Just hold on.*

"I didn't expect any of this," Tav murmured behind her. "For him to be so . . ." He sighed. "I didn't know he'd kept so much from me."

Kajal tried to imagine keeping so many secrets from Lasya and couldn't manage it. Her sister had always seen straight through her. "It's not your fault, Tav." Her thumb worried at the saddle's stitching. "Maybe it's fate. Maybe the asura really is destined to be evil."

Tav tightened his grip on the reins, making the horse's ears flick. "My brother is not evil."

His voice was controlled, but hiding a bitter anger that Kajal recognized in the way her own veins sang with it.

"He was doing something he thought was right, but he was tricked by Bakshi. He was *wrong*, but that doesn't make him evil. Just as yakshas can be malicious and rakshasas can be benevolent, the asura is not destined to be wicked simply by the circumstances of their birth, and the deva is not destined to be good."

When Tav spoke, she felt his words pass from his chest and through her back. "He's trying to undo his mistakes. It's my responsibility to help him."

Kajal's throat had tightened again, making it difficult to swallow. "I'm sorry."

"Don't be sorry." He paused, then pitched his voice even lower. "You . . . didn't tell me. That Lasya was your twin." An unspoken accusation: *We had this in common, and you said nothing.*

She closed her eyes. "I'm sorry," she said again. It was the only thing she *could* say. Everything was too jumbled and broken, slipping formless off her fingers. She was a bowl holding too much when all she wanted was to be a sieve.

Tav's gentle squeeze on her arm grounded her. "You don't have to explain now."

So she didn't.

They stopped when dusk matured into evening. Based on the Sodhis' reports, the group of Vadhia soldiers were still a few hours away. They'd have to make the rest of the trip in the morning.

The Sodhis had given them bedrolls, food, and enough supplies for a campfire. Advaith kept Lasya close to him as he discussed perimeter checks with his aides, and Kajal would have marched up to them if Jassi hadn't appeared at her side.

"Kajal," she whispered. "Can I talk to you?"

Kajal swallowed the first biting words that sprang to her lips. "What do you want?"

"To apologize for what happened. He—"

"He forced you," Kajal said blandly. "I know."

"I was given your notes. I studied them carefully and made sure to reactivate every chakra. But I couldn't do it on my own." Jassi frowned. "I needed whatever power he has to activate it."

Kajal thought of Jassi's concern about whether any physician could revive a dead body. Now she'd proven that wasn't true, unearthing a bigger question: Who *could*?

"I wanted . . ." Jassi fiddled with her hands, rubbing her knuckles. "I wished I could do it. By myself."

"So you can revive your father one day?"

Jassi confirmed it with a grimace. "It's difficult for him to take care of my little sister as his health declines." She blinked quickly, though the firelight emphasized the dampness of her eyes behind her glasses. "I can't leave Nishaa alone. I can't . . . I can't say goodbye yet."

Kajal was suddenly struck by how young Jassi really was, despite being one of the oldest here. Some of her anger fled, seeing in the professor the same desperation that had claimed her after Lasya's death.

"I understand," Kajal murmured. "I'm sorry it didn't work."

Jassi took a deep breath, her shoulders drooping. "Do you think he can really manipulate the blight?"

Kajal watched Advaith laugh at something Vivaan had said. The laugh was bright and bell-like, absurdly boyish. It made Tav look up with soft eyes, as if recalling a different time.

"We'll see," Kajal whispered back. She flinched when Jassi pressed something into her hands. "What—?" She cut herself off at the sight of a hooked needle and a bobbin of thread.

"I resutured the wound on Lasya's stomach," Jassi said. "But I'll leave the rest to you."

Kajal took needle and thread with a rush of gratitude. Before she could thank Jassi, the professor hurried off.

Steeling herself, Kajal approached Advaith. "I need to speak with my sister."

"Sure. Just don't go too far." When Kajal frowned, he made a shooing motion. "It's not a trick. Go."

Still uncertain, Kajal took Lasya by the hand and drew her far enough away from everyone else that the edges of the campfire barely touched them. Kutaa followed, eyes gleaming in the darkness.

"Did he touch you?" Kajal demanded once they sat cross-legged in the grass, facing each other. Kutaa settled down beside them. "Did he—?"

Lasya laid her hand on Kajal's knee. "No. He was respectful. He's just . . ." Lasya contemplated until she settled on "Afraid."

"*Afraid?* He's the one ordering all of us around, laughing it up like this is some sort of game. The only thing he should be afraid of is my fist in his face."

The smile on Lasya's face could have split Kajal in two. She'd missed that smile so much.

"This was your first success?" Lasya asked as she scratched Kutaa's chest. The dog contentedly leaned into it.

"He was."

"And a very handsome one at that." Lasya stroked the back of her finger up the soft fur of Kutaa's snout. "I knew you could accomplish anything you set your mind to."

Kajal forcefully cleared her throat and took out the needle, thread, and the pouch. "Give me your hand."

Her sister obeyed. Kajal glanced at the stub with a swell of hatred. Tamping down the urge to throttle Vivaan, she took the finger from the pouch and brushed off the dirt, rubbing it clean on the hem of her kurti.

"The ring is gone," Lasya murmured sadly, gazing at the band of greenish skin the copper ring had left behind.

"I'll get you another one." Kajal threaded the needle and lined up the finger with the stump. "You might not have sensation in this finger again, or be able to move it."

"That's fine."

Kajal gritted her teeth. It *wasn't* fine; none of this was fine. Her hand began to shake, the needle catching gleams of orange from the campfire.

Lasya caught her hand. "It's all right."

She shut her eyes. "Stop saying that. It's *not*. I made you—" She forced the words past her throat, clawing on the way up. "I turned you into a bhuta."

Lasya's fingers squeezed hers. They sat in heavy silence, the murmuring of the others faded and obscure. They may as well have been alone in the field, the two of them out in the wilderness like it had always been, them against a wide and cruel world.

"Do you . . . remember?" Kajal asked. If Tav didn't, maybe Lasya would be similarly spared.

"It's strange." Lasya studied the stump of her finger. "I remember most things. The names of villages we passed through. How certain foods taste. I remember you giving me the ring, but not why you looked so remorseful about it. Some memories feel like they're underwater. I can sense them, I know they're there, but I can't dredge them to the surface."

Lasya was quiet a long time before adding softly, "But I remember being a bhuta."

Her sister, brilliant and gentle, remembered her hands around Kajal's throat. Remembered the horror of the Harama Plain. Remembered taking the lives of Gurveer Bibi and Gurdeep and Riddhi.

All because Kajal had been racked with guilt and denial. Because she had been the one to survive, and Lasya hadn't.

And like always, Kajal's plan to fix things had only broken them further.

Lasya's other hand cradled the side of Kajal's face. "Behan."

"Don't," Kajal whispered. "Don't comfort me. You should be furious. You should curse me out, shout at me, hit me."

Tears fell silently down Lasya's face, and that dark, lurking thing was back behind her eyes. Her stare went straight through Kajal—not the way it normally did when her sister read her so easily, but in a way that dismissed her completely.

It turned the blood in her veins to snowmelt. She'd already guessed that having memories of the bhuta would do irreversible damage, but to actually see it, to see the trauma as a physical thing possessing her sister's body—

"Sorry, I don't mean to interrupt."

They turned sharply at Tav's appearance. He carried two bowls in his hands, which he set down in the grass beside them. Kutaa sniffed at the one closest to him. "I, um . . . Food."

"Wait," Lasya said when he turned to leave. She had thawed, the hard line of her mouth softening. "You're the deva." She quirked an eyebrow. "The one with the yaksha butterflies."

He seemed torn between wanting to admit or deny it. "Yes."

The two of them stared at each other. Kajal's discomfort grew, though she couldn't fully explain why.

"Thank you," Lasya said, her tone grave. "For protecting Kajal."

Tav glanced at Kajal, something heavy and unspoken in the set of his jaw. "Of course."

Of course?

He'd turned on his heel and retreated before Kajal could think to say anything. His iron bangle caught the firelight in a wheel of orange. Kajal wondered if the metal had played a part in suppressing his memories of being a bhuta; if Lasya, without a bangle of her own, hadn't been afforded the same mercy.

"He's oddly shy, but I like him." Lasya picked up one of the bowls and looked inside. It was filled with rice gruel made with lentils. "Oh. This is . . ."

This was Lasya's first meal since dying. Lasya deserved far grander than this—deserved an entire feast, or at least a meal she could season properly with her spices.

Kajal watched her sister sniff the porridge like Kutaa had, then scoop some with her fingers and push it into her mouth with her thumb.

Lasya chewed carefully, staring off at nothing, and Kajal was horrified when tears spilled from her eyes. "It's missing asafoetida."

It was so unexpected that a laugh burst out of Kajal. Lasya jerked, then laughed as well. There was a wild edge to the sound, not amusement so much as incredulity, as if surprised they could laugh at all.

The next morning, Kajal watched Lasya run her fingers over the small, precise sutures around her reattached finger as they shortened the distance between them and the Vadhia. Though there was far more they wanted to say to each other—so much more to work through together—some of the crushing weight in Kajal's chest had lifted.

But the trepidation remained. It trawled through her the way it did whenever she'd been forced to face an ordeal, the teeth-rattling anticipation of staring death in the eye.

She'd thought of trying to slip the bitter almond extract into Advaith's porridge that morning, but Vivaan and Sezal guarded him too well. They had even kept the dakini's dagger, tucked now in Sezal's belt.

When they stopped near a line of trees for water, Vivaan and Sezal went to scout the area. Not much later, Kajal heard a scuffle from the trees before Vivaan returned holding two people by their collars.

"Guess who decided to follow after us," Vivaan drawled, shoving Vritika and Dalbir to the ground.

"How *dare* you manhandle me," Vritika snarled. "Give me back my crossbow!"

Vivaan had brought it along on the trip, attached to the saddlebags of his horse. "Since you asked so nicely . . . no."

Dalbir raised their hands placatingly. "Hey, I'm just here to bear witness. Don't mind me." Yet there was a glint in their eyes that told Kajal what they really meant was *I'm going to get such good content out of this*.

Advaith gave another of those ringing laughs. "I shouldn't be surprised. You *did* have some interesting things to say about halahala," he said to Dalbir. "And we're near enough that I can't spare anyone to travel back to the estate with you. You may as well come along."

Jassi hurried forward. "They're just children who don't know what they're doing." Vritika bristled, but Jassi shot her a warning look. "Please, allow me to escort them back."

"No," Advaith said simply. "Vaan, be sure to bind the hunter."

Vritika put up a decent fight, but she was no match for a disguised danava.

To everyone's surprise, Lasya walked toward the girl while her hands were being tied.

"Lasya," Kajal hissed, but her sister ignored her.

"Are you Vritika?" Lasya asked.

"Yes. Not that it matters to you." Though Vritika was noticeably uncomfortable, her voice dripped venom. "You're the one who was the bhuta."

Kajal growled, prompting Kutaa to do the same. A single glance from Lasya subdued them both.

"I take it my actions in that state have caused you grief."

"You killed my friend. Riddhi. Do you remember her?" Vritika's eyes shone. "Do you remember stealing the breath from her lungs and stopping her heart?"

"I remember." Lasya, her face blank, sank to her knees and bowed deeply, touching her forehead to the earth. "No apology can make up for your loss, but please know that I am truly, eternally sorry."

The discomfort on Vritika's face grew. "You—"

"It's not enough, I know. Nothing ever will be."

Vritika turned her face away. "Stop it. I . . . Sorry."

Lasya straightened. "Why are *you* saying sorry?"

Kajal could tell Vritika was flushed. "I don't know. Just . . . get away from me."

Lasya obliged. Kajal gripped her arm.

"You didn't have to do that," Kajal whispered.

Lasya stared at the ground. "I did."

Sezal returned shortly after. She noticed Dalbir and Vritika with surprise but quickly shook it off and turned to Advaith.

"They're near," Sezal said.

The sky was dark with clouds when they reached a crest overlooking a sloping valley. Half a mile away sat an encampment, dozens of tents propped against the sharp wind from the mountains, the blue and marigold of Vadhia uniforms bright against the gloomy setting.

With quiet instructions from Advaith, they dismounted and tied their horses to the nearest trees. Everyone was nervous save for him, his mouth upturned like a curved bow as he knelt at the lip of the crest and observed the camp. "How many do you think there are, Vaan?"

Vivaan made a silent assessment before answering, "Thirty-three."

"Hopefully, that'll be enough." Advaith stood and edged back. Though he wore a smile, his gaze was stern. "Kajal?"

His tone was an invitation; the order underneath, anything but. Her fingers twitched as the outer rings of his irises burned scarlet.

Beneath the earth, something stirred. Like the dark thing behind Lasya's eyes. Like the misgivings within her own heart.

For years, she had been running from something she hardly understood. Some would call it fate, or dharma. Only she had ever considered it a curse. Considered it to be the reason why Lasya was good and she herself was not, why it felt so satisfying to give in to violence and disorder, whether in the form of throwing a brick through a window or imagining her hands around someone's throat.

It was easier to run. To ignore. To deny. To starve the weak, pleading parts of her.

But Kajal suddenly decided that she was very, very tired.

She didn't want a repeat of Siphar. Didn't want the chaos and the guilt, the fear that dogged her like her own personal blight. Didn't want Lasya and Tav to be caught up in something that was her responsibility, no matter how much she wished otherwise.

So it was with her own unfeeling smile that she looked back at Advaith and said, "It won't work."

"Figures that you're a pessimist," he said, unconvinced. "Let's try, shall we? The sooner I enter Patala, the sooner I can locate Lord Dukha and get answers about how to stop halahala." He nodded to Tav. "This is what we want." He said it in a way that suggested he was in the habit of making choices for Tav, and it only bolstered Kajal's irritation.

"Even if it's what *you* want, it won't work," she said again. "Because I've already tried."

Lasya's arm brushed up against hers, a silent bulwark.

"What do you mean?" Advaith asked slowly.

Kajal took a deep breath, smelling the cold mountain air and the hint of the camp's fires.

"I also thought about manipulating the blight. To concentrate it in one place and force the gates of Patala open. But in the end, it wasn't possible." Her heart beat a sickening rhythm beneath her sternum. Lasya's hand found hers and squeezed. "And it cost me everything."

That horrible day in Siphar, black vines had writhed up from the earth and smashed into the nearby cave, causing it to collapse and kill the six miners inside. But even with Lasya yelling in her ear, Kajal had persisted, unable to let go once she'd had a glimpse of the outline of an obsidian gateway.

The overwhelming tamas had infected the miners, their gray hands scrabbling uselessly against rock. The energy had swelled higher and higher until the gateway had blasted apart, a hunk of it striking Lasya in the stomach and nearly bisecting her.

There was movement in the corner of her eye now as Tav came closer. She kept her focus on Advaith's growing smile.

"Why would you try to open the gates to Patala?" Tav asked softly, so softly it hurt.

"Tav," Advaith said with exasperation, "isn't it obvious just from looking at them?"

The crown prince gestured to Kajal and Lasya, alike and opposite, morning and night, harmony and war, life and death.

"They are the asura and deva of this generation."

Chapter Twenty-Eight

THE FIRST SOUND that broke the silence was a laugh. Dalbir slapped a hand over their mouth.

"Sorry," they said, muffled. "Sorry, but . . . this can't be right."

"I didn't think it was possible either," Advaith said. "After all, there have never been *two* asuras and *two* devas in existence at once. And yet, here we are."

Jassi's brow furrowed as she scrutinized Kajal and Lasya, as if she could see the power in them if she stared hard enough. Vritika looked like someone had smacked her over the head. The demons showed the least amount of surprise; in fact, Vivaan seemed smugly validated, yet another of his suspicions proving true.

And Tav . . .

Kajal couldn't bring herself to look at him.

"It made sense, though, when I thought about it," Advaith went on. "Tav and I died. An asura and a deva must be born to each generation. As soon as our lives were severed, the wheel of dharma spun on without us." He twisted the iron bangle on his wrist. "And spat out our replacements."

"But you still have your powers," Vivaan said, the shade of a question.

Advaith held out his hand, ringed in crimson light. "Yes." He turned pointedly to Kajal. "Do you?"

Kajal's hand was clammy in Lasya's grip. This wasn't supposed to be her role; Lasya was the talker, the charmer, the one who got things done. But Lasya said nothing, her fingers tightening in encouragement.

"I don't know." Kajal struggled over the words, hating how weak they sounded, easily carried away by the strident wind. "We weren't . . . We were never . . ."

Advaith huffed in disbelief. "The demon lord didn't summon you? No rakshasas came to train you?" Kajal shook her head, and he shared a frown with Tav.

When Kajal finally saw Tav's face, she immediately wished she hadn't. He may have forgiven her for not telling her about Lasya, but *this*—this was a whole other level of deception. She could see it in the way his gaze held hers, filled with silent questions, a hurt that went beyond shallow lies.

"Tav . . . I . . ."

She didn't know how to explain, so Lasya did it for her.

"We were orphaned young," Lasya picked up, and Kajal sagged in relief. "We wandered through our hometown for years, taken care of by neighbors, until we were old enough to travel. Not long after, a pujari found us."

Kajal slipped back into the memory like wading into cold water, something that stung yet had numbed with time. Even now, she could picture the elderly wandering priest happening upon them sleeping under a banyan tree, the way he had stared and stared, his eyes rheumy with age.

They had sat, frozen, as he knelt and pressed each of his thumbs to the center of their foreheads. He'd closed his eyes, and Kajal had felt a curious sliver of something stirring and waking inside her. He told them he'd been drawn to this spot, answering a quiet prayer.

Before they had fallen asleep, Lasya had wished for food to fill their aching bellies.

It was the only time a pujari had been the one to give *them* something. He had taken a mango from his pack and presented it to them with both hands, calling them Holy Deva and Blessed Asura, and they had been too scared to say anything in response before he'd tottered off to deliver the rest of his puja to the nearest shrine.

They hadn't believed it, of course. What little they knew of the asura and deva came from stories they'd overheard, depicting larger-than-life figures powerful enough to carry the moon on their shoulders or dry up every river in Dharati. They were guardians and warriors, and the humans' only links to the heavenly and subterranean planes.

Kajal and Lasya were just two young girls—small, poor, and weak. They did not have the capacity for such greatness.

Then yakshas and rakshasas started to approach them. Kajal and Lasya had been terrified by the array of unusual creatures, from sharp-toothed chimeras to wildcats made of braided cattails, but they were only tentative and curious, never meaning them harm. Eventually, the two of them grew bolder; Lasya asked the rivers to give up fish for their dinners, and Kajal called on ghost lights to whisper stories to them while they fell asleep.

In this way, they slowly began to believe.

But they could only learn in inches. In the stories, the asura and deva were each representatives of Patala and Svarga respectively, yet no one came to fetch them or tell them their duties.

"We thought we had to train ourselves," Lasya said. Her thumb rubbed over Kajal's knuckles in a wordless question. Kajal nodded. "There's a town in the south called Kusala with a large shrine many pujaris travel through. It's notable because they pray not only to the yaksha deities, but also to the demon lord."

"Which is how it was always supposed to be," Advaith interrupted. "Until towns started destroying their shrines to Lord Dukha."

"Kusala celebrates the old ways—or at least they did then. The two of us stood at the shrine and prayed for guidance. To have some sort of confirmation that we were meant for more."

That day had been hot, the eyes of passing townspeople heavy alongside their angry murmurs demanding why two girls were causing such a disturbance.

Kajal couldn't bear to hear Lasya say the next part, so she continued, "When there was no reply, I got angry. I yelled at the shrine, yelled that the asura and deva were ready to serve, that we wanted passage to the other planes. A couple of Vadhia came to shoo us away. When one grabbed Lasya, I attacked him." She'd lunged at his face, leaving scratches down his whiskered cheek with her nails. "So they whipped me."

The words were flat, emotionless, but her chest kicked at Tav's short, furious inhalation.

"We did everything we could think of," Lasya said. "But still no one came for us."

Lasya had claimed she was content to simply live their lives, but Kajal knew she hurt. It was the same hurt Kajal carried, the same yearning to belong somewhere, to be part of something bigger. Kajal's spark of hope had flamed into resentment, wondering if they were being kept out for a reason—if they were not good enough, not smart enough, not strong enough. Kajal's entire focus fell toward proving that wrong. She would force her way into Patala if she had to.

And then, Siphar.

Any trace of Advaith's previous humor had fled. "This doesn't make sense," he muttered. "When Tav and I were old enough, we were brought to the yaksha deities and the demon lord. Why wouldn't they do the same for you?"

Tav wrenched his gaze away from Kajal with effort. "We need answers from Lord Dukha."

Advaith nodded distantly, turning back to the encampment. "You're right." He paused. "Do you think he . . . ?" He shook his head. "No. We have to focus on the task at hand."

"Your task will fail," Lasya said. "When Kajal attempted to control the blight in Siphar, it backfired." She laid her other hand on top of her sewn-up stomach. "It'll backfire now."

Advaith stared at Lasya's hand until his expression shifted. "It was you." He spun toward his aides. "You said the blight started after the battle at the Harama Plain, but only recently has it escalated."

Understanding dawned across their faces, the same conclusion now twisting Kajal's stomach. She bent around it, all the breath kicked out of her.

Halahala, the nagi had said. *It must be a clash of power . . . Of opposites.*

Of the asura and deva.

"No," she murmured to the grass, to the world, to the girl who should be dead at her side. "No, no, no—"

The first tendrils of blight had sprouted when Advaith's blade pierced Tav's flesh. It had been a slow yet inevitable threat, creeping deeper into Dharati's soil by the year. No one had therefore been prepared for the sudden rearing of its head, for its skulk to turn into a sprint.

Because of what she'd done that day. Because she had been so impulsive, so wounded, so overconfident.

Because she had killed her sister.

"Fields of crops decimated," Advaith whispered. "Poisoned yakshas and infected humans. Bakshi's soldiers trawling the countryside for witches to blame. Because of me . . ." His eyes were fever-bright when he turned them on Kajal. "Because of *you*."

You *are to blame for this disease on our land,* Jagvir had snarled at her. *And it can only be cleansed with your death.*

Kajal's hand slipped from Lasya's as she sank to the ground. Someone made a sound of dismay, but she couldn't tell if it had come from her own mouth.

Knowledge. What a dangerous thing—what an unwieldy weapon. The shape of it in an unfamiliar vessel could drive one to madness: a woman who sang while she worked, her voice so sweet and rich that she must be casting spells; a widow who lived alone, her womb empty of children, who must have killed her husband to consume his flesh and live forever; a young girl who stared at others and accurately guessed their ailments, a perversion only fire could cleanse.

All of them monstrous and unknown. All of them a scourge.

All of them poisoned by the wellspring she had dug with her own two hands.

A figure knelt before her. She was too numb to feel their touch on her shoulder.

"You didn't know," Advaith said quietly. If it weren't for the rasp of his voice, she could have mistaken him for Tav. "Just as I didn't know the extent to which halahala could spread. Without anyone to guide you, how could you have guessed what would happen? It was a mistake." He held out his other hand. "But it's one we can fix together. There's still a way to redeem ourselves."

Sweat rolled down her neck. Below her, blight was spindling like roots through crust and soil, fingers prodding into the dark to seek out any trace of life. Kutaa sensed it too, lifting up each paw as if the ground had turned hot beneath him.

She stared at the plain of Advaith's palm, the calluses of his fingertips. She couldn't feel herself take his hand.

Advaith's smile was surprisingly gentle as he pulled her to her feet. "We've both misstepped and suffered for it, but I'll ensure it never happens again. We want the same things, in the end." He brought her to stand beside him on the crest. "After we cleanse Dharati of halahala, I'll teach you how to wield your powers. Tav can teach your sister."

Kajal stared at the encampment, at the small figures of the Vadhia soldiers going about their chores.

Remembered the grin of the Vadhia who had whipped her.

The shock and pain on Jagvir's face as his chest had gaped open.

Gurveer Bibi, and Gurdeep, and Riddhi.

Perhaps the asura is merely doing what they do best, Riddhi had once said in a university classroom. *Being evil.*

"Do you feel it?" Advaith whispered. And Kajal *did*, could pinpoint each diseased vein below their feet. "It won't take much. Perhaps a little blood, or a mantra."

She was standing in the dakinis' forest, her bloody palm pressed to rough bark as she summoned the tamas of the dead absorbed by the twisted pines.

Easy. It would be so easy. She did not know how to be an asura, but this—she knew this. She knew *death*.

There is a difference between making the right choice and having a choice at all, Ruhi had said.

The longer she stood there doing nothing, the cloudier Advaith's face grew. "Don't make this difficult," he murmured.

No more, she thought, the phantom press of the bhuta's fingers against her larynx, Siddhi's wails ringing in her ears. *No more.*

The asura is not destined *to be wicked simply by the circumstances of their birth,* Tav had told her.

What Advaith wanted was control.

What Kajal wanted was a choice.

"It's funny," she said at last, staring at the encampment as her hand slipped into her pocket. "How much my life has followed the same pattern. Suspicion, capture, waiting for a trial. I've survived every ordeal, you know. Had to cheat my way through them, of course."

Advaith said nothing. Behind them, the others were deathly silent.

"But I managed to escape each one. Even an ordeal of poison." She huffed a quiet laugh. "Or so I thought."

Quickly, before anyone could stop her, she uncorked the vial of bitter almond extract and downed it in one go.

There was a shout, a bark, and someone grabbed her, but she held her hand to her mouth and swallowed it all. The poison was sharp and tingling on her tongue, numbness already trickling down her throat in its wake.

"Get it out of her," Advaith demanded, grip frantic and tight on her elbow. "Vaan—"

Kajal pushed his chest, and her hand lit up crimson. Advaith was sent flying backward, skidding over the grass.

"Kajal!"

She wobbled and fell into Tav's arms. The poison was circulating far faster than she'd thought it would. Lasya knelt on her other side.

"What did you do?" her sister cried, feeling for her pulse. *"Kajal!"*

She wanted to apologize; she really did. She hadn't meant for it to come to this. But just as they had taken her dagger away, sometimes it was better to remove a weapon than wait to see how it would be used.

She was an asura. She was made for destruction.

Hard to destroy anything when she was dead.

"Don't," she gasped, holding on to Lasya's arm. "Don't let him revive me. Burn—"

Lasya shook her head wildly as Tav ripped Kajal's collar to have better access to her neck. Kajal tried to grab his wrist, but already it was a struggle to lift her hand.

"Don't," she breathed again, and Tav looked down at her with eyes blazing blue.

Warmth seeped into her skin, but it wouldn't be enough. It only made him that much more determined. "Help me," he pleaded of Lasya.

"I— I don't know how," her sister stammered, face ashen. "I never—"

"Do what I do. Focus your energy through your hands."

Kajal was already cold, her insides twisting sharply as short, pained gasps escaped her. Her skin prickled with needles, her blood boiling in her veins. She wondered if any of the bhuta's victims had felt like this, before the end.

She wondered if Lasya had felt this much pain.

It was fitting, in a way. It was what she deserved. A life for a life for a life for a life.

Her vision shrank. Tav and Lasya loomed over her, and if they were the last things she saw on the mortal plane, she'd be content with that.

Lasya was sobbing. Kajal had always hated seeing her cry, so she locked eyes with Tav. He wore the same piercing look as when he'd tried to revive the lake yaksha, running up against the hard barrier of what his power was and wasn't capable of. Her heart struggled under his hand, and he dug his fingertips into her chest as if to claw through bone and muscle to reach it.

"Kajal," he whispered, his voice faraway. Something slipped out from under his shirt, swinging in front of her face. The amber pendant with its lotus petal.

Her shaking receded, and the cold turned into a sweet drifting sensation, like a boat taken out by the tide. She stared at the amber pendant, its edges limned in blue light.

There was a song in her memory, in her framework, notes hidden between her ribs and under her nails and behind her teeth. She blindly turned toward it, the music of her blood and marrow.

She followed the path of it home.

Chapter Twenty-Nine

"Divya, come here."

She looked up from where she crouched before an array of cups, fascinated by their various shapes and patterns. She'd been told each spirit that arrived in Patala required a specific one, but no one knew which until the right moment.

Following the sound of Bijul's voice, Divya left the shelves and entered the main chamber. It was wide and cavernous, its dark walls encrusted with glittering jewels that winked in a mosaic of ruby and peridot and spinel and topaz. Beyond the gaping mouth of the chamber lay a stretch of black sand with specks of white diamond. An avenue of looming black trees led to a lake, its surface gleaming like burnished silver.

Around the lake, a few nagas were peering curiously at whatever had risen from its depths. It wasn't often a spirit caught their attention like this, and it made Divya's heart beat faster.

She peered up at Bijul. The back of the nagi's hood was carbuncled with amethyst and cast her eyes in half shadow. The nagi smiled down at her, revealing fangs.

"You are young and haven't experienced this before," Bijul said in her soft sibilance. "It is likely you won't experience it again. Pay attention."

Divya pouted. It was true she was young—five this year, according to

Martya's measurement of time—but dakinis aged slower and lived longer than humans. Who was to say she would never see the same thing twice?

She had already seen far more than the other dakini children. Dakinis tended to inhabit caves on the borders of Patala, but one day she had snuck all the way down to Nagaloka, the lowest realm, where the nagas watched over the lake through which spirits entered the netherworld. Hidden among the shelves, she had observed one such spirit rise from the lake and drift into the chamber, nothing but a small ghost light. Bijul had cupped it between her green-gray hands and judged it in silence.

"They have met a certain amount of dharma," Bijul had announced. "They will be reborn in Martya to complete it."

The ghost light formed into the figure of a man. He was old, his eyes closed, and he was leaning slightly forward with hunched shoulders. Bijul wandered among the shelves of cups until her fingers paused over one of copper, small and unassuming, with a cow etched along its side.

The other nagas lifted the lid off a large cast-iron pot. The steam rising from the liquid inside smelled of cardamom and anise, of clove and pepper. The forgetting tea. Bijul ladled some into the copper cup and held it to the spirit's lips. Once the man had drunk, he let out a sigh like the wind moaning through trees, then dissipated into wisps of white fog.

Hands clasped sedately before her, Bijul had watched until the last slip of soul was gone. Then she'd called, "You may come out now and ask your questions."

Divya had burned with embarrassment at being caught. But she'd been taught to be deferential to the nagas, so she'd crawled out and stammered an apology. Bijul had only smiled. She'd known better than to ask why Divya's mother had let her out of her sight; among the dakinis, there was no emphasis on *mother*. Everyone took care of the children equally, regardless of whose womb they'd grown in.

Since then, Divya had been allowed to come to Nagaloka whenever she pleased, so long as she didn't get in the way. She had seen many more spirits take the forgetting tea, their souls dispersing to return in another form among the planes. Few had been sent on to Svarga, and fewer still had reached enough enlightenment to be removed from the cycle of reincarnation altogether. Some had been violent and disturbed, and Bijul had sent them to Naraka, where their souls would be trapped for an eternity of punishment.

But this was the first time Divya had seen such fuss. Two spirits rose out of the lake, barely rippling the surface, their forms the same ghostly pale as all the others had been.

Divya blinked. No, there was something strange about them, something *new*. One spirit swirled with a fretful crimson energy, and the other radiated a gentle azure.

The contingent of nagas escorted the two spirits down the avenue of trees and toward the judgment chamber, thick tails making waves in the black sand. Bijul was focused in a way that made Divya's back straighten.

When the two spirits entered the chamber, Bijul prostrated herself before them. Divya started; Bijul had *never* done that before. The other nagas smoothly followed suit.

"Holy Deva, Blessed Asura," they murmured as one, "we thank you for your gifts and guidance."

The asura and deva? She had heard of them from the other dakinis, but she had never caught a glimpse, let alone met them. And now they were dead.

Bijul rose on her tail and carefully, so carefully, cradled each spirit within her palms. The energies within them seeped out like milk from a broken pail, fretful red and gentle blue, until they formed their own small orbs.

"Your dharma is complete," Bijul intoned. "May you find peace eternal."

The ghost lights, separated from their colorful energies, formed into the figures of two women, identical in every way, save that one had long hair and the other short. Unlike most of the other spirits Divya had encountered, their eyes were open. They had reached enlightenment.

The spirits inclined their heads and vanished into sighing fog. Only the red and blue lights were left.

Bijul smiled at her. "Can you guess what these are?"

Divya stepped closer. The red light scared her a little, zipping restlessly here and there. Instead, she reached for the blue light. It obediently floated into her small hands, casting her brown skin silver, like the lake.

It was . . . warm. It felt like holding a cup of cha, the heat seeping into her palms and fingers, delving down and taking root in her stomach. She grinned and held the orb against her chest to protect it.

Bijul laid her hand atop Divya's head. "These are the essences of the asura and deva. Although the humans who carried them are now gone, the cycle of the asura and deva is ongoing. Unending."

"So they'll be reborn? Like spirits?"

"Precisely."

Divya nodded in understanding. There were no souls attached to the energy, the essences, but they had to go *somewhere*.

Reluctantly, she let go of the blue light. It drifted back up to its sibling, which pressed in closer as if it had missed the other. Bijul cradled them in either hand.

"Go and journey into Martya," she said to them. "Find those who would house you, feed you, cultivate you. We will wait patiently for your return."

With a sense of loss, Divya watched the lights fade away.

One day, she was traveling down to Nagaloka when she sensed something unusual.

She was currently in Sutala, where Lord Dukha's palace sat within the city of Bali. Divya had never gone into the city, but she greatly enjoyed the land surrounding it. Each of Patala's seven realms was said to be more beautiful than Svarga, and Sutala was no exception; here, the ground was blanketed in purple sands and sparkling black grasses, strewn with waterfalls that spilled over dark rock formations, and overhead were far-flung gems even brighter than the stars in Martya. Trees grew tall and thick, their black branches shivering with leaves of silver and gold. She liked to pluck the round red fruits they grew, which were always perfectly ripe, their juice bright and tart. Bijul often clucked her tongue while wiping Divya's sticky, grinning mouth with a wet cloth after she'd eaten them.

She was halfway to reaching for one such fruit when a sensation skittered across her nape. Not as if she were being watched, though the elder dakinis had taught her what to do in such a situation.

If someone follows you with ill intent, or touches you without your consent, you teach them better, one had said while presenting her with a curved dagger. *We will show you.*

Divya liked to practice the moves whenever she was alone, but this feeling meant she was *not* alone, so she abandoned the fruit and dove behind a large boulder covered in glittering moss. Soon after, a figure emerged from the trees.

It was a boy. He was young, perhaps her age, which in Martya time meant he was twelve or so. Her hand settled on her dagger as he came closer to her vantage spot, chewing on his lower lip and casting his gaze around in wide-eyed apprehension.

Divya gawked. It was a *human* boy, one who had clearly never been here before. It was rare for humans to enter Patala, though not unheard-of. But one as young as him, without an escort?

The more she stared, taking in his short dark hair and amber eyes, the more she wondered if she *had* seen him before. But certainly not—the dakinis did not cross paths with human men if they could help it.

A memory tickled the fringes of her mind. Standing in the judgment chamber with Bijul, cradling azure warmth between her hands, overcome with a rare and remarkable sense of peace.

Divya grinned wide. *Hello again, little light.*

Unable to hide any longer, she hopped onto the boulder and put her hands on her hips. "Where do you think you're going?"

The boy gasped and stumbled. One of his hands fell to a knife at his belt.

"Wh-Who? I . . . I'm not—" He swallowed hard and whispered, "Please don't hurt me."

Divya threw her head back and laughed. The boy balked as if she were some towering daitya with a cudgel rather than a scrawny young dakini.

"Why would I hurt you?" She nimbly jumped off the boulder and approached him. "You're the deva."

The boy lost some of his tension, hand dropping from his knife. "How do you know I'm the deva?"

"Because I'm omnipotent. I know *everything*." Her cheeks puffed out with the effort not to laugh at his bewildered face. "I could tell you what you're thinking right now. I could tell you what you had for breakfast this morning. I could tell you when you last emptied your bowels."

"Don't," he choked, with a deepening flush.

The laugh that tumbled out of her was so strong she had to hold on to her sides. "No, no, none of that's true. We've actually met before."

This only flustered him more. "We have?" His gaze darted from her long braid to her black, pointed fingernails to the third eye upon her forehead. "I . . . don't remember meeting you."

"You wouldn't be able to. But we're meeting now! Officially." She bounced on the balls of her feet, teeming with an overflowing sense of joy. She was often told by the elders that she had too much energy, but she'd never agreed until this moment, when she was filled crown to toes with it. As if she could run through all of Patala and hardly be out of breath.

Was that the effect of the deva? Or was it merely delight at reuniting with that warm, soothing light?

"I'm guessing you're lost," she went on. "Is this your first time in Patala?"

The boy nodded. "My brother and I are supposed to be paying our respects to the demon lord. But . . ." He scratched the back of his neck. "There was an interesting flower. I lost him."

Divya scoffed. "There's *plenty* of interesting flowers here. If you go wandering off to look at them all, you'll spend your whole life lost."

"I know that now," he muttered.

"There's a lot to see in Patala, you know. You could go up to Vitala and see the goblins who mine mountains of gold. Or visit all the palaces built by the demon architect. But do *not* go to Atala!" She shuddered at the memory of stumbling upon that realm even after the dakinis had warned her not to, the tableau of depravity forever seared into her mind. "They have different appetites there." That's what one of the elders had told her, anyway.

The deva stared at her with lips parted, either awed or overwhelmed. Perhaps both. Taking pity on him, she grabbed his hand and tugged him forward.

"Come on, I'll show you to Bali," she said over her shoulder. "That's where your brother was going, isn't it? The asura?"

"Y-Yes," he stammered, his fingers twitching within hers. "But it's all right. Really. I can—"

"*There* you are!"

Another boy ran toward them, his face—so similar to the deva's—contorted with worry. Purple sand kicked up from his boots as he skidded to a stop, looking between Divya and his brother.

"You shouldn't have let me continue on like that!" he scolded, panting from his run. "Here I was chatting away, only to realize I was talking to myself!"

The deva hung his head. "Sorry."

The asura sighed. "No matter. At least I found you." He bowed to Divya, and she dropped the deva's hand in surprise. "Thank you for escorting him."

"I didn't really do anything." If she concentrated, she could sense within him the restless energy she'd seen in the judgment chamber. That fussy red essence, so unlike his brother's. It didn't feel bad—just different.

"Still." The asura trotted back toward Bali, gesturing for his brother to follow. "Come on, Lord Dukha is waiting."

The deva hesitated. He chewed his lower lip again, chapped from the habit.

"All those things you talked about," he murmured. "In Patala. Are those really things I can see?"

Divya brightened. "Of course. I can take you to all the realms. I know the best shortcuts."

The boy's expression softened with a smile. Divya's breath caught at the sight of it, and again she was filled with that soothing warmth.

"I'd like that," he whispered.

"Tav!" his brother shouted. "Hurry up!"

The boy uttered a quick goodbye and took off. Divya stood staring after them long enough that the newly lit fire in her chest dwindled down to popping embers.

It was months before she saw him again.

She'd started lingering in Sutala, in case she caught him journeying to Bali. She crouched in the grass and ate fruit until her mouth dripped red, sometimes scanning the roads and valleys for hours before giving up.

Of course it was a day she didn't plan to linger that she ran into him. In fact, both of them were standing before one of the lakes, admiring the veil of rushing water that spilled over the gleaming rocks. The asura, talking nonstop, had an arm perched on his brother's shoulder, and when the deva replied the asura erupted into laughter.

"I'm sure it's not poison!" she heard once she'd crept close enough to eavesdrop over the roaring of the waterfall.

"You don't know for certain," the deva murmured, shifting on his feet. She remembered the name his brother had called—Tav—and wondered what would happen if she shouted it.

Before she could draw in a breath to try, the asura whirled around. His jovial face fell to wariness, his brown eyes ringed crimson. Divya scurried back, but within a couple of blinks, his eyes returned to normal.

"Oh, it's you," he said. "The one who helped Tav last time."

If she didn't know any better, she'd say the two of them were happy to see her. Divya allowed that to bolster her as she stepped out of the long grass.

"Divya," she said.

"Divya," the asura echoed while his brother silently mouthed the name beside him. "I'm Advaith. Me and my brother were arguing over whether the lakes here are poisonous."

"Why would they be poisonous?"

Advaith nudged Tav in the side. "See?" Tav whacked his arm away. "I wanted to go swimming, but *someone* was too scared."

Tav sighed. "I was being careful. We're in *Patala*. You know how people talk about rakshasas."

Divya frowned; what did they say about rakshasas in Martya?

"Baa-Ji said—"

Advaith blew a raspberry at his brother. "Baa-Ji isn't the asura or deva, is he?"

"Adi."

"What? It's true." Advaith grinned at Divya. "So? Is it safe for swimming?"

She nodded, not quite sure what to make of the conversation.

With her assurance, he shimmied out of his kurta and shoes. Left only in his trousers, he leapt into the lake with a splash. Divya had never interacted with humans this closely before, wasn't sure how they typically acted outside the stories the dakinis told her. She'd never heard any stories about them loving water like this.

Advaith surfaced and crossed his arms on the rocky ledge along the shore. "Well?"

Tav glanced at Divya and blushed, but he pulled his kurta over his head. Then, rather than jumping in like his brother had, he slowly eased into the water.

"Oh," he said. "It's warmer than I thought it would be." He gazed up at Divya. "Are you coming in?"

What a strange question. The thought must have shown on her face, because his shoulders crept up.

"You don't have to if you don't want to," he mumbled.

"Well, it's not about wanting." She sat on the smooth rock below her. "I don't know how to swim."

Advaith, who'd been floating on his back, squawked and flailed, accidentally splashing Tav. "You don't know how to swim?"

"That's what I said."

Tav gave a retaliating splash. "Not everyone does. It's fine."

"But—" Advaith sputtered. "You *have* to learn! Come in, we'll teach you!"

Divya burst out laughing. Before she could explain why she found this so funny, two young danavas appeared out of nowhere. She reached for her dagger.

"Your Highness, what are you doing?" the boy danava asked of Advaith, bewilderment in his voice. "Who's this?"

"I'm Divya," she said, annoyed that he didn't ask her outright.

The girl danava smiled, showing off curved fangs. "Hello, Divya. Thank you for looking after them."

"I wasn't—"

"Vaan, do you know how to swim?" Advaith demanded.

The boy danava, Vaan, blinked. "No?"

Advaith made a despairing sound, lifting his arms out of the water. "I have to teach you too! Come on, all of you get in."

The girl danava laughed, and Vaan rolled his eyes at Advaith's theatrics. "Unfortunately, we can't," he said. "Lord Dukha is waiting."

Advaith and Tav froze.

"I forgot," Advaith whispered.

"We can still make it," Tav said, hoisting himself out of the lake. "I'm sure he won't be mad. Time passes differently here anyway."

Divya tried not to show her disappointment that they were leaving so soon. After Tav pulled his kurta back on, he lingered at her side, eyes flitting between her forehead, her shoulder, her chin.

"You said you could show me more of Patala," he said at last. "If we come back in a few days . . . ?"

She beamed, awash in that now-familiar heat. "Yes! We'll meet here." She would wait all day for them if she had to. "What do you want to see first?"

When she told Bijul about her new friends, the nagi paused. Bijul didn't usually pause, her every movement calm, sinuous, purposeful.

"They feel like their energies did," Divya went on, buzzing with anticipation. "But different also. And so different from each other!"

Bijul gave a soft sigh and put a steady hand on Divya's shoulder.

"I am glad you're having fun," the nagi said, "but remember that their powers are unique. Their dharma is unique. They will often find themselves at the center of conflict. Please . . . be careful."

Divya nodded eagerly, thinking this was an easy promise to keep.

Chapter Thirty

DIVYA QUICKLY LEARNED that Tav and Advaith weren't merely the asura and the deva—they were also royalty, which in Martya was considered important and rare.

But it was easy to forget when she was in their company, jostling and laughing and traveling through Patala's realms together. They gaped at the towering mountains of gold in Vitala, the residents adorned with gleaming bits of gilded jewelry and armor. Divya helped them sneak close enough to see the wide, wending river that snaked through the whole realm, its surface rippling due to the winds that constantly swept through the valleys.

Much later, she took them to Talatala, where the famed demon architect, Mahit, had constructed vast, magnificent palaces, which largely stood empty. After building Lord Dukha's palace in Bali, he had been given an entire realm to do with as he pleased. Sometimes those from other realms came to stay, but the architect was content with his solitude and never-ending supply of materials.

"It's even bigger than the palace in Malhir," Advaith breathed as they trooped through one of the abandoned citadels. Advaith's danava aides had come with them, the girl—Sezal—ogling, and Vaan quietly impressed. "I wonder what Baa-Ji would make of this?"

Tav turned from where he'd been peering through a latticed window to make a face at his brother. "What, do you want to live here instead?"

Vaan perked up, as if intrigued by the idea.

Advaith's laugh echoed brightly off the walls. "It wouldn't be so bad, would it? I like Patala."

"I hate to ruin your plans, but Mahit is very territorial of his work," Divya said. "He gives petitioners extravagant tasks and only grants them permission to live here if they prove themselves worthy."

Tav shuffled away from the window. "Does that mean we shouldn't be here?"

Divya flapped a hand at him. "He doesn't mind *looking*. How else would others admire his art?"

"I'm sure they would love to have you in Bali, though," Sezal said, Vaan nodding at her side. "If you really wanted to stay here."

"But the whole point would be having a palace to myself!" Advaith complained. "I'm the asura. Surely that's enough of a reason?"

"You have *two* palaces back home," Tav argued.

Every time they met, Divya took them somewhere wondrous and new, more than happy to show off her home to those who would appreciate it. From how they spoke of Martya, she gathered that most humans lived in fear of rakshasas, even those who went out of their way to help humans. It made no sense to her. She could tell it bothered Advaith too, and they sometimes shared a commiserating look.

One day, almost a year after their first meeting, they were exploring a market in Mahatala—where many of the nagas lived—when Divya heard the telltale lilt of a storyteller.

She dropped the bracelet she was examining, ignoring the vendor's irritated hiss, to turn and grab each brother by an arm. Despite their confusion, they allowed her to drag them through the throng of nagas toward the storyteller.

"This'll be a treat," she said as they joined the crowd, pushing their way to the front.

A space had been cleared for the storyteller under an awning strung with bells and flower garlands. She was a nagi with a hood spackled in emerald, her upper half wrapped in a finely embroidered uttariya. Beside her stood a danava, silent and stern-faced, with curved horns and skin so dark it was nearly black.

The nagi spread out her arms. "It begins, as we all did, with the ocean."

The crowd instantly hushed. Even the bustle of the street dimmed in respect for the storyteller's voice, clear and ringing across the multicolored pathways of the market. Those around Divya sighed and settled.

"When the planes burned as mere specks within the cosmos's eye, there were bridges tentatively linking them, feats of great and subtle power. The earth was one—rich soil, strong roots, vulnerable flora. It connected Martya with Svarga, light and growth. From this connection came the great yaksha deities."

Tav's eyes gleamed with intrigue. Divya was sure he'd heard of the yakshas' origins before, but storytellers were famed for a reason: They cast their words as spells, creating tapestries out of history and myth and legend.

The danava beside the storyteller moved their hands. Danavas were skilled in illusion, and as the storyteller spoke, images formed before the crowd.

"The Elephant, for wisdom and luck. The Serpent, for guardianship and grievances. And the Tortoise, for stability and health." The storyteller gestured to the image of each god with a graceful flourish. "Together, they worked to ensure Martya's development and foundation. Once they were satisfied, they blessed the soil so it would continue their work and retreated to Svarga to oversee their heavenly duties."

The danava spun another illusion, and with it came a sudden crashing sound that made Divya startle. Water filled the small clearing, rushing over the crowd's tails and shins and splashing up against the nearest buildings. Some cried out while others laughed. Divya clung to Tav, worried the water would rise higher.

"And then there was the ocean," the nagi went on. "A great, churning bed of restless water and teeming life, dark and deep and dignified. It was from within these depths the first rakshasa was formed, a being of no discernible name or race. Some claim he was born in the shape of a snake, and that the slitted pupils in his eyes give this away."

Advaith drew in a breath. When Divya glanced at him, he was smiling, completely enraptured with the story.

"No matter his form, he was a being with immense power. But unlike the yaksha deities, he was completely alone. He writhed and suffered under the crushing water, in the dark, while the cosmic energy within him turned dark as well. He had no place to direct it, and so it turned inward, festering, until it became a toxin to himself and to others."

Blackness spread through the water. Tentacle-like tendrils wrapped around the nagas' tails and around Divya's ankle, making her shriek. Tav reassuringly patted the hand that was crushing his.

"This toxin came to be known as halahala," the storyteller said, "and that was what the progenitor rakshasa was called before he chose his own name. The yaksha deities, learning of Halahala's predicament, grew worried and sought to help him. They wove the energies of Svarga through a celestial loom until it produced the substance known as amrita. The immortal nectar."

With a twitch of the danava's fingers, the water receded. A beautiful glass jar containing a silvery-blue liquid now wove before the storyteller. Divya's mouth watered at the sight of it; it certainly looked good enough to drink.

"They could not travel to Halahala themselves, so to deliver it, they recruited a physician who understood the cosmic energies. This physician became the founder of Ayurveda, a medicinal practice celebrated within

Martya. With his vast knowledge, he was able to enter the ocean and help Halahala consume the nectar.

"After the ingestion of amrita, the toxin within Halahala was put to rest, settling into a power that was both dark and heady, as destructive and beautiful as the ocean itself. With this power, he was able to open the way to the third and final plane, Patala, where he took up residence. Brahimada, the Universal Divide, was finally complete." She nodded to the danava, who produced a new image of an intricately wrought throne of gold and starry obsidian. "The tormented being known as Halahala chose the name Dukha, and he has ruled Patala ever since."

Advaith's smile had grown a little bigger. Divya wondered what the demon lord was like. She herself had never laid eyes on him, and Advaith wasn't allowed to share what they discussed.

"As thanks to the yaksha deities for rescuing him from his isolation, he allied with them to oversee Martya, which was ruled by humans." The storyteller's amber eyes landed on Tav and Advaith with a subtle smirk. "But this was not all that resulted from that fateful drinking of amrita."

The next image was of two balls of light, one blue and one red. Divya gasped, remembering that day in the judgment chamber with Bijul.

"The meeting of halahala and amrita produced new threads of cosmic energy, eager to be stitched within the tapestry between worlds. From halahala being touched by life came chaos, and from amrita being touched by darkness came healing. Each spun into new forms, as bright and hungry as stars. Those energies became the first asura and deva."

On either side of Divya, Tav and Advaith shifted awkwardly. The storyteller's smirk grew.

"The asura fell to the patronage of the demon lord; the deva, to the yaksha deities. But it was only when they worked together that they could accomplish feats of greatness. At last, Martya had guardians of its own. The asura and deva worked in harmony, and the human race flourished.

"Martya's soil was so potent that lesser yakshas had grown to care for the land, the water, and the skies. The yaksha deities, out of an abundance of fondness, shared amrita with them so that some could join the deities in the heavens. Svarga prospered with these celestial beings while Patala remained empty. The demon lord, wanting subjects of his own, petitioned the asura and deva to help him. But they learned that the celestial loom the yaksha deities had used to create their nectar of immortality had been destroyed, as they no longer had need of it."

The danava formed an image of two faceless human forms, one blue and one red, facing each other. "And so the asura and deva worked together to determine how to produce amrita themselves. They labored tirelessly, unceasingly, until their combined efforts came to fruition." Another bottle of the silvery-blue liquid appeared between the figures. "Yet despite their powers, the asura and deva are, unfortunately, only human, and susceptible to human vices."

The figures' positions changed. One held the trishul; the other, the sudarshana chakra. It seemed as if they were about to fight each other. Divya frowned while Tav and Advaith shifted again.

"The asura and deva fought over the nectar of immortality." The storyteller shook her head. "And when they clashed, it was reminiscent of the dark churning power of the ocean, and toxin spread from below their feet in black ribbons of disease. Halahala existed once more, and it threatened all of Martya even as it gave birth to the rakshasas.

"The yaksha deities sent the celestial physician to put a stop to their fighting. He took the amrita they had produced and poured it over the halahala. It was through this pool of blended toxin and nectar that the nagas were born, waterlogged and immortal."

A pool of that silvery liquid spread before them, and the ghostly shapes of nagas crawled out of its depths. The crowd murmured and smiled.

"And so the demon lord got his wish, and the nagas and other rakshasas took residence in Patala under his rule. But the asura and deva had committed a grievous wrong, betraying one another in their greed. Since it was the asura who had struck first, the yaksha deities, sorrowful, enacted justice by taking the asura's life."

Advaith tensed. Tav reached across Divya to grab his wrist.

"Not long after, the deva succumbed to heartache and died as well. The deities decreed that a new asura and deva would be born to carry out the incomplete dharma of the first. And so it is the fate of the asura and deva to be eternally reborn in different avatars until they can provide proper penance for their greatest sin."

The blue and red figures returned, standing side by side.

"Some say they are always born as twins, perpetually bound together. Some say that when the celestial physician spilled the amrita, the asura stole a drop, giving them a hint of immortality."

She spread her hands again, and the illusion fell away.

"But this we know for certain: That we are forever bound to the water, and to the asura, and to the demon lord. That we have both halahala and amrita to thank for our lives. That the planes cannot exist without both darkness and light."

Her tone gave clear indication that the story was finished. The crowd cheered and tossed gems toward the nagi, who humbly inclined her head in thanks.

Advaith had begun to tremble. Divya took his other hand, dismayed by the expression on his face. She was so used to his smiles and laughter that the reverse was alarming.

"It was a long time ago, Adi," Tav whispered. "It was the *first* asura and deva. Since then, they've all worked peacefully together. We're not like that."

Advaith and Tav shared one of their silent conversations, the kind that Divya found herself oddly jealous of. Eventually, Advaith sighed and nodded.

"I know," he murmured. "I just . . . didn't like hearing about it. Even the *thought* . . ." He gently extracted his hands and reached toward his mouth. "Do you think it's true that the asura had a drop of amrita? What does a hint of immortality mean?"

Tav shook his head. "I don't know. We could ask the storyteller. Or you can ask Lord Dukha when you see him next."

Advaith dropped his hand, but his face remained clouded. "Maybe I will."

Chapter Thirty-One

EVER SINCE THE day with the storyteller, there were small, unexpected moments when Advaith grew quiet. He was still the same boisterous Advaith, ready to laugh at the drop of a pin and often teasing his brother and Vaan (with Divya's help on most occasions). But Divya noticed times when he would simply stare off, his mouth a flat line and a divot between his brows.

Over the next few years, Tav was often requested both in Svarga and Martya for matters pertaining to injured yakshas and failing crops. Meanwhile, Advaith's missions tended to be more in the vein of settling disputes, such as the eternal feud between the nagas and the garudas. While the dakini elders taught Divya how to use her dagger and all the ways in which to apply her third eye (though they claimed she was too unfocused to properly perceive with it), both of the princes were trained in combat and learned how to use their legendary weapons.

She watched Tav summon his sudarshana chakra with a mantra, a blue light in the shape of the weapon that solidified into metal. It consisted of a long stock with a large golden disk at the end, its edges ridged in sharp points like the fangs of a beast. There was a hole in the middle of the sun-shaped disk, and all along the inner perimeter was a ring of small gems, with a pearl at their apex.

He swung it like a lance. The disk at the top detached and spun forward in a violent blur, chopping a tree in half. It then obediently spun back around to reattach to the stock.

Divya clapped. "I feel bad for the tree, but you're getting better!"

Tav scratched his head with a sheepish smile. "I'd rather stick with my sword, but . . ."

Divya had seen him wield a sword as well, and he was impressively swift and precise with it. The focus he got in his eyes when he trained made that familiar warmth well in her chest and stomach.

More and more, it had just been her and Tav. Advaith was always busy, and whenever the two visited Patala, he had to report to Lord Dukha first thing. After, he barely hung around.

"It's because he's the crown prince," Tav had explained when Divya expressed her annoyance. "He has more responsibilities than I do."

"You're *both* princes."

"Yes, but he's the one set to inherit everything."

Human politics were so baffling. "What about you, then?"

He'd shrugged and turned his face away. "Well, no one knows I exist, so—"

"Wait." She'd grabbed him by the shoulders. "No one knows you *exist*?"

"No one in our country, I mean. When we do missions, we cover our faces. Baa-Ji . . ." He'd paused. "It's just easier this way."

Divya hadn't understood then, and she didn't understand now, but perhaps she wasn't meant to. Those were human affairs, and she had barely left Patala, only going a small distance beyond the dakinis' caves into Martya before losing her nerve.

Tav let the sudarshana chakra disappear and turned to her. As if he could read her mind, he asked, "Have you ever thought about visiting Martya?"

Divya chewed on her lower lip. She'd picked up the habit from Tav, which made the elder dakinis click their tongues at her. "Of course I have. You and Advaith make it sound so strange."

But if she were to journey to Martya, would the humans try to hurt her? She knew there were clusters of dakini communities that had made Martya their home, but they lived far from dense human populations.

Tav rubbed a hand up and down his arm. "You've shown us so much of Patala. Maybe I can . . . I mean, I could, if you wanted to . . . I'd return the favor? But you don't have to. I'd protect you. I mean . . ."

Divya felt a smile spread slow and sweet as honey across her face. "Yes."

He forcefully cleared his throat. "I, uh, found a nice place recently. I'd like to show it to you."

Even if it was the only bit of Martya she could bring herself to see, it would be enough, she thought, if Tav had chosen it especially for her.

Tav met her a few miles from the dakinis' cave, far enough that his smell wouldn't alert the elders. It was already the farthest she'd been, and she answered Tav's smile with an uncertain one of her own.

"We can turn back anytime," he reminded her, and she nodded, silently grateful.

They went the rest of the way on horse. Divya had never ridden one before, and she and the horse were equally wary of each other until Tav gently took her hand and pressed it to the horse's broad, soft forehead. The horse nudged into her palm, and a breathy laugh escaped her. Or maybe it was from the flurry in her stomach at Tav's touch.

Riding was uncomfortable, especially considering how close they had to be, but she quickly found it was more than worth it. As they crested a grassy knoll, Divya gaped at the sprawling floodplain below.

There was a river so wide and lazy the water was practically still. Although the sky was studded with slow-moving clouds, the river's surface glinted the way the gems within the judgment chamber refracted the ghost lights. It smelled verdant and wild here, from the sun-warmed grass to the algae that had dried on the rocks along the river's shore.

And there were flowers. Dozens of them, *hundreds* of them, all held open like cupped hands, their petals long and flushed a deep pink that paled to white at their centers. They rose on long, thin stalks from wide green leaves and flat pads.

Tav helped her down from the horse, and she briefly lingered on the sensation of his hands on her waist before her attention was caught once more by the river. She walked toward it, wrapped in the warmth of sunshine and Tav's expectant gaze.

"They're called lotus flowers," he said when they stopped near the river's edge. Their smell was gently fragrant, sweet, like the air of Patala. "We get them in our lakes and rivers, but I've never seen one so completely overrun before." He admired the field of pink petals. "I like it, though. How untamed it is."

She took a deep breath, then another. She couldn't seem to get enough of that heady scent, enough of Tav's voice and how he sometimes looked at her the way he was looking at the river now.

"I like it too," she whispered.

They visited the river often.

They mostly sat on the shore and enjoyed the view, talking about nothing of consequence while Tav carved funny little figurines, or discussing Tav's responsibilities as both the deva and a prince in hiding. He told her stories about when he had to pretend to be Advaith—usually when the crown prince was away on missions—and how he had offended no fewer than five Malhirian nobles when he had accidentally mixed up their names.

"It's not *my* fault I don't see them often enough to remember who's who," he grumbled while Divya laughed. "I'd rather be out in the training yards. Or here."

The last part was said softly, and Divya immediately stopped laughing due to the flush blazing across her face. It was all she could do not to dunk her entire head in the river.

Another time, she braved the shallows to stand ankle-deep in the water as the sun beat down on her shoulders. It was hot and humid that day, the air pressing in close. Tav had decided he was *too* hot, and he had waded into the river in his salwar. She now watched him make lazy strokes, rippling the glass-like surface and making the flowers bob up and down.

She wiggled her toes, silt shifting beneath them. It was unsettling yet oddly satisfying.

Gathering her resolve, she called, "I want to swim."

Tav stopped and turned. "What?"

"I want to swim. To learn, I mean." She swallowed. "To . . . do what you're doing."

He returned to her. As he emerged from the water, his salwar clung to his legs, sitting low on his hips. Divya looked away.

"You want me to teach you how to swim?" he asked slowly.

Staring at the nearest flower, she nodded. She felt a tap at her hip and forced her gaze over to where Tav had rested a finger on the sheath of her dagger.

"Leave this on the shore," he said. "Everything else you can keep on."

Despite being fully dressed, she felt exposed as Tav took her hand gently, so gently she wanted to cry, and led her deeper into the river. Her heart pounded at the wet, silken caress of it, her instincts screaming that one wrong move and she could go under. If she drowned, would she immediately emerge from the lake in Nagaloka as a spirit?

She recalled the storyteller years ago, the illusion of the ocean's waves, the way her words had painted a picture of Dukha's origins. *Destructive and beautiful,* the nagi had said. *We are forever bound to the water, and to the asura, and to the demon lord.*

But though Divya knew that was objectively true, she wondered at the fate of those who were bound to the deva instead of the asura, going against the nature of the dark. She *was* a dark thing, which in Martya seemed to be bad, but Patala's enchanting passion would forever be in opposition to Svarga's structured perfection. That was just the way of things.

Did Tav see her as something chaotic? Something *bad?*

Yet he held her so carefully in the water, letting her adjust to the strangeness of it, the overwhelming loss of control as her feet left the riverbed and floated on their own. She wrapped her arms around his neck with a strangled sound, and even her braid limb reached out to grab hold of his arm.

"You're all right," he assured her, but there was amusement in his voice, so she pinched him with her long nails. "Ow! What was that for?"

"You're laughing at me," she muttered.

"I am not. You're doing a brave thing. It's commendable."

She really couldn't handle this. At a loss, she ground her forehead into his shoulder, making another strangled sound. He rubbed her back in sympathy.

"Once you're ready, we can start."

"I'm ready." She wasn't, but she had to move away from this conversation or else suffer a demise worse than drowning.

"All right. Start kicking your legs through the water, like this." He demonstrated, something she could feel more than see. "This is how you'll stay afloat, though if your body's anything like mine—or, rather, a human's—you'll float naturally. It's when you fight against it that you go under."

She kicked her feet the way he was showing her. He held her somewhat apart from him, but she was too focused on her movements to mourn it.

He pulled her this way and that, the water both possessive and aloof in how it slid over her legs and hips.

She was so busy concentrating that it took her a moment to realize Tav had let go. She was treading water on her own. Divya immediately squeaked and flailed, and Tav rushed forward to hold her again. The nearby lotuses nodded up and down in the current.

"Remember what I said about fighting against it?" Tav said. "You were doing well!"

"I was surprised!" she argued. "I can do it again."

His eyes flashed with something that wasn't amusement, but more like he was . . . pleased. With her.

"Show me, then," he said, and never one to pass up a challenge, she did.

It was after another lesson that they were lying on their backs on the grass, letting the sun dry their clothes, when Divya heard Tav humming.

The humming itself wasn't unusual; he tended to hum melodies he'd learned at home, marching chants and yaksha hymns and folk songs. Divya enjoyed hearing them, had even memorized a few, but this was one she'd never heard before.

She opened her eyes and blinked against the dazzling light. They only visited the river in the morning and early afternoons, when the lotuses were in bloom. Everything smelled like sun and water, the grass prickling her bare forearms and feet, and if she moved her hand a couple inches to the right, it would brush against Tav's leg.

He had sat up at some point, leisurely whittling a piece of wood. The shape in his hands was slowly resolving into the figure of a dakini. Some of his yaksha butterflies hovered around him, finding perches on his shoulders. She only ever saw them in Martya, as yakshas could not enter Patala, and she delighted in their bright wings and tiny tickling feet.

She pushed herself onto her elbows. Tav wore a small, easy smile, the kind she was certain he wasn't even aware of. A smile born out of pure contentment, natural and enduring.

Her heart clenched. He was content here, with her.

She wanted to say something about how she was content too. That their visits to the river were the best parts of her week, that the elders narrowed their eyes (all three of them) at her because she was filled with buzzing energy in the hours leading up to their meeting. That she often thought of him when he wasn't there and wished for his company always.

Instead, she asked, "What song is that?"

"Hmm?" He seemed dazed, lost in his peaceful whittling.

"The song you were humming. I haven't heard it before."

It was hard to tell if the color in his cheeks was a blush or a natural tint from the sun. "I didn't even realize I was humming it."

Intrigued, Divya sat up and crossed her legs. A yaksha butterfly landed on her knee. "What's it called?"

He raked his hair away from his face. It was a little longer now, nearly to his shoulders. He'd grown it out because Advaith kept his hair that length. "It doesn't have a name. Not yet, anyway."

"What do you mean? All songs have names."

"Well . . ." He plucked at the nearby grass. "It doesn't have a name because I wrote it."

"You *wrote* a song?" She scooted closer. "I didn't even know that was something you could do!"

"It— It's not a *good* song," he mumbled, ducking his head. "When we come here, I feel peaceful. More so than in any other place. One day, a melody popped into my head, and I thought . . . that's it. That's the feeling the river invokes in me."

Sometimes Divya's third eye allowed her to perceive the dormant energy within Tav, the steady blue light at the core of him. She sensed it now, radiating power and tranquility, the warmth she had been chasing since the fateful day she'd first felt it.

She was so full of it now that speaking was impossible. She had to stare at the river, the riot of pink and green, as she burned and burned and burned with it.

"*Lotus Blossom*," she blurted.

"What?"

"A name. For the song."

He thought it over until that small, contented smile returned to his face. "*Lotus Blossom*," he agreed. "It's perfect."

The dakinis quickly grew tired of her humming the same song over and over, to the point where once they heard the first few notes they groaned and ordered her to get into trouble somewhere else in Patala instead.

Bijul didn't have a problem with it. When Divya asked her what she thought of when she heard it, the nagi indulged her by closing her eyes before replying, "Harmony, and rest. Something with which to soothe the heart."

Divya told Tav this, and he seemed touched by Bijul's words. "You should meet her," Divya insisted. "Although I suppose, technically, you already have. And you will again, one day."

Tav coughed. "I suppose that's true."

Humans were touchy on the subject of death, she'd noticed. They dwelled in the past and feared for the future, sometimes forgetting to live in the present.

She sort of understood, though. Whenever she came here with Tav—and Advaith, on the rare occasion—she dreaded the moment they parted, the world suddenly not as vibrant or colorful, the air too quiet, her skin colder. If she could trap a day like this forever, she would.

It was silly, but she was afraid of Tav forgetting her. As they got older, he took on more and more responsibility, and their visits became less frequent. The dakinis complained about her moping, but she couldn't help it.

What if she was away from him for so long that she became unimportant?

During their next visit, she carefully cut a lotus flower from its stem and brought it home with her. She searched for the right materials within Patala, then asked for Bijul's assistance. The end result wasn't pretty, but she was proud nonetheless.

Still, she was silent with mortification when she thrust her hand at Tav the next time they met. He uncurled her fingers out of their fist and made a sound of surprise.

"Did you make this?" he asked, lifting the pendant from her palm, warmed from her skin. It was a rectangular blob of amber; encased within was a single petal from the lotus flower. The rest lay pressed and dried among her belongings.

"It's not very good," she muttered. "You don't have to keep it."

"Why wouldn't I keep this? It's lovely."

She scowled and finally looked at him, ready to snap that she didn't want to be patronized, but she froze at the expression on his face. He cupped the pendant within his hand as if it were something precious, his eyes soft and slightly unfocused.

And then he moved those eyes to her, as if *she* were the precious thing, and something within her broke apart and healed at once.

Not knowing what else she could possibly do, she turned and ran. His startled laughter followed after.

She was humming *Lotus Blossom* when Bina looked at her askance.

"You really know no other songs?" the nagi drawled.

Bina was Bijul's daughter and often helped in the judgment chamber. Over the years, she and Divya had fallen into a comfortable friendship where they demanded little from each other.

They were cleaning the shelves where the various cups were stored. Divya held one made of silver with two handles. Bina polished one of porcelain covered in intricate floral engravings.

"This is the song I like best," Divya said imperially, setting the cup back in its proper place. She had spent a long time wondering which of these cups would be hers. She had picked one out—a large gem-studded goblet of gold—and Bijul had visibly held in her laughter.

"You do not choose which cup will be yours," she'd explained then. "The cup chooses you. It best represents how you lived your life."

Divya had pouted. "Well, if I can't choose my cup, then I'll never die."

Bijul had put a hand upon her shoulder. "Nothing eludes us forever," she'd said. "Not even death."

Divya sighed now and picked up the next cup, thick and wooden, more of a bowl. "It's been weeks."

Bina seemed confused until she grumbled in understanding, "Since you've seen the deva, you mean."

"*Tav*, yes."

"Not all of us are on such casual terms with him."

"Jealous?"

"Why would I be? I have no use for human men. Unless it's to eat them." Bina showed off her fangs in a wide grin, making Divya kick at her tail.

"You're still frequently seeing the deva?"

They both winced and turned toward Bijul. She was as calm as ever, though her gaze was troubled as it landed on Divya.

"Not *frequently*," Divya mumbled, holding the wooden bowl closer. "Not anymore, at least."

Tav had warned her he'd be away for longer because of some worrying development in his country. He wouldn't lie to her, but a small, niggling part of her mind kept whispering that she had become unimportant.

"We've been receiving an influx of spirits from Martya," Bijul said. "Specifically from Dharati."

"Why is that?" Bina asked.

"They have died by violent means. It could mean raids, or the typical skirmishes for land. Or, potentially, the first stirrings of war."

A flash of hot dread stung Divya's chest and stomach. Bina gave her a concerned frown that mirrored her mother's.

"I hope this is not the case, but if it is, the asura and deva may be caught up in it." Bijul addressed Divya alone when she said, "Please be careful."

It used to feel like an easy promise. Now Divya nodded guiltily, knowing it had never been a promise at all.

Chapter Thirty-Two

DIVYA DIDN'T UNDERSTAND how dire the situation was until the day she was waiting in Sutala—restlessly pacing, a new habit that tested Bina's patience—and Patala's gates suddenly opened before her.

She had only seen the gateway once or twice. It rose impossibly tall and dark, stone and obsidian and material not of any world, black and gleaming like an insect's eye or the farthest reaches of Martya's sky. When the gates swung open, Divya shielded her eyes against the flood of light. Several figures tumbled through, and the ground rumbled as the gates resealed themselves and disappeared.

Divya ran forward. Tav was kneeling beside Advaith, both of them bloodied and panting harshly. Advaith clung stubbornly to his trishul, the trident's three wickedly sharp prongs dripping red. The asura's aides fretted over his injuries. As danavas, their illusions allowed them to craft glamours that made them pass as human, which they dropped now that they were safely back in Patala.

"I'm *fine*," Advaith growled, trying and failing to push Vaan away.

Vaan grabbed his wrist. "You're *hurt*," he said, and there was no mistaking the fear in his voice. "You don't have to run to Lord Dukha immediately."

"Collect your breath, at least," Sezal added.

Tav pressed insistently on his brother's shoulder, making him sit. Sezal swung her pack off her shoulders to root for medicine while Tav held a hand to the wound on his brother's side, closing his eyes and channeling his energy. His hand shone cerulean against the trickle of Advaith's blood.

Divya could only kneel there and watch. Useless—she felt so useless.

Once Tav was done, he nodded to Sezal, who descended on the asura with linen bandages and poultices. Tav started at the sight of Divya, as if he hadn't noticed her until now.

"What happened?" she whispered, chest tight.

Tav sighed and was about to scrub his hand through his mussed hair before realizing it was drenched with blood. "There was an ambush close to where we were. An outpost. Bakshi's army's been taking control of them throughout the kingdom, and we sent more soldiers, but . . ." He heaved another sigh, this one deeper and dispirited. "Even with us there, we were overrun."

Divya had heard that name muttered a few times: Anu Bakshi, a man in Martya who desired the same sort of power that Tav and Advaith had. That was how she understood it anyway.

"I tried to summon the nearby rakshasas," Advaith muttered, wincing as Sezal tied the bandage firmly around his torso. Divya couldn't be sure from this angle, but she thought Vaan might be holding the crown prince's hand. "But the commotion's driven both them and the yakshas away."

"Lord Dukha isn't offering help?"

Tav shook his head. "No. The yaksha deities aren't either, though we plan to appeal to them again."

Advaith was gazing out at the landscape with that distant expression. It seemed different now. Harder.

"I'm not going to Svarga," Advaith decided.

"Adi—"

"I'm staying here. You go."

A tense silence followed. Eventually, Tav said, "Fine."

Divya licked her suddenly dry lips. "If Patala and Svarga won't help, then how can you fight back?"

Tav touched a spot on his chest, an unconscious gesture. She realized she could make out the shape of the amber pendant beneath the part of his shirt that wasn't covered by armor.

"In any way we can," he answered.

It only got worse.

The demon lord didn't send Martya aid, as this was considered a "human affair." The yaksha deities were similarly unwilling to get involved. Even though their realm was tied to the life in Martya, they were wary of the violence of humans, which bred chaos. So the warlord known as Anu Bakshi continued to plunder his way through Dharati.

"He kills those who oppose him but treats everyone else with respect and generosity," Tav explained. "He recently sat down to tea with the officials of a large town in the north to discuss a peaceful transition of power. They practically handed him the town on a gilded serving tray."

Tav and Advaith were stretched thin. Divya hardly ever saw Advaith anymore, and when she did, he was always with his aides and looked grim. He had lost weight, and his eyes were haunted, as if something were eroding him from the inside out.

Whenever she managed to see Tav, he was similarly exhausted, pulled between the deva's duties to ensure the yakshas' safety and a prince's duty to protect his people. Once, they met up near the caves only for him to fall asleep on the grass. Divya let him sleep for hours, loath to wake him for anything, despite the ache deep within her that longed for his gaze and his voice. She instead contented herself by brushing the hair out of his face and whispering words she wasn't brave enough to say while he was conscious.

On a warm afternoon not long after, when she prowled the edges of Martya, a white yaksha butterfly fluttered onto her shoulder. Though she couldn't understand them, the message was familiar: Tav was waiting.

He was quiet and drawn, as he typically was these days, but he smiled when he saw her. Her steady thrum of anxiety eased.

They rode to the river. Since it was later in the day, the lotuses had closed up, and the sinking sun set the water on fire, creating a mosaic of pinks and greens and oranges and reds. Divya inhaled deeply when she saw it, something within her settling like disturbed silt floating back to the riverbed.

The two of them sat and enjoyed the view. Butterflies flitted around them, some landing on the lotuses and serenely opening and closing their wings.

Finally, when the sun was a mere sliver on the horizon, she turned to him. "I know you're going to war."

Tav closed his eyes. The amber pendant was resting outside his shirt today, glowing gold in the last rays of light. It was a long time until he spoke.

"Our father is dead." He kept his eyes closed, as if unable to face the world now that the words existed in this place that was only meant for peace.

Divya didn't understand what it was like to have a father, didn't know what sort of grief losing one would entail. She knew both he and Advaith had dearly loved their parents, and their mother's death years ago had left Tav bereft. She felt a great deal of distress when she imagined losing Bijul, but imagining and living through it were two wholly separate things.

She placed a careful hand on his arm. He shuddered and took a broken breath, and it shattered the fragile wall around him. Divya wrapped him in her embrace, holding him while he rested his head on her shoulder and wept. Here, he didn't have to be a prince or the deva; he could merely be a boy who was sad and hurting, who didn't know how to navigate a cruel world on his own.

Her fingers were tangled in his hair, and the first stars had freckled the sky by the time he'd calmed down. He was warm and pliant against her, having exhausted himself on heartache. Divya leaned her head on his, lips skimming his temple. Again, she felt helpless, not knowing what he needed, what she could do to make this better.

But maybe it wasn't supposed to be better. It simply *was*, and she now had to figure out how to support him through it.

"Where's Advaith?" she whispered as the insects in the grass trilled their nighttime songs.

"We sent him to the fort in Suraj days ago." He swallowed hard. "He was furious, but Ranbir and the others forced him to go."

Between the two brothers, Advaith had always been the more explosive one. Of course he would hold a desire to avenge their father.

"But Bakshi's intentions are clear." Tav leaned back, his eyes red and his expression grave. "He wants the throne. He wants total conquest of Dharati. My father's troops have been cut down, and now Bakshi's army makes its way toward Malhir." He didn't look at her as he said, "I'm the last line of defense against him."

It took a moment for Divya to understand what he was saying. She grabbed his arms, her long nails puncturing the skin under his sleeves.

"No." It was a growl. "You can't."

"I have to. Someone has to stop him."

"Can't Advaith fight with you? What about the rakshasas, the yakshas? If I— I can go to the dakinis, ask them to join you—"

"We can't let Bakshi know we're the asura and deva. He could use it against us somehow." Tav brushed the hair that had fallen out of her braid behind one of her pointed ears. "And I wouldn't want the dakinis to put themselves in danger for a human affair."

"It's *not* just a human affair!" she argued. "If Dharati falls to him—if the asura and deva fall to him—that will affect Patala and Svarga."

Tav dropped his hand back to his lap. "Perhaps." His voice was hollow, as if crying had drained him of emotion until all that was left was blank acceptance. "But even if I fall, Advaith will live. There will still be an heir. He can take shelter in Patala under Lord Dukha's protection and petition again for aid."

"Even if you fall? How can there be an asura without a deva? Don't you care if you live?"

His gaze dropped, as empty as his voice had been. Divya fisted a hand in the front of his kurta.

"*I* care," she hissed. "I care if you live!"

A flicker of raw anguish crossed his face. "I don't know what else to do. How else to stop him."

"Then let me come with you. I can help. I can *fight*."

He was already shaking his head. "I've been training with these soldiers all my life. They know what we're facing. You haven't seen battle, and I never want you to. The risk is too great."

"Nothing eludes us forever," she said, echoing Bijul's words. "Not even death."

"You can elude it for a long time yet. I'm not going to have you jeopardize that for my sake."

But it seemed more than that. "It's because of what I am, isn't it? A rakshasa fighting by your side would scare your soldiers."

"Divya—"

"I don't *care* what they think!" she shouted, disturbing the butterflies that had settled on the river. "I care about protecting you!"

Tav pulled her into his arms with a harsh sob. He held her tightly, painfully, but she welcomed the ache. She fought against her own tears as she clung to him, savoring the crush of her ribs and the way her chest was pressed against his, as if desperate to share a heartbeat.

"Please," she kept whispering. "Please."

He leaned away slightly. Despite his fatigue, despite his grief, he was stunning in the moonlight. He looked at her as if she were the moonlight itself.

When their mouths met for the first time, it already felt like the last. Divya hadn't known what it would be like, but she'd guessed it would be warm. And it was—his lips were soft on hers, shy and slow. They found an unhurried rhythm, and he tasted like the fruit in Sutala, like the sugared candy he'd brought her from the city, like the deep humid heat of summer.

It settled into the core of her, nestled away like a hoarded bit of gold. Like she could pluck the sun from the sky and swallow it, and it still wouldn't be this warm. He held her so carefully, his hands framing her face, holding her hips, the back of her neck. She wondered if this was what it was to be treasured. Her hand had settled upon his chest, her thumb rubbing over the surface of the amber pendant.

They lost themselves in touch and the orchestra of nightfall. Every time he whispered her name or pressed his lips to the curve of her neck she shivered, his attention overwhelming. He was everywhere. She wanted to keep him that way, but her kisses grew lazy and off mark. Tav cradled her jaw and brushed fingertips over her cheek, his eyes flashing blue for just a second.

She fell asleep to the sound of him humming *Lotus Blossom*, a song that promised harmony and rest. A song for a place that belonged only to them. She wanted him to promise he wouldn't go, at least not without her, but she was out before the words could form.

When Divya next opened her eyes, the sky was pearlescent with dawn and Tav was gone.

She sat up with a curse, the last vestiges of sleep burning away in the tide of her panic. She touched the ground where Tav had been lying. It was cold.

"No," she breathed. The horse was gone as well. She was alone. "No— Tav—"

She scrambled to her feet. The elders had tried to guide her in using her third eye beyond its natural perception, to pierce the veils of past, present, and future. But it required focus and composure, and they'd deemed her incapable of such a feat. That didn't stop her now as she closed her eyes but kept the third one open, searching frantically for where he'd gone, trying to sense the warmth of him like a heat map to his location.

But all she sensed was her own panic. Even if she ran as hard and fast as she could, for as long as she could, she knew she wouldn't reach him in time.

Her throat squeezed shut. Her chest hitched with quick half breaths. Useless—she was *useless*.

She didn't see the sleeping lotuses bob or hear the faint ripple of the water. It was only when a voice called her name that she whirled around, hand flying to her dagger.

Bina had risen from the river, hair wet and expression grave. "Maa was worried about you," she said, inching closer to shore. "She sent me to find you."

Divya had told Bijul of the lotus river, trying and failing to describe its beauty. She was thankful for it now as she hurried toward the nagi.

"There are rumblings in Patala," Bina went on, reading Divya's dire expression. "They're saying a great battle is happening in Martya."

"Take me there," Divya said without hesitation.

Bina's eyes widened. "*Why?*"

"Tav, he . . . The deva is in trouble. I have to go to him."

She was a second away from unspooling, from dissipating into mist from the sheer force of her anxiety. Bina wavered, caught between her mother's orders and Divya's determination.

"If you won't help me, I'll find a way myself," Divya snapped.

"Maa said—"

"Bina." Her voice broke. "Please."

The nagi hissed and beckoned her toward the water. Divya gracelessly splashed into the shallows, allowing Bina to drag her farther in and then pull her completely under.

Chapter Thirty-Three

SHE HAD NEVER traveled the way the nagas could—creating pathways through various sources of water, from the smallest puddle to the ocean itself. Divya's lungs ached as the dark water surged around them. She had to fight the instinct to struggle, Bina's hand a tight clasp around her wrist.

They were pulled this way and that, riptides sucking them in and spitting them out. Divya's head spun, and her stomach roiled, her vision blackening until Bina finally tugged her upward and they broke the surface.

She clung to the nearby rocks, coughing and retching. Bina dragged her from the swollen creek before the rushing water could carry her downstream.

Once Divya caught her breath, she stumbled forward on shaking legs.

She heard them before she saw them. The great, tumultuous roar of a many-headed creature interspersed with the clanging of metal and the screams of the dying.

"Divya," Bina said behind her. "You cannot help them. Not here, at least. We should be going back to Maa to assist her with all the spirits that'll find their way to Nagaloka after this."

You cannot help them.

Divya snarled and took off. Bina cried out after her, but she was filled with a brass-bound resolve, which lifted the last of her fugue and gave her new purpose. She was going to find Tav, and she was going to get him out of here.

The battlefield was muddy with spilled blood. Bodies lay contorted and forgotten across the plain, but Divya couldn't stop; she had to keep moving—forward, forward.

"Tav!" she screamed, spinning around as she desperately searched the pockets of fighting. *"Tav!"*

The nearest soldiers saw her and recoiled. They touched their foreheads and flicked their fingers at her.

"Kill it!" one of them yelled.

Divya unsheathed her dagger. Two men charged at her, but she quickly disarmed one and hamstringed the other. She didn't know whose men these were—she didn't know the Dharatian colors, or Bakshi's—but they intended to kill her, and the elders had taught her what to do in such a situation.

One of them got her dagger in his heart. She slit the other's throat. Her face warm with their blood, she continued deeper into the battlefield.

Those wearing green had been largely overwhelmed by those wearing blue. Many of the latter were riding away from the field, not in retreat but in preemptive victory. Divya killed a couple more in defense as she wandered, lost, through the mayhem. The kills themselves were quick and clean and did not linger in her heart, though she had the distant feeling they were supposed to.

But in this moment, nothing else mattered.

White fluttered in the corner of her eye, a small contingent of butterfly yakshas. "Where is he?" she demanded.

They zoomed ahead. She followed, dagger dripping at her side.

She found him soon enough. His head was covered with a helmet, yet she recognized the way he held his sword and wielded it like an extension of his body. Divya ran faster as Tav finished off a blue-clothed soldier with a bloody spray. He was panting heavily, on his way to exhaustion.

At Divya's arrival, he spun and lifted his sword only to stumble at the sight of her, his eyes round beyond the chain-mail curtain of his helmet.

"Divya? What are you— You can't be here!"

"You left without me!" she shouted back, tightening her hold on the dagger. "You *left*."

Pain flashed across the parts of his face that were barely visible. "I *had* to. I have to do this. I—"

"But you don't have to do it alone! Your duty isn't more important than your life!" She grabbed his arm and pulled. "We'll find Advaith and hide, wait for things to settle before making a plan to attack."

Tav hesitated. Her heart leapt in hope; she was already imagining the two of them riding away from here, away from the thick, bitter tang of blood and the wails of the fatally injured.

Then a butterfly fluttered near his ear, and he tensed. He turned away from her and toward the figures of two approaching men. Their pace was leisurely, as if they could not be touched by the surrounding turmoil.

Divya didn't recognize the older man. His face was mature and handsome, with a glossy black beard and dark eyes, his body packed with muscle under his armor. A massive sword was slung across his back, a smaller mace bumping against his hip. She knew at once this must be Anu Bakshi, the warlord who had been making his campaign across Dharati for the past several months.

And beside him . . .

"Adi," Tav whispered, and the anguish held in his brother's name could have felled Divya right then and there. "What are you doing?"

The asura stood at Bakshi's side, his expression neutral save for the pinch of his eyes. The trishul he held in one hand was nearly as tall as he was, gleaming brassy gold. The fact that he didn't bother to hide the holy weapon meant that Bakshi must have known who they were. *What* they were.

"You're supposed to be in the fort," Tav said slowly. The rest of the battle didn't exist at that moment, the four of them caught within a bubble. "Did he . . . ?"

"He hasn't kidnapped me, Tav. I'm here willingly."

"Why?"

Advaith sent a pleading glance to Bakshi, who nodded at Tav with only the vaguest hint of respect.

"Greetings, Holy Deva," he said, his timbre clear and deep. "It is unfortunate we must come to blows."

A burst of laughter escaped Tav, and Divya was startled into half lifting her dagger. "*Unfortunate?* Look at your great work!" He swung his arm out, gesturing to the horror of the plain. "You've burned our land and killed its people. You want to destroy the royal family and claim this ruined country as your own!"

"Tav, wait." Advaith stepped forward, his free hand held out before him. "I can explain later, but I'm here under Lord Dukha's orders."

"Lord Dukha?" Tav repeated.

"Yes. I have to . . ." His voice failed him, and he aggressively cleared his throat, no longer looking at his brother. "It won't make sense now, but I promise it will. This is for the good of Martya and Patala. Good for the rakshasas."

"What good does this do for the rakshasas?" Divya asked.

Advaith frowned at her. "This is between the asura and the deva. You don't need to know."

Divya's ears rang. In all the time they'd known each other, in all the time they'd been friends, he'd never spoken to her this way.

"Then why is he here?" Tav demanded, pointing his talwar at Bakshi. "He *killed* Baa-Ji!"

Advaith flinched. "I said I'll explain later." His words were starting to sound rushed, desperate. "Tav, please, you have to trust me."

"I always trust you," Tav said. "But I need *answers*."

"Our chance is slipping away," Bakshi said, eyeing the remnants of the battle. "Do it now."

Divya's chest constricted, ready to move depending on what the asura did next.

But she wasn't prepared for what happened. For Advaith to sprint forward, trishul raised, straight at Tav. For Tav to merely stand there and watch, stunned, as the brother he loved more than anything sank his weapon into Tav's abdomen.

A scream built in Divya's throat and refused to leave. Instead, it shrieked like a howling, battering wind inside her as she stared at the trishul, two of its three prongs puncturing through Tav's armor to the flesh beyond. Tav took hold of the trishul's stock, gaze never leaving his brother's.

"What?" Advaith's eyes burned cinnabar, wide with terror. "No . . . Tav, you were supposed to . . . Why didn't you block me? Why didn't you fight back? *You were supposed to fight back!*"

His voice was an anguished howl by the end. Tav had begun to glow blue, but the light was already stuttering around him, like a struggling heartbeat. He sank to his knees, pulling Advaith and the trishul down with him.

"Adi," Tav whispered. He released the trishul and reached up, cradling the side of Advaith's face, smearing blood across his cheek. "Veera. Why would I ever fight against you?"

Advaith sobbed for breath. "You were supposed to . . . He told me it was the only way to do it . . ."

Divya was too cocooned within her shock to notice it at first, but his words stirred a memory inside her of a storyteller's measured cadence. Learning of halahala, the product of the asura and the deva clashing.

Already, she could detect fine, nearly invisible threads of black stirring from the spot where Tav's blood had spilled. Bakshi smiled to himself.

That broke the spell on her. Divya came back to herself like a lightning bolt, all suddenness and heat.

The scream lodged within her roared free as she ran forward and plunged her dagger into Advaith's chest.

The force of it pushed the asura away and loosened his hold on the trishul. Advaith gasped like she had only said something shocking rather than struck him through with steel. When the pain finally registered, it flooded his face, transformed his disbelief into an almost childish fear. He scrabbled over her slippery hands in a futile attempt to pull the dagger out.

"Divya," he whimpered. "Please . . ."

Above them came a deep laugh.

"You've done my job for me. I suppose I should thank you for that."

There was a blur of silver, and Advaith's head went flying. Divya stared uncomprehending at the empty spot where his tearstained face had been, blood spurting from the severed neck and onto her face, her chest, her arms.

Bakshi loomed over them, greatsword in one hand. Advaith's blood coated its curved blade as the asura's dismembered body fell limply to the ground.

"Still, precautions need to be taken," Bakshi went on. "It'll take some time for the halahala to fully spread."

Divya longed to be numb. To succumb to the relief of unfeeling, to escape to a place where no thought or emotion could touch her. But rage and fear trawled through her bloodstream. She smelled of death, and this man was the reason why.

Ancient impulse took over. The third eye upon her brow opened fully, casting its glare upon Anu Bakshi.

The nazar hit him so forcefully it buffeted him backward. He roared and clutched his bloodied face as a dark miasma swirled around him, seeping into his skin. He shuddered, and when he dropped his hand, his right eye shone black with a red mark burning where his pupil should have been. The symbol for ajna, the third eye, but inauspiciously reversed.

"You are cursed, Anu Bakshi," she said hoarsely as he lifted his sword and stalked toward her. "For the rest of your days, you will suffer pain and uncertainty and bear the mark of the evil eye so that everyone knows you are destined for the greatest misfortune."

She laughed.

He sneered down at her, blood dripping off his upper lip, mismatched eyes narrowed with that promised pain. He had conquered a kingdom and been cursed for it, and yet the greatest offense of his life must have been this mere dakini, this mere girl, laughing at him.

He didn't bother to address her again before he shoved his sword through her chest, shattering bone and cleaving muscle. And though the agony was unlike anything she'd ever felt, she kept laughing, blood pouring from her mouth like the juice of Sutala's fruit.

Bakshi kicked her off his sword, and she landed in the mud. Her mind caught up to the truth of her shattered body, and the last of her weak laughs turned into wretched gasps. She could barely move, could barely do anything but twitch and turn her head to one side.

Tav lay only a few feet away. The chain mail of his helmet had fallen to reveal half his face. His eyes were partly open, fixed upon her.

His lips moved slightly. Shaping her name.

Divya gritted her teeth and used her braid limb to push herself off the ground. She whined at the searing pain, setting every nerve on fire as she dug her fingertips in the mud to crawl to him.

"Tav," she whispered, but it was hardly even a sound. Her own heart had quieted from a drumbeat to a murmur.

She lost strength halfway there. She collapsed, one hand held in front of her, reaching for him. Tav tried to move his arm to grasp it, his breaths coming quicker and quicker, the pupil of his visible eye dilating.

Like so many times before, she didn't know what to do. So she did the only thing she could: She started to hum.

The melody was broken and warbling, scarcely audible, but it reached him nonetheless. Tav held her gaze as their song floated between them, occupying all the spaces they could not, bringing him back to the place that was waiting for them. Harmony, and rest.

He closed his eyes, the lines of his face softening. And then all the tension left his body at once.

For the first time since she'd met him, Divya felt cold.

Her humming scattered like disturbed butterflies. She screamed breathlessly into the mud, writhing against the agony of her body and her heart, and all the parts of her she'd taken for granted. All around them, the ground seeped with the first toxic stirrings of poison. In front of her lay a boy who had deserved better.

And inside her was nothing but frost, rime, snowmelt.

Unable to feel anything beyond the cold, she didn't know when hands grabbed her and dragged her away. Eventually, a familiar face materialized above her, dripping water onto her chest.

"Divya." Bina was sobbing, clutching onto her shoulders. "Foolish thing! I told you not to go!"

She couldn't argue, couldn't speak. There was no point.

"It— It will be all right," Bina stammered as Divya's sight darkened.

"I'll burn this body to release your soul. We will meet again."

We will meet again.

She thought of sunlight on water, of gently waving lotus blossoms, of a place now beyond her reach that would forever be hers. Even if she looked upon it with a new pair of eyes, it would still be hers.

Theirs.

We will meet again.

For a while, she was nothing.

She didn't know for how long, but that wasn't important. Nothing was important anymore, and she was content with merely floating through the long dark. It was peaceful, even pleasant.

But it couldn't last forever. She was dimly aware of the flow of water, of murmurs and jewels, and a beautiful face beneath a hood coated in amethyst.

"Divya," she heard, a familiar voice so full of sorrow it nearly penetrated the shell of her peace. "My girl. I am so sorry."

Something was placed within hands she no longer had: a cup of black crystal, veined with streaks of red and dark pink. It reminded her of something delicate and beautiful and temporary.

When it was lifted to her lips, liquid flowed through what remained of her. It was strong and fragrant, and with every sip the hint of memory faded and faded, until only a wisp remained.

But something stopped her from taking the last sip. The cup was removed, and the spirit did not fight it.

"We need her to remember," came the voice the spirit once thought of as familiar but was no longer. "If she is to come back to us. Even if it's only a little bit."

"But what if she comes back as a human, or a yaksha? What if she can no longer come home to Patala?"

The spirit regained a fraction of awareness. Two figures, one hooded and one not, shadowy and dim. Between the hooded one's hands was a small orb of fretful crimson. The other hissed but didn't stop the hooded figure from approaching the spirit again.

"I am sorry," the figure whispered before handing over the red orb. The spirit held it as it had held the cup, and it was energy and fire and passion, wild and restless. So completely different from the peaceful journey the spirit had made here.

Yet the spirit allowed it to fuse together with whatever matter it was made of. Already there was a strange pull, as if something, someone, were calling from a distant place.

"We will meet again," the spirit heard as it let go, back to the darkness of quiet unbeing.

Quiet, that is, until there came the sound of two hearts beating side by side.

Chapter Thirty-Four

KAJAL'S EYES FLEW open.

At first, she was still mired in the darkness, the cosmos spanning between her heartbeat and Lasya's, lined in crimson and cerulean. But she could feel her chest expanding, her lungs a bellows. She could feel her heart pumping, a miracle crafted from blood and tissue.

And she could feel her throat, burning without pain. As if she had swallowed a star, sheltering its glaring warmth underneath her skin. That warmth pervaded her, making pathways of her veins, putting the sun itself to shame.

When her vision cleared, she was aware of two figures leaning over her. Familiar, beloved. She turned first to Lasya, tears drying on her face, focused so intently on sending her energy through Kajal. And Kajal recognized it, the way she could recognize her sister's walk and voice and scent. It had always been there.

The other . . .

She turned toward Tav. Remembered holding the core of him within her hands.

Realizing she could move, she reached up and curled one of those hands around the pendant swinging between them.

"Nothing eludes us forever," she said softly. "Not even death."

He shut his eyes—not in despair but whatever was its opposite and equal, an understanding that tore, then mended.

"Divya," he whispered. His touch moved from her throat to the side of her face, searching her features for the signs of one who'd been lost. "I wondered, but . . ."

Kajal almost laughed. He was always so good at drawing conclusions.

"Not Divya," she corrected. "Kajal."

He nodded, but his eyes gleamed with unshed tears, with rekindled hope. She saw in him now the boy he used to be, sweet and shy and smiling, and it made the ache in her chest all the greater.

"I remember her." His thumb brushed over her cheek. "But not what happened to her. I didn't know for sure that you . . . that she . . ."

For a second, Kajal tasted the forgetting tea on her tongue, clove and anise, the promise of a new beginning.

Tav leaned over her. "How—?"

He was pulled away, and the pendant's chain snapped between them.

"That was stupid of you," Advaith growled as he knelt and grabbed a fistful of Kajal's kurti. "You really think killing yourself is a better alternative to killing the enemy?"

Lasya kept hold of her, and this was partly why Kajal wasn't afraid. But the other part, the larger part, was because of the memories running rampant through her, the sensory recollection of how it felt to slam her dagger through his chest.

Slowly, with the hand not currently gripping the pendant, she pressed her fingers to that exact spot.

"Did it hurt," she said, mimicking his own words, "when my blade found you here?"

Confusion darkened his eyes. Then they flashed red as he recoiled in recognition.

"You . . . ?"

Lasya helped Kajal to her feet. "I know Lord Dukha ordered you to fight Tav to make halahala," Kajal said. "I know Tav refused to lift his blade toward you, which cost him his life." A humorless grin spread across her face. "And now you want to return to Lord Dukha to finish what you started. Rakshasa dominance, is that it?"

Divya may not have understood, but Kajal did. Lord Dukha wanted to overwhelm the plane of Martya with rakshasas until it fell under his control, then do the same to Svarga. And, unable to make amrita without the yakshas' celestial loom, the best way for him to create more rakshasas was halahala.

Advaith was too stunned to reply, Tav equally silent behind him. Vivaan and Sezal waited for the asura's next command while the three humans watched on in bemusement.

Kutaa bumped into Kajal's side with a whine. She gave him a reassuring scratch behind his ears.

"He told me Patala's numbers were weak," Advaith said quietly, more to himself than to her. "That the yakshas would outnumber them. Then Bakshi began his campaign, and somehow Lord Dukha roped him into it."

"He killed thousands of our people," Tav seethed. "He killed *Baa-Ji*. Why would Lord Dukha involve him in this?"

"I . . ." Advaith put a hand to the sutures around his neck. "I don't know. He never told me the full plan. Just my part in it."

Staring at the sutures, Kajal's mind spun.

Advaith's faint heartbeat. Punching out of her own coffin in Siphar. She had wondered so often why she had lived and Lasya hadn't.

The storyteller had said the first asura may have taken a drop of amrita. *A hint of immortality.* The reason, perhaps, why Advaith could remember everything and Tav and Lasya could not. Why Bakshi—whether under Lord Dukha's orders or otherwise—had split Advaith's body into three pieces so he couldn't revive himself.

Tav and Advaith hadn't been reincarnated because their bodies hadn't been burned, their spirits trapped in soil. Instead of fully parting from them, the energies of the asura and the deva had merged into the spirits who would become Kajal and Lasya.

She was too lost within her thoughts to realize Advaith had moved until he spoke.

"We won't get answers until we return to Patala," he said firmly. He stood again on the crest's edge, surveying the encampment. "These soldiers are using halahala as an excuse to tear our country apart. *I won't let them.*"

He held out his hands, and they lit up crimson.

Tav started forward, but Vivaan blocked him. Kajal tried as well but found her and Lasya's way impeded by Sezal.

The earth began to darken and wither. Veins of sickly black rose to the surface like pungent tar. Kutaa laid his ears flat. Kajal could sense the halahala even through the soles of her shoes, toxic and wrong. The product of conflict. Death.

"Adi, don't!" Tav fought out of Vivaan's hold. But as he got close to Advaith, his brother's energy lashed out, pushing him backward.

"Don't stop me, bhara," Advaith warned. "They deserve this."

The Vadhia only realized something was wrong when the veins reached the encampment. Kajal heard their cries of shock and fear, saw the way they scurried to fetch weapons and horses. But Advaith forced the halahala out of the ground. It burst upward into snakelike beings, towering over the Vadhia.

"No!" Lasya cried, but it was too late. The vines of halahala descended, striking down each and every soldier. Chests were caved in. Skulls were crushed. Limbs were ripped from bodies.

Satisfaction, dark and jubilant, bloomed within Kajal. As much as she longed to deny it, the sight of the Vadhia afraid and in pain pleased her. Whether it was the part of her that was the asura, thriving on chaos and disorder, or the part of her that was a girl trying to survive in this wretched world, she couldn't say. Maybe they were one and the same.

Advaith's forehead shone with sweat as the poison seeped into the soldiers' bodies, covering them in that tar-like substance. The air was so thick with blight-touched tamas that both Tav and Lasya cringed. Kajal could smell it, taste it on her tongue. It brought her back to that moment before Lasya's death, when she had attempted to open the gates on her own. But she had been an asura with no training; Advaith had had years of it.

Only when all the soldiers were dead did they rise and shamble toward the crest. Kajal had once likened Tav's connection to animals as a puppet master with his puppets, but she could see now that was wrong. *This* was what a true puppet master looked like.

Advaith shook while he struggled to maintain control. The ruby ring upon his finger lit up with his power. "Div— Kajal, please, help me."

But Kajal refused to move, too stricken with the memory of killing the Vadhia soldiers near the dakinis' forest. How the halahala had answered some silent summons of hers, caused by fear or rage or both.

She hadn't meant to kill them, just as she hadn't meant to kill the miners, or Gurveer Bibi, or Gurdeep, or Riddhi. Just as she hadn't meant to kill Lasya. Just as she hadn't meant for her mistakes to lead to the murdering of innocents by the Vadhia.

As a dakini, she hadn't cared, but she was no longer that person.

Kajal was only dimly aware of Jassi ushering Vritika and Dalbir away, now that the demons' attention was elsewhere. The corpses shuffled without direction, jaws hanging slack and eyes white and unseeing. Two of them tore at each other's diseased flesh with piercing cries, their sattva corroding while the tamas around them swelled higher.

"Now," Advaith ground out.

In the air before him came a faint sheen of black and silver. The gateway to Patala. The one Kajal had tried so hard to summon.

The gates that flickered into existence were wide and tall, made of glittering black stone that didn't look of this world. Their surface was studded with jewels and engraved with various species of rakshasas and night-blooming flowers, the symbol of a trishul standing as the keystone. With a deep rumble, the gates opened ajar, a sliver of beckoning shadow beyond.

Advaith was starting to flag. He groaned around gritted teeth, his energy sputtering as the veins on his wrists blackened.

Lasya tried to get past Sezal, but the danava blocked her way.

"Why are you allowing him to do this?" Kajal demanded of the aide. "He didn't tell you about his plans with Dukha and Bakshi. He kept you in the dark, and look what happened!"

Sezal wavered. "We need him. He's the asura."

"*I'm* the asura," Kajal said.

Sezal looked at her with mounting uncertainty.

"Do you really think this will lead to a cure?" Kajal gestured at the dead, wilted ground. "Or do you want to find another way?"

Sezal glanced between her and Lasya. Vivaan called to her, but she ignored him. A moment later, the danava stepped to one side.

Before Kajal could act, Lasya ran out ahead. With her revenant strength, Lasya landed a powerful kick to Advaith's side, sending him flying across the blackened grass. Lasya's hair stirred in the wind, her face eerily blank, and Kajal almost despaired that she hadn't been resurrected after all—that she was still the bhuta out for blood.

But her sister's eyes glowed blue, not red. As Advaith righted himself with a grimace, emotion flitted across Lasya's face. It was an emotion Kajal had never seen on her, and at first she couldn't be sure she'd seen it at all.

Fury.

"Don't make me do this." Advaith put a hand on his sword hilt. The veins on his wrist remained black, as if he'd taken in some of the halahala to better control it.

"I will kill you before you try," Lasya said. The words made Kajal feel like *she* was the one who'd been kicked.

Advaith unsheathed his talwar at the same time Lasya flew at him. Red and blue clashed, searing even behind Kajal's eyelids. They were both matched in strength, but the wind around Lasya was phantom and strange, smelling of grave soil.

Advaith lined his sword with violent red energy and struck. But Lasya dodged and spun with inhuman speed, aiming a punch at him. He jumped away and her fist smashed into the diseased ground, forming a small crater that steamed with blue-and-black mist.

"Careful," Advaith said, lifting his glowing talwar. "You don't yet know how to control those powers."

Lasya's eyes narrowed. Silently, she spread out her arms, fingers curled upward like claws. Behind her an azure light grew and flickered like a flame.

It resolved into the birdlike figure of a garuda. The phantom yaksha spread its wings wide and released high-pitched cries from its three heads before it plummeted toward Advaith like descending upon a serpent.

The prince barely put up a crimson shield in time. The garuda slammed into it, wings buffeting and talons scratching at the surface. In Advaith's weakened state, his shield stuttered long enough for the phantom yaksha to slice a long gash under his collarbone.

"Advaith!" Vivaan cried. Kajal could already see the knife in his hand, ready to plunge it into Lasya's unprotected back. Kutaa growled and clamped his jaws around Vivaan's leg to keep him in place.

A crossbow bolt whistled through the air before landing deep in Vivaan's shoulder. The danava cried out, the bolt's blessing sending white flashes like lightning across his chest. Kajal whirled around; Vritika had taken repossession of her crossbow, already nocking another bolt.

Advaith retaliated by reaching for the halahala, raising new vines from the earth that undulated around him. One by one, they struck at Lasya, and she dodged and blocked as best she could. Kajal yelled when one came close to hitting her, but the phantom garuda dove in front of it, shrieking as it scattered in a burst of blue light.

Lasya's eyes flared red, and she shoved a hand out before her. Advaith dropped his talwar and fell to one knee as he clutched at his sutured throat, struggling for breath. Kajal touched her own throat, remembering how it felt to have the bhuta choking her. The deadened earth beneath them turned darker, bubbling with toxin.

"Stop!"

Tav got between Lasya and Advaith, arms flung out on either side.

"Stop!" he begged again. "Please, don't—don't make the halahala worse."

Lasya slowly lowered her hand and released her hold on Advaith. The glow left her eyes, but the bhuta's wind still whipped around her like an agitated cat's tail.

"He's caused so much devastation," Lasya said.

"And he'll attempt to fix it. *We,*" Tav corrected, looking over his shoulder at his brother, "will attempt to fix it."

Kajal took a step forward, but she already knew she couldn't prevent what was coming.

"I'll go with you," Tav said to Advaith. "To Patala. We can solve this without you killing yourself on your own power." Eyes filled with remorse, he glanced at Kajal. "Just promise me you'll leave them out of this."

The surge of hope on Advaith's face was painful. "You'll go with me?"

"Yes. We'll find Lord Dukha and ask how to reverse halahala. And if he truly is working with Bakshi, then we will find a way to unseat them both. We're in this together."

We're in this together.

Tav had spoken those same words to her. They had made her feel, at least for a little while, less alone.

She had been a fool for believing them.

Advaith nodded eagerly, sheathing his talwar to grab Tav by the arm. "Yes. *Yes*. We're the asura and deva. We don't need anyone else getting in our way. And I can— I can make all this up to you."

Tav lifted his fingers to Advaith's face like he had on the Harama Plain with his brother's trishul impaling him.

"I know, Adi," Tav whispered.

Vivaan had broken off the crossbow bolt. Though he was clearly in pain, he took Advaith's wrist and grimly examined the black lines there.

"Heal him," Vivaan ordered Tav.

Kajal saw the moment Tav recalled the blighted yaksha in the lake. The way his powers hadn't been able to reduce even a vein of pollution.

"I can't," Tav confessed. "I can keep him from being in pain, but . . . the blight is beyond me."

Vivaan turned toward the humans. "He will need a physician."

Jassi stepped in front of Vritika and Dalbir. "If you promise to let my students go, I'll come with you." Her voice shook only slightly. Vritika and Dalbir started to argue, but the professor quieted them. "It's all right."

Vivaan let go of Advaith's wrist. "Very well. Sezal, come. His Majesty needs us."

Haltingly, Sezal took her spot at Kajal's side. "I serve the new asura."

Vivaan reeled as though she had run him through. He opened his mouth, but Advaith lifted a hand.

"She is free to serve whomever she chooses." Yet Advaith's parting nod to her was stiff, and he could barely conceal the hurt in his expression. "I wish you well, Sezal."

She ducked her head.

The corpses below them stilled, and the edges of the gateway faded. "There isn't much time," Advaith said. He looked at Kajal and Lasya with some reluctance, despite his insistence that they would only get in his way.

She knew Advaith would allow her to go with them, if for no other reason than to have access to another asura's power. She could finally enter Patala and join their mission to track down the demon lord.

But Advaith had chosen a path of destruction, even if he'd done so thinking it was for the greater good. And she was so tired of destroying everything she touched.

She and Lasya would figure this out on their own, as they'd always done.

Noting their resolve, Advaith frowned and dismissed them.

Vivaan gestured for Jassi to enter the gates. The professor wavered at the sight of the darkness beyond, casting one last glance at Vritika, Dalbir, and Kajal before steeling herself and stepping through. Vivaan allowed himself a resentful glare at Sezal before he followed. Advaith waited for Tav to do the same.

Instead, Tav turned back to Kajal. There was an apology there, and regret, but also steadfast determination. He believed he was doing the right thing, and perhaps he was.

Yet the part of her that remembered being Divya couldn't help but think he was once again choosing his brother, his duty, over everything else. They hadn't even had a chance to speak. Not with the truth exposed, her past opened up to her. He knew who she was, and again he was leaving her.

"Tav." Advaith reached out an impatient hand. "Leave them."

Whatever Tav saw in Kajal's face made his own shift, as if something inside him were breaking.

I'm sorry, he mouthed.

As if she hadn't lied to him over and over. As if she deserved an apology from anyone.

He and Advaith turned to the darkness and let it swallow them together. Before anyone could think to follow, the gates sealed shut and vanished.

✦✦✦

As if Tav's presence had been the only thing keeping her upright, Kajal fell to her knees. Lasya's wind died and she crouched beside her, Kutaa approaching on her other side.

"You shouldn't exert yourself," Lasya said, patting down Kajal's hair.

Kajal's laugh was mirthless as she steadied herself against Kutaa's bulk. "You should talk."

Lasya touched Kajal's throat. "There's a ring around your neck. It's blue."

Kajal's fingertips bumped against Lasya's. The spot was right over her throat chakra. Tav and Lasya's combined healing must have altered it as they'd burned away the poison.

Watching Kajal closely, Lasya moved her hand to her shoulder. "We'll find our own way to Patala. We'll stop him."

But there was so much more to it than that. It was the life she remembered that Lasya hadn't been part of. It was the enormity of halahala's devastation due to her own pride and pain. It was that she still didn't know how to use her powers to their full extent.

Useless.

Kajal shook her head. She couldn't think like that. Those kinds of thoughts had gotten her killed the first time, and an overabundance of confidence had gotten her killed the second.

Sezal knelt before her, head bowed. "Blessed Asura, I am yours to command."

Kajal took a deep breath. "Can I have my dagger back?"

Sezal blinked, then pulled it out of her belt and handed it to her. Kajal savored the heft of it. She'd thought it was foreign before, but now it couldn't have been more natural.

"Is it over?"

Dalbir and Vritika joined them. It was Dalbir who had spoken, gaze fixed on the spot where the gates had been.

"For now," Lasya answered. "Until we figure out how to follow them."

Vritika pointed at the ruined encampment, where the corpses had fallen motionless to the ground. "What, and do *that* again? We need to rescue Professor Jassi, but if this is the cost—"

"That's not the only way."

Everyone started at the new voice. Everyone except Kajal, who looked up sharply.

Several paces away, standing where the halahala ended and the grass grew green, was the same nagi who had harassed her under the hawthorn tree, recited the poem in the lake, and stopped the Vadhia soldiers.

"Bina," Kajal whispered.

The nagi's eyes widened before she let out a husky laugh. "So you finally remember."

"Remember?" Lasya frowned. "Remember what?"

"It's a long story," Kajal murmured. She nodded to Bina. "I assume you have an idea?"

"A few."

"Will I like any of them?"

"No."

Kajal huffed. But so long as she could avoid spreading halahala further, so long as she could prevent more hearts from stopping, she would listen.

"We will ensure that one of them works." Bina smiled slightly. "Maa is waiting for you to come home."

Kajal's hand curled around the dagger's sheath. Something else dug into the palm of her opposite hand, and she unfurled it. The amber pendant gleamed against her skin, housing its solitary lotus petal.

She wondered if she would ever return to the river. If she would be alone or have someone at her side. If she would ever reclaim the feeling of peace she'd once coveted.

But everything was different. *She* was different.

As she stared down at the pendant, a butterfly yaksha landed on her finger. It flapped its wings serenely, unbothered by the deva's disappearance.

Tav claimed that no one else could hear the butterflies, but if she concentrated, she thought she could detect the faintest whisper.

Trust me.

She closed her watering eyes. When she opened them again, the butterfly was gone.

She got to her feet and assessed the others. They all watched her, as if waiting for her to give them an order. The spot between her eyebrows prickled. She remembered sitting under a banyan tree with Lasya as a pujari knelt before them, his thumbs pressed to their foreheads, saying their titles for the first time.

Kajal had wanted a simple life. A life that didn't demand anything of her, a life that allowed for her and Lasya to be together forever. She'd known even then that it wasn't possible.

Now, standing there with a dakini's dagger and a pendant crafted by hands she no longer possessed, Kajal accepted that she was the asura, and that demons bowed to her.

That she was halfway a demon herself.

And that one way or another, she would return home.

Author's Note

The Mutability of Myth

WESTERN MEDIA HAS familiarized many readers with a spectrum of fantasy staples: elves, dwarves, dragons, and even demons and angels. There are so many interpretations of these tropes spanning countless books, movies, and shows that some readers might forget they originated in religion. In fact, one of the most formative pieces of fantasy literature, *The Lord of the Rings*, was inspired by Norse mythology.

Just as Norse mythology is tied to ancient faith, so, too, is Hindu mythology tied to religion—a religion that's very active, beloved, and sacred to many today. In that vein, this book is not meant to teach you Hindu mythology, which is incredibly nuanced and varied. Rather, I've created an Indian fantasy in the way some authors take mythological cues when developing their secondary worlds.

However, for those who are not as acquainted with these specific mythological cues, I have the responsibility to explain how they deviate from their origins.

But first: spelling. There are a variety of ways to spell Indian words, especially since there are hundreds of languages across the subcontinent. I've used the spelling I found most intuitive where possible, and I chose the Punjabi version of words where I could, as that is my family's native language.

In the world of *We Shall Be Monsters*, there is no Hindu pantheon. The faith of this world is largely Buddhist in nature with an undertone of Sikhism, and the gods that exist are ones I have made up myself, as well as many of the demons and spirits, like the aga ghora. Similarly, while Nagaloka is indeed the nagas' kingdom, Bijul's lake and the forgetting tea are my own spin on samsara (the cycle of reincarnation, which spans several Indian religions). The Brahimada is also my own term, inspired by Brahmanda, although Patala and Svarga are familiar concepts in Hindu and Vedic lore. And, while bodies are typically cremated in India, the use of coffins in the story is my own addition.

But the biggest shift from original myth comes down to the main characters: the asura and the deva.

In Hindu (and even Buddhist) mythology, *asura* is a word attributed to an entire race of demonic beings, much like the rakshasas. They are demigods in constant conflict with the devas, another race of divine beings, who are considered more benevolent than the hotheaded, passion-driven asuras. In Vedism, an ancient religion that was a precursor to Hinduism, texts used *asura* and *deva* to describe any creature considered supernatural. Yet over time, the asuras came to represent wickedness and the devas came to represent goodness.

It's important to note that some aspects of Hindu mythology, such as the villainous portrayal of rakshasas and asuras, originate in caste discrimination. The frequent celebration of the gods being victorious over demons (who are typically shown as ugly and darker of skin) contribute to a rigid depiction of good versus evil. This has led to violence and social stigma against marginalized communities in India, such as those of different castes and practitioners of other religions. While there is no caste system in this book, many of its echoes can be found in how background characters view rakshasas, and should be acknowledged.

We Shall Be Monsters is a very loose reimagining of the myth of Halahala, in which the asuras and the devas worked together to churn the Ocean of

Milk and make Amrita, the elixir of immortality. However, in the churning, Halahala—a deadly toxin that spread into the ocean—was also produced. The god Shiva was called upon to help the asuras and the devas, and in answer to their pleas, he consumed the poison. His wife, Parvati, held his neck to prevent the poison from traveling to his stomach, which turned his throat blue.

Because mythology is multilimbed, there are several variations to this myth. In one, Vayu, god of the wind, produced a gale that lessened the toxic fumes. In another, the asuras and the devas were guided by Brahma to form a pact to make Amrita, because the asuras had a sage to bring them back to life, and the devas did not.

In any case, when Amrita was made, the devas and the asuras returned to their old ways and attacked one another. It was Vishnu's interference—in the guise of Mohini—that broke up the fight. Mohini craftily distributed the Amrita only to the devas, giving them advantage over the asuras.

This clash—and the timeless, global theme of good versus evil—was something I put at the heart of *We Shall Be Monsters* and dissected in my own way, in my own world. What is the line been good and bad? Where lies the difference between human, demon, and god, and who gets to decide which is which?

As Dalbir says in the book: Mythology is a mirror of humankind. I wanted to explore what would happen if supernatural beings, already prone to the folly of human nature, were humans themselves. After all, we cannot help but see ourselves in characters and try to understand the world through their actions and points of view. In that way, I hope the story I've told is one that feels both familiar and new.

Acknowledgments

BOOKS ARE DIFFICULT no matter how many you've written. In fact, it seems the more I write, the harder they get, which is distinctly unfair. Thankfully, I have a great community that makes sure the task, daunting as it may be, is never impossible.

For this particular book, the very first person I need to thank is Dhonielle Clayton, who gave me the initial spark of what this story would eventually become. Back in 2016, Dhonielle tweeted that she wanted to see me tackle an Indian *Frankenstein*, and my immediate response was "Bet." Now here we are, eight years later, and I can only hope you like the finished result.

Never-ending thanks to my editor Caitlin Tutterow, who approached every draft with unfailing enthusiasm and understanding. I consider myself very lucky to have found someone who loves these characters and this story as much as I do. Much gratitude also to Stacey Barney, who saw the potential of this horror fantasy and took a chance on it. And to Nancy Paulsen, who oversees it all and gave me a space in which to tell my silly little stories.

I have tremendous appreciation for the Nancy Paulsen / Penguin Teen crew: Nicole Rheingans for interior design, Maria Fazio for cover design, Sierra Pregosin for publicity, Kim Ryan for subrights, and the digital marketing team of Felicity Vallence, James Akinaka, Shannon Spann, and

Alex Garber. Thanks also to copyeditor Elizabeth Johnson and proofreaders Janet Rosenberg, Misha Kydd, and Ariela Rudy Zaltzman for catching all my embarrassing mistakes.

A heartfelt thank-you to Amrit Brar, the artist of not only the amazing cover of *We Shall Be Monsters*, but also my favorite tarot deck. Your work inspires me so much, and it's an absolute honor to feature it alongside my own.

Victoria Marini, thank you for putting up with my anxious text messages and emails alike. Thank goodness you're a double Taurus.

Traci Chee and Emily Skrutskie, what would I do without you? I love our Whines and Cheeses and trying to solve overcomplicated puzzles together. Traci, I'm always grateful to be friends with someone so talented and compassionate. Emily, get bent.

I have such a wonderful writing group that I would be lost without, so oodles of thanks to the Cult of Shrek: Janella Angeles, Ashley Burdin, Alex Castellanos, Kat Cho, Maddy Coli, Mara Fitzgerald, Amanda Foody, Amanda Haas, C. L. Herman, Meg Kohlmann, Axie Oh, Claribel Ortega, Katy Rose Pool, Akshaya Raman, and Melody Simpson. Katy and Alex, extra thanks for all the Nertz games, even though I lost the majority of them. Unaffiliated yet an invaluable resource nonetheless, thank you to Margaret Owen for letting me ask you all sorts of questions concerning matters both written and visual. Graphic design is not my passion.

To Cirque de Merque, aka Yev, Sara, Eurus, and Solana: You're the best adventuring party an awkward tiefling rogue could ask for, despite the whole getting arrested thing. I'm so excited to go to hell with you. Many, many hugs for Jamie Lynn Saunders for being such a great DM and also a champion of my books over in Ireland.

And speaking of being book champions, the loudest thanks of all go to YOU, my readers, especially those who've been with me since the beginning. Your support means the entire world to me, and I wouldn't be able to do this if it weren't for you. Blessings upon all your crops and coffers.

Endless gratitude to my family, the Sekhons and Gills and Sims, for always being there.

To my cats, even if you walk all over my desk and prevent me from getting work done.

And to my parents: Thank you for your love and pride, and for sharing stories that have shaped my own. I love you.